Praise for N

"Written by a giant of the geni....ighly recommended."
—Lee Child, author of the Jack Reacher novels

"I have been a fan of Maxim Jakubowski for years. There just is no finer mystery writer and editor anywhere. Find a comfortable chair and a strong drink and prepare to be enthralled."
—Alexander Algren, author of *Out in a Flash: Murder Mystery Flash Fiction*

"A stunning collection, simply the best short mystery and crime fiction of the year and a real treat for crime-fiction fans. I highly recommend!"
—Leonard Carpenter, author of the Conan the Barbarian books and *Lusitania Lost*

"Maxim Jakubowski is deeply experienced in the field... Sometimes a brief zap of great writing is just what you're in the mood for or have time for. That's when anthologies like his are ideal... intellectually outstanding."
—*New York Journal of Books*

THE RETURN OF

Sherlock Holmes

THE RETURN OF

Sherlock Holmes

Further Extraordinary Tales
of the Famous Sleuth

Edited by Maxim Jakubowski

mango
PUBLISHING
CORAL GABLES

Cover Design: Roberto Nuñez
Layout & Design: Katia Mena
Interior Illustrations: AdobeStock (MoreVector, Rawpixel.com, channarongsds, unorobus, Morphart, amorroz, Natalya Levish, Oleksandr Babich, pteshka, alhontess, Hein Nouwens)

For permission requests, please contact the publisher at:
Mango Publishing Group
2850 S Douglas Road, 2nd Floor
Coral Gables, FL 33134 USA
info@mango.bz

For special orders, quantity sales, course adoptions and corporate sales, please email the publisher at sales@mango.bz. For trade and wholesale sales, please contact Ingram Publisher Services at customer.service@ingramcontent.com or +1.800.509.4887.

The Return of Sherlock Holmes: Further Extraordinary Tales of the Famous Sleuth

Library of Congress Cataloging-in-Publication number: 2021938480
ISBN: (print) 978-1-64250-636-5, (ebook) 978-1-64250-637-2
BISAC category code FIC022050

Printed in the United States of America

Table of Contents

Introduction   10
By Maxim Jakubowski

The Silver Lining   12
By Bonnie MacBird

The Curse of Carmody Grange   38
By Eric Brown

Sherlock Holmes and a Case of Humbug   62
By Paul A. Freeman

The New Messi   79
By Nick Sweet

The Adventure of the Talking Board   93
By John Grant

The Booby's Bay Adventure   117
By O'Neil De Noux

The Adventure of the Red Dress   136
By Ana Teresa Pereira

The Wargrave Resurrection   154
By Matthew Booth

The Case of the Waterguard   172
By Jan Edwards

The Adventure of the Bloomsbury Pickpocket   192
By David N. Smith

The Dulwich Solicitor   213
By Martin Daley

The Adventure of the Missing Master   231
By Phillip Vine

The Pale Reflection   255
By L. C. Tyler

Sherlock Holmes and the Butterfly Effect   275
By Cristina Macía with Ian Watson

The Case of the Secret Assassin   296
By David Stuart Davies

About the Editor   316

About the Authors   317

Introduction

By Maxim Jakubowski

The initial volume of brand new Sherlock Holmes stories in our series of anthologies for Mango Media attracted such tremendous interest from talented contemporary writers all over that we received a score of wonderful stories we were unable to include in *The Book of Extraordinary New Sherlock Holmes Stories*. So a vote of gratitude is due to Chris and Brenda at Mango who quickly agreed to a second volume (and a fifth book in the series).

In addition to the stories held over from our first round, it gave me an opportunity to solicit new material from a handful of authors new to the series, including writers from Spain and Portugal—proof if ever there was that the life and times of the sage of Baker Street and his familiar cohorts and adversaries are of universal appeal. And how could I say no to return appearances from some of our esteemed regulars for whom any theme in the crime, thriller, and mystery genre represents a worthy challenge!

So, freely dip into these pages as the game is yet again afoot, and investigations, puzzles, ratiocinations, and thrills are served up on a plate in a further fifteen stories that bring the Sherlockian canon to life in all its Victorian splendor and excitement.

Encounter fog-surrounded streets, the eternal battle of wits between the great detective and his new foes, and yet more dastardly crimes which our hero is compelled to solve, even when it repeatedly pits him and his faithful sidekick Doctor Watson against forces of darkness and evil.

Better critics and academics than me have tried to explain why the adventures of Sherlock Holmes have proven so popular for well over a century and "speak" to every new successive generation of readers, in every single country of the world, ranging across race, language, and age, and why the subtle art of detection proves such a wonderful draw for the imagination. But it's elementary, dear reader, and the answer is their charm, their sharply unforgettable characters and perfectly engineered, clockwork-like plots, and dollops of acutely drawn atmosphere.

So welcome back to the unique and wonderful world of London's most famous consultant detective. You will not be disappointed.

The Silver Lining

By Bonnie MacBird

T here was a satisfying snap as I popped open the crown of my new silk opera hat. I had purchased it the day before at Lock and Co. on St. James, an extravagance to be sure, but if I had to accompany my friend Sherlock Holmes to the opera, I might as well find some amusement in the doing.

It had been a long evening of Verdi, at least for me, but seemed to raise my companion's spirits, which had been ragged of late. And for *that* silver lining in the voluminous clouds of music that had inundated us, I was grateful.

Afterward, as we joined the crowd descending the grand staircase at the opera, my ears were ringing from the overdose. A strident female voice from behind us suddenly cut through the murmur. "Mr. Sherlock Holmes! Is that you?" The accent was clipped, patrician.

I turned back to see a dark-haired, beautiful woman in her late thirties cutting through from above, gesturing with her decorative fan. She exuded privilege, from her costly beaded dress and elaborate coiffure to the manner with which she parted the *hoi polloi*, or so she seemed to regard them, to reach us. With her was a very handsome and much younger man.

In a moment she stood on our stair, blocking all behind us.

"I am the Countess Rameau," announced the lady. "Call me Elena. And I need you to solve my little problem." Her eyes flicked over to me once, then again, and lingered just a moment too long.

A man directly behind me on the stairs harrumphed impatiently.

"Madam," said Holmes with a smile. "I came to enjoy Verdi. I conduct business on Baker Street." He pulled a card from his jacket, handed it to me over his shoulder, and without a further word continued down the stairs. The lady looked after him in dismay.

"Sincerest apologies," I said with a little bow, presenting her the card. "Here is the address." Her young man snatched it from my hand.

She took the card from her gentleman and her eyes met mine. She glanced over me a third time and appeared pleased at what she saw. "And you are?"

"Dr. John Watson, Mr. Holmes's colleague."

She smiled warmly. "Sir. I will come to see *you*, then." As they departed, her young man flashed me an angry look.

She was true to her word. At ten the next morning, Mrs. Hudson announced a visitor "to see *you*, Doctor! A very fine lady, the Countess Rameau!"

A moment later the magnificent countess stood before us, intent on some mission, and with a large silk reticule at her side. Her luminously pale, beautiful face and sharp hazel eyes were dramatically set off by a bright hyacinth silk dress, embroidered in silver and white. Our modest flat seemed dingy with this elegant flower in its midst.

I rose to greet her, but Holmes remained seated, busily attending to his pipe.

"Dr. Watson, and the rude Mr. Holmes. I have come on urgent business," said Countess Rameau.

"Please be seated, Madam," I said, gesturing to a chair near the window. "May I offer you a tea or coffee?"

"Put that infernal pipe away," she commanded Holmes. "I abhor tobacco." She sat.

He looked over at her in amusement and paused mid-light. "And yet your husband's fortunes depend on several tobacco plantations in, I believe, Virginia?" he drawled. He nevertheless set the pipe down. He had looked her up, no doubt.

"That is of no matter. I have come for help, not what passes for wit in this dreary place."

"Of course, Madam," said I. "Please, tell us your problem."

"Silver! Silver is my problem! I have a great deal of very special, unusual, *unique*, rare silver. The set is a family heirloom. It is Baroque, original, of great beauty."

"A great many adjectives," remarked Holmes. "Stolen, I suppose?"

"Yes. From our home in Belgravia."

"All of it?"

"No, select pieces only."

"Belgravia, you say. But you and the count reside in Bedfordshire, do you not? Flintwood Hall? A grand place, they say, Watson."

"Our London pied-à-terre is in Belgravia."

That area of London was an enclave of the very wealthy. I wondered at the size of this "pied-à-terre."

"When did this silver go missing?" Holmes asked.

"Recently."

"When, exactly? Did someone break in? Were locks or windows forced? Any witnesses? Specifics, Madam, if you would like me to help you," Holmes said.

"No, no, nothing like that. No break-ins. The butler noticed it last week. He and I believe it to be someone in the household. In fact, I am sure of it."

"Last week! What did the police have to say?"

"I have not notified the police."

"Why not?"

"Because, well, I know the thief." She paused, and Holmes waved her to continue, as though encouraging a child. "It is, I am sure, Clara," said she. "A new lady's maid hired to look after our female guests."

"You are certain of this? How?"

"A woman knows." She glanced over at me with undisguised coquetry.

"Madam. That is insufficient. Why do you suspect this maid particularly?" said Holmes.

"Several costly items have appeared in her room. New dresses, and so forth."

"Gifts rather than purchases, perhaps? That is what we call circumstantial evidence. It will not hold in a court of law. What has Miss Clara to say of the matter?"

"We have not spoken of it."

Astounding, I thought. "Mr. Holmes might discreetly question this young lady," I suggested.

She beamed at me. "A lovely idea, Doctor!" Then her face took on a childish pout. "But you cannot question her. She is…she is with my husband at Flintwood."

"Ah," said Holmes. There was a pause.

The lady exhaled softly and smoothed her skirts. With a little toss of her head, she continued. "I don't care about that. It will be over by Christmas. That is our pattern." She turned to me with a warm smile. "My husband spends the autumn in the countryside at Flintwood, hunting, and…and so on. I spend the season here for the opera and ballet. And to make new friends, Doctor." Her gaze lingered on me and she smiled. Beyond her, I could see one of Holmes's eyebrows lift in amusement.

She turned back to him and he was all innocence. "How can I help you, Countess?" he said.

"First, Mr. Holmes, find this silver, wherever it is, and buy it back for me. Here are photographs of the missing pieces and money to purchase them." She removed a small brown envelope from her reticule, followed by a small suede pouch, and handed them both to me. I looked inside the pouch to see a wealth of gold sovereigns. I handed both to Holmes. "Mr. Holmes, *find out who sold my silver.* Prove that I am right."

Holmes eyed the photographs. "These are unique pieces. Quite beautiful." He handed them to me. They were serving pieces, ornate but odd, with boars' heads, foxes, and elven faces woven into the curling, leafy designs.

Holmes emptied the pouch onto the table next to him. The gold sovereigns gleamed in the morning sunlight streaming in off Baker Street. He frowned. "I fear this sum will be insufficient for both the silver, and the information."

"Good. I see you know the value." She took out a second pouch and dangled it in the air. Once again I stood up and ferried the thing to Holmes. It was a peculiar dance we were doing in this meeting.

"A description of the maid, if you please?"

"Clara is short. Dark hair, slender, pretty. Oh, and she has a large mole on her right cheek."

Holmes stood. "Your delay in this matter is unfortunate. But if we are in luck and the silver is still in London after a whole week, I shall have it back for you by the morning. Good day, Countess."

The lady rose with a smile. "You may keep all the money that you do not use in the purchase," said she. "Oh, one other thing. There is an auction of fine silver, midday at Sotheby, Williams and Hodge. I plan to attend, but I will need someone to accompany me. My usual friend is unavailable. Dr. Watson, might you join me?"

"Your silver will not be there, Madam, if that is what you are thinking," said Holmes. "That august organisation does not operate as a venue for thieves. They are quite careful about provenance."

"Oh, I know," said she. "I go for enjoyment. I do love beautiful things. I may pick up something that takes my fancy. Dr. Watson?"

Normally, I would be inclined to meet such a request, but the plan made me uncomfortable for reasons I could not articulate.

"I'm afraid I must—"

"Watson, I see no harm, I will not need you for this simple matter," said Holmes. My back to the lady, I glowered at him. He smiled innocently.

Two hours later, I sat next to the countess in the large, airy auction room of Sotheby, Wilkinson and Hodge on Wellington Street, just off the Strand. The room buzzed with anticipation. Surrounding us were a swarm of wealthy bidders, colourfully attired in the latest fashions, coiffed, perfumed, polished. In addition, there were a number of scholarly types, scanning the catalogue, reference books and lists in hand.

There was nothing quite so eager, I thought, as a collector in search of a mismarked treasure, unless it was a very wealthy individual on the hunt for a bargain.

I was seated on the aisle of a row of folding wooden chairs, the countess beside me. Disconcertingly, her arm had remained looped through mine.

We were receiving several amused glances. She had become a tittering schoolgirl, pointing out this and that well-dressed bidder, and whispering gossip into my ear, all the while clinging to me as though we were two young lovers who had temporarily escaped from our chaperone. Again and again, her bidding paddle flew up and down as she gleefully bid on several frivolous items, won two of them, and had me collect them for her, rather than arranging for later delivery.

At one point I stood to let someone into our row, and just as they passed, she playfully tapped me on the buttocks with that same paddle, giggling.

"Madam!" I said. I heard a "tsk" from the row behind us and sat down. I could feel myself flushing with embarrassment.

But it was as if I had thrown kerosene on the flame. She leaned in and kissed my cheek. "You are adorable!" She then turned to the people behind her and said, "Handsome, isn't he? Don't you wish you were me?"

A tight-laced woman directly behind us snorted in derision, but an elegant, older man with a monocle and glittering smile leaned in. "Countess Rameau, I have always wished to be *with* you!" he said with a tip of his hat.

"Take your place in the queue, Baron," said another, younger man, glistening in pomade and with a flower in his buttonhole. He winked at the countess.

It was with utter relief that I later deposited "Elena," as she asked to be called, at her home in Belgravia, declined her invitation to linger over a sherry, and retreated to the safety of 221B. No man dislikes being called handsome, yet I had felt less cherished than on display.

A glass of good whisky and a smoke set me quickly aright, and I was in decent enough cheer when Holmes returned at seven, carrying a large, heavy carpetbag. He looked tired, but I read success on his keen features. "The silver?" I asked.

"It took some doing, but yes. I have all of it in hand. And a partial description of the seller—hooded and attempting to conceal herself, but female, small, pale, with dark hair and, I am sorry to say, a large beauty mark on her right cheek."

"The silly young thing was foolish enough to try to sell the goods herself!" I said.

"And yet she must have lugged that amount of silver with some difficulty," said Holmes thoughtfully.

He dashed off a note to the countess and sent it to Belgravia with our page, Billy. As I poured him a celebratory whisky, I noticed some newspapers and periodicals open on the table. I caught a glimpse of an article titled "The Rambunctious Rameaus" in some scandal rag. I looked up to see Holmes staring at me with unusual interest.

"Survived the afternoon intact, I see?" he asked with a smile.

"Really, Holmes! You knew what she was like, didn't you?"

"Watson, all of London does. The countess and her husband are in a famously permissive marriage. They regularly take lovers, throw discretion to the winds, and are seen everywhere about town with them. I've been doing a little research. You are, apparently, Madam's type."

"Oh, for God's sake—"

"You are a brave man, Watson."

"Ha! That must be my attraction," I said. "That and my biceps, apparently."

There was a pause before we both burst out laughing.

We were in Belgravia at nine the next morning, but to Holmes's surprise, the butler informed us that the countess had left for her country estate the previous evening. A note addressed to me directed us to meet her at Flintwood with the silver, as she had decided to confront Clara after all.

Outside, on the pavement before Eaton Square Gardens, Holmes and I decided we would take the train to Pebblewirth, the nearest station to their country seat. "But later this afternoon, Watson. I have a few inquiries to make before we travel to the lair of the philandering Rameaus. I will be happy to wash my hands of this business."

"Perhaps you should go on alone," I suggested.

"I wouldn't think of it, my dear Watson," said he. "Besides, I would like a witness when I disclose the sizeable payment I have managed to retain from the initial two batches of sovereigns."

At the end of the afternoon, after an hour's train ride and another hour in a hired carriage to the estate, we stood on the steps of a grand, three-storey stone and marble edifice at the end of a long driveway lined with poplars. The trees whipped about in the wind that had come up, and dark grey clouds had made their appearance on the horizon. I shivered, having only a light coat with me. A foolish error for an Englishman in this unpredictable season, but it had been mild and sunny when we left London. I hoped we would not be long in this place.

We were not expected. Holmes's name meant nothing to the sour-faced butler, and to our surprise, the countess was not at home here, either. The man, Peterson by name, advised us to take lodging in the nearby town. "Madam may arrive sometime in the next few days. You might try back then."

Peterson then refused to provide a carriage, and despite the incipient storm, directed us to walk to the main road a mile away and try our luck with some passing vehicle. This was surprisingly inhospitable, I thought.

Holmes indicated the large carpetbag he had placed at his feet. "We have something to deliver to the lady, and I don't wish to have it hanging about an inn. It is precious silver from the count and countess's home in Belgravia."

Just as he said this, a tall, elegant man appeared behind the butler. "Peterson," he said sharply, "what is this about our silver?"

Minutes later, Holmes having introduced us and stated our business, we faced Count Rameau across an enormous low table in a salon lined with gigantic oil paintings. Through the French windows behind him, a formal row of rosebushes shuddered in the brisk wind.

The count reclined and, as we spoke, continuously smoothed luxurious wings of black hair away from his face. He seemed as vain as any theatre actor. But his eyes kept darting to me. Odd, I thought.

Holmes related the countess's story, leaving out her suspicions about the specific maid. He opened the carpetbag to reveal the treasure within. The count glanced down at it and waved a hand.

"Yes, that is ours. Hers, really, as she said," He looked Holmes over. "You have come a very long way to deliver it, so I presume you are here for payment?" He rang for the butler who appeared in an instant. "Peterson, take this silver, list the contents, lock it in the pantry." The fellow departed. The count turned back to Holmes. "All right, you've done your little job; now what do we owe you for your service?"

"My fee has already been paid. Don't you wish to know how the silver came to be missing, Count?" asked Holmes.

The count shrugged. He then leaned back in his chair and once more languidly appraised me without any attempt to hide it. I felt distinctly uncomfortable under the man's gaze.

"Who are *you*, again?" he suddenly demanded of me. His gaze flicked between Holmes and me and he smiled. "Friend and colleague? What does that mean, exactly?"

"It means precisely what it says, Count Rameau. Dr. Watson assists me in my investigations. Do you have a young lady on your staff, a lady's maid named Clara?" Holmes said.

The man ignored the question. He continued to stare at me.

"Doctor, eh? Have you met my wife on the occasion of her hiring your 'friend and colleague'? If not, I feel certain the countess would enjoy meeting *you*. Elena is due to arrive tomorrow." The count turned back to Holmes. "This could be amusing," said he. "I am of a mind to invite you to stay."

"No, really, I don't think—" I began.

"Thank you, we will accept," said Holmes. "May I interview your maid, Clara?"

"Why?"

Holmes said nothing. The inference was clear.

"Oh, I see. My wife is trying to pin the theft on the little 'robin redbreast,' is she? Well, I doubt Clara did it." He smiled and rang. The butler appeared, and he sent for the maid. I puzzled over the "robin redbreast" comment.

In a moment the girl appeared, bobbing her head in respect, and lingering in the doorway until the count bade her enter. She was slender, pale, dark-haired, perhaps seventeen or eighteen, with a large beauty mark on her right cheek. Her starched maid's costume was unusual in that it featured no typical high, ruffled collar, but instead a plunging décolleté. It was as though she were costumed as a French maid in a West End farce.

I glanced at Holmes, who was taking all this in, and probably a great deal more.

The girl stood before us. As she did so, the count moved to her side and put his hand on her shoulder. It was less a gesture of protection than it was of ownership. I did not like it. She seemed to shrink, but the count gave her a sharp look. In response she straightened up, and met our eyes with a forced but steady gaze.

"Clara," said the count. "This gentlemen wishes to question you. Please answer him as best you can." His hand remained on her shoulder. Clearly the man cared nothing for propriety, but this seemed to be a family trait.

He patted her shoulder, and the pat turned into a caress. The girl held steady as though nothing odd were happening…but began to flush—not just her face, but her neck and chest went red as well. "Robin redbreast" he had called her. I found myself hot with embarrassment. I glanced at Holmes. He gave little indication but I sensed that even he was uncomfortable at this bizarre display.

"Gentlemen," said the count. "She is all yours. Ask her what you will. Clara, answer Mr. Hearns."

"The name is Holmes. I prefer to interview her privately."

"No," said the count.

There was a pause. The count's hand remained on Clara's shoulder. I could have been mistaken, but I thought I saw it tighten. My stomach lurched.

"All right, then. What is your family name, if you would, Miss?" asked Holmes gently.

"Smith."

"Miss Smith, how long have you been in the employ of the count and countess?"

"Four months next week, sir."

"And who hired you, Miss?"

"Sir did." She glanced sideways at her employer then looked down. His hand caressed her shoulder.

The girl kept her reactions well masked, yet I thought I noted fear in her eyes. Holmes observed her closely. "Count," he asked, "are you in the habit of hiring lady's maids who work for you? Is this

not usually the purview of the housekeeper, or indeed the lady of
the house?"

"I choose them when it suits me to do so. But that is hardly
any of your business, Mr. Holmes. Are you finished with
your questions?"

"No. Clara, do you normally have access to the silver in the
Rameau household in Belgravia?"

For the first moment, the girl looked blank. "The silver?" she
said. "No, why?"

"Some went missing, and the countess seems convinced that you
took it." Holmes shrugged as though that were the silliest notion, but
he was obliged to say it.

She did not reply but looked confused, and glanced up at her
employer. He shook his head.

"I don't know any silver," said she. "And I have no reason to
touch it. I am a lady's maid. Butler locks it up, I think," said the girl,
suddenly uneasy.

"Then you do know of it?"

"Only as I have seen it on the table, sir."

"So you see. Clara is no thief," said the count. "We are finished
here. Leave us, Clara."

At the command, the girl started, then fairly dashed from the
room as he rang for the butler. "I have changed my mind. I ask that
you leave Flintwood now," said the count.

There was the sound of thunder and, over our host's shoulder,
I could see that a downpour now pummelled the gardens. Peterson
appeared at the doorway.

"Peterson, pay Mister—what was it—'Holmes' for his trouble.
Ten pounds. Then send these two off to Pebblewirth Station in our
carriage," said the count. "You have got what you came for, Mr.
Holmes. Good day."

"Sir?" said the butler. "The carriage is away fetching provisions
for the countess's arrival tomorrow. And our landau is in town with

the wheels in repair. All we have available just now is the dog cart, or the two field ponies. Your hunters are at the farriers."

The count relented. "All right. I suppose you must spend the night. Peterson, have James take them to…"

"The blue room is available, sir," said Peterson.

The count nodded sharply. "Perfect."

The "blue room," as it turned out, was a dismal little space tucked away under the eaves in the chilly north end of the house, with blue wallpaper peeling from the walls, and the wind rattling through cracks in the window. Two hard single beds, a lone armoire, and a washstand with two threadbare towels were the only amenities. A single, half-burned tallow candle sat on a rickety table between the two beds.

We had passed numerous guest rooms, their doors open to reveal sumptuous furnishings. All of these, of course, had stood empty.

"Holmes?" I said.

"One night only, Watson."

"I did not plan for an overnight stay."

"Nor did I. But we have little choice, unless you would care to walk back to Pebblewirth through this." He waved to the window. An icy rain beat down on the verdant landscape, now growing grey under the settling dusk.

The small fireplace was cold and empty, nothing to burn. In an hour, two dried sandwiches and two bruised apples arrived at the room, along with a carafe of cloudy water and a pot of lukewarm tea. I have dined better in a pauper's house.

And so at we began a restless and chilly night, sleeping in our clothes on the hard beds, with one thin blanket each.

It was after three in the morning when I was awakened by Holmes shaking me by the shoulder. He held the candle, guttering in the cold, drafty room. He was drenched, and cold droplets from his sleeve hit me on the neck. "Watson, come. There is evil afoot. We have work to do. I will explain later."

I leapt from the bed and threw on my thin coat. We ran out into the rainy night like two thieves, my blood rising to the challenge of the chase. Crossing a wide yard, our footsteps crunching on the gravel, we proceeded downhill over a soaked lawn, then down a brick path, to the stables.

The downpour had dwindled to a cold spitting rain, and a watery moon glowed faintly silver through the clouds. Now I, too, was soaked. The stables were black and, as we approached, I heard a horse nickering softly at our presence, then another, in answer. We continued around to the back, to an elaborate construction previously hidden from view. Once out of sight of the main house, Holmes carefully lit a dark lantern he had evidently procured somewhere on the estate.

The structure appeared to be a new addition, one large room, with pipes for indoor plumbing at one end, and a single window. From it, a warm light burned through closed pink curtains. We moved toward it, and I could see through a sliver of an opening a young woman in her nightclothes, sitting on an enormous bed with velvet coverlets and many pillows.

Clara. She was alone in what was clearly a hideaway.

Unlike the other servants, who were usually housed under the eaves in the main house, as we were, Clara had been isolated here.

In spite of the hour, the girl was awake, sitting on the edge of her bed, rocking and nodding, whether with joy or to comfort herself, I could not tell. I moved closer to the window, but Holmes's thin fingers grasped my arm and pulled me back.

"Watch where you step! The footprints!" He pointed to the mud below the window, under the eaves, and thus protected, a little, from the rain.

"What? Whose? I squinted. "Looks like a woman's shoe."

"Watson, I believe this girl is in danger. We must go in there and interview her apart from the count."

"But this is terribly improper, Holmes. The girl is alone, in her nightclothes. Can't it wait 'til morning?"

"That is why you are here. I need a witness. This girl's life may depend on it. The count had her up in his room for over an hour this night."

"Why, this place here seems to be designed for—"

"Exactly. But while Clara was there, your friend the countess arrived, and—"

"—she is not my friend!"

"Shh. It was then about two. She entered the house, careful to make no sound. Clara was still with the count. I expected some confrontation, but instead, the countess shortly exited the house, carrying an umbrella and a small sack. I followed her down to the stables here, and watched as she peered through the window, entered Clara's empty room, lit a candle, and placed something in the back of the lowest drawer over there."

"She is trying to set up the girl with another 'theft'!" I exclaimed.

"You astound, Watson. She then left and returned to the main house. I meant to retrieve whatever it was she left but—don't step there, I said!"

"Sorry. Is this the countess's footprint, do you think?"

"Of course. Keep your voice down. I meant to go in and fetch the item, but the girl returned before I could."

"But this has already been tried, and it failed," I pointed out. "The count will no doubt defend the girl as he did today, with us. He doesn't care if she's a thief!"

"Something has changed, Watson; the countess has raised her game. It was she who sold the silver disguised as the girl, I would wager, though it will be difficult to prove. This couple has broken more than a few hearts. Their antics are games to them, but dire to some they have seduced."

"Do you really think the girl is in actual danger?"

"I do. Depending on what is in that drawer, the girl could hang for the theft."

"My God," I cried, but just as I did, the pink curtains were yanked open and the face of Clara Smith stared out at the window at us, only inches from our own.

She screamed.

It seemed I had been asleep only minutes when Holmes shook me awake a second time. Shortly, after a discussion with Clara in her hideaway, he'd insisted I return to our room while he attended to "a few small matters."

"What time is it?" I asked. Bright sunlight now flooded through the small window of our awful room. I blearily took in his utterly soaked clothing. "What have you been up to?"

"Later. Come! We are to join the countess for breakfast in the Orangerie. Say nothing of our visit last night."

In the Orangerie, we found Countess Rameau seated at one end of a long table. On a sideboard were silver dishes of fruits, pastries, and sausages, along with a tureen of scrambled eggs. She looked up to smile warmly at me, then gasped when she noticed the state of our clothing. I was still quite damp, but Holmes was literally dripping.

"Oh, Doctor, you must be chilly! Come here, sit by the fire, near me! I take it you brought the recovered silver, Mr. Holmes? And identified the thief?"

"The silver is here," said he. "And…the seller had a mole on her cheek! We are very fortunate in this distinctive identification!"

The countess smiled and was about to reply when the count burst into the room all in a fury, and near hysteria, Peterson anxiously trailing him. "Find it! Find it! Search everywhere. The servants' quarters! Everywhere!" The count seemed surprised to see us all there. "Elena! When did you arrive?"

"In the night, darling."

"Er, when exactly?"

"Maybe five, six this morning? What is the matter, dear?"

"My inkwell! It has been stolen! Dear God, someone took *the inkwell!*" He keened in agony, nearly tearing out his hair.

"Oh, dear," said the countess, arising and rushing to her husband. "Not *the* inkwell?" The count nodded and covered his face with his hands. She turned to us. "A precious antique! The inkwell that was used by William Shakespeare! It sits on the count's desk. He writes his daily list from it every morning. That remarkable item is the pinnacle of our family's collection!"

Holmes and I exchanged a small glance. That old thing we discovered in Clara's drawer must have been this! The girl could indeed have hung for such a theft. I had sensed at the time that Holmes knew more but had explained nothing to me. I had no idea what he had up his sleeve.

"Shakespeare's inkwell!" said my friend with a smile. "Now that *would* be a treasure. Acquired by you, I understand?"

"Gone! Gone! It was there when I retired," shouted the count.

"Darling, I think I know who might have taken it," said the countess. "Mr. Holmes, will you please report what you have found about the missing silver?"

The count looked up from his despair, to bark at her, "Peterson already has your damned silver. Yes, I know that he found it, Elena. That is nothing compared to this inkwell. Nothing!"

"But, darling, our silver was sold in London, and Mr. Holmes can describe the person who did so. Perhaps the same thief stole both! Mr. Holmes?"

"I can indeed describe the seller of your silver, sir," said Holmes. "The buyer identified her as a delicate, dark-haired lady."

"That could be anyone—" moaned the count.

"But…with a distinctive mole on her right cheek," added my friend.

The count looked up in surprise.

"I told you, darling. Clara! She is a thief," said the countess.

"If so, you may find the inkwell in her room, I would imagine," said Holmes.

I grew nervous at this, but had learned to keep faith with Holmes's odd plans.

"Yes, of course," said the countess. "It must be there!"

"Everyone, follow me. Peterson, call the police!" shouted the count. I noticed the hint of a secret smile from the countess as her husband dashed off.

In a minute the four of us, followed shortly by Peterson and a footman, arrived in the secret room. It was empty!

Stripped bare. Drawers open, armoire gaping. No clothes. Nothing.

The girl was gone, along with all of her things. Even I was surprised at this.

The count and countess stared at the empty room, united in their dismay. The count sank down upon the bed, covering his face. The lady was first to recover. "We must search. Perhaps she…perhaps she left it behind!"

Holmes had positioned himself in front of the small chest of three drawers. The top drawer lay on the floor, empty, the second was wide open and also empty. The bottom drawer remained closed. The countess edged toward it, mesmerized.

"It is of no use, Madam, the girl has gone," said Holmes, as if he did not notice her strange attention to the one closed drawer he was blocking. "If she stole it, she would have taken it with her."

"But…we have not looked everywhere!" cried the countess. "That drawer, closed, behind you."

"The girl has gone, Elena. Gone with my treasure," moaned the count.

"She will head for London, no doubt," said Holmes.

But the countess continued to stare at the chest of drawers. "But that drawer. The one closed behind you. Step aside, Mr. Holmes. Step aside, I say," said she.

Holmes did not move. "Really, Madam, do you think she would clean out the room entirely and leave this one drawer?"

"Step aside!" she shouted.

Holmes was strangely calm. "Yes, Madam." He moved off.

She ran to the drawer and yanked it open. It was empty, except for a small envelope of pink paper. She grabbed it, read what was printed upon it, and went white. She closed her eyes and staggered to the bed, sitting down upon it next to her husband. Then, as if realising where she sat, she leapt up, horrified.

"Pull yourself together, Elena. What does that say?" asked the count. He stood and snatched the pink envelope from his wife's hands. "Oh, just some advertisement." He dropped it on the floor. "Dear God. That girl absconded with my...how could she..." his face suddenly lit up with the force of a brilliant idea.

"Mr. Holmes! You found the silver. Do you think I could employ you to find the inkwell as well? Do you think you could? Oh, please! I would pay anything to get it back. Name your price. Anything. She cannot have gone far. You could trace her, could you not? If you start at once?"

Holmes paused and eyed the tearful count and countess. "I believe I could," said he. "But is it the inkwell, not the girl, that most interests you? Would you pay two hundred pounds for its return?"

"I would pay you five hundred pounds! More! Name your price!"

"Five it is, then. Please write your check now, and arrange for our ride to the station. Unless it has disappeared into thin air, I will be able to deliver the inkwell to you in short order." The count and countess swept from the room.

"Watson, bring that little pink envelope, if you would?" said Holmes, with a quick smile. I retrieved it from the floor and followed him, still in the dark as to his plans.

Moments later, we stood in the count's study as he tearfully wrote out a check to Holmes. My friend took it, folded it in half, and placed it in the one dry spot in his clothing, the inside pocket of his jacket. "Thank you." He smiled.

"Peterson, the carriage! Mr. Holmes and Dr. Watson must be on the next train to London," said the count. He looked up at Holmes. "You feel certain she went there?"

"If I were to sell the authentic inkwell of William Shakespeare, that is where I would go. Within days, hours perhaps, it might be en route to the Continent, or even to America."

"You could trace such a thing?"

"I make it my business to track many aspects of criminal London, sir."

"If it leaves the country, I would never see it again!" cried the count. "Hurry, please. Peterson, the next train is in an hour! Gentlemen, you can just make it."

Holmes patted his pocket. "This fee is for the return of your item, correct?"

"Yes. I said so. And I must know the thief."

"No matter when? No matter who?"

"Of course! But the sooner the better. I'll see her hang for this!" cried the count.

Holmes and I looked at each other. He turned back to the count. "Miss Smith could indeed hang for stealing an item of such apparent value. But, of course, she is of no concern to you. What about you, Madam?"

"What do you mean?" said the count.

But Holmes stayed fixed on the lady. "I understand several of the count's young 'friends'—er, your lady's maids—have been through a similar adventure to Miss Clara Smith. A Miss Isabel Christie? And, oh, yes, a Miss Caroline O'Herlihy. Do you know what happens to a maid when she is dismissed without a reference? They are often condemned to living in destitution on the streets. As those two currently do."

"What? How do you know this?" said the countess.

"What has this to do with my inkwell?" shouted the count.

Holmes continued staring at the lady. She cleared her throat. "Henry!" said she, accusation in her tone. "You were to provide references for them."

Her husband waved her off. "I may have forgotten once or twice. That is not my concern." He turned to Holmes. "But your spying on me is! How do you know about these girls? What is your game, sir?" said the count, staring at Holmes in growing fury. "Give me back my check."

"I made it my business to understand your family's patterns, Count. You and your wife are well-known in London. Many people follow your adventures avidly. Whole columns in the papers have been devoted to them. But I think you are aware. You cultivate notoriety…because you can. Even your inkwell has been written up and pictured in the papers."

"What? Are you attempting to blackmail me? It is of no use. I hide nothing."

"Blackmail you? No." Holmes held back a laugh. "Even if I were to stoop to such tactics, there is little I could reveal which would exceed your actual reputation."

The count paused, took a deep breath, and composed himself. The countess put her arm through her husband's, as if to present a united front. "But the inkwell, Henry, the inkwell. It is missing. The girl is gone. Clara stole the silver. She must have stolen that!"

"Madam, *you* stole the silver," said Holmes. "Will you confess, or need I go on?"

"Darling, you stole your own silver?" said the count.

"No, of course not. Mr. Holmes has identified the seller. She had a mole. It was Clara!"

"Madam, you force my hand. And since you have not made the inference, Count, the pink envelope, if you please, Watson. Kindly read what it says."

I pulled it from my pocket. I read that inside are "Twelve Fancy-Dress Ball 'Mouches' or 'party patches.'"

"What are those? And what does this have to do with anything?" asked the count. I was wondering the same.

"These are false beauty marks—or moles—made of velvet," said my friend. "In vogue in the last century and used today for fancy-dress balls."

The count looked confused. "I thought Clara's beauty mark was real! The duplicitous little wench!"

Holmes laughed. "Clara's? No, hers *was* real. These false patches were in Madam's cosmetic case. She used one when she sold the silver."

But of course!

The import of this gradually dawned. The count turned to his wife. "*You* were the seller? You stole your own silver?"

The countess shrugged. "Oh, darling. I was justified. You crossed a line with Clara. You know you did. Bringing her to your own room. But the girl is a thief, after all. She took your inkwell. I certainly didn't."

"Ah! Madam, you persist beyond all logic!" cried Holmes. "All right. I *saw* you place the inkwell in the drawer last night. The drawer you so insisted on opening just now."

"That *was* odd…" said the count.

"Liar! You have no proof. Your word only." The countess stood firm, defiant. "Why would I deign to come to *that room* in the middle of the night?"

"Why indeed? And yet I watched you do so while the occupant was elsewhere." Holmes reached into the carpetbag, which lay at his feet, and unwrapped a dainty green embroidered shoe, stained badly with mud. "This shoe matches a print under the stable house window. Yours, Madam."

"You have been inside my room!" cried the countess.

Holmes laughed. "You already know this, Madam. Where else would I have retrieved the pink envelope?"

"I shall have you up on charges for trespassing!" she snarled.

"Interesting," said Holmes. He turned to the count. "You must have noticed your wife's great concern with the drawer. That is where I saw her place it."

"Oh, Elena, why?" cried her husband. "*Why* would you take the inkwell?"

The countess paused. But she was not finished. "Fire with fire. I know you, Henry. You fell in love with this one. I had to do something."

Exactly as Holmes had surmised.

"But then, where is it now? Elena, *where is it now?*"

"That little strumpet must have found it and taken it. Because, oh, all right, I admit, I left it there. But you cannot deny, the girl is gone, and so is the inkwell! Was the inkwell still there in the drawer when you placed the pink envelope in it, Mr. Holmes?"

"Yes. When I opened the drawer, there it was."

"So you see. The girl is still a thief!" cried the woman.

"I shall never see it again!" moaned the count.

"I dare say you will," said Holmes. "It was in the drawer when I opened it, but not when I closed it." He reached into his carpetbag, removed the inkwell, and set it on the table. It was a small brass item, struck from a mould. Ornately carved, originally, but quite worn, and with a sizeable dent.

The count snatched it to his bosom with a gasp, which turned into fury. "What? You trickster! Give me back my check. I'll have you arrested for theft. And perjury! My wife is no thief. We are just playing a game. The courts will uphold this. Peterson, call the police!"

"I have done so some time ago, sir," said Peterson, calmly.

"I have produced your item and named the thief. Those are the terms. There are witnesses," said Holmes. He gestured to me, and to the butler. I nodded. To my surprise, so did the taciturn servant.

"But you had it all along!" cried the count.

"So did many others."

"What? What do you mean?"

"You will recall that the London papers mentioned your great family treasure. It took me but two hours yesterday—while Madam enjoyed the company of Dr. Watson here at an auction—to learn what I needed. Let me clarify. Here, too, is your inkwell."

Holmes reached into his bag and placed a second, identical inkwell on the desk. "And here." He reached in again and retrieved a third, placing it next to the first two.

The count gasped. He set down his precious inkwell next to those on the table and stared open-mouthed at three precisely identical items. I could see even from where I stood that the dents in them were perfectly matched.

" 'Shakespeare's inkwell,' " said Holmes, "is a specialty item known among certain dealers of antiquities along the Portobello road. They are a relatively cheap reproduction. The maker of these keeps the price high by only releasing them very, very selectively to… certain types of buyers, such as yourself. Another inkwell resides with a man in San Francisco, and a third in Moscow."

"I paid a king's ransom for that!!"

"Oh, darling!" cried the countess.

The count wheeled on us, his face a bright red. Not like a robin, but rather like a cardinal, I thought.

"Get out of here! I never want to see either of you again!" he shouted.

"Nor I," chimed in his mate.

But the count did not demand the return of his check, and within a few minutes we were climbing into the couple's finest carriage, which had been brought round to the front of the house on the butler's command. Just before the door shut, Peterson handed in a large picnic hamper. I opened the top. Inside was a veritable feast of pâté, cheeses, cakes, chocolates, and wine.

"For the ride, gentlemen," said he with a small bow. "And thank you."

A week later, Holmes and I sat before a roaring fire at 221B, an icy rain again bucketing down onto the street below. Winter was full upon us. My friend had been out often in the intervening days but had spoken not a word to me of where or why. We were perusing the newspapers when I read aloud a small mention of the Count and Countess Rameau having left England to winter in the south of France.

"There to wreak more havoc," I said bitterly, feeling the pair had gotten off unscathed from their callous and criminal behaviour. I thought again of the Rameaus' three young maids—without work, without references, bereft in the freezing London winter.

"That couple is largely untouchable, I am afraid, Watson. However, there is a silver lining to this case after all. Take a look." He handed me a paper, and I laughed at the choice of periodical. Of course I'd seen him read them all, from *Ally Sloper, Lucifer, Horse and Hound*...to the *Times*. Today it was the *Lady*.

A small advertisement in the lower left corner of one page, read "Silver Lining: A Royal Fashion Service. For the discerning woman who would like to be treated and attired like royalty. Three former lady's maids offer a private service to update and maintain your dress, cosmetics and coiffure on a daily, weekly, or monthly basis. Be exquisitely groomed, beautifully *au courant*, and the envy of all your friends, while we remain your secret! Taste, discretion, and impeccable references. Ask for Miss C. Smith."

"Holmes! Is this what I think? Clara Smith?"

He nodded. "I approached Miss Smith to offer her a large share of our fee. The business was her idea, and I convinced her to take on the other two maids as well. I also secured references in writing from both of the Rameaus, and several of their friends."

"Well done, Holmes!" said I. "You have been a busy man. A toast, then, to this new enterprise!" I moved to the sideboard and poured us both a celebratory whisky.

"Yes, a toast, Watson." Holmes smiled as he raised his glass. "To the Silver Lining!"

The Curse of Carmody Grange

By Eric Brown

On referring to my notes, I am reminded that the winter of 1890 was exceedingly severe, with a cold snap gripping the land and a fall of snow covering the city of London to a depth of six inches. On the morning of January 23, having been called out in the early hours to minister to the needs of an ailing major in Bloomsbury, it was almost eleven by the time I returned to find Holmes toasting his thin hands before the blazing fire.

"There's breakfast on the sideboard," said he. "I would ask Mrs. Hudson to reheat it, if I were you. She was all for taking it away, as punishment for an assumed drink-fuelled late night, but I prevailed upon her to show mercy and explained that you had been called out to Major Fotheringay."

"How the deuce do you know I was over at Fotheringay's, Holmes?"

"Simplicity itself. You mentioned the major's gout last week, and when I arose I observed that your bag was not at its usual station in the hall, and that the magnesium was absent from your rack of medical supplies. The deduction was therefore obvious: you had been summoned by the major."

I glanced at Holmes as I sat down and tucked into the bacon. "I won't bother Mrs. Hudson," I said. "Cold breakfast never harmed anyone. Got quite accustomed to lukewarm kedgeree in Afghanistan."

I paused, chewing thoughtfully, and observed a certain vim in my friend's demeanour as he rubbed his hands together and turned to roast his backside before the flames.

For the past fortnight Holmes had been sunk in a slough of despond, with frequent recourse to his 7 percent solution. Holmes was at his very worst when his brain was inactive, which produced in him a physiological lassitude ameliorated only by his fondness for cocaine. But now his eyes sparkled, and a vitality informed his movements, brought about not by drugs, I surmised, but by some intellectual puzzle presented to tax his intellect.

"I say, Holmes, are you working on a case?"

He turned his aquiline visage and favoured me with a sardonic glance. "From time to time, Watson, your powers of observation astound me."

"Out with it, man!" I demanded, ignoring his heavy-handed sarcasm.

He seated himself in his armchair beside the fire and crossed his long legs. "This morning," said he, "I was called upon by a young lady and presented with a pretty problem. You have heard, I take it, of Oswald Carmody?"

"Of course. His volumes on the occult are famous, though I rather think there has been nothing new from his pen for a decade or more."

"Just so. And pray tell, what do you make of his work?"

"Well… His books are first-rate examples of their kind—if you go in for that type of thing."

" 'That type of thing,' " Holmes repeated with scorn. "Trifling accounts of the supernatural: tales of ghosts and ghouls and things—

to employ the cliché—that go bump in the night. In other words, poppycock."

"Quite," I said; "but what has all this got to do with your lady visitor?"

He stared into space, a long forefinger stroking the line of his jaw, before he replied. "Amelia Carmody claimed that her father's stories are based on fact: that the many and various shades, spectres, and apparitions that appear in his lurid little accounts do in actuality exist. More to the point, she also made the claim, before she returned to Hampshire on the ten o'clock train, that the occult had a direct bearing on her father's sudden disappearance three days ago."

"Oswald Carmody has disappeared?" I exclaimed.

"Vanished clean off the face of the earth, according to his daughter," he said, "and according to the report in yesterday's *Times*." He glanced up at the carriage clock on the mantelshelf. "There is a train leaving Waterloo at a little before one o'clock, Watson. Are you game?"

"Need you ask, Holmes?" said I.

"Then pack an overnight bag, and I will recount what Miss Carmody told me once we are ensconced in the carriage to Winchester."

"Oswald Carmody was in the habit of working well into the early hours," said Holmes as the train raced through the snow-bound shires southwest of London. "He favoured a large room on the ground floor of the Jacobean manse that had been the family seat for almost three hundred years. His study was a book-lined room with a single door giving onto a passageway, and a pair of French windows overlooking a lawn to the rear of the house. He was in the habit of locking the study door while he was working, and the French windows were kept locked at all times. On evening of January 19, just over three days ago, he retired after dinner at nine, as was his wont, and locked the study door after him. This was the last that Amelia saw of him, for the old man did not show himself at breakfast the following morning. As eight o'clock came and went, and then nine o'clock—and no reply to his daughter's increasingly desperate queries issued from within the room—she summoned the manservant, who succeeded in forcing the lock. To their consternation, they found the room empty: Oswald Carmody had vanished. The key was still in the lock on the inside of the door, and the French windows were likewise secured. Moreover, it had snowed the previous evening, but no footprints were to be seen leading from the French windows and away from the house. Amelia, as you might imagine, was beside herself with fear and consternation, emotions still on display when she sought my services this morning and recounted the fateful episode. She was distraught at the thought of what might have happened to her father—and fearful of the agency that had caused his disappearance. For she was convinced, Watson, that he had been spirited away by demonic forces. I agreed to take on the case, for, quite apart from finding it a pretty little puzzle, I am determined to prove to the poor girl that her father's predicament, far from being the result of occult machinations, has a perfectly rational explanation."

"That's all very well, Holmes, but if both doors were locked from the inside, and no footprints were to be observed leading away from the French windows…"

My friend bestowed upon me a knowing glance. "I see," he said; "you are playing the Devil's advocate. But there are many explanations to account for the anomaly, Watson, as we shall find in due course. Now, I do believe that this is our station."

From the country halt just outside the city of Winchester, we hired a trap to take us the three miles to the village of Thurston Marriot, on the outskirts of which stood Carmody Grange. The going was treacherous, the narrow lanes being blocked in places by deep snowdrifts, and it was almost an hour before we turned into the driveway and the Grange came into sight.

Surrounded as it was by the lowering shapes of ancient oak trees, with a caul of snow-filled cumulus overhead, the Grange presented a dour aspect that had nothing at all to do with my knowledge of its being the domicile of one of the country's most revered writers on the occult.

If the house itself was dank and drear, then its present incumbent—Miss Amelia Carmody—proved to be quite the opposite. She was a tiny creature with a pretty face and a vital, becoming manner, notwithstanding the situation in which she found herself.

She greeted us at the door with a ready and grateful smile, and ushered us into a large if dowdy reception room. Holmes made the introductions, and Miss Carmody took my hand and murmured that she was delighted to make my acquaintance.

She turned to regard my friend. "You cannot begin to imagine my gratitude at your agreeing to look into this matter, Mr. Holmes," she went on. "The local police have been little more than useless: they insist that my father has wandered off of his own accord and will turn up in due course. But forgive me—you must be cold and tired. You will, of course, remain at the Grange as my guest for as long as the investigation takes. I will summon Jefferies to show you to your rooms."

The old man ushered us through the rambling house, along creaking passageways that M. R. James himself might have described in his tales of the uncanny. No sooner had I unpacked my overnight bag than Holmes came knocking upon my door.

We proceeded downstairs and met Miss Carmody outside her father's study. The passage was narrow and gloomy, and laid with cold flagstones, the door itself black and warped with age. Splintered wood showed where the manservant had succeeded in forcing an entry.

Miss Carmody pushed open the timber door, and we stepped into the hallowed chamber.

The instant we crossed the threshold, my friend was pacing hither and thither like a bloodhound on the scent. He strode the length of the room, taking in its accoutrements and furnishings, and then, as I had seen him do on countless occasions, he fell to his knees and began a minute examination of the floor of the chamber.

With its gloomy mahogany panelling, its shelves of leather-bound volumes, its multitudinous examples of the taxidermist's art, as well as the bountiful paraphernalia of the occultist—crystal balls, pentagrams drawn on musty charts upon the walls—the room was the very manifestation of the *sanctum sanctorum* of a man who had devoted his life to the study of the dark arts.

Miss Carmody stood beside the desk, a hand resting lightly upon the leather inlay, as she watched with curiosity—and not a little amusement—the antics of Sherlock Holmes as he went about his business.

The moment found him tapping at the walls between the bookcases with his long, agile fingers, his ear pressed to the uneven plasterwork. As he worked, he fired questions over his shoulder.

"As I recall, you mentioned that you have a brother. Is he resident at the Grange?"

"Indeed, sir; George has no other option for he is, sadly, bed-ridden."

"His condition, if I might ask?"

"He is consumptive and stricken with regular brain fever."

"Nevertheless, I will have to question him, if this can be arranged."

"I am sure he'll be amenable to such a request, Mr. Holmes; he has few visitors, and will be eager to make your acquaintance."

"Beside your brother, yourself, and your father, who else is resident at the Grange?"

"Only Jefferies, the manservant."

"No cook, kitchen staff, valets?"

"Mrs. Hopkins from the village comes in and cooks and cleans for a couple of hours every afternoon."

"You mentioned that you are employed as a governess for a lawyer in Winchester," said Holmes. "When precisely are your days of work?"

"I work three days a week—Mondays, Tuesdays, and Wednesdays—teaching his twins French, German, and Latin."

"The rest of the time you are domiciled at the Grange? So you were present the day before your father's disappearance, on Friday last?"

She assented to this, and Holmes went on. "Did your father receive guests during the week leading up to the fateful day, pray tell?"

"No… That is, yes—his brother Jasper dropped by on the Tuesday, although I was out at the time."

Holmes repeated the name. "On what business, might I ask?"

"That I cannot state with any certainty, Mr. Holmes; though I do know that my father and Jasper share an interest in the occult."

"I will find Jasper in the village?"

The young lady shook her head. "He has a small cottage in the grounds of the house; it was the groom's, in the heyday of the estate, when my ancestors kept horses for hunting. Sadly, the stable yard is much overgrown these days."

"Might I ask why your uncle resides in the groom's old cottage, when there are ample rooms to be had in the Grange?"

"My father and Jasper did not, at one time, see eye to eye; indeed there was a falling-out over the provision of my father's will. Happily, that has been resolved, and they are on equable terms once more. Nevertheless, Jasper still prefers the solitude of his own cottage."

His examination of the four walls complete, Holmes moved to the desk before the French windows and stared down at its disorganised burden: maps and charts sat in heaps, weighed down with an eclectic array of oddments—an ancient dirk, an old meerschaum pipe, and what I recognised as the scapula of a fully-grown man.

Beside the desk stood a walnut bookcase bearing an array of two dozen volumes which on closer examination proved to be those from Oswald Carmody's own pen, with such sensational titles as *The Terror of Hadleigh Hall*, *Ghosts I Have Known*, and *The Devil's Accomplice*.

Holmes looked up from the hugger-mugger of objects on the desk. "Are you close to your father, Miss Carmody?"

"I hold him in deep affection, if that is what you mean. He is in many ways a reserved man, little given to a show of emotion. This I explain by the early death of his wife, taken when I was just an infant; indeed, I can hardly recall Mama."

"And your brother, George; is he close to your father?"

She compressed her lips. "I am afraid not. They do not see eye to eye, and never have. George finds my father's obsession with the occult nothing short of ridiculous; he is an arch rationalist, a man of science. He was studying physics at Oxford before he fell ill."

Holmes nodded to himself and opened the cover of a stout ledger which occupied pride of position on the desk. Looking over his shoulder, I made out a neat copperplate hand covering an expanse of feint-ruled lines.

"My father's journal," Miss Carmody explained.

My friend read a few lines, then, in a flurry of excitement, riffled back a few pages and resumed reading with increased absorption. A minute later he looked up at me, a gleam in his eye. "What do you make of this, Watson—most especially the passage here?"

His finger indicated the final entry in Oswald Carmody's journal, and I stepped forward and began reading.

...approaching a critical juncture in our research. There can be little doubt that all the evidence, ably abetted by the observations of Jasper, leads to the manifest fact that we have come upon a significant clue as to the very location of the portal ultimum. *There can be no doubting, also,*

that a passage might be effected. I shall inform Jasper without delay, and God willing I shall prove to the world...

Holmes turned to the young woman. "Have you read this, Miss Carmody?"

She shook her head. "I was never allowed into his study, and I wouldn't dream of—"

Holmes interrupted. "Would you kindly cast an eye upon this passage?"

She did so, a hand to her mouth as her eyes raced across the lines. At last she looked up at my friend, her expression puzzled. "I...I cannot for the life of me fathom its meaning..." She took a breath and went on, "What can he mean, the *'portal ultimum,'* and 'a passage might be effected'?"

Instead of replying, Holmes moved around the desk and stood before the French windows, staring out at the snow-clad grounds. He spent long minutes examining the frame, and then the lock mechanism at the foot of the door, and finally the huge iron key that hung on a hook beside the windows.

He consulted his fob-watch, and said, "Now, Miss Carmody, I would like an audience with your brother, if I may, after which I think there might be time to pay a visit to your uncle before dinner."

The young woman ushered us from the study, up a grand staircase, and along a warped corridor into the west wing of the house. There she knocked on a door and, receiving a summons, opened it and introduced Holmes and myself to a sickly-looking youth who was sitting up in a four-poster bed. Saying that she had to supervise the cook in the preparation of dinner, she slipped from the bedchamber.

"Please forgive our intrusion," Holmes said as he drew up a chair. "Your sister had the wisdom to enlist our aid in the matter of locating your errant father, and there are one or two questions I am obliged to ask."

"Amelia mentioned that she was travelling up to London to petition the great Sherlock Holmes," George said. "I am at your disposal."

As I took a seat, I observed the youth more closely: he was in his twenties, and thin to the point of emaciation; his blade-like face was deathly pale and covered in a sheen of perspiration. His hands, which lay upon the counterpane, were claw-like, with veins outstanding, and twitched from time to time with involuntary, galvanic spasms.

"If I might begin by asking about the events of the morning of the twentieth," Holmes said.

"Amelia came to me," George said, "beside herself with worry. She reported what she had found in pater's study—or rather what she had not found—and I did my best to console her and vouchsafe the opinion that my father, deep in the throes of creation, had left his study and gone for a long walk."

"And the small matter of his study being locked from the inside?"

"Simplicity itself, Mr. Holmes. The only explanation can be that my father had a spare key for the French windows, and used this to let himself out on that morning."

"Notwithstanding the fact that the snow behind the Grange was untrodden?"

"It was snowing heavily that night," said the youth; "I venture that he went abroad early, and that a fresh fall of snow covered his tracks."

A light gleamed in Holmes's eyes, and it came to me that this explanation had occurred to him, too, and he was applauding the young man's rationality.

"And the fact that he has failed to return?" Holmes asked.

"I fear my father might have succumbed to illness while abroad, or slipped and fell. Uncle Jasper said that he would summon the local constabulary and have them conduct a search which, due to lack of manpower, was scant, according to Jasper himself."

"I take it you give little credence to your sister's explanation that a supernatural agency might have been responsible for your father's disappearance?"

George gave a heartfelt sigh. "My sister is as credulous as my father, Mr. Holmes. We were brought up in an atmosphere steeped in the occult and the supernatural: whereas I repudiated such tomfoolery and sought a more mechanistic explanation for the workings of the universe, my sister was not so fortunate. She took my father's preachings on the supernatural as gospel."

"Are you aware of his latest investigations, pray tell?"

The young man laughed, but without mirth. "He has been obsessed with this for the past ten years," said he. "He abandoned his other writings and bent all his efforts to investigating the portal, and the curse that is said to hang over the Grange."

This pricked my friend's interest: he became even more alert. "The curse? But Amelia said nothing of this."

"My father thought it wise to protect her feminine sensibilities on the subject."

"I would like to know more about this so-called curse," said Holmes, leaning forward in his chair.

The young man waved a languid hand in eloquent disgust. "It is arrant nonsense, Mr. Holmes. My father claims to have uncovered some writings of a distant forebear dating from the 1600s, in which a curse is mentioned. I don't know the details, but my father says that the owner of the Grange back in the 1690s discovered the entrance to the netherworld, and was taken by the creatures that dwelled within. One hundred years later, in the 1790s, Sir Pelham Carmody happened to vanish, again in peculiar circumstances. From these incidents arose the ridiculous story of the curse. The fact is that Pelham was a notorious rake and ne'er-do-well, with considerable debts, and it was in his interests to go to earth and so confound his creditors."

"Still and all," Holmes mused, "an interesting little fabulation."

"But that's all it is, mark my word," said George. "If you really wish to know more, then my Uncle Jasper is your man. He worked with my father on his investigations: he is just as besotted with the story."

"I understand that at one time your father and your uncle were in dispute over the former's will?"

George said, "This was many years ago, following the death of my grandfather, who left the estate to my father, despite my uncle being the elder of his sons."

Holmes frowned. "Did your grandfather explain the reason for this decision?"

The young man shrugged. "I understand that my uncle was, at the time, given to drink, and so earned the mistrust of my grandfather."

"But a rapprochement between your father and uncle has been achieved?"

"To the point where they now happily work side by side," said George.

"Do you happen to know the provision of your father's will?" Holmes enquired. "I take it that you, as his only son, are his main beneficiary?"

The young man inclined his head. "So I understand, Mr. Holmes, though I am assured that adequate provision has been made for my sister."

My friend stared through the mullioned window to the darkening skies, lost in thought for the moment. At last he stirred himself and rose to his feet. "We will keep you no longer, young sir; I thank you for your time."

We moved to the door, whereupon Holmes turned and asked, "I wonder…we are dining with your sister this evening: will you be able to leave your bed and join us?"

"From time to time I make the effort," said George, "and on this occasion, with such esteemed guests at the table, it will be my honour to dine with you."

"Capital," said Holmes as we took our leave.

We made our way downstairs and along the gloomy corridor, then stepped outside and crossed the snow-covered lawn toward the stand of bare trees at the far end of the garden.

"You asked George about the provision of his father's will," I said as we entered the margin of trees and proceeded through the woodland; "but surely you can't suspect George of doing away with his father?"

He stopped beneath a dripping elm and stared at me. "If we rule out a supernatural cause, which we have," said he, "and if we allow that foul play is possible, then one of the suspects must therefore be George, and the others Jasper and Amelia—if, that is, the culprit is not someone from beyond the Grange itself."

"Good God, man!" I cried. "You don't seriously think that Amelia might be behind this, do you? Why, she's a mere slip of a thing!"

"You are making the grave mistake of allowing your emotional bias to blind you to the very real possibility that Amelia might be responsible. I have said before, Watson, that the fairer sex are capable of crimes just as heinous as, and worse than, any male." He pointed through the trees. "And this must be our destination."

We had passed several tumbledown outbuildings in our progress through the woods, and now before us, in a clearing, stood a tiny cottage with a low thatched roof and the illumination of a welcoming oil-lamp burning behind a mullioned window.

Our summons was answered by a tall, perilously thin, and cadaverous man I judged to be in his eighties; he wore a smoking jacket and a high-collared shirt, with a pair of half-moon glasses perched upon the bridge of his thin nose.

"Miss Amelia told me that she had hired the services of the illustrious Sherlock Holmes," said he by way of a greeting, though with a touch of acerbity in his tone.

We followed the old man into a tiny front room which, like Oswald Carmody's study, was packed with ancient books. In the middle of the room stood a small table piled with leather-bound volumes and scrolls; evidently we had interrupted Jasper Carmody in the process of writing, for a quill stood in a pot of ink and a square of blotting paper covered a quarto of vellum.

"If you would care to take a seat, gentlemen—"

He stopped abruptly as Holmes, with unaccustomed clumsiness, stumbled into the table. In doing so he brought down the folding leaf, sending an avalanche of books and papers to the floor.

"My apologies!" my friend cried. "How clumsy! Please, allow me to…" Bending down, Holmes picked up a pile of books, along with a bundle of papers, and restored them to the table. Fortunately the pot of ink did not spill, and, order restored, we took our proffered seats before the fire.

"It's a pretty problem and no mistake," Holmes began. "Amelia ascribes her father's disappearances to some supernatural agency while, conversely, her brother will have no such truck with the idea. I understand that you," Holmes went on, "subscribe to the former?"

The old man's skeletal face gave a thin smile. "I know full well the fate of my brother, Mr. Holmes."

"Ah, the 'portal ultimum'…?" Holmes said.

"So you have been reading Oswald's journal? Stirring stuff, is it not?" The old man stared at us, excitement visible in the light of his bright blue eyes. "We have been working toward this for well nigh a decade, and soon the world will be cognizant of the true facts of the case."

"I take it," said Holmes with ill-concealed amusement, "you refer to the Curse of Carmody Grange? If you might enlighten me as to the exact nature of the curse, my friend?"

"In the 1600s, a distant forebear of ours, one Geoffrey Carmody, dabbled in the dark arts and summoned a demon. It was this demon, so the story goes, that cursed the man and took him thither, never to be seen again. A curse was placed on the family: whosoever dabbled in the dark arts would be likewise taken. In 1790, Sir Pelham Carmody met a similar fate…"

"And yet," said Holmes, "this did not deter your brother—or indeed yourself?"

"Far from it, sir! Unlike our forebears, we are well versed in magicks black and white, and Oswald judged that the time was upon us—was it not a century since Sir Pelham Carmody vanished from the very woodland behind the Grange? From our exhaustive investigations, we knew that soon the portal would open, and Oswald ensured that he would be present when it happened."

"Do you mean to say…?" I began, staring from my friend to the ecstatic visage of the old man.

"I saw it, sir, with my own eyes, on the morning of the twentieth. An effulgent glow of lapis lazuli light emanated from the mighty oak not half a mile north of this very cottage, and with a cry of elation my brother stepped through the portal, embraced by its lambency…"

"But, confound it, man," I cried, "what the deuce happened to him?"

The look that Jasper Carmody bestowed upon us confirmed to me that indeed the man was out of his mind. "He stepped across the threshold of this world," he said in trembling tones, "and into the next."

"The *next*?" Holmes said, sitting back in his chair and regarding the old man with dispassion.

"The reality that underpins the material world as we know it," he said, "the realm of spirits, sprites, and, yes, the undead."

"I take it that you did not worry Miss Amelia with this?" Holmes said.

"I thought it wise to remain silent on the matter," Jasper said. "When she rushed here to inform me of her father's disappearance, I did my best to calm her. I returned with her to the Grange, assuring her that all would be well and that soon her father would return."

Holmes leaned forward. "Return? How could you be certain?"

Jasper smiled and pointed across the room to a small table before the window. A mortar and pestle sat upon it, and next to them a pack of Tarot cards. "I have been in contact with those from beyond," he said, "and they have reassured me of Oswald's safe return to this world."

Doing his best to hide his smile, Holmes asked, "And when might this be, Mr. Carmody?"

"When the time is auspicious," the old man said; "I suspect within the next day or so."

"I would be grateful if, when you have precise intelligence of his return, you would kindly inform me," Holmes said, his tones larded with sarcasm. "I should like to be on hand to witness this...*miracle*."

The old man inclined his head. "It would be my pleasure, sir."

Shortly thereafter, Holmes thanked Jasper Carmody for his time and we took our leave. As we hurried through the darkness toward the Grange, I said, "What did you make of that, Holmes? Confirmation, if any were needed, that Jasper is quite clearly insane, what?"

"On the contrary, Watson, I think friend Carmody is quite remarkably sane—as we shall find out in due course."

Holmes would vouchsafe no more on the matter, and we arrived back at the Grange in time to dine with Miss Amelia and George. Talk was desultory at first, with all parties reluctant to broach the very topic that had brought us here; I regaled our hosts with a story or two of my service in Afghanistan, and it was only toward the end of the meal that Amelia brought herself to enquire as to the progress of the investigation.

"It proceeds satisfactorily," said Holmes; "and I very much hope that the affair might reach its resolution on the morrow."

Citing an early start in the morning, Holmes would not be drawn to elucidate, and soon thereafter he bade our hosts goodnight and retired; I followed him shortly thereafter.

I spent a sleepless night, kept awake not only by all the recent talk of ghosts and ghouls, but by the manse's ancient timbers creaking and groaning like those of an old galleon on the high seas. It was well into the early hours by the time sleep at last claimed me.

I was awoken from a fitful slumber at seven the next morning by an intemperate tapping at the door. I opened it to find Holmes fully dressed and impatient to be away. "Come, Watson," said he; "we are leaving."

"Leaving?" I said, casting about for my clothes and quickly dressing.

"I have told Miss Amelia that we will continue our investigations elsewhere," he said, "and she is rousing Jefferies to ready the trap to take us to the station."

I saw, from the damp state of my friend's brogues, and the droplets covering his cape, that Holmes had ventured out that morning. When I questioned him, he said, "We'll make a detective of you yet, Watson! You're right—I had a little job to conduct in the woods. But more of that later."

Within fifteen minutes, having consumed a hurried breakfast of coffee and crumpets, we took our leave of Miss Amelia and boarded the two-wheeler. I was surprised to see that the snow had vanished during the night, washed away by a drizzle that still precipitated and soaked the land.

My friend was silent until Jefferies reined us to a halt before the station, turned the trap, and cantered off. Holmes consulted his pocket watch and exclaimed with satisfaction, "Not yet eight—we are in time, Watson, to meet the four o'clock slow train from Waterloo."

"What is all this, Holmes—our hurried departure, and now this? You said we are to meet the train?"

"Or rather someone who will be upon it," said he, and proffered a small sheet of paper by way of explanation.

It was a telegram, and in some state of confusion I read the short message thereon: INTRIGUING! ARRIVING AT EIGHT. CHESTER ATKINS.

"I noted the edge of the telegram obtruding from beneath the pile of books on the table in Jasper's cottage yesterday, with Atkins's name upon it," said Holmes. "My curiosity piqued, I contrived the trip to dislodge them and pocket it." He waved the telegram. "Note the name—Chester Atkins."

"The reporter from the *Times*?"

"No less. The very same young fellow who assisted us in the Pendlebury Poisonings just last year," Holmes said, as we hurried onto the platform in time to meet the slow train pulling into the station.

Chester Atkins, a rubicund young man with ginger pork-chop sideburns and an ebullient manner, descended from the carriage and hurried, panting, along the platform. "As I live and breathe!" he cried in pronounced Cockney tones. "If it ain't Sherlock Holmes hisself, and Dr. Watson! But what in heaven's name brings you to this Godforsaken place?"

"The very same that brings you, young sir," said Holmes. "Come, I will apprise you of the situation on the way to the Grange."

We boarded a four-wheeler in the station forecourt, and minutes later were barrelling back the way we had come, Holmes in hushed confabulation with the young reporter. The fellow could barely contain his amazement at my friend's account. "A singular tale and no mistake!" declared Atkins; "but not quite the story I was expecting."

We arrived at the Grange, and Holmes led the way around the house and through the woods to the cottage of Mr. Jasper Carmody. The old man whipped open the front door and greeted us with elation. "Mr. Atkins! And Holmes and Watson—you're just in time. Oh, the miracles you are about to witness, sirs! The veritable wonders that are about to assail your senses! But there is no time to lose—I have had confirmation from the spirits themselves that the *portal ultimum* will open within the hour! If you would kindly follow me this way…" So saying, he pulled on a greatcoat and hurried from the cottage, with young Atkins giving Holmes a startled look as we gave chase through the woodland.

"As I mentioned in my original missive, Mr. Atkins," Jasper said breathlessly over his shoulder, "four days ago my brother Oswald entered the *portal ultimum*—the very portal through which passed his ancestors."

"I understand that those ancestors never returned," Atkins panted as he attempted to keep pace; "so what I want to know is, how come Mr. Carmody has managed to elude the ghostly horde on the other side?"

"Because," said Jasper, "my brother went forewarned, with a vast knowledge of the occult and the means with which to best those that dwell thither!"

We plunged ever deeper into forest, the trees crowding together and shutting out the daylight, and if ever a stage had been designed for the culmination of our eldritch investigation, then this was it. We came at last to a clearing, in the centre of which stood a vast stunted oak: its great bole had split into two, and over the decades one trunk had contrived to bend over to form a perfect parabola, an archway fully ten feet high and just as wide.

Jasper Carmody halted and spread his arms. "Behold!" he cried. "The *portal ultimum*! The gateway connecting this world to the next!"

As his words rang around the clearing, despite myself, I shivered: there was an almost palpable atmosphere of imminent menace in the air. The oak appeared at the same time mighty and yet stunted, resembling one of the grotesquely contorted growths that grace the illustrations of Arthur Rackham, and I half expected a phalanx of ghosts and ghouls to come tumbling through the arch at any second.

Startling me, Jasper gave a cry in Latin, whipped a long dagger from beneath his greatcoat and, raising it into the air before him, stepped slowly but with purpose toward the oak tree, chanting as he went.

He then proceeded to move widdershins around the tree three times, all the while beseeching the demons to release his brother in magic. He disappeared around the contorted bole for the third time, and from behind the tree we heard his heartfelt cry: "*Behold!*"

I took a step forward, my heart beating wildly, quite taken with the old man's theatrics.

"Look!" said Atkins, pointing toward the arched trunk.

As he spoke, I beheld what I can only describe as a feeble splutter of sparks from around the archway such as might be produced by defective fireworks; indeed, the phrase "damp squibs" comes to mind. At the same time, still hidden behind the tree, Jasper intoned, "Behold, the portal opens, and Carmody returns triumphant!"

To say that the culmination of his pronouncement was anti-climactic would be an understatement. As the feeble sparks spluttered out, silence reigned, and the portal signally failed to open. All was as it had been before Jasper's portentous words and the sad display of fireworks.

Sherlock Holmes stepped forward, clearing his throat. "You can come out now, Jasper—the game is up."

Jasper Carmody emerged from behind the tree, his smile now sickly. "I…I cannot fathom what might have happened. The spirits were specific—my brother was to return! What can have become of him?"

"If you would care to follow me," said Holmes, "I will show you precisely what has become of Mr. Carmody. Watson, be so good as to take a firm grip on friend Jasper's arm so that he might not elude us. This way!"

Doing as he said, I marched Jasper Carmody through the woods in pursuit of Holmes and young Atkins, the old man muttering pitifully as we went. We moved toward the Grange and came at last to the tumbledown outbuildings. A small stone building stood in their midst, the only one still quite whole, and an odd sight then greeted our gazes.

The building possessed no windows, only a single door, and to the handle of this door was attached a rope which stretched from the handle to a nearby tree, around which it was securely tied. That the rope was an effective means of keeping the door securely shut was attested to by the curses and thumpings that issued from within the rude stone prison.

Holmes stepped forward and, taking a pen-knife from his pocket, sliced through the rope and pushed open the door.

The dishevelled figure of a bald-headed man, in a febrile state of rage, stood upon the threshold.

"Gentlemen," Holmes announced, "I present to you none other than Oswald Carmody."

"It was a cruel and feeble ruse you attempted to play," Holmes declared. We were in the front room of Jasper Carmody's cottage, with Oswald and Jasper seated side by side on the settee like a pair of miscreant schoolboys.

Atkins sat to one side, eagerly taking down Holmes's words in his notebook.

"How you came upon the idea," Holmes said, "is a matter of conjecture. Did a decade of investigations into the Curse of Carmody Grange come to nought, Oswald? Did you thus decide, with the aid of your brother, to stage the little pantomime in the hope of convincing Mr. Atkins, and the world, of your miraculous sojourn in the netherworld? Did you then plan to write up your escapades in a tawdry volume for the scurrilous delectation of a gullible and feeble-minded public?" He waved this away. "Whatever, it was a cruel jape to play on Amelia and George. You thought nothing of their consternation at your disappearance, only of the glory you would attain upon your miraculous return."

At this point Atkins interposed a question. "What made you suspect it was a ruse, Mr. Holmes?"

My friend smiled. "It was wonderfully ironic, Mr. Atkins. My suspicion was aroused by the very impossibility of ascribing Mr.

Carmody's vanishment to the occult. There had to be a rational explanation for his disappearance, and I had my first clue when I discovered that you, Jasper, were upon the scene soon after, bringing Amelia back to the Grange and assuring her that her father would soon return. My suspicions were further stirred when I discovered the telegram you received from Mr. Atkins, whom you had contacted with the tale of Oswald's abduction by spirits and his miraculous return through the *portal ultimum,* instructing the reporter to come this morning." Holmes gave a grim smile. "What in fact happened was that Oswald left his study on the evening of the nineteenth and spent the intervening days lodged in his brother's cottage while the world read the *Times's* account of his mysterious disappearance, only this morning retiring to the outbuilding in order to be close to the so-called portal."

"And the fact that the French windows were bolted from the inside?" I asked.

"Simplicity itself," said Holmes, turning to the brothers. "When you pulled the French window shut after you, Oswald, the force with which you did so dislodged the bolt, which was aligned vertically at the foot of the door. It slid into place, effectively securing the door from within."

Holmes smiled around the gathering, and continued. "At dawn today, I hurried into the woodland and located the mighty oak. I had a little time to wait, but in due course witnessed Jasper himself arranging small piles of sulphur, charcoal, and saltpetre in the recesses of the tree trunk, linked to a fuse wire leading out of sight behind the tree. Once I had seen Jasper return to his cottage, it was a simple matter for me to dampen the mixture and thus effectively render it useless. I reasoned that Mr. Carmody must be in hiding not too far away, and on searching the few outbuildings in the wood, I soon located his dwelling place, signalled by his snores from within. I then secured the door with a rope to ensure that he would be going nowhere. You know the rest, my friends."

Atkins shook his head and, closing his notebook, said, "It will make a goodly column or two for my paper, Mr. Holmes—"

At this, Oswald Carmody looked up suddenly and exclaimed, "You can't! I would be ruined! The reputation, the work of a decade…" He spluttered to a halt at the idea of his defamation in the eyes of the public.

"I think," said Holmes, "that perhaps the story might be best kept from the wider world—if, that is, Mr. Carmody, you will make two promises."

Carmody looked up at Holmes with an enraged expression. "And they are?"

"One, that you will return to the Grange and explain to Amelia and George that, in the early hours of the morning of the twentieth, you let yourself out of your study by the French windows, using a spare key you had cut a while ago, with the bolt slipping into place as I earlier described. Thereafter, musing upon your work, you wandered through the woodland, where you fell and struck your head. Insensate, you managed to drag yourself to a shelter and there lay, passing in and out of consciousness, until this morning."

"Very well," Carmody muttered, "and your second proviso?"

Holmes gave a grim smile. "That you write not one word, for public consumption, pertaining to the Curse of Carmody Grange— on pain of my good friend Mr. Atkins here making public the story of your duplicity."

Almost weeping with frustrated rage, Oswald Carmody had no option but consent to my friend's terms.

There is little more to relate of the matter. We returned to the Grange, leaving Jasper Carmody sulking in his cottage and Chester Atkins to make his way back to London, suitably recompensed by Holmes for his time and effort. It was with a swelling heart that I beheld the expression of disbelief, closely followed by joy, on the face of Amelia Carmody as her father stumbled into her embrace.

"Why, Mr. Holmes," she said, pulling away from her father and staring tearfully at my friend, "however might I thank you?"

Holmes, who my readers well know was little given to exhibitions of overt emotion, was clearly moved by the sight of the reunion. "The evidence of your happiness at the successful outcome of the affair is sufficient gratitude in itself, Miss Carmody."

Later that day, on our return to Baker Street, we warmed ourselves by the fire and my friend observed, "A salutatory little affair, Watson; and one which, I take it, will at some point find itself recounted in the annals of my exploits?"

"The episode does contain elements that the public might find salacious," I allowed, "once Mr. Oswald Carmody has shuffled off his mortal coil, that is: a comely young woman in distress, a family curse, a hint of the occult, and not a little chicanery."

"Let it be an object lesson," said Holmes, "in the triumph of rationality over the woolly-mindedness of superstition. And now, if you please, would you be so kind as to pour me another glass of brandy?"

Sherlock Holmes and a Case of Humbug

By Paul A. Freeman

One frigid December twenty-fifth, once the plum pudding of our Christmas dinner had been consumed, my friend Sherlock Holmes discarded his party hat with a flourish and said: "My dear Watson, enough of this coercive frivolity. In yesterday's *Gazette* there appeared a most curious article. It concerned a miserly old moneylender residing at 12A, Gilforth Yard, who on Christmas Day last year became suddenly munificent and sociable."

" 'Tis the season…" I said with a shrug, paraphrasing the popular Christmas carol.

"That may be so," my friend continued, unaffected by my evident indifference. "However, the transformation coincided with the seventh anniversary of his business partner's death. Do you not find any of this suggestive?"

"Not in the slightest," I replied, at which Holmes's eyes gleamed mischievously.

"Oh, no!" I protested. "Not on Christmas Day."

"Get your coat and muffler, Watson," said Holmes, gleefully rubbing his hands. "And if you wouldn't mind, perhaps bring your service revolver with you. I have done some preliminary legwork on this matter, so we should be back in time for the Yuletide concert at Westminster."

Shortly afterwards, Holmes had secured a hansom cab and we were on our way through the falling snow toward the City. And what wondrous sights we beheld along our route. It was as if Christmas had transformed the rude urban populace, sprinkling upon them the essence of kindness. Gangs of good-natured youths ran amok throwing snowballs at passers-by, laughing heartily when their victims retaliated in pretended outrage. On every street corner stood carollers, their voices ringing out in the crisp, cold air, collection boxes before them as they raised alms for those less fortunate than themselves. Outside every bakery, lines of common London folk waited patiently to place their geese in the shop's ovens and to cook up a sumptuous, once in a year, Christmas dinner. Meanwhile, the more pious of the Town's denizens, dressed in their finest, made their way to church, as if drawn by the pealing bells. Everyone, it seemed, had a "Merry Christmas!" on their lips and a smile on their ruddy face. The ruthless rough-and-tumble and the selfish cut-and-thrust of daily life in the great metropolis had indeed been suspended on this anniversary of our saviour's birth.

My companion, however, was his habitual, thoughtful self. "You know, Watson," he said, "it has been statistically proven that the festive season, what with its financial stresses and the emotional strain of being compelled to turn the other cheek, is the most propitious time of the year for murder to occur."

I rolled my eyes. "And a merry Christmas to you, too, Holmes."

My friend chuckled at my deadpan reply, reached into the pocket of his coat, and withdrew the newspaper article from the previous day's *Gazette* which he had mentioned back at Baker Street. "Do me the favour of reading this aloud," he said, "and let me have your thoughts."

The said article, from the *Gazette* of 24 December, 18--, read as follows:

Heartwarming Tale of Skinflint Turned Philanthropist

A year ago today, Mr. Ebenezer Scrooge, a counting-house proprietor in the City of London, turned over a new leaf. Claiming that, after visitations from four ghosts (the first phantom being that of a business partner who had died exactly seven years earlier), the notorious miser, famous for his short temper and disagreeable manner, became a philanthropist overnight.

On this, the first anniversary of Mr. Scrooge's reformation, I interviewed him in his modest apartments at 12A Gilforth Yard.

"The spectre of my old partner, Jacob Marley, advised me on the joys of altruism," Mr. Scrooge explained to this reporter. "Being but a shade, he was impotent in his efforts to physically assist the poor and needy. And so, weighed down by the chains of selfishness and avarice he had forged during his lifetime, he told me I should change my ways or else suffer a similar fate.

"In an endeavour to bring about such a change, three more spirits visited me—the ghosts of Christmas Past, Christmas Present, and Christmas Yet to Come. They showed me the error of my ways and taught me that kindness to my fellow man was my only salvation."

Mr. Robert Cratchit, the accounts clerk at Scrooge and Marley and a resident of Camden Town, was all praise for his employer. "Gawd bless him," he said. "Never in my wildest dreams would I have believed that such a heartless, grasping, blood-sucking vampire of a man could have altered so considerably if I hadn't seen it with my own eyes. The gent has a soft spot for my youngest, my Tiny Tim. If it weren't for Mr. Scrooge's munificence, my boy wouldn't be able to walk about, what with the polio what's afflicted him since birth."

Without warning, Holmes burst into laughter, slapping his thigh as if he had heard the funniest of jokes.

"My dear Holmes," I said, "what an unseemly reaction. This Scrooge fellow has reformed from his wicked ways, and his benevolence is to be commended. Yet here you are, laughing about a disabled child and a grateful father."

With some effort, Holmes collected himself, and his guffaws subsided. "Quite so. I'm sorry. But you see, all might not be as it at first appears, my good Doctor. As I told you earlier, I have already done a little digging around, so I am in possession of several salient facts you are not yet privy to. Pray, continue with this most entertaining article."

With a sigh of annoyance, I resumed my reading:

When asked about his plans for Christmas Day, Mr. Scrooge said: "Just as happened last year, I'll send the prize turkey from the nearby poulterer's to my clerk and his family, and then drop in for Christmas dinner and charades with my til' recently estranged nephew, Fred."

Still wearing a supercilious smirk on his face, Holmes raised his hand, indicating I should stop relating the uplifting story of Ebenezer Scrooge's return to the fold of humanity.

"We're here," he said—without elucidating as to where "here" might be—and rapped on the roof of the cab with his cane.

We had stopped in the vicinity of London's Royal Exchange, the building's columned portico and ornate pediment a monument to Victorian architecture. And yet this was not our destination. Instead, Holmes led us through a warren of dilapidated tenements and assorted hovels, to a district of seedy moneylending establishments. The single bright spot in this grimy corner of London was the newly painted signage of Scrooge and Marley, the former penny-pincher's counting-house.

"What nerve this Scrooge has," Holmes remarked obscurely. "He's even kept his dead partner's name on the signboard. I warrant a week ago the façade of this moneylending premises was as grubby as the other such establishments in this street," he added, sniffing at the aroma of fresh paint in the freezing air. "He seems to be preparing to expand his business portfolio. Tell me, what do you deduce from what you see here, Watson?"

Above the heavy oak entrance door to Scrooge and Marley, a horseshoe had been nailed onto the lintel. "How ironic," I observed, "that a symbol of good fortune smiles down on those poor souls entering his office in hopes of borrowing a sum to cover their ill luck."

"But lucky for Scrooge, hey! What else?"

I peered through the lead-lined diamonds of glass in the bay window, into the gloomy depths of the counting-house. "Apart from the essential furniture and accoutrements of a city office, the establishment is quite bare."

"Exactly. Mr. Scrooge's liberality does not apparently stretch to the refurbishment of his business premises, and yet its veneer has been recently upgraded. Most elucidating. Anything else, Watson? What about the far wall of the good gentleman's offices?"

I leaned up close to the window, until my nose almost touched the glass, and shaded my eyes. "It doesn't look as if the wall's been painted in decades. And yet there's a lighter patch at eye level—the outline of something that once adorned the wall. A picture, perhaps."

"Or a mirror," said Holmes.

The contours of the outline, though symmetrical, were not rectangular, and indeed did resemble the shape of an ornate mirror. I conceded as much, and Holmes proceeded to hammer home my ignorance.

"I wrote a monograph on the subject of antique mirrors several years ago. The one which adorned this wall was pear-shaded and gilded—an eighteenth-century French Rocaille mirror, if I'm not mistaken." He took out his pocket watch and frowned at the time. "Come along, Watson, it's time to see the district where Mr. Scrooge resides and to make the old bird's acquaintance. Just keep in mind the horseshoe and the missing mirror."

With that, Holmes led me at a swift and rather exhausting clip through some of the narrowest streets and one of the most squalid quarters in London, until we arrived at Lime Street, a veritable thoroughfare in its width when compared to the filthy lanes we had just traversed. Except for a loitering street urchin who was stamping his feet and breathing warmth into his hands, the place was deserted. Presumably, the good folk of London were relaxing at home after the gluttonous excesses of Christmas dinner.

Hearing our footfalls, the lad turned his dirty face to us. "Allo, Doctor! You look pooped," he said before turning to Holmes. "Where've you bin, guv? The church bells 'ave just chimed two o'clock."

"Quite so, Wiggins," said Holmes, addressing the youthful leader of the Baker Street Irregulars. "However, I'm here now. No sign of our mark?"

"Not yet. Mr. Scrooge must still be at 'is nephew's."

Holmes nodded thoughtfully. "And the letter I gave you this morning for Inspector Lestrade?"

"Delivered as instructed, though 'ee weren't too 'appy being disturbed at 'ome on Christmas Day."

Whilst I was still catching my breath, I listened to this exchange in complete perplexity.

Noting my bafflement, Holmes explained. "Since yesterday I've had the Irregulars out and about, keeping an eye on Scrooge's apartments and his counting-house. They've also been to Camden Town, sniffing out the abode of Robert Cratchit, Scrooge's accounts clerk, snooping around, and reporting back anything of interest."

"Which we did last night, Doctor," said Wiggins. "And today, as per Mr. 'Olmes's request, I've been stationed in this charming spot of the capital, keeping me eyes and ears open." The young urchin pointed to the entrance of a nearby yard, Gilforth Yard. "Down there's where Mr. Scrooge lives. Number 12A. Not much to look at from the outside, and from what I've 'eard not much to look at on the inside. If 'ee's a rich geezer, then I'm the king of bloomin' Prussia."

"Well, your majesty," said Holmes, with unaccustomed good humour. "Here's a sovereign for yourself and your streetwise cohorts."

Skeptical at his good fortune, the little scamp tested the validity of the gold coin with his teeth, and, once reassured, said, "See the tavern across the road. Every day, without fail, Mr. Scrooge partakes 'imself of a tankard of grog and a gander at the newspaper."

And with that, Wiggins tipped his hat to us and headed off to whatever jollifications he and the other Irregulars had in store for Christmas Day.

Holmes indicated with his cane the Old Goose Inn, the dingy-looking tavern Wiggins had pointed out to us. "If we wish to acquire more information about this Scrooge character, and perhaps make the erstwhile skinflint's acquaintance, this is where we should hang our hats for an hour or so."

After our pell-mell perambulating, I was quite happy to put my feet up and smoke a pipe or two before the warming hearth of a hostelry. So we crossed Lime Street and Holmes pushed open the door to the private bar. Once inside, he ordered two glasses of bitter from the corpulent, ruddy-faced landlord, a fellow who, fortunately for us, was much predisposed to chitchat.

The opening sally was Holmes's, though. "I see you have many of the capital's daily newspapers available for your patrons to enjoy," he said, pointing to a newspaper rack beside the roaring fireplace. "I could not but notice that Ebenezer Scrooge, a local resident of this district, was the subject of a heartwarming article in the *London Gazette* yesterday."

"Oh, yes," said the landlord. " 'Ee lives in that yard just over the road, guv'nor; but don't believe all you read in them tabloids, nor the broadsheets; 'ee's just as mean as 'ee's always been. Leastways, 'ee is with me. And I don't mean 'ee's just mean with his money, even if 'ee does sup 'ere most ev'nings on our finest fare."

"Not much of a recommendation," I mumbled under my breath, looking around the sordid drinking establishment with distaste, at which Holmes tapped me most painfully on the shin with his cane.

"Pray, what are you referring to when you mention Scrooge's meanness?" the great sleuth asked. "Presumably you're alluding to some meanness of spirit."

"Well, the last time 'ee showed a bit of temper was to me cat, Esmeralda, sir. Usually Ezzie's moochin' about in the public bar, gettin' fussed over by the customers. The other night, though, she strayed into the private bar, where we are now. Mr. Scrooge was occupying 'is usual place, in the booth over there." At this juncture our host pointed to a partitioned spot by a window in which two un-upholstered benches faced each other, separated by a rickety oak table on which sat a salt cellar. "Any'ow, Ezzie comes over to 'im, all friendly-like and purring, rubs 'erself up against 'is leg as 'ee's 'eading back from the bar to 'is booth, and 'ee kicks 'er 'alf way across the bar."

"My goodness!" I ejaculated. "I can only imagine his excuse is that he has an allergy and that the hair of a feline brings him out in a rash."

The landlord shrugged. "Maybe 'ee's just a cruel old geezer what don't like cats."

I noticed that Holmes had that peculiar twinkle in his eye which can occur either when a new fact confirms his favoured theory or when I've said something particularly dim-witted.

"Tell me," said Holmes. "Is Esmeralda by any chance a *black* cat?"

"She is, actually," said our host, "Black as the Devil 'imself. You don't reckon Mr. Scrooge believes in witches and broomsticks and black cats and all that mumbo-jumbo, and that 'ee got the 'eebie-jeebies from Ezzie?"

"Not at all. I'm sure there is a much simpler explanation," said Holmes and, turning to me, he continued, "Now, Watson, let's get the weight off our feet and seat ourselves in the booth our friend Mr. Scrooge daily monopolises."

The landlord made a half-hearted protest, insisting that it was close to Scrooge's customary time of visitation when not a workday. However, Holmes was adamant, and to assuage our host's concerns, he tipped him a florin.

Once we had ensconced ourselves opposite one another in the booth beside the window with our glasses of beer before us, and while I ruefully contemplated the flaming fireplace, devoid of any customers enjoying its heat, Holmes said: "Never mind, old chap. Eyes on the prize turkey. By now Mr. Scrooge should have left the home of his nephew. From our present vantage point, we'll be able to spot this miraculously metamorphosed skinflint as soon as he turns the corner of Leadenhall Place onto Lime Street."

I nodded at the sensibleness of occupying Scrooge's booth, and then, leaning forward with earnest curiosity, asked him: "The cat. How did you know it would be black?"

"My dear Watson, apply the observational and analytical methods which you have chronicled so often in your somewhat fictionalized accounts of our adventures. Remember, Mr. Scrooge was not sitting down when he encountered Esmeralda, but was walking toward his habitual window seat."

"The black cat crossed his path!" I said, with the abruptness of an epiphany.

"Exactly! Now bear in mind that Scrooge lives at 12A, Gilforth Yard. Is there anything in that which strikes you as significant?"

"Why, of course," I said, feeling the triumph of sudden deduction that is so routine to Sherlock Holmes. "12A is often used by householders with an aversion to the number thirteen."

"And what was nailed above the doorway of Scrooge and Marley's counting-house?" asked Holmes, thoroughly enjoying himself by now.

"Why, a horseshoe!"

Holmes leaned back against the headrest of the bench, grinning at my obtuseness in not recognising earlier that Ebenezer Scrooge was morbidly superstitious.

"But how does this help you in investigating whatever nefarious or criminal activity you believe the man's involved in?" I asked.

Holmes was about to answer, but instead gave a brisk nod toward the window. "Here comes our bird," he said, "from the direction of his nephew's home. Wiggins gave me a detailed physical description of him yesterday."

An elderly man had hoved into sight. Dressed in a fashionably cut ulster and with an Angora scarf wrapped about his throat, he strode with a stiff, business-like gait down Lime Street, his heavy cane swinging with every stride. As he approached us, I can honestly say his was one of the least friendly countenances I had ever beheld. His nose was sharp, its tip pointed at the end, and his cheeks were sallow and shrunken. As he crossed the empty road and approached the Old Goose Inn, I saw that his lips were thin and blue and his eyes an angry red. Apart from the rime of white hair crowning his head, colouring the arches of snowy eyebrows and infusing the goatee clinging to his pointed chin, his appearance was the antithesis of grandfatherly benevolence.

When the old man entered the inn, Holmes sprang to his feet and said cordially, "Mr. Scrooge? Mr. Ebenezer Scrooge?"

"Yes," said the newcomer. "What of it? And what are you doing seated at my table?"

"My name is Sherlock Holmes, and this is my friend and confidant, Dr. Watson. Perhaps you have heard of me."

"I have," Scrooge said guardedly, his shifty eyes flitting between myself and Holmes. "A meddlesome fool who by all accounts thinks he's better than the police. What do you want with me?"

Holmes pulled up an empty chair and placed it at the end of our table. "Why don't you join us and drink a toast to your partner, Jacob Marley, who I believe died on this day eight years ago?" he said and instructed the landlord to bring Scrooge's usual beverage.

The moneylender eyed us suspiciously. However, curiosity had got the better of him, and he sat down and leant his cane against the table.

"A wise decision," said Holmes, and as he resumed his seat, his elbow jogged the salt cellar, knocking it over and causing a small quantity of salt to spill onto the tabletop.

The change in Scrooge's composure at this accidental spillage was profound. His breath quickened, his eyes widened, and his face blanched. I was about to offer my professional attention, when his hand shot forward and righted the salt cellar. Then, between his thumb and forefinger, he took a pinch of the spilled salt and threw it over his left shoulder, only just missing the approaching landlord.

"I see you're of a superstitious inclination," said Holmes, as the landlord placed a tankard of ale before Scrooge before retreating back behind the bar counter.

"Everyone is superstitious to an extent. Would you deliberately walk beneath a ladder, Mr. Holmes? Would you, Dr. Watson?"

I was about to tell Scrooge that my friend would willingly act contrary to every known superstition in the world in order to prove them fallacious; however, Holmes held up a hand to stay me.

"My own beliefs are irrelevant in this matter," said Holmes. "Yours, however, are most certainly relevant, especially with respect to the mirror that once hung from the wall of your offices and which brought you seven years of bad luck."

At these words Scrooge leapt to his feet, grabbed hold of his cane, and with an apparent feat of willpower resisted swinging it at us. "You have nothing on me," he spluttered, "and I won't sit here any longer listening to your couched innuendoes and spiteful allegations."

With that, the moneylender marched out of the Old Goose Inn, slamming the door behind him, and without so much as a backward glance disappeared into Gilforth Yard.

"Well," said I, "I'm as much in the dark now as I was at the beginning of this escapade. What has been achieved by this contrived interview with Ebenezer Scrooge, except to forewarn him that you suspect him of involvement in his business partner's death?"

Holmes rubbed his hands together triumphantly. "Exactly. You finally do seem to be getting the hang of this amateur crime detection business, Watson. Oh, and when you write up this case, kindly remember to make a note of my improvisation with the salt cellar to expose Scrooge's superstitious bent. A deft touch, if I do say so myself. Now all that remains is to let Mr. Scrooge stew for a while. In the meantime, we're off to Camden Town, to the abode of Robert Cratchit. Scrooge will soon realise that his clerk's residence should also be his own next port of call, to ensure the man's silence. So let's hurry. There's not a second to lose."

Holmes paid the landlord for Scrooge's untouched ale and for our own half-finished glasses of beer, and we hastened off to nearby Fenchurch Street. There, as the sun set and twilight set in, we took a hansom to Regent's Park Road in Camden Town. The street proved to be close to the capital's famous zoological gardens, and even though Holmes stopped the cab at the unfashionable end of the road, the residences were still quite respectable terrace houses, not the dilapidated tenements one would expect a lowly accounts clerk to inhabit.

"Are you sure this is where Cratchit lives?" I asked.

Instead of answering me with a yes or a no, Holmes asked, "How much do you imagine an accounts clerk earns?"

"Around fifteen shillings a week," I hazarded.

"According to the proprietor of a rival moneylender's whom I spoke to yesterday, that was indeed Bob Cratchit's weekly salary until eight years ago. Then, after Jacob Marley died of blunt force trauma to the head in an accidental fall, his salary tripled to just over two pounds a week."

"It's a princely sum," I remarked as we clambered down from the hansom cab and paid off the driver.

"And yet," said Holmes, "as the *Gazette* noted, Scrooge's conversion to munificence occurred only one year ago. What does that suggest to you?"

"My God! Cratchit has been blackmailing Scrooge over the circumstances surrounding Jacob Marley's death. But how will you prove it?"

"Yes," said a voice close by us. "How *will* you prove it?"

"Ah, Inspector Lestrade," said Holmes, totally unsurprised at the policeman's sudden appearance. "You got my message. How good of you to join us. Are you armed, and do you have your handcuffs on your person as instructed?"

"I do, indeed," said the tenacious Scotland Yard inspector, tipping his hat to us by way of greeting.

"Then let us proceed at once to number thirty-two, Regent's Park Road, and hopefully extract a confession."

Before we had moved a couple of yards, though, a young lad swung past us on crutches. In an instant Holmes thrust forward his cane and swept one of the crutches away. I dare say my look of dismay mirrored that of Lestrade's, and yet, instead of falling headlong onto the paving stones, the boy stumbled, regained his balance, threw down his crutches, and glared at Holmes.

"What the 'ell do you think you're doing?" said the youngster. "You could've crippled me. I'm telling me dad on you."

"Timothy, isn't it?" said Holmes, picking up the boy's crutches. "Yes. Do lead the way to your father."

As we followed the boy, Holmes explained. "Wiggins and his compatriots discovered the whereabouts of the Cratchit household yesterday. They also spotted the purportedly disabled younger son, Timothy, a.k.a. Tiny Tim, some distance from here, running around playing football with a group of roughs. Ironically, they were using his crutches to mark the goal posts."

"But to what end would he pretend to be crippled?" asked Lestrade.

"Let us ask the young charlatan's father," said Holmes.

Timothy Cratchit had stopped on the doorstep to number thirty-two and was in animated discussion with a balding, middle-aged man dressed in a silk shirt and finely tailored trousers.

We stood by patiently while the darkness grew around us and the gaslights were being lit.

"My boy has nothing to do with this affair," said Robert Cratchit eventually, and instructed Tiny Tim, "Go to your aunt's house. Your mother and your siblings have gone there for Christmas evening." Then, once Holmes had handed Tiny Tim back his crutches and the lad was disappearing down the road, Cratchit stood aside, letting us enter his home.

He directed us to sit in three ostentatiously upholstered armchairs in the living room. He, however, sat before us on a simple, straight-backed chair, looking dejected and penitent.

Myself and Lestrade watched as Sherlock Holmes took in the room's rich décor, which included a Welsh dresser filled with Royal Doulton china and silver cutlery. However, it was the glassless, eighteenth-century French Rocaille mirror on the wall, one side of its metal frame buckled, that captivated his attention.

"It is my habit, if you will indulge me," said Holmes, once he had introduced himself, Lestrade, and me, "to reveal what I already know and what I have deduced. If you wish to be treated leniently by the authorities, I advise you to fill in any gaps."

"I am in your hands," said Cratchit. "This reckoning has been a long time in coming. I've not had a proper night's sleep since the business with Mr. Marley started."

Leaning forward, his fingers steepled as if in prayer, Holmes began. "Eight years ago, an altercation occurred between the two proprietors of the Scrooge and Marley counting-house. Scrooge took the heavy French mirror from the wall and smashed Marley over the head with it, staving in his skull, and, in the process, damaging the mirror. Cratchit witnessed all this from the adjacent cell where he was working. I also see that he retained the murder weapon as a bargaining chip. However, I must confess I'm a little hazy about the cause of the altercation."

"Money," said Cratchit. "Marley had always been as stingy with money as Scrooge, but came to believe that when he died, he would be punished for his tight-fistedness. A change of heart came over him. Until then, Scrooge and Marley had been the sole beneficiary of one another's wills, but now Marley planned on writing a new will and giving his fortune away to the needy."

Holmes nodded and continued. "Marley's sudden demise left Scrooge still sole beneficiaries. But there were three problems. Firstly, the murder had been witnessed. The solution was for Scrooge to pay the monetary consideration Cratchit demanded to corroborate his employer's version of events, *vis-a-vis* that Marley fell by accident and hit his head. Hence Cratchit's inflated salary and salubrious living conditions. Am I right so far?"

The accounts clerk nodded.

"Secondly, during the perpetration of Jacob Marley's murder, the glass in the mirror shattered. To Scrooge's superstitious mind, seven years of bad luck was now attached to the small fortune in gold which I have learned Marley kept in the Coburg branch of the City and Suburban Bank. Scrooge could not therefore access the windfall bequeathed him until seven years had elapsed."

"And thirdly?" said Lestrade, enthralled by the great detective's skillful reasoning.

"Thirdly," said Holmes, "Scrooge needed a cover story once the seven years was up, to explain away his changed spending habits after a lifetime of parsimony. He therefore concocted a fairy tale about Christmas, and ghosts, and redemption to give credence to any uncustomary spending habits that might throw suspicion on him. These sprees of spending included money to treat Tiny Tim's fictitious affliction—money which in reality went into your pocket, Bob Cratchit—and a few charitable donations. However, this was merely camouflage to mask the investments Scrooge has been making this past year in acquiring London tenements and purchasing shares in South African gold mines using the inheritance money.

"How am I doing so far, Cratchit?" asked Holmes.

"You have me, sir," he said unhappily, "for the cowardly blackmailer and extortionist I am. And as for Mr. Scrooge…"

As Cratchit spoke, there came a loud rapping on the front door, causing Lestrade to jump out of his seat.

"That would be Mr. Ebenezer Scrooge," said Holmes, and instructed Lestrade to admit him.

The scene that followed unfolded swiftly. Scrooge barged past the police inspector, saw us in Cratchit's living room, and knew the game was up and that he had been betrayed. He was not about to go quietly, though.

"Fiends!" he cried, and aimed a blow at poor Bob Cratchit's head with his cane, knocking the man senseless.

It took the three of us to wrestle Scrooge away from his vengeance, and only then because the villain perceived that myself and Lestrade had drawn our revolvers.

"The picture is complete," said Holmes, once Scrooge had been subdued. "What good is it to you now that you hoarded the assets of your murdered partner for seven years, fearing the money cursed?"

Scrooge was unrepentant. "You've got nothing on me, Holmes!" he shouted over his shoulder as Lestrade led him away in handcuffs, and as I tended to the cut on Cratchit's forehead. "The question of who murdered Jacob Marley is my word against Cratchit's, if indeed it can be proven not to have been an accident."

"Then we'll need a confession from you, Mr. Ebenezer Scrooge. May I suggest that Inspector Lestrade incarcerate you in cell number thirteen in the basement of Scotland Yard until you come to your senses?"

Suffice to say that within an hour, Lestrade had extracted a full written confession, and shortly after Scrooge had dotted his last *i*, Sherlock Holmes and myself were sitting in the nave at Westminster Cathedral, enjoying the annual Christmas carol concert.

The New Messi

By Nick Sweet

Holmes might have been secretly jealous and wounded by the thought of Watson's forthcoming marriage; but then, when little Leroy was abducted, the green-eyed monster that had risen in the great detective's breast disappeared without trace.

Young Leroy was the product of a liaison, as brief as it was doomed, that his mother, Julia, had with a Black tribesman-*cum*-rapper she became involved with while carrying out research in the Congo; and the man disappeared from her life before he had the chance to learn he was on the road to becoming a father. Enter dear Watson, who met and promptly fell in love with Julia, some eight years later, after her return to London; and being the warm-hearted sort that he was, he took young Leroy to his heart, too. He duly asked Julia for her hand and she accepted his proposal of marriage, and they were to be married in June.

But now the boy, which is to say Watson's beloved stepson-to-be, had been abducted.

"It had to happen *now* of all times," Holmes said.

Watson's eyes widened as he leaned on his cane. "Is there ever a *good* time for an innocent child to be snatched off the street?"

Sensing he had hurt his friend's feelings, Holmes hastened
to explain. "This is clearly the work of our old friend Professor
Moriarty," he said. "He's taken the lad because he's got wind of the
fact that I'm on the verge of putting paid to his plans to bankrupt the
world economy."

"But what the blazes are you talking about, Holmes?"

The great detective set about bringing his dear friend up to
speed. What he had to say took in the way Black Friday, back in
March, had brought down all the major banks and all but crippled
the nation, as well as the rest of the world. He hardly needed to tell
Watson that bankers and businessmen had jumped out of office
windows, leapt into the Thames, or blown their brains out all over
London, from Cheapside to Hampstead, and from Hoxton to
Chelsea, since the capital was rife with stories of such dire ends. And
who else was behind all this misery other than the fiendish Moriarty?

Holmes went on to explain how he had dedicated his every
waking hour since Black Friday to trying to save the planet.
Having rightly assumed that Moriarty must have hit upon some
near-infallible equation which, when applied to the workings of
the economy and the stock market, would enable him to drain
the nation, and indeed the world, of its monetary wealth, Holmes
promptly set about seeking first to discover what such a formula
might entail, so that he could then find its "antidote" in the form of
a second equation that would work to counterbalance and right the
wrongs wrought by his archenemy.

And just when Holmes, who had gone ninety-six hours without
sleep, felt himself to be near to solving the puzzle, Moriarty had
come up with his latest dirty trick in a heinous bid to distract him.

Having heard Holmes out, Watson said, "But why the
blazes should Moriarty have wanted to go messing with the
world economy?"

"For the same reason that has prompted him to perform all the
other evil deeds he has blighted our paths with down through the
years—for the hell of it, Watson." A slender, quixotic figure, he

puffed on his clay pipe, so that his intelligent eyes became torchlights in a mist as he gazed at the doctor. "The man is easily bored and his genius needs to perform evil acts in order to enable him to assuage the ennui that would otherwise pitch him into despair."

"Do you mean to say the blasted fellow only does these things to keep himself *entertained*?"

"Why else?"

Watson thumped the table with his balled fist. "Little Leroy's such a wonderful fellow that I really can't bear the thought of what's happened, Holmes," he said. "It really has got the better of me." He set about drying his eyes with his handkerchief, but to no avail. "He's just an innocent child. Who would do such a thing?" His big eyes appeared to stare deep into the abyss, where he no doubt fancied Moriarty had contrived to set himself up in business. "The dear boy's a great footballing talent, you know," he said. "Performs all sorts of fantastic tricks with a ball at his feet." The tears were streaming silently down his face. "Has quite a sense of humour, too. Cheeky little chappie, he is. When I asked him once how he does all these tricks with a ball, he had the gall to tell me it was all quite elementary, my dear Watson."

Holmes knew better than to laugh, and indeed the next moment his dear friend began to sob his heart out. "Don't worry, dear chap, we'll get him back."

"But how?" the doctor wailed through his tears.

"Moriarty won't have taken him for nothing. He's sure to get in contact before very long."

"So do you mean all we have to do is wait until he does?"

Holmes nodded. "Well, *you* do," he said. "And in the meantime, I have work to do." He poured his friend a stiff Scotch, and helped himself to a snort of cocaine to calm his nerves, before he went back to his computer and applied himself once more to the search for the missing *x* that had denied him any sleep these past few days, and which went some way toward explaining the dark patches under his eyes that stood out in gross contrast with his ghostly pallor. And the line of cocaine that he had snorted may or may not have helped him along the road toward reaching the longed-for eureka moment.

"I say, Holmes, I fail to see how you can be so insensitive as to sound happy, and even *celebrate*, at such a terrible time. I swear I love that dear lad with all my heart."

"But I've cracked it, Watson."

"Cracked *what*?"

"The economy will live to fight another day, and the world will be dragged back from the brink—don't you agree that such news is cause for celebration?"

"But what about poor Leroy?"

Before Holmes could reply, his mobile rang. He stared at it for a moment as if it were a rattlesnake, and then he snatched it up. "Hello?"

"Sherlock Holmes?"

"Indeed…and it is with Professor James Moriarty that I have the pleasure of speaking, I assume?"

"Who were you expecting, Doctor Livingstone?"

"Now you're going to tell me you've got the boy."

"And *you're* going to tell *me* you've found a way to stop me destroying the economy."

"Am I, indeed?"

"Yes, and you're going to tell me the equation you will have devised to prevent me from putting my scheme into action—or you will if you want to see the boy again alive."

Holmes wondered briefly how such things might be valued: the life of a single beloved child against the nation's, or indeed the world's, economy. But there was only ever going to be one winner. "You shall have my equation," he said, "once we have the boy back safely."

"Okay, so this is the way we're going to do it."

Holmes listened as Moriarty gave him directions; then the evil professor hung up.

"Come on, Watson." Holmes put on his tweed jacket and deerstalker. "Don't just sit there crying into your drink."

"But where are we going?"

"To get young Leroy back."

They took a taxi down to the embankment, out past Twickenham, and presently a helicopter came into view. "Here he comes," Holmes said. "If I say *shoot*, then do so without hesitation."

"Of course."

No sooner had the helicopter landed on the lawn next to the Green Man pub than Holmes hurried over to it. "Give me the boy," he yelled, in an effort to make himself heard over the sound of the craft's engine and rotor.

Moriarty gestured for him to climb up into the cockpit.

So it was an exchange the man was after. It made sense: with Holmes out of the way, Moriarty would be free to do his worst quite unhindered. Holmes had little doubt that this rat of a man was doing his utmost to scupper his own attempts to curb global warming, and he suspected that the rapid melting of the North Pole, while also caused to a degree by the effects of mankind's carbon footprint and other factors, had been helped on its way by the evil professor.

Right now, though, Holmes was in no position to bother about such matters, and had no alternative but to climb up into the helicopter. No sooner had he done so than he felt the cold barrel of a gun pushing against the back of his head.

At that point, sensing the need for action, Watson took out his gun and fired at the evil professor, but his shot went astray and ricocheted off the body of the helicopter.

Holmes urged little Leroy to jump down out of the helicopter and run to safety, but the lad seemed not to want to listen. Just then, Moriarty fired back at Watson, and as he did so Leroy spotted the opportunity to come to Holmes's aid by biting the evil professor's wrist.

Moriarty cried out in pain and dropped his gun, which fell out of the helicopter and landed on the grass; then Holmes hit the evil professor on the nose with a real whopper of a punch. Sensing that the professor had lost the upper hand, his pilot applied himself to the controls and the helicopter left the ground; then, realising that it was now or never, Holmes grabbed Leroy's hand and they both jumped from the craft.

They landed awkwardly on the wet grass, and by the time they clambered to their feet, the helicopter was already heading back over the river, carrying Moriarty off to safety. "There goes the most evil man in the world," Holmes said, in the manner of a man who is talking to himself.

"All I know is that his clothes smelt of mothballs and he has bad breath." No sooner had Leroy said this than he ran over to Watson, and, seeing that his benefactor was wounded, the lad began to cry in alarm; but Holmes soon established that his dear friend would live to fight another day, the bullet only having got him in the arm.

"We'd better get you to a hospital, old bean," Holmes said, taking out his iPhone, and he dialled 999.

"We sure showed him," Watson said hours later, when he came round after the bullet had been taken out.

"Yes, Leroy, and the world economy have been saved." The skin over the great detective's forehead, which appeared to be stretched tight as a drum, creased in a frown. "Now all we have to worry about is the melting ice caps."

Leroy came and threw himself on his beloved Watson once more, the lad's emotions having got the better of him. The doctor chuckled fondly and said, "Now, how's the next Messi doing, then, eh, what?"

"I was worried about you," the prodigy sobbed.

"No need to worry about me," Watson chuckled. "It was only a scratch."

"Anyway," Holmes said, "I had better get going."

"Not without me you don't."

"But you need to stay here and recuperate, and I have no time to waste."

"I'll be all right," Watson said. "They've dressed the wound and put my arm in a sling, so I can't see the point in hanging around here any longer." He swung his legs over the side of the bed. "Always did hate hospitals." He was now changing out of his pyjamas and into his day clothes, which had been neatly folded and placed in the bedside cabinet.

Holmes wondered if his friend were really in a fit state to go with him in search of the evil professor, but Watson assured him that he had never felt better. "I want to help you find that blasted snake if it's the last thing I do. Some causes are worth fighting for, even dying for, after all—and the apprehension of Moriarty is just such a cause."

"Yes, indeed," Holmes concurred. "It was he, after all, who was behind all the meddling in the last American election that you will have read about in the *Times*. The crippling of the banks is really just another branch of his overall plan, which is to bring the Western democracies to their knees."

"Yes, I seem to remember you saying one time, Holmes, that you thought Moriarty was behind the introduction of that awful punk rock, which so blighted the music industry back in the seventies, too."

Holmes nodded. "It was he who coached that cad Sid Vicious to sing 'My Way'. "

"I rather liked old Frank Sinatra's version, back in the days before he lost his voice. Whereas that Vicious fellow made a right pig's ear of it, if you ask me."

Holmes, whose toleration of music stretched only to certain works of Scarlatti and Handel, and even then only in the smallest and most infrequent of doses, eyed his friend with a mixture of disbelief and something like alarm. "Anyway, we don't have time to stand here talking about music."

Little Leroy asked them to wait for him. "But you need to stay here until your mother comes to pick you up," Holmes told the lad. "She's on her way."

"No, I want to go with you."

"You're too young."

"But you need me."

The two men appeared mystified as they gazed at him; then Holmes asked the boy what on earth he meant. "You won't find Moriarty in the North Pole," Leroy said, "you can be sure of that."

"And what makes you so confident of what you're saying?"

"I heard him say where he was going."

Holmes's eyes narrowed as he tried to decide whether to believe the boy. "Why would he have spoken of such matters in front of you?"

"I suppose he could hardly have expected me to be fluent in Lingala, now, could he?"

"In *what?*" Doctor Watson demanded to know.

"One of the languages spoken in the Congo region of central Africa," Holmes set his friend straight, without taking his eyes off the boy. "Professor Moriarty is a master of numerous tongues, among other things." He said this as if even his archenemy's great skills as a linguist could be taken as further evidence of his inveterate evil. "What strikes me as odd is that you should also speak it, Leroy."

"Mum first met my father in the Congo, when she was over there working on her doctorate," the lad explained. "Then afterwards she decided it was only right to teach me my father's language." He shrugged. "I suppose she reckoned it would give me a better sense of my roots."

"Yes, quite." With that Holmes and Leroy proceeded to speak in Lingala, until Watson demanded to know what the blazes the pair of them reckoned they were about. "We were merely talking in Leroy's father's native tongue, Watson."

"All sounded Greek to me."

Holmes might have launched into a detailed disquistion on the differences between Lingala and Greek, but there really was no time for such nonsense. Addressing himself to Leroy, he said, "So what did you hear Moriarty say?"

"That he was heading for the Congo."

"Is that a fact?" Watson said. "Blazes, so we'd better get ourselves over to central Africa on the double, then."

"Indeed," Holmes assented. Then to Leroy: "Did he say exactly whereabouts in the Congo? It's a big region, after all."

"He reserved a room in the Hotel Relax, in the capital, Kinshasa."

"That's useful to know."

"Does that mean I can go there with you?"

"Most certainly not," Watson said.

"I'm sure I would be of great help to you, with my knowledge of Lingala," Leroy said, looking at Holmes.

The great detective considered the lad's proposition for a moment. While his own grasp of Lingala was pretty good, it was certainly the case that it suffered in comparison with his command of Swahili and Yoruba, not to mention any number of other languages. In truth, his Lingala was a little rusty in places, a fact that was scarcely surprising since he had not set foot in the Congo since he had gone there some fifteen years ago, when he was busy investigating the case of the missing emeralds. Young Leroy's command of Lingala, on the other hand, was much more assured. For this reason, it seemed to Holmes that the lad was right in what he had said: he might be a great help to them, were they to take him along. "All right, Leroy," he said. "You can come with us, so long as you do just as I say."

"But of course."

With that, the trio left the hospital, and Holmes waved down a taxi and told the driver to take them to Heathrow. "And there's an extra twenty in it for you if you can get us there in less than fifteen minutes."

Having landed in Kinshasa, they hired a Range Rover and had little trouble in finding the Hotel Relax. "Now what, Holmes?" Watson wanted to know.

"We wait here and see if the professor comes out."

Which he duly did some forty minutes later, and they trailed him out into the brush along a road that soon became little more than a dirt track. Seeing Moriarty's jeep pull to a halt up ahead, Holmes stopped, too, and just hoped the evil professor hadn't realised that he was being followed. By now it was pitch-dark, and no sooner had the three of them climbed out of their vehicle than they found they were surrounded by a number of natives armed with spears.

Meanwhile, Moriarty had turned his jeep around and was now driving over to where they were being held. The evil professor climbed out of his vehicle and barked orders in a Lingala that Holmes could not help but admire for the precision of the speaker's accent and grammar, even if the sentiments behind his words were far from praiseworthy; for Moriarty had just ordered the natives to take their captives and boil them up for dinner.

Holmes ignored Watson's enquiring gaze, since he realised that informing him as to the meaning of Moriarty's instructions would only cause his friend to worry unneccesarily. Knowing the doctor as he did, Holmes knew just how outraged the man would be, were he to discover Moriarty's plans for the three of them. He could just imagine how Watson would hold forth on his being an Englishman and a gentleman, and how it was not an Englishman's place, or a gentleman's for that matter, to end up as anyone's dinner.

Holmes was an Englishman, too, of course, but he was an altogether different version of such an article, and rather than waste his time by mouthing pointless oaths, he asked Moriarty what his intentions were. "While you are being dined upon by my jolly friends here," the evil professor replied, "I shall be launching my laser bombs."

"I assume the destination of these laser bombs is the North Pole, Professor?"

"How bitter is knowledge that cannot be acted upon, Mr. Holmes." Moriarty permitted himself an ugly, bitter laugh. "Once the laser bombs sink into their target, they will send out rays of heat that will melt what ice remains at the Pole within minutes," he said. "That in turn will have the effect of sending massive tsunamis in all directions, I am most happy to say." He laughed again. "New York and Washington will be history by midnight—as indeed will the whole of the East Coast of the United States. Needless to say, your beloved London will be sunk, too, as will most of the rest of the civilised world."

"Why, you evil madman," Watson hissed, "this just isn't cricket. Do you really mean to say—"

"Quieten yourself, Watson," Holmes said. "This is no time for amateur dramatics."

"I never said it was, but—"

Holmes said, "And what about your beloved Russia?"

"Just because I have been on Russia's payroll, you should not make the mistake of thinking I have any feelings for that nation."

"Are you saying Russia will be for it, too?"

"You are learning, Holmes."

"So what's in it for you?"

"With the major nations all either under water or at best plunged into utter chaos, I shall then set about ruling what's left of the world from my base here in the Congo."

"Have you quite taken leave of your senses, man?" Watson wanted to know.

Instead of answering the doctor, Moriarty merely said, "And now, please excuse me while I leave you in the very capable hands of these friendly tribesmen."

With that, Moriarty turned his jeep around and set off in it, and
the tribesmen dragged the reluctant trio over to a huge cauldron,
which was suspended over a lighted fire. Holmes realised that he had
better think of a plan, and do so fast, if he and his two companions
were to have any chance of surviving their current ordeal. He
searched his mind for an idea, but nothing occurred to him.

And then, just as they were about to find themselves being
lifted up and dropped into the cauldron, where they were to be
unceremoniously cooked, he turned his head to look at Leroy and
said, "I hear you are a superb footballer?"

"I'm not b-b-bad," Leroy replied modestly, trying his best not to
show his fear, even though his teeth were chattering.

"I believe I saw you put a tennis ball in your pocket earlier at
the hospital?"

"Yes, but what of it?"

"Tell the tribesmen that you're going to show them a trick,"
Holmes said. "Then take out the ball and do what you're good at."

"But what's the p-p-point?"

"You never know what effect a few tricks of the sort I've heard
you're capable of might have on these fellows."

"That's a point," Watson concurred. "These fellows haven't
had the benefit of being educated at a top prep school and then
public school, followed by Oxford or Cambridge, after all. Dash it,
some of them look like they wouldn't even have been accepted by
Charterhouse in their day."

"You'd better hurry up about it," Holmes said, feeling the heat
from the fire on his face. "Time is of the essence, old chap."

With that, Leroy shouted at the tribesmen, and his mastery
of their rather guttural tongue was such that, as had been the case
earlier, Holmes once again found himself admiring the young
lad's wonderful command of the language, despite the ever-closer
proximity of the most horrendous of destinies. Then, having told the
tribesmen that he was about to show them a trick of such immense
skill that they would be amazed, young Leroy took the tennis ball

from his trouser pocket and dropped it onto his right toe, before he proceeded to execute a number of what he called "keepy-uppies."

"I say," Watson said, as he saw the way the tribesmen then prostrated themselves on the ground before the prodigy.

"He's not the new Mess*iah*," Holmes said, "but the new Mess*i*."

"So it would appear."

Having prompted his audience of tribesmen to bow down to him and then begin to chant in the form of a prayer, Leroy realised that he had saved the day: instead of ending up as the tribesmen's dinner, he was now their master, having clearly assumed a godlike status in their eyes. Such was his proficiency with the tennis ball at his feet, that the tribesmen, simple fellows that they were, had become convinced that he was possessed of supernatural powers.

"Tell them that you are their god and they must listen to you and obey your every word," Holmes told the lad.

Leroy relayed this message to the tribesmen, speaking in their native tongue once more.

"Good, now order them to find Moriarty straightaway and destroy his laser launchers before he uses them."

Leroy did as Holmes had instructed, and with that the tribesmen all got to their feet and went running off, holding their spears aloft as they did so. They ran so quickly that Holmes and his two companions had their work cut out to catch up with them.

Minutes later, they found Moriarty in a moonlit clearing, where he was about to activate his launchers and thereby set in train a series of events that would devastate the greater part of the civilised world. The tribesmen were confused and clearly unsure as to what Leroy expected of them; but the great detective was able to call on his detailed knowledge of rocket science, gleaned from his investigations with the aid of the internet, to deactivate the launchers.

No sooner had Holmes breathed a sigh of relief after saving the planet, than he wondered as to his archenemy's whereabouts. He stopped tribesmen at random to ask them where Moriarty was, but they ignored him, clearly being minded only to listen to their newfound god; and by the time Holmes finally managed to find Leroy in the darkness of the African night, he learned that the lad had seen no sign of the evil professor, either. "Tell the tribesmen to find and detain him."

Leroy gave the tribesmen orders to this end; but, sad to say, despite searching for hours, it finally became clear that Holmes's archenemy had somehow managed to flee into the night.

Holmes could congratulate himself on having got Leroy back safe and sound, as well as on having saved the world—for the time being at least; but he knew only too well that it would not be long before the evil professor perpetrated his next outrage.

The Adventure of the Talking Board

By John Grant

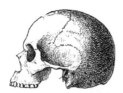

"I think this is the silliest idea I've ever come across," said Heather as she lit the cluster of red candles at the centre of the table. "What are we, Jim? Still fourteen years old?"

"Just think of it as the equivalent of a ghost story for Christmas," I told her. "Just a bit of innocent fun."

She raised an eyebrow. " 'Innocent fun'? My father wouldn't have agreed with you there." Her father, God rest his soul, had been a moderator of the Church of Scotland.

I stood back to look at our handiwork. Heather had insisted on coming over to the house early to help me set up, but really there hadn't been very much setting up to do. I'd opened a couple of bottles of red wine to let them breathe, and there were more where those came from, although I didn't think we'd need them. There was Pinot Grigio in the fridge in case of emergency, plus some Perrier in case anyone had an attack of abstemiousness. I'd put two cheeseboards on the table to either side of the candles, plus a big wooden bowl of crackers and a little stack of plates and knives.

Also on the table was the ouija board, still in its fancy box. I'd eschewed the gaudily packaged cheapies on sale in the local toy shops and ordered up a rather grand model from an online vendor. The board's letters were inlaid in mother-of-pearl. The movement of the pointer—the planchette, to use the professional term—promised to be as near frictionless as dammit, the roller ball underneath it being made of some synthetic rubber that had been developed for use in the Space Shuttle. The box itself was like an extra-large wooden cigar box, with the word "OUIJA" seemingly burned into the lid using a red-hot poker.

"Well, I still think it's silly," Heather fussed. "You might find yourself playing with forces you can't control. Evil forces." She shuddered theatrically, then glanced at her watch. "The others will be here soon."

I smiled affectionately at her. Of all my friends—and I don't make friends easily—she was the one I was fondest of. We went back a long way—far further than she knew, in fact—and if the courses of our lives had run differently, we might have been preparing for an evening with kids and grandkids rather than just a bunch of friends.

I poured her a glass of the Cabernet, and one for myself. "I think we'll be safe enough."

Just then the doorbell rang.

Bill Davisson had brought his wife, Greta, but the other two arrivals, Johnny Cuthberts and David Cloke, were both multiple divorcees who'd vowed the single life was in future the life for them. All four, after they'd taken off their coats and scarves and gloves, stood on the hearth in front of the log fire, rubbing their hands and talking about how cold and icy and foggy the streets were. Greta was the designated driver—I'd been right to lay in the Perrier—but the other three went after the wine with a will.

"So it's going to be a ouija party?" said David after a while, nodding toward the box on the table. "A séance? Where's the medium?" he added. "I was expecting a daft old lady with gin on her breath and a glassy stare."

Greta snorted. "Ooo, spooky. When's the table going to start tilting?"

I puffed my chest out pompously. "It depends on whether or not the spirits of the departed will wish to communicate with us."

"Yeah, right," said her husband. "And there are fairies at the bottom of every garden."

We all laughed.

I made a great show of drawing the board and planchette out of their box and skimming through the sheet of instructions that came with them. Of course, this was all just make-work. I could remember from childhood how to operate a ouija board—it's not exactly rocket science, after all—and, besides, I'd done a little advance swotting last night in case there were any wrinkles I'd forgotten.

Heather, despite her skepticism, was clearly becoming quite interested. "Who's going to be it?" she asked me.

" 'It'?"

"The person whose hand's on the planchette. The person who asks the questions."

"We all do," I said. "We each put a finger on it. That way we can be sure no one's cheating—that it's the spirits moving the planchette around, not one of us."

"And who decides when the spirits are likely to be ready?" Greta said.

"I'm probably the one best qualified for that. After all, I had a Welsh grandmother. I think. On my mother's side. Mom always told me her mother was Welsh."

"What's your hypothetical Welsh grandmother got to do with it, Jim?" said Bill, sitting down with a thump on one of the upright chairs around the table. "Anyway, I thought you were as American as apple pie, ancestors sailed there on the Mayflower, all that sort of thing."

He'd piled a plate with crackers and slices of cheddar and Stilton. Greta had already seated herself and was picking, birdlike, at her own consignment of food.

"She had the second sight," I explained, ignoring the issue of my ancestry. "Otherwise she'd have been a traitor to her kind. It's an essential characteristic of grandmothers up there in the valleys, see, boyo?"

"If she existed," he said with a jowly grin. Even though he and I have never liked each other, he was making an effort to get into the spirit of things. It was Christmastime, after all, the season when it's socially obligatory to be jovial or die trying.

"If she existed," I agreed. "There's always that."

Soon all six of us were sitting around the table, glasses and plates full. I got up and switched off the electric lights, leaving the candles and the log fire in the hearth as the room's only sources of illumination. As I reseated myself, I saw the reflected flicker of the candles gleaming in the bulbs of the wine glasses and the eyes of my companions.

"Shall we get started?" I said.

"If you think the spirits are ripe for questioning," Johnny said with a nervous chuckle. Of all those here, he seemed the one most susceptible to fears of ghoulies and ghosties and long-legged beasties.

"I sense they're gathering." I waved my hands in what I imagined was an evocative manner, and picked up the planchette.

The fire spat, and we all started.

"Good timing," said Bill. "Do you write your own scripts, Jim?" He took a glug of his Cabernet.

"Maybe it's a sign from the departed," I said in a cod-sepulchral voice.

"Ooo-ee-ooo-ee-ooo," contributed Heather.

I placed the planchette on the board. "Ready?"

Each of us rested the tip of a forefinger on the little heart-shaped device. Johnny was last, still looking uncertain whether he wanted to take part. We all leaned forward, focusing on the board.

"Nothing's happening," said Heather after a minute or two.

She was right. A sense of anticlimax went around the circle.

"I guess the souls of those who've gone before us have taken off early for Christmas." There was a hollow note to Bill's attempted heartiness. We still kept our fingertips on the planchette.

And then we all felt it. A distinct little tug on the planchette as if someone were trying to catch our attention.

Heather gave a quick intake of breath. "Holy crap. Did you feel that?"

It was obvious we all had.

"Who's there?" I asked the empty air.

There was no answering reaction from the planchette.

"Wrong question, maybe," said Greta. Now she was sounding as scared as Johnny.

I tried again. "Is there anyone there?"

This time the response was immediate. Moving smoothly on its high-tech roller ball, the planchette slid over to the big "YES" on the left-hand side of the board.

"Holy crap," said Heather again.

I'd gleaned from the leaflet in the box that the ouija board was in fact an American invention. I'd always thought, based on the name— the combination of the French and German words for "yes"—that it must have originated somewhere in Europe, but no: it was a Maryland inventor called Elijah Bond who patented the device in 1890. There'd been other forms of "talking board" before then, but it was Elijah Bond's variant that caught on. Even so, it was just a parlour game at first. It wasn't for another quarter-century that the spiritualists adopted it for communicating with the dead.

I'd been going to tell my guests about this—after all, everyone expects Americans to brag about their national achievements, don't they?—but something held me back. A bit of sneakiness, I think.

I had a fairly thick Boston accent, whereas the others, aside from Heather, had upper-crust English accents you could have used to grate celery. Heather's accent was upper-crust too, but it still retained enough of the Islay lilt that somehow it didn't jar as much.

Not that I cared about my guests' poshness, not any longer. Besides, I had more money than they did. I'd been one of the lucky ones who'd gotten in on the home computer industry early, when monitors had six-inch screens and weighed half a ton and could display any colour you wanted so long as it was green or black.

Heather had played first violin in the London Symphony Orchestra before arthritis put a premature end to her career. Bill had gone into the family export business, following in Daddy's footsteps and wondering how long it'd be before he got his peerage, but then the company went belly-up and he'd been living on the proceeds of selling bits of inherited property ever since. Johnny did something mysterious in the civil service, and David fiddled figures in the City.

None of them were short of a bob, as they'd have put it themselves, not even Heather, but they weren't *rich* rich, like I was. Yet I knew that Bill and Johnny and David looked down their noses at me. I was the commoner, and a "colonial cousin" on top of that; they were bluebloods.

Yet another reason to derive satisfaction from a petty revenge.

Sometimes I wonder if I ever really grew up.

"Ask them who they are," hissed Johnny, his eyes wide.

"You can do that yourself," I told him.

"No, you do it."

But the planchette had already started to move again.

Heather read out the letters as it paused briefly at each of them. "S-H-E-R-L-O-C-K."

Greta began to giggle. "That's ridiculous!"

David and Bill joined in with the laughter, as did I.

"There's only one known Sherlock," said Bill, his fleshy face covered in a grin. "The sage of Baker Street. Is this a...a visitation from Basil Rathbone, do you think?"

Johnny and Heather looked far less amused.

"What if it's a surname?" said Heather.

"What do you mean?" Bill asked her, his expression switching from amusement to a surprising belligerence.

"The Sherlock we immediately think of," she explained, "is for obvious reasons Sherlock Holmes. Who is, of course, fictional. But there've been plenty of people with the *surname* Sherlock. You must have heard of the architect Cornelius Sherlock, surely? And there was a bishop called Sherlock, wasn't there?"

"And I'll bet there are other Sherlocks around, too," said Greta, her face sobering. "You know, 'Wendy' wasn't even a name until J. M. Barrie invented it for *Peter Pan*, yet fans started calling their kids that, and now it seems there are Wendys everywhere you look. I'm guessing there must have been a few fans who named their kids Sherlock."

She looked pointedly at the ouija board. "Are you one of them?"

The planchette moved decisively. "NO."

"Then who are you?"

Again Heather read out the letters. "H-O-L-M-E-S."

More laughter.

"You gotta be kidding," sputtered Bill. "Who's pushing the pointer?"

Johnny gazed at him coldly. "I don't think any of us is, Bill. We'd be able to tell, wouldn't we?"

"I suppose."

I took a sip of wine, then cleared my throat—bringing the meeting to order, so to speak.

Once all the fingertips were back on the planchette, I said, "What message have you got for us?"

The little platform paused for a moment and then moved with far greater speed than before. This time Heather didn't bother reading out the letters individually, just said the result at the end.

"Alexander Midgeby."

"Who's Alexander Midgeby?" said Greta and I, almost in unison.

Johnny's face had become even more ashen than when the planchette had first started twitching. David and Heather weren't looking too good either. Bill was staring at the planchette with an intent frown, as if expecting it to whisper a secret tipoff to him.

"Sandy Midgeby," he said quietly. "Now there's a name I never expected to hear again."

"Yes, but who *is* he, dear?" said Greta, grabbing his elbow.

"Was," said Johnny, before Bill could answer. There was a dull edge of despair in his voice. He looked down at his hands, knotted in his lap. "Maybe still is. Someone we all knew a long time ago."

"Not all of us," Heather corrected. "Just the four who were at Oxford. Bill, David, and Johnny at St. Loys. Plus me at Humboldt. The three boys were all on the same corridor. I was Bill's girlfriend, back then, so I was on the corridor quite a lot too." She looked at Greta. "I assume he's told you?"

Greta nodded with a weak smile. "Water under the bridge."

Johnny was clearly oblivious to this interchange.

"That thing with Sandy Midgeby," he mumbled, more to his hands than to the rest of us, "that was the rottenest thing I was ever involved in. I wish I could forget it ever happened, but I can't."

"It was a long time ago," Bill protested, half-rising to his feet. "Leave it alone. Like Greta said, water under the bridge."

Johnny shot him a dirty look. "I've told the story to three different shrinks and they've said that having faced up to it, I'd feel better. Only I didn't feel better. Well, I've had enough wine tonight, or soon will have, to see if telling it to real people, not medical professionals"—he spoke the words fastidiously—"will do the trick."

"It's not of interest, Johnny," said Bill, jabbing at him in the air with a finger. "Nobody cares any longer. Nobody but you."

"I care too." Heather spoke quietly. "We should get all this out in the open between us. We've all bottled it up for too many years."

I looked from one face to another. "Please, explain it to this poor unenlightened Yank."

Johnny told most of it, refueling his determination from time to time with Cabernet. Heather told parts of the story, with David reluctantly chipping in from time to time. Bill, aside from the occasional grunt of anger, maintained an intimidating silence.

"Back in the day," Johnny began.

Back in the day, St. Loys—St. Aloysius de Gonzaga College, to give it its full name—was the snootiest of the Oxford colleges. Not that it had the academic record to back that up, or even the best port. But somehow into the tapestry of its tradition had been woven the conceit that it was a cut above the others. All the best families wanted to send their sons there. The heads of government departments tended to look kindly on CVs that featured the name of St. Loys, even if the applicant had managed only an Upper Third. At any one time, the cabinet had at least a couple of St. Loys alumni, and they had a disproportionate presence in the Lords. As people were fond of saying, you didn't go to St. Loys to swot, you went there to swank.

There were a few exceptions. One of those was Sandy Midgeby.

Sandy Midgeby was the son of a children's librarian, Alice Midgeby, who'd borne him after throwing her boyfriend out of her life on discovering he was securely married and had no intentions of becoming otherwise. She'd raised Sandy on her own, with the help of her mother as a constantly-on-tap babysitter, Dad having died some years before. On the days when Mum couldn't manage the child, Alice brought him with her to the library. As a result, young Sandy could read by the time he got to kindergarten, and the advantage never deserted him: all through his school years, he was educationally a year or more ahead of his classmates. He got As in four of the five A-levels he sat and a B in the fifth, which was history. St. Loys was the winner in a university contest to give the boy a scholarship.

Which was why he ended up on a corridor with Bill and Johnny and David.

All of whom despised him soundly because he wasn't of the proper stock and came from Scunthorpe.

Well, those were the reasons they admitted to, anyway. The other was that, academically, they were lucky if they were even in his slipstream. The subject he'd elected to read was maths, and his tutors reckoned that somewhere down the road there was likely to be a Fields Medal—the Nobel of maths, as it's often called. The blueblood trio regarded maths as a subject suited to mechanics and accountants, which made them revile Sandy all the more.

Come finals week, the three decided the hour was long overdue for them to exact their revenge upon the upstart. The expectation was that Sandy would sail through the exams and be snapped up for postgraduate work at somewhere prestigious like MIT. That wasn't the sort of fact that Bill and David and Johnny enjoyed facing. They themselves were aspiring to Lower Seconds, if they were lucky, and then to relying on family influence.

There were dungeons beneath St. Loys—as apparently there are under a couple of the other Oxford colleges, relics of an earlier era, when the university authorities could resort to sterner means of disciplining their recalcitrant charges. This was a fact known to the cleaning staff and the dons, but to few of the students.

One of the few was Bill Davisson.

With his two cronies, he hatched a plot to destroy the future of the commoner they all loathed.

The night before finals week began, Johnny Cuthberts ran into Sandy Midgeby, as if by chance, in Broad Street. Johnny had been, on the surface, the only one of the three who offered any measure of friendship to the outsider.

"Ho there, Midgeby."

Sandy smiled politely. "Hello to yourself, Cuthberts."

"Where're you off to?"

"Back to college. To swot."

"On a fine afternoon like this?"

"When better? Tomorrow's the big day." Sandy Midgeby grinned.

"You should take an hour or two off," Johnny told him. "Give the old brain a bit of a rest."

Sandy looked as if he were about to ridicule this idea, then paused. Maybe Johnny wasn't so far off the mark. After all, Sandy probably already knew all there was to know about four-dimensional functional analysis—more than his tutors, if anything. Perhaps he could indeed do with a little R&R.

"What do you suggest?" he said.

So Johnny told him about the dungeons in the bowels of St. Loys, and about how he and David and Bill were planning an expedition there this very night. Would Sandy like to come along?

Yes, indeed, Sandy would.

That night the four of them, flashlights in hand, crept down to the college's basement. Although the area wasn't officially out of bounds, they sensed that officialdom would disapprove of their being there, so they didn't talk much. Sandy, as the only one of the four who hadn't been down here before, kept looking around him inquisitively, as if each fresh turn in the corridors might have a new secret to reveal. Johnny wore a mask of apprehension: breaking the rules went against the grain for Johnny, Sandy reflected, or perhaps he was just in a funk. The other two were cheery enough, prattling in soft voices as they led the way.

Most of the doors to either side of them were locked and covered with the grime of the ages. Sandy paused to shine his flashlight through a couple of the small, square barred windows set into the doors, but couldn't see much. No skeletons of long-ago skirkers, no thumbscrews or iron maidens or chains dangling from the walls.

In the flickering illumination from their flashlights the four students walked on, turning this way and that as the corridors took them. There was a musty smell in the air that reminded Sandy of cinnamon in the way that it made his nostrils tingle.

They must have been exploring for half an hour or more when they came to a door that was different from the others. Situated at the end of a narrow passage, it had the same heaviness in its frame as the rest, but its solid wooden panels had been wiped clean of the grey-green filth of time and a new steel hasp had been fitted just above the metal handle. From the latch dangled a shiny padlock.

"Looks like there've been other people down here recently," said Bill lightly.

"Maybe an international gang of crooks has been using the place to store contraband," said David in the same breezy tone.

Sandy led the way to the door, his pace slowing as he advanced. David was right. Maybe they'd stumbled across something criminal. The wisest thing they could do was beat a hasty retreat and tell a porter, or even the police, what they'd seen. Even so, it'd be a pity not to find out first. Besides, there could be a perfectly innocent explanation, and they'd look like fools if they raised a hullabaloo for nothing.

He pushed the door cautiously, and it creaked open.

There was nothing to see inside except an empty, stone-walled cell. The floor had been swept clean sometime recently, and there was a bucket in the corner.

Sandy took a couple of steps forward and shone his light around, then turned back toward the doorway.

"Hey, you guys—" he began, but stopped as he saw the door closing firmly. Outside he could hear the rattling of the padlock, then some soft sniggering.

"So long, sucker," came Bill Davisson's sneering voice at the little barred window. "I'm guessing they're going to have to have finals week without you."

And then they were gone.

Sandy Midgeby looked around him. He supposed he should be grateful they'd thought to leave him the bucket. There was no use in shouting for help, because there was no one who'd be able to hear him. He wondered how long the battery in his flashlight would last and, as if in reply, the light flickered and yellowed a little.

He sat down in the corner opposite the bucket, leaned his back against the wall, switched off his flashlight, and shut his eyes.

There was no sense in raging or panicking. That would just make his plight worse—he'd be out of his wits by the morning.

The morning.

He assumed his tormentors would let him out then, if not before.

A little eddy of concern crossed Sandy Midgeby's mind that his three false friends might simply put him out of sight, out of mind— that he might be here all week before it finally occurred to one of them to come down into the dungeons to set him free. He knew they despised him, for reasons he found unfathomable, and he knew they had the cruelty of the privileged. But did they perhaps hate him enough to want him gone for good?

Don't panic, he told himself again, shifting his behind on the hard, unforgiving floor. *Just force yourself to stay calm. This ordeal will be over soon.*

I hope.

"God help me," said Johnny, clutching the stem of his wine glass so fiercely I was worried he might break it. He was staring down into the red liquid with all the intensity of a scryer expecting to see some vision of eternity. "God help me, but that was perhaps the shittiest thing I've been a part of in my life."

He shot a furious glare at Bill, then drained his glass.

"It was not," admitted Bill, "our finest hour."

"Maybe you've done so many shitty things that this one doesn't stand out particularly," Johnny told him. "But I haven't."

Bill chuckled and made a little movement with his hand as if waving away an inconveniently attentive insect. "Just youthful hijinks."

Johnny appeared not to have heard him, but now looked instead at me like I were some kind of father confessor...or one of his shrinks. "There was worse to follow, you see."

The next morning Johnny clambered early out of his hard college bed. He had a slight hangover, something distinctly not recommended at the outset of finals week, but it was nothing he couldn't cope with. What had roused him so early was guilt about what he and David and Bill had done to that poor little pleb Sandy Midgely the night before. Lord knows but Midgely was a rebarbative little sod, with his shifty hesitancy and his constant look of someone who'd accidentally put on the clothing of someone just a little bigger than himself, and, worst of all, that frightful accent of his. But, even so, he didn't deserve to have his whole future destroyed by a sadistic student prank.

As Johnny hurriedly threw on clothes, brushed his teeth, and ran his fingers through his hair, he reflected that at least Midgeby had his intelligence to bail him out. He'd probably still sail through with First Class Honours despite a sleepless night.

Johnny stumbled down the corridor and hammered on Bill's door.

After a few moments, it opened a crack, and Bill peered out. He looked as dishevelled as Bill felt.

"We've got to let him out," blustered Johnny.

"You mean the squirt?"

"Midgeby, yes."

"Oh, he'll be all right where he is for a few hours longer."

Bill began to close the door, but Johnny put his foot in it. "Don't be such a bastard, Davisson!"

"What time is it, anyway?"

"Quarter past eight," sang out Heather's voice from within. As she so often did, she'd spent the night here in St. Loys. "Johnny's right, Bill. You've got to let the guy out. It wasn't a very funny joke to begin with, and it's getting less funny by the minute."

For a moment Bill looked as if he were prepared to argue the toss with them both, but then he relented. "Just wait 'til I get some togs on."

He turned away, leaving Johnny fuming in the corridor.

Twenty minutes later, with Heather in tow, Bill and Johnny were once more down in the college cellars. It didn't take them long to reach the door Bill had equipped with the new hasp and padlock he'd bought along with the metal bucket earlier in the week from the big B&Q in Abingdon.

"Wakey wakey, rise and shine, happy campers!" shouted Bill sardonically as he strode toward it. "Time to face the world, Mr. Mathematics!"

There was no response. It was then that Johnny began to get really worried.

Bill pulled the glittering little key out of his pocket and undid the padlock. He pushed the ponderous door open.

"Okay, Midgeby, you've had your—"

His voice tailed off as he looked around him in disbelief.

The little chamber was empty. Instinctively Johnny went over and looked into the bucket. It hadn't been used. Could there somehow have been *two* cells prepared like this? It didn't seem possible, but then neither did the fact that Midgeby had managed to escape from a securely locked room in the middle of the night.

"You're not pulling my leg, are you?" said Johnny, turning angrily to Bill. But Bill appeared to be every bit as dumbfounded as Johnny himself was.

"There's only one key, and it's been in my trouser pocket all night long."

Johnny stuck out his jaw. "You didn't have second thoughts and come down here in the middle of the night and let him out?"

"I slept like a babe until you came battering on my door this morning to wake me up. Ask Heather."

Heather, clinging to the door frame behind Bill, her dark hair framing her face, nodded agreement. She was gazing around the room with a look of anxiety. "Where the hell can he have got to?" she said.

A very nasty thought came to Johnny. Assuming there was no magic going on—and Johnny, for all his follies, didn't believe in magic—Midgeby had somehow contrived to free himself from his prison. Johnny didn't *like* Midgeby, but he was a clever little sod, and Johnny wouldn't have put it past him to devise some Houdini-like means of escape. Suppose he'd done that, then. What would he do *next*?

Well, one of the things he might do was go straight to the college authorities and tell them what had happened. He could even go to the police, if he felt so inclined—what his three corridor-mates had done to him was, after all, a crime in anyone's books. If Midgeby did either of those things, Johnny and David and Bill—and, right now, Johnny didn't give much of a monkey's about David and Bill—wouldn't be spending this week doing Finals. If they were *lucky* they'd be packing up their belongings and going home to try to explain to their parents why St. Loys had chucked them out on their ears. So much for those hoped-for Lower Seconds.

Johnny felt as if his whole world were falling to pieces around him. His palms were sweating. He glanced sidelong at the bucket in the corner and wondered if he should go puke in it.

"First thing first." Bill's voice had adopted a decisive tone. "We have to get out of here. Yes, it's a mystery where the little bugger's gone to, but we're not going to solve it by standing around with our thumbs up our rears. So far as the world is concerned, we were never down here, haven't seen Midgeby since dinner last night, don't know anything about nuffink—understood?"

Bill stared challengingly at Johnny and Heather in turn. "We have to go and eat our breakfasts and then head for the exam halls as if there was nothing different about this morning than any other. Midgeby will turn up, you'll see, and the little turd will have fun lording it over us tonight as he tells us how he did it, how he put the shits up us."

"But if—?" started Heather.

"No ifs. Grab the bucket, Johnny—we'll find somewhere to dump it. Let's get moving."

"So that's what we did," said Johnny. "We pretended there was nothing the matter, but of course the one set of people we couldn't pretend to was the examiners. Heather was all right—besides, it wasn't really anything very much to do with her—but the rest of us just about scraped through, no more. We've done all right since then—family, you know—but I for one have been haunted ever since by not knowing what the hell happened to Midgeby. You see," he said, now addressing himself to Greta, "Bill was wrong. Midgeby didn't turn up that night to rub it in our faces that he'd outwitted us. He didn't turn up at all. He'd vanished from St. Loys. A few days later the porters cleared out his belongings from his room— there wasn't very much to clear out, poor devil—and since then, so far as any of us know, no one in the world has seen hide or hair of Alexander Midgeby, Esquire."

Greta was staring at her husband as if he were an especially unpleasant lizard, as if she didn't want to know him any longer and was disgusted they'd ever met.

"Did the cops not investigate the disappearance?" I said.

"Not much," said Johnny. "They tended to dismiss it as just another case of an undergraduate folding under the pressure of the big week. They probably kept an eye on the river, in case he turned up there, but that was about it. He was an adult, after all, and adults are allowed to disappear if they choose to."

He drew a deep breath and let it out slowly. "And ever since then, you see, it's been hanging over us. How the hell did Sandy Midgeby get out of that goddamned dungeon, and where did he go to? Sometimes I wake up in the middle of the night and think I see him sitting on the end of my bed, playing with a sharp knife or a piece of rope and with this horrible vengeful leer on his face…"

"We could ask Sherlock Holmes where he is," I said, nodding at the ouija board. The others seemed to have forgotten about it.

Bill snorted. "How old do you think we are? There aren't any spirits and there's never been a Sherlock Holmes. Johnny should have kept his mouth shut, though after all these years I don't suppose it makes any difference what we did to Midgeby."

"That's what you think, buster," I heard Greta mutter.

"Still, there's no harm in asking," I pressed. "Humour me. At the very least, it'll take our minds off Johnny's spooky story."

"One spooky thing in place of another," David said, clearly trying to lighten the atmosphere.

I smiled. "You could put it like that."

Greta didn't want to have any part of it any more, but the rest of us gathered round the board and dutifully put our fingers on the planchette.

"Are you still there, Sherlock?" I asked the empty air.

The planchette moved promptly and easily, as if the spirits had been waiting for the question.

"N-O S-H-I-T," it spelled out.

"Our friend has a sense of humour," observed Heather drily.

"I'm not sure I want to know the answer," said Johnny, looking as if he were about to pull his hand away.

"Don't break the circle!" Heather hissed. "It's better to find out the truth, even if it's a truth you don't like. Do you really want to spend the rest of your life the way you've been up to now, constantly looking back over your shoulder in case the spectre of Sandy Midgeby comes leaping out of the woodwork?"

Johnny grumbled under his breath, but didn't remove his finger from the planchette.

"This is ridiculous," said Greta from the far side of the room. "Just take a look at yourselves. Grown men and women—well, grown men and *a* woman—asking the nonexistent ghost of a nonexistent private detective if it can help you."

"Hush," said Johnny, with surprising vehemence.

"All right," I said. "Here goes. Mr. Holmes, could you tell us what happened to Sandy Midgeby?"

There was a long silence, and Heather shivered as if the room had suddenly grown a little colder. Then the planchette began to move again, speeding between the mother-of-pearl letters on the board.

" 'Once you eliminate the impossible, whatever remains, no matter how improbable, must be the truth,' " said David, when the planchette had stopped. He began to laugh—a nervous, high-pitched, self-conscious sound.

"Oh, for God's sake shut it, David," growled Bill. "What the devil can Sherlock mean by that?"

"He means that, in any investigation, you—" Johnny began doggedly.

"I know what the *sentence* means, you oaf. I'm not a *complete* illiterate. But what does the remark mean in the context of Sandy Midgeby's disappearance?"

"Maybe," I said, "Sherlock's trying to tell us that all these years you've been looking for a complicated explanation for the man's disappearance—an impossible explanation, really, because you'd have known if somehow he'd been able to break down the dungeon door, and he could hardly scrabble his way out through thick stone walls, could he?—when really the answer was staring you in the face the whole time. That's the problem with locked-room mysteries, as they're called. Everyone looks for an elaborate mechanism when really the easiest way in and out of a locked room is to unlock it."

"But Midgeby didn't have a key," Bill protested. "There was only one key to that padlock and it was in my trouser pocket all night long."

The planchette moved again, making a noise like paper being cut as it moved from one letter to the next.

"Holmes wants to know," I said once it had paused, "how you can be so very sure of that."

"Because I—"

A light dawned in Bill's eyes, and he turned to look at Heather.

"*I* never stirred from my bed that night, not even to go for a pee," he said. "But *you…*"

She smiled in an embarrassed way and dropped her gaze to the tabletop. "I couldn't bear the thought of that poor boy stuck miles underground in a dungeon with no way of escape, knowing the exams on which his future depended started the next day. Johnny had the right word—it was a truly shitty thing you lot did to Sandy Midgeby. You boasted to me about it and thought it was a great joke but, though I laughed about it with you, like your loyal little woman, I didn't think it was so hilarious. So as soon as you were asleep, Bill, I crept out of our bed, grabbed a flashlight, and retrieved the key. Luckily no one saw me as I went down the stairs to the cellar. From there, it was easy enough to follow where the dust had been disturbed until I found the room where you'd imprisoned him."

"And you let him out?" said Bill.

"Yes."

"And you never told the rest of us?"

"No. I thought it was *your* turn to suffer. You'd been happy enough to ruin poor Midgeby's chances in the exams, so my conscience suffered not at all at the thought of you three being in a cold sweat all finals week. I let him out, and I apologised for my pig of a boyfriend and my pig of a boyfriend's piggish friends, and then the two of us went back up to the corridor together. He vanished into his room while I crawled back into bed beside you, Bill. In the morning, you were none the wiser. It was the last time we ever slept together, Bill. Did you ever wonder why?"

"The fact that you dumped me during finals week didn't help my results. Though, with everything else that was on my mind..."

"You shit," David snarled at Heather. "All the time we were suffering the torments of the damned, you were laughing up your sleeve at us."

"It's all right, Jim," said Heather, putting a hand on my arm. "I don't mind what he calls me. The feeling's entirely mutual. There's hope yet for Johnny, who's always had pangs of guilt about what happened that night, but as for the other two—*pfft*. They're pathetic.

"Mind you," she added, "I was as puzzled as anyone else when Sandy failed to appear the next day. I'd expected to see him at breakfast, or at the latest in hall for dinner. But then I thought maybe he was just so revolted by the people he'd found himself among that he wanted to put as much distance between them and him as he could. Who could blame him? Wherever he went, wherever he is in the world now, I hope he's doing well for himself. My guess would be that he is. He was so much *brighter* than the three upper-crust stooges who looked down their noses at him."

Understandably, my little soirée didn't last too much longer after that. The guests all left together in something of a rush, the men braying at each other in loud voices as if to let the world know they hadn't been humiliated this evening.

From the way Greta was acting, my guess was that Bill would be looking for a hotel room by this time tomorrow. I felt sorry for her and wished she hadn't been among those hurt. It wasn't her fault the man she'd married had poison at his heart. I wondered idly what all those other shitty things were that Bill might have done.

Heather didn't leave with the rest but hung back on the pretext of helping me tidy up.

"I've guessed, you know," she said as I stooped to pick up the overturned plate of cheese and crackers David had left on the carpet in his haste to leave.

"Guessed what?"

"Don't play games with me, Sandy."

"Jim," I said. "I've been Jim for a long time now."

"It was the way you pursed your lips as you leaned over the ouija board. That was the final straw. Often enough over the past few years you've done something that's rung a bell, but I've discounted it because, after all, there's only a limited range of mannerisms that human beings can display. But tonight, when the subject shifted around to Sandy Midgeby, I put everything together. I recognised you."

I spread my hands and looked at her in my best aw-shucks fashion. "Guilty as charged, ma'am. At least the accent's genuine. Since I got back to this country and managed to insinuate myself into your circle, Heather, I've been expecting at every moment that you'd spot me for who I am—or was." I paused, then said, "Are you going to tell the others?"

"Why should I? I enjoyed playing along with your game tonight. And I don't care if I never see them again. I wouldn't like to lose sight of *you*, though, Sandy. Jim."

"The feeling's mutual. Back at St. Loys, you were just about the only reason I stuck it out. After that dreadful night, when I got back to my room, I looked around, decided I could never attain you and there was nothing else to keep me there, and so I lit out for good. Worked my passage across the Atlantic on a liner and set out to make my fortune in California. By the time their immigration people caught up with me I'd gotten myself a green card. I'm a citizen now."

"So it was you pushing the planchette?" she said.

"None other. It's easy enough to do—surely you learned that when you were a kid. Everyone else is trying so hard not to influence the pointer that the slightest little shove you give it will be amplified by the others and, presto change-o, the spirits are spelling out a message."

"And you convinced those poor goofs they were in touch with the afterlife shade of Sherlock Holmes?" She began to giggle. "No wonder they were lucky to scrape through with Thirds." She patted the couch beside her. "Come here."

I obeyed. "There's only one thing," I said as I settled myself. "You're wrong to think of Sherlock Holmes as a fictional character."

"Oh, pull the other one, Jim." She gave my knee a playfully cross little slap.

"I'm not trying to kid you, Heather. People say Conan Doyle based Holmes on a surgeon he'd known at the Edinburgh Royal Infirmary called Joseph Bell, but that's not strictly true. Well, maybe it's true in part. You see, my grandma's maiden name was Holmes. She married a Midgeby."

"I know the other three are stupid," said Heather, "but please don't put me in the same bracket. I've had enough of tall tales for one night, Jim. It was fun watching you pull the wool over the eyes of those dimwits, but I don't relish the notion of your thinking you can do the same to me."

"I'm not. I'm telling you the truth. My mum's grandpa was a Welshman named Sefton Holmes. He didn't wear a deerstalker or play the violin, and so far as I know he didn't have a cocaine habit, but he genuinely was a private detective. He lived in Edinburgh for a while and that was where Doyle met him. Later in life, when Doyle was trying to establish himself as a writer, he got in touch with my great-granddad and suggested they could write a book together—really, that Doyle would ghostwrite my great-granddad's

autobiography. The adventures of a private detective, Doyle
said: what could be more guaranteed to grab the attention of the
reading public?

"Holmes disagreed, and besides there was the matter of his
clients' confidentiality to think about. But he allowed Doyle to
follow him around for a few weeks to garner some ideas, telling
people Doyle was his hired assistant—his dogsbody."

"His Watson," said Heather.

"You got it in one. They even shared a profession, Doyle and
Watson. Doyle wanted to give his fictional detective the same name
as my great-granddad, but Holmes—the *real* Holmes—refused to let
him do that. So Doyle changed the forename to the obviously bogus
'Sherlock.' And there you have it."

"I'm not sure I entirely believe you," said Heather thoughtfully.

"I'm not sure I entirely believe me either," I said. "But that's the
story as it was handed down to me by the family."

"And you think maybe we got in touch tonight with the spirit of
your great-grandfather?"

"I very much doubt it. Like I said, it was my finger that was
pushing the planchette, not some ectoplasmic extrusion from the
great beyond."

We sat in silence together for a while, side by side. Her hand was
still on my knee.

"We've wasted a lot of time, you and I, haven't we, Sandy?" she
said at last.

"Years and years and years," I said. "Far too long."

The Booby's Bay Adventure

By O'Neil De Noux

O ur latest visitor stepped in, paused, and looked at me for a moment before turning her gaze to my friend leaning against his oversized chair.

"Mister Sherlock Holmes, I presume?"

Holmes stood straight and said, "Miss Emily Topping." He opened a hand to me and added, "This is my friend, Dr. John Watson."

The young woman nodded at me and looked back at Holmes, and I made mental notes so I could describe her in what I expected to be another of my friend's adventures.

Emily Topping, five foot six inches, blue eyes, yellow blond hair worn in a bouffant.

Miss Topping wore a slim blue dress which showed her willowy figure, but it was her face which kept my eyes on her. There stood a beautiful young woman with an almost angelic face, wide eyes, full mouth, high cheekbones, and a small chin.

"I received your note, Miss Topping." Holmes pointed to the chair across from his as he sat and crossed his leg.

She sat.

"Your note stated that I was the only one who could help with a matter most urgent."

Mrs. Hudson brought in a tray of tea, fixed a cup for me and Holmes each as we liked it, and turned to our guest.

"Milk? Sugar?"

"Both."

Mrs. Hudson left and we sipped our tea.

"Back to the note," said Holmes.

Emily put her cup down. "I need your expertise, Mr. Holmes. Your expertise in the paintings of Gowan Gindick. I believe I have located the lost *View of Bay near Trevose Head.*"

My aloof friend tried not to show his excitement at hearing this, and I sat back, astonished that Holmes was expert in the paintings of…what was the name? I took the notebook and a pencil from my jacket pocket and wrote notes.

"Continue," Holmes told the young lady.

"I have traced it to Halmouth Abbey, on Booby's Bay just outside the village of Bushly, Cornwall. Within view of Trevose Head."

My olfactory sense picked up a hint of the lady's light perfume, a welcome scent in a room smelling of burned tobacco.

To me now, Emily said, "Gowan Gindick died in 1622. There are only ten known paintings by this Scottish painter, a contemporary of the great Johannes Vermeer. There are only thirty-four confirmed works from Vermeer's brush. Gindick's final work, finished shortly before he took his life, has been lost for over two and a half centuries."

"A suicide?" I asked.

Emily raised her cup and said, "Gindick's torrid infatuation with young Alice, Lady Febland, was unrequited, and he wrote her a final letter and leapt from a high cliff at the Mull of Kintyre. Alice was a cousin of the future King Charles I, the beheaded one. She would marry Lord Smyth-Grader, who was killed at the Battle of Saint Fagans."

A torrid infatuation?

Back to Holmes—"Money is no object, Mr. Holmes."

"What do you propose we do?"

"If you can authenticate the painting, I shall make such a generous offer, the owner would be unable to refuse."

Holmes raised his chin, looked down his nose at the pretty woman.

"Why? Gindick was a good painter, but hardly Vermeer."

"Gowan Gindick was my great-great-great-great-great-great-great-great-great uncle."

I lost count of the greats.

"I am the last of the Gindick line."

Holmes finished his tea, sat back.

"Cornwall? Will you accompany me, Watson?"

"Of course."

"There is a complication," said Emily as she took another sip of tea.

"Complication?"

"Halmouth Abbey is a nudist resort. The Booby's Bay Nudist Resort. Once we arrive, we must disrobe and wear no clothing during our stay."

Holmes blinked twice, sat back in his chair, and closed his eyes, his face as stern as I've ever seen it. The lady turned to me.

"I am a physician," I said. "Nudity does not bother me, although I am not used to traipsing around naked."

"Neither am I," she said. "But I am not shy. I think it shall be… liberating. I dislike wearing corsets."

Holmes cleared his throat, stood, and went to his pipe stand atop the fireplace mantel.

"Well, Mr. Holmes. Will you accompany me? I will double your usual fee."

Holmes filled his pipe and spoke to it.

"An unusual predicament."

I could not resist and said, "We were just discussing our recent lethargy. My good friend Holmes had just commented that our minds were becoming mired in malaise."

The lady withdrew a white envelope from her purse and put it on the small table next to her teacup.

"An advance," she said as she stood. "I think this predicament will stimulate your mind, Mr. Holmes."

And everything else—I thought. *Yes, life is full of whimsy.*

"I can make reservations for us as soon as you are ready to go, Mr. Holmes," Emily added.

Holmes took a few moments before clearing his throat.

"Um, yes. Miss Topping." Holmes looked in her direction, then at me. "Yes, we shall accompany you."

"The day after tomorrow, then?"

Holmes agreed.

I led her to the door and closed it behind her, smelling her perfume again, the scent swiftly covered by Holmes's cherry-scented pipe smoke as he sat in his chair.

"A descendant of a lost painter searching for a lost painting," he said. "I have studied all nine Gowan Gindick paintings. Wrote a paper on them. Published in Crumplehorn's Art Journal. All of the paintings are here in England. Five in small museums, the others privately owned. Like Vermeer, Gindick's art is characterized by a compositional balance and special order, illuminated by pearly light. He was a much finer painter than art experts concluded years ago."

I sat and poured the rest of the tea into my cup, mixed in milk and sugar, and had to say, "I did not realise you were an art expert."

"I am not. I am a Gowan Gindick expert. There are many talents hidden in me, my dear Watson."

"How does one authenticate a painting?"

"It is complicated. First and simplest is the visual examination of the art by someone expert in the artist's work, someone who can recognise the brush strokes, the paints, the use of light. A minute examination of the rear of the canvas can aid in revealing its age and authenticity."

A thought occurred to me and I said, "In case you fear someone recognising you going around nude, you can wear one of your disguises."

Holmes shot me a squint-eyed look. He settled back and, after a minute, his voice softened.

"I worry if I see Miss Topping—" He cleared his throat. "And other women in the nude. I may become..."

"What? Erect?"

His lips stiffened.

"I worry I shan't," I said.

His eyes opened wide.

"Is that a joke from the eminent doctor?"

"I'm not joking."

He settled back, and I picked up the volume of Kipling I had been reading. Sometime later, I saw his eyes were closed. Later still, he muttered, "The lost Gindick."

Miss Emily Topping wore tan jodhpur riding trousers for the trip, with a cream-coloured blouse and short brown boots, topped with a smart Bohemian ranger hat, which she removed before the train left the station.

"More comfortable than a dress with petticoats and a slip and corset and other undergarments. This is an expedition, after all." She touched her hair, obviously making certain the hat did not alter it. "One hat. One pair of boots. One change of jodhpurs and blouse for the return trip."

Holmes lifted her suitcase onto the shelf above her head as I sat across from Emily and removed my top hat. Holmes sat next to me and took off his deerstalker hat. Her perfume was there again, light and sweet in the confines of the coach.

"Booby's Bay lies west of the River Camel estuary, and Halmouth Abbey stands on a rise above the bay. The nudist resort is surrounded by a white wooden fence. Lord Alfred Thelemgotten, Sixth Earl of Aldestowe, established the resort twelve years ago. He and his wife, Lady Prudence, are leading proponents of nudism. We disembark in the village of Bushly, where a carriage will take us to the resort."

Holmes asked, "How did you learn the missing Gindick was there?"

"A friend visited the resort. She said it was in one of the three libraries. She could not remember which. The painting almost hidden. I find that odd."

"Why?" I asked after a few moments.

"If I had a Gindick, it would be where everyone could see it."

"If he wanted to hide it," Holmes said, "it would be locked away from sight."

The rain started as soon as we crossed into Cornwall, and we ate in a dining car peppered by rain against the windows. Even dressed in trousers, Emily drew the gaze of nearly every man in the car. One man stopped and asked if he'd seen her on the stage. London.

"No."

The rain finally relented as the train tracks made a sweeping crescent along the seashore.

"Booby's Bay," Emily announced, and we looked out at rolling breakers and bright blue-green water, a rocky shoreline with occasional beaches.

"I say, Holmes, did you know women's breasts were sometimes called boobies in the late seventeenth century?"

"I missed that fact, Doctor. You are a fount of obscure information on occasion."

Emily snickered. "You two are funny."

Which drew a "harrumph" from my good friend.

We disembarked at Bushly, where we found no porters to assist with our luggage. Holmes snatched Emily's suitcase, along with his portmanteau, and led us to a landau for hire, where I stored my portmanteau and assisted Emily in while Holmes loaded their luggage. Emily informed the driver of our destination, and the old man perked up as he got his horses moving. Cool air, rich with the smells of spring grass, gave way to the thick, salty scents of the sea as the sun beamed down on us.

The landau turned through the open gate of a white fence and moved up a rise to Halmouth Abbey, hovering tall against the blue sky. Small groups of naked people stood on either side of the three-story fieldstone building. The landau pulled up in front, and a young man wearing only a tie and boat shoes came out for our luggage. Holmes paid the driver as four nudists came around the side of the abbey, led by two buxom women.

"Aye," said our landau driver as he watched the group approach. "Always a pleasure to come here."

A lean naked man who appeared to be around forty sat behind a desk in the foyer. He wore a tie as well. He looked up our names in the reservation registry.

"Ah, yes. Mr. Reynolds, Mr. Shane, and Miss Guard."

Emily stepped forward and presented the man with a white envelope, and he checked the bills inside as Emily stepped back to us and whispered, "Do you really want to be registered as Sherlock Holmes?"

"I am Reginald," said the man as he held up their keys. "Billy will show you to your rooms. The gentlemen in a double room, the lady in a single room. I am certain you will enjoy our accommodations. To summon staff, pull the purple sash next to your beds. Lunch is served in a half-hour." As we turned away, he added, "Once you unclothe upstairs, remember clothing is not permitted. We revel in our nudity."

On our way up the wide, spiral staircase, Emily said she would meet us at the bottom of the staircase in a quarter-hour.

Our spacious room had two large beds with nightstands, a long dresser, two standard dressers, three cushioned chairs, a small writing desk with chair, two wash basins, two closets, and windows overlooking the wide lawn behind the abbey. Three small groups of nude people strolled there, several with umbrellas to protect them from the sun. Peering down, I observed a wide awning covering the area at the rear of the abbey. Three white gazebos dotted the lawn, two occupied by more naked people.

"I thought there might be only a dozen people here at most," Holmes said as he stood next to me.

I stepped to my side of the room and began disrobing. Holmes moved to his side of the room and began taking off his clothing.

"If you write this tale," he said, "please be good as to leave out your usual detailed description of me."

We waited at the bottom of the stairs, keeping our gazes focused on the faces of those who passed until two young men stopped and looked past us up the stairs. Both let out long breaths, and we turned to view Emily in all her naked beauty descending the stairs on the balls of her small feet, a hand on the rail.

I shall not describe Holmes in the buff, but the reader should not be cheated out of envisioning one of the most beautiful women I have ever seen. Her golden hair, still in a bouffant, picked up the sunlight streaming through the front windows, her face trying to hide a little smirk as she descended. She indeed needed no corset with such a narrow waist, her full breasts rose high with pale pink areolas and small nipples, her belly flat, her pubic bush a shade darker than the hair on her head, her legs long and slim.

"Hello," she said as she arrived, and Holmes and I turned to lead her to the dining room.

"Hello," I said, and stopped. I had no idea which way lay the dining room.

Holmes called out to a young woman wearing only a maid's white bonnet on her head. She was lovely as well, a full-figured young woman with a broad smile. She directed us to the dining room as Emily stepped between us, and I realised the fear of my body not reacting as any man would to such a vision was wrong. Holmes stepped up the pace and moved stiffly in front of us.

During our lunch of mutton and new potatoes, I noticed Holmes did as I did and kept focused on Emily's face as we spoke. Of course I could not telescope my eyesight so narrowly and found myself looking at those marvelous breasts. Halfway through our meal, a couple who had been moving between the tables and greeting diners stepped up to our table.

"Do not let us interrupt your meal," said the man.

They were in their fifties, the man stocky with brown hair gone grey, the woman full-figured with reddish hair.

"I am Lord Thelemgotten, and this is Lady Prudence."

"We came to welcome you," said the lady.

"Excited to meet new temporary members of our society," said the lord.

"We hope you enjoy your stay and return many times."

"Lord Alfred," said Emily. "Do you know how Booby's Bay got its name?"

"No."

"I would think," Lady Prudence said, "it was named for the bird. The seabird. The booby."

"But boobies are not native to the British Isles," said Holmes.

"That may be so." Lady Prudence stiffened her back. "But they can visit."

Emily asked his lordship, "I've heard you have an excellent art collection here at Halmouth. Is there anyone who can show us around, so we do not miss anything?"

The lord smiled down at her. "My secretary Rosamonde conducts tours of our art and other treasures upon request. I shall make sure she contacts you prior to tea time."

After our meal, Emily declared she would walk around. "I want to feel cool grass underfoot. Care to join me?"

"I'll be in our room," said Holmes.

I was about to agree to accompany our lovely client until she rose and eased around the table, stood next to me and raised her hands to touch her bouffant, her breasts rising, and I told her I would return to the room as well. My libido threatened to rise. I thought maybe Holmes and I should snoop around, maybe find this small library, maybe locate the lost Gindick. I waited until we were up in the room to mention this to Holmes as he filled his pipe.

"I shall wait to traipse around when we are taken on the tour."

The sky outside darkened and clouds hovered overhead. I moved to a window and spotted Emily walking to a gazebo followed by a young man, then another and a young couple. Lightning forked in the distance.

"A most difficult case." My friend sat back in his chair in his robe, his eyes closed.

"Yes." I thought about it, then asked, "Why? We simply locate the painting and you examine it."

"I do not mean that part of the matter."

I moved to my dresser, where'd I'd emptied my small suitcase, and put on my robe.

Holmes spoke, but I missed what he said and asked him to repeat it.

His voice came soft. "When she came down the stairs."

"Oh, yes."

"Walking around like this is difficult."

"But you shall rise to the occasion."

His eyes snapped open.

"More humour? I was going to say the case has challenges both mental and physical simultaneously."

"Indubitably."

"Indubitably?" He shook his head and closed his eyes again. "I do not believe I will read whatever you write about this adventure."

A thunderclap turned me to the window to see Emily and the others hurrying back to the abbey. A few seconds after they disappeared from view, a wall of rain washed in from the sea.

At a quarter until four o'clock, a rap at our door drew me to answer to find a young, dark-haired woman with her hands behind her back. I tried to focus on her pretty face as she smiled and said, "I am Rosamonde." She leaned so she could see into the room. "His lordship asked me to take you on a tour after tea." She went up on her toes. "I am thrilled to meet Mr. Sherlock Holmes." She waved at Holmes and put a finger over her lips.

"Mum's the word on your secret identity, Mr. Holmes. His lordship recognised you and has informed no one beyond Lady Prudence and me."

Rosamonde looked back at me and rolled her shoulders, her breasts moving in a mesmerizing sway before she turned and walked away.

I was a physician. Yes. But this was no medical examination. This was a pretty woman standing naked in a hall, and I remembered that my grandfather once commented we had Norman French blood in our ancestry.

Holmes gave me a weary look.

"It appears our cover is blown," I told my friend.

"Indubitably."

At tea, Holmes stared at me sitting across from him—no doubt hoping no one else recognised him. It seemed to me a few looked our way more than once, but it was most likely Emily who drew their attention. After tea, Rosamonde led us to the foyer. Emily moved next to Holmes and asked him what was wrong.

"They know who I am."

I almost said it, but gritted my teeth, almost reminded him I suggested he wear one of his infamous disguises. A wig, a moustache, a limp. We had a few canes back home.

Rosamonde led us into a large room across from the dining room, a room filled with books on two walls and paintings on the wall facing a line of windows. A mix of paintings from ornate Rococo art to neo-classical to the English Norwich School, even Japanese paintings of ducks and other birds. The only names I recognised were John Crome and watercolour artist John Thirtle. In the smallest library upstairs, Holmes spotted the lost Gindick on a wall between two bookcases. He moved straight to it as Rosamonde began her tour of the room near the door. Emily followed Holmes, and I stepped over as he went up on his toes for a better look.

The painting was the largest in the abbey, a blueish-purple sky above a dark blue sea with whitecaps breaking over turquoise water near a tan beach creeping up to grey rocks, a steep headland along the right side, all bathed in a pearly light. The *View of Bay near Trevose Head* stood nearly a yard square.

When Rosamonde reached our area, Holmes asked if the painting could be brought down for a closer look.

"Oh. Oh, no. His lordship does not allow examinations of his paintings."

"Why not?" Emily asked.

"I do not know."

Rosamonde shrugged and led us away with, "I saved the best for last."

We held back until Emily grabbed Holmes's arm and, in a low voice, said we'd return after midnight.

The final room had only two paintings, and Rosamonde explained that this was the room with his lordship's greatest treasures. She led us to a glass case and stood over it until we collected around the case, filled with four gold bracelets, gold rings, silver rings, necklaces, and his lordship's most prized possession, a nine-inch Saracen dagger in a solid gold scabbard encrusted with diamonds, rubies, and emeralds.

"This is astonishing," Holmes declared.

It occurred to me as we departed that, while the case seemed formidable—thick glass and what appeared to be an excellent lock—the jewelry inside should be in a safe.

Emily invited us to join her outside, as the weather had cleared, but Holmes said he faced a three-pipe problem and I went upstairs with him, opening the windows as Holmes filled the room with pipe smoke.

"I could simply ask his lordship," said Holmes as he sat in his chair, his robe wrapped around him. I donned my robe and stepped to the window to look down at the nudists milling behind the abbey. A large black dog raced from one gazebo to the next and back again in a frolicking gait, tail wagging.

"I could ask his lordship for a closer look at the Gindick." Holmes took a hit from his pipe. "But I feel something is amiss, my dear Watson. Why will he not allow examinations of his paintings?" He looked at me. "I wonder if his jewels are real?"

"His estate is real enough."

Rain returned in the early afternoon, and we had a delicious dinner of beef soup, roast goose, and green peas, followed by a tart lemon blancmange. Emily insisted we dine at a larger table, where Holmes and I sat at the quiet end while she and two young couples conversed, the young men talking of rugby and diamond mines in Natal and the young women talking of Parisian fashions and the Rational Dress League, explaining to one of the men how the league professed to rid women of corsets and extra undergarments.

After dinner, Emily remained with the ladies for hot cocoa, while Holmes and I skipped brandy and went to our room.

"We leave in the morning, Holmes. What shall we do? Sneak back upstairs with your magnifying glass or ask his lordship outright?"

"We shall discuss it when Miss Topping comes tonight."

"You are certain she will come?"

"Shortly before midnight, Watson. Shortly before midnight."

I looked at the clock when the soft knocking came at our door later. It was almost midnight.

"Come in, Miss Topping," said Holmes.

Emily peeked in, then stepped in.

"I've reconnoitered," she said. "We should go up the back stairs."

Holmes stood with his magnifying glass in hand.

"Come, Watson. We shall need a lookout."

Emily put her hands on her hips and said, "The robes."

We left our robes, and Emily led the way up the narrow staircase. I kept my head down, as her rear end was at face level. I did not see her stop and turn at the top of the stairs, and I almost bumped into her bush right in front of me. She put a finger over her lips and tiptoed, and we followed her down the hall to the room. We went in, and Emily told us to stay still as she skipped over and opened the curtains, letting in enough moonlight for us to see. I whispered for her to stay by the door while Holmes and I carried a cushioned chair over and took down the painting. We took it to a table, and I switched places with Emily.

"Dr. Watson," Emily said. "Bring us the torch."

"What torch?"

"The one ten feet to your left, in the nook next to the encyclopedias. I hid it after dinner."

I brought it to them.

"Where did you find the torch?"

"It was in the nightstand in my room. Do you not have torches in your nightstands?"

I never looked.

"Watson." Holmes nodded to the door and I returned to guard it as he examined the painting. Three minutes into the examination, he and Emily turned the painting over and he inspected the back side. They turned it over again and he studied the painting once more, moving around it until he stood and shook his head.

"It looks genuine from a distance, but, I am afraid, this is not a Gindick."

Emily stood with her mouth open.

"Are you certain?"

"Quite." Holmes bent over the painting with his glass again. "I am sure you are aware your ancestor used light brush strokes and never used raw paint, undiluted paint, as in this painting. Even the signature is incorrect. Gowan Gindick always dotted the first *i* in his name, but never the second *i*. One of his peculiarities." He stood. "And the canvas is not from the seventeenth century."

The door opened and struck my arm, and I turned as Lord Alfred and the black dog I'd seen on the lawn came in, followed by a young footman. His lordship and the footman carried torches, the dog bounding over to Holmes with a wagging tail.

"Good boy, Brutus," his lordship said. "You've sniffed them out."

He turned to the footman. "Take Brutus into the hall, Geoffrey."

The footman, whose torch lingered on Emily, led the dog into the hall, and Lord Alfred closed the door.

"Mr. Holmes. I am disappointed in your taking advantage of my hospitality."

Holmes stood stiffer as his lordship crossed to them.

"I am astounded at myself as well, sir. I apologise for my conduct and surrender to whatever reproach you feel necessary."

His lordship reached over and took the magnifying glass from my friend's hand.

"I know you are not here to purloin this painting." He raised the magnifying glass. "We must reach an agreement, Mr. Holmes."

"Your lordship?"

"You say nothing about this painting, and I shall forget what happened tonight."

Holmes nodded.

"It is not a genuine Gindick, is it?"

"No, it is not."

"As I always suspected." His lordship turned to Emily, glanced down her body. Not subtle.

"I always suspected it was not a genuine Gindick, which is why I would never sell it, never wanted anyone to examine it. I rather like people believing I have the lost Gindick."

Emily asked, "Where did you get it?"

"Cairo. At a small shop off the main bazaar. Nearly twenty years ago."

He looked at Holmes now and it occurred to me again—this was why I was a good chronicler of Holmes's adventures. I was present, but not involved.

"I paid little for it, and it does look very much like the Gindicks in the Queensberry museum."

His lordship offered his arm to Emily and said, "How about a nightcap, darling?"

Emily stepped to Holmes and wrapped her arm through his.

"Thank you, but no, milord."

Holmes tried his best to keep his face expressionless, and I was not about to lower my gaze.

A London rainstorm greeted us upon our return. Holmes, dressed in his travelling suit and deerstalker, hired us a coach. He instructed the driver to drop us on Baker Street and take the lady on to her house. Baker Street was clogged with traffic. Holmes grew impatient as the rain slackened to a light drizzle a block from 221B and insisted the coach driver turn off and take Emily Topping home.

"I shall come see you soon," said Emily. "Settle up what I owe you."

She smiled and touched our arms as we climbed out, and I was relieved to see the smile return to her lovely face. She had been unsmiling on our return trip. Holmes climbed out and I followed, and we went around and grabbed our luggage. Holmes urged the driver on, and the carriage pulled away as we hurried off. It was not until we were in our rooms that I noticed Holmes had mistakenly taken Emily's suitcase when we hurriedly snatched our luggage in the rain.

"I did not take it mistakenly. She will come for it in a few minutes."

I professed I did not understand.

"Lift it."

I did, and it felt heavy.

"You recall when we boarded the train at Bushly, I carried Miss Topping's suitcase into the station, put it on the shelf on the train."

"Yes."

Holmes cleared a small table and placed the suitcase in the chair next to it. He opened it and pulled out the blouse and jodhpurs Emily wore to Halmouth Abbey—she had worn black jodhpurs with a pale pink blouse for the return trip. He drew out a black silk sack, which jingled. He poured the contents on the table and four gold bracelets tumbled out, as well as gold rings, silver rings, and necklaces. Holmes reached into the bottom of the suitcase, withdrew another black silk sack, and took out Lord Thelemgotten's most prized possession, the nine-inch Saracen dagger in a solid gold scabbard encrusted with diamonds, rubies, and emeralds.

"It is a heavy item," he said, placing it next to the other jewelry. He went into our bedroom and came out with a pillowcase, which he draped over the booty. He put the clothing and sacks back into the suitcase and closed it, filled a pipe, and sat in his chair.

"Miss Topping's small suitcase doubled in weight on our journey." He lit his pipe.

I sat in my chair.

"Holmes. That is how you solved this…caper? The suitcase weighed more."

"From the beginning I thought this was much ado about little. While you focused on Miss Topping's lovely body, I paid attention to her eyes and felt something amiss there. Her nudity was an eager distraction for everyone save Sherlock Holmes. Standing next to the glass case, while you were looking at the jewels and glancing at her abundant and exquisite bosom, I watched Miss Topping's eyes and saw lust there, more lust than the looks the men were giving her. It was merely keen observation on my part."

Presently, a knock on our door produced Mrs. Hudson and Emily Topping.

"Come in, my dear."

I nodded a thank-you to Mrs. Hudson, who withdrew.

Holmes cut off Emily as she started to talk, waving a hand at the suitcase.

"Here it is," he said.

"Oh, I am so relieved, Mr. Holmes."

She crossed the room, smiling toward me on the way, and reached for the suitcase.

"But that is not all you came for, is it, my dear?" Holmes took a puff.

"No?"

"No."

Holmes rose and stepped to the small table and lifted the pillowcase.

Emily let out a gasp, took a step back, and looked at me. She took another step back.

"How?" Her voice sounded scratchy. "How did you know?"

"Years." Holmes dropped the pillowcase atop the loot and smiled. "Years of careful observations."

Emily turned to the door and I moved to cut her off. She pulled a small, nickel-plated handgun from her purse and pointed it at me, a steely look in her eyes, as she backed toward the door.

"Let her go, Watson." Holmes sat and raised his pipe. "Goodbye, Miss Topping."

Emily continued to the door and then out.

Holmes chuckled.

"No sense taking a bullet, my dear Watson."

"But she is getting away."

"We have recovered the loot for Lord Thelemgotten."

"But Miss Topping."

"We've seen enough of her, wouldn't you say?"

The Adventure of the Red Dress

By Ana Teresa Pereira

John had dreamt of the tower again. He was going up the narrow staircase. The image was repeated on the cover of a book he hadn't yet written, and the ending of a film nobody had yet directed. It happened sometimes, these strange connections, in the endless world of his nights. Same as the idea that red hair and blue eyes were characteristics of vampires.

Like the men in his books, he liked to walk along London streets at night. So many times, when he was not sure how to begin a novel, there was a man walking near Regent's Park. A man who looked like him, perhaps taller, with his hands in the pockets of his overcoat. The streetlamps, like signs in the fog, were his only direction. There was rain, too, not heavy rain, the never-ending rain that accompanied him all his life.

Suddenly he realised where he was. The narrow street, the dark shops—why didn't they leave some light in the windows?—the old trees, and the silence that always made him feel, even though

he was in the centre of the city, that he was in a solitary lane in
the countryside.

He had convinced himself he needed a quiet place to work, but it
wasn't true. There was the library at home, his paintings, his books,
the familiar disorder, and a dinner the cook had left for him in the
kitchen—she took care of him like a mother when his wife was away.
And there was Fay's apartment and the corner she had arranged for
him, just a table near a window, a lamp, a watercolour of the Thames
discovered in one of the antique shops she liked to visit. But, even if
she was on the other side of the room revising some screenplay, he
could feel her presence, that kind of warmth, though her skin was
always cool. And her scent, that mixture of orange and flowers she
ordered from Paris. Are the red hair and the blue eyes characteristic
of the vampires?

The building was old and, since he rarely went there during
the day, he had no idea who lived in it. He opened the door. The
entrance was illuminated by a single bulb, and the flight of stairs was
always in the dark. No smell of food, no sound of children's voices.

His room was at the end of the corridor. The smell of his pipe.
The window opened to an even narrower and darker street. He lit the
ceiling bulb and the lamp on the table. As usual, he looked around,
wondering what he was doing there. It was as squalid as could be. A
narrow bed, a table with a typewriter he had bought second-hand,
two chairs. He had thought of buying a cheap painting to warm
it a little, but instead had put some theatre bills on the wall. Two
shelves where he had some books, a bottle of whisky, and two glasses.
There was a bit of whisky left in a glass, and he washed it in the tiny
bathroom. He had a drink and only then took off his overcoat and
hung it behind the door. The room was freezing, as always, so he left
his scarf on.

The editor of the *Strand* had commissioned a Sherlock Holmes
story, perhaps remembering that he and Adrian had planned to write
a collection. He had to deliver it the next day but wasn't too worried.
He was accustomed to deadlines. Besides, he had most of the story

by now. It would be narrated by Watson. Still from the time he and
Holmes shared the apartment on Baker Street. A new client. A young
man who owned a bookshop specializing in poetry. A girl named
Violet. Why were so many girls in Holmes stories called Violet?

He took the small book of Shakespeare's sonnets that Fay had
given him from his pocket. He opened it on the first page. To
John from F.

He needed a verse. Something that would leave Holmes
metaphorically at sea. A story of lost souls. Damn Holmes and his
rational mind. The old fool was as lost as the rest of us.

"For thy sweet love rememb'red such wealth brings—"

I lifted my eyes from the newspaper and stared at Holmes. I
didn't know if he was speaking to me. He had a letter in his hands. I
made an effort to remember.

"That then I scorn to change my state with kings."

We were sitting at the breakfast table, having a final cup of
coffee. It was autumn, a dark autumn day, the continuation of a long
dark night. The streetlights were on, and the fog muffled the sounds
of voices and carriages.

Holmes didn't answer. I couldn't help smiling. Apart from the
Shakespeare plays we saw once in a while, and his favourite quote,
"There are more things in heaven and earth…" Holmes didn't seem
much interested in our Bard. And I don't even think he owned any
edition of the sonnets. But then his library was a kind of labyrinth,
where one could find the most surprising things: from old numbers
of pulp magazines to some eighteenth-century treatises on vampires.

"We'll soon have a visitor, Watson."

He gave me a small card. "Lawrence Mason. Mason Bookshop.
Specialist in Poetry."

I took a final sip of coffee.

"So, Holmes, can we expect an old librarian, smelling of old books and pipe smoke?"

"No, Watson. A young man, an aspiring poet, and probably very much in love."

"Come on, Holmes. That's a wild guess."

"I never guess, my dear Watson. You should know that by now. Take a look at this envelope and this note."

I examined them.

"Well, very absent-minded, I'd say. He addressed it to 220 Baker Street."

"Yes. It seems that I live in the shop next door."

"And he says he wants to talk to you about a red dress."

"And its owner, I presume."

"But…this is interesting…on the other side of the page, he had been scribbling. Squares inside squares, something resembling a maze. And a few words: 'But thy sweet love.' All right, Holmes. This doesn't seem at all like a letter from an old librarian. A young man, rather absent-minded and thinking about a woman."

"We'll soon know. Someone is arriving."

Two minutes later, Mrs. Hudson introduced a young man into our drawing room. He was rather tall and handsome; his suit, although perhaps too light for the season, was well cut and discreet.

"Mr. Holmes, I presume."

"Yes, you got the right door."

My friend was having fun; he smiled the way he did sometimes, only with half his mouth, and only for a second. The young man seemed to realise that, too.

"Yes, Mr. Holmes. I am the kind of person who often gets lost in the fog."

"It would be worse had you lived before Turner."

"I suppose I would have fallen into the river a few times."

They were talking very seriously, and Holmes must have noticed that I looked perplexed.

"You should read Oscar Wilde, my dear Watson."

"Fairy tales?" I asked defensively.

"I understand you want to talk to me about a red dress," remarked Holmes. "I must tell you I'm no expert in women's dresses."

A sudden shadow passed over the young man's face. He took a silver cigarette case from one of his pockets.

"It's a long story, Mr. Holmes. The strangest story you've ever heard."

"Oh, I doubt that. But please begin, my friend," said Holmes. He had his fingertips together and his eyes on the ceiling.

"My name is Lawrence Mason. My father died two years ago, just after I left college. I was planning to travel for a year or so. I've only been to Paris and Berlin, and I think a writer, a poet, should know the world. But my father owned a bookshop and I had to take care of it. I love the bookshop, ever since I was a child. I spent long hours there, and it was my idea of a magic place. The corridors full of books, the books on the floor, the mysterious visitors, my father holding a new book, smelling it, examining it with his magnifying lens. There is a small apartment upstairs, so I had a place to live. Apart from some money, my father also left me our family house in Hampshire. It's a lovely cottage. Like something from a painting. The walls are a faint red, and almost covered with leaves, the porch has a few steps where I still like to sit in the evening. And the sounds…the birds, the water of a nearby spring, a kind of sigh when the fog surrounds it. I spent my childhood there until I went to a private school. And I always went back in the holidays."

He lit a cigarette and looked at the window.

"For two years I led a quiet life. I have some friends from college days. I like to go to a pub and the theatre occasionally. But most nights, after dinner, I went to my room and wrote or read until dawn. I had a few liaisons, but nothing serious, until I met Violet last spring."

"I met her at a party. She was not prettier than the other girls, she hadn't read many books, she hadn't travelled at all… Maybe her hair looked softer, and I liked her voice; the next day I woke up thinking of her and tried to locate her through my friends. I asked her to lunch, then we went for walks in the park, and almost without noticing it, I was engaged. Violet didn't have any family and earned her living as a typist. We married last summer and spent a few days in Edinburgh. When we came back, we lived in our house in Hampshire. I hired the couple who had worked for my family years ago and still lived near the village. They gave Violet a puppy, a curly-haired spaniel we called Jasper. She didn't seem lonely when I spent a few days in London. She would welcome me in one of her new dresses, Jasper would jump at me, and Mrs. Danvers would have a nice dinner prepared for us. We were perfectly happy."

"And yet, and yet…"

"About a month ago, something happened. I had been in London the whole week and returned on Friday afternoon. I arrived at dusk, and I walked home as usual. It is a beautiful walk, and it was autumn… Everything was submerged in yellow leaves: the path, the bridge, the spring. I noticed the wooden gate of the cottage had been painted afresh. The garden was full of autumn roses. Danvers was clipping some hedges and greeted me as usual. I could see Mrs. Danvers through the kitchen window; I could even smell dinner. I went in, and Violet came downstairs to meet me."

"And…" said Holmes.

"It wasn't Violet. At least Violet as I remembered her."

"You don't mean you had forgotten your wife's face in a week, Mr. Mason." But Holmes wasn't smiling now.

"No… You see, Violet, as I remembered her, was a brunette, with a round face, not very tall… The woman that came to meet me was as tall as I, slim, with long copper hair and the bluest eyes I had ever seen."

Holmes remained silent for a few minutes, with his fingertips still pressed together, his long legs stretched out in front of him.

"You had never seen her before?

"No."

"Are you certain?"

"She isn't easy to forget."

"Ah!"

"Mr. Holmes, when I was a boy, I got lost in the fog twice. I liked to walk for hours, follow the streams, discover hidden waterfalls. And plants. To find a rare flower and bring it to my mother. And I got lost. The first time for a few hours. The second, an evening and a night. They had been looking for me, and I arrived at dawn. The strange thing is I couldn't remember what had happened. I mean, I had no notion I had been away for so long, I had small bruises on my knees and I didn't remember falling… I couldn't understand why everyone was making such a fuss. That's how I felt that day. I was arriving home, but everything before that was vague, uncertain."

"Your sense of reality was gone."

"Yes. I went upstairs and changed, then I came down for dinner. Mrs. Danvers looked perfectly natural, the dog was under the table, and I was telling the woman I didn't remember which books I had bought during the week, what novel I had been reading at night, what play had just opened in the closest theatre."

"Mrs. Danvers and her husband were behaving as if everything was normal?"

"Yes. I was tired and went to my room early; I think I fell asleep almost at once. The next morning there was a girl sleeping in the bed next to mine, her hair was in disorder and she smelt nice."

"And life went on…"

"In a way. It was as if I was playing a part, and the actress had changed. And the whole world seemed different."

"The whole scenery."

"Well…yes. The lighting was different. Then I was in London and things were normal, too. Are you familiar with Mr. Edgar Allan Poe, Mr. Holmes?"

"Fairly."

"All we see and all we seem are but a dream… That's how I felt."

"You'll soon be quoting *Alice in Wonderland.*"

"I guess."

Holmes said slowly, as if he was thinking aloud, "But who was dreaming all that?"

"And the dream lasted a month?" I asked.

"Almost a month."

"What happened to wake you up?" asked Holmes.

"Last Saturday, I brought her to London to see a play. She looked lovelier than ever, with a string of pearls and a red dress. That's… what made me regain consciousness, Mr. Holmes. My wife would never wear a red dress."

Holmes was silent for a moment.

"I see. What do you expect me to do?"

"I am going to Hampshire this afternoon. I wonder if you would come with me. And Dr. Watson, if he wants to. I'll send a cable saying we have two guests for dinner."

"I think we can arrange that. Watson?"

"I wouldn't miss it for anything in the world."

The young man seemed relieved.

"I'll be at the station a few minutes before seven. It's a nice journey."

That evening, we had a carriage just for us on the seven o'clock train. Holmes seemed absorbed in the papers but, from time to time, I noticed him looking through the window. The phantom beauty of the English countryside is always touching; but maybe he was wondering about the criminal impulses of the people living in the scattered cottages. Our young friend had opened a blue-covered book, but he, too, glanced occasionally at the landscape, with the familiar fondness of an owner. We finally saw the tower of the Winchester cathedral.

The train left us at a small station with the customary beds of red geraniums. After engaging two rooms at the inn, we walked to Mason's cottage.

It was twenty minutes' walk among trees and hawthorn, and fugitive curlews; at a certain point we crossed a stone bridge. Holmes, who claims to be completely indifferent to landscapes, has a strange fondness for bridges. This one was very old, and the water under it was clear and bluish, perhaps because of the grey stones and the moss.

"Have you ever noticed how certain words seem to coincide with the things they name? Bridge, water, stone, moor, fog," said Holmes.

I looked at him, astonished. But Mason seemed to find those thoughts familiar.

"It's the same thing with certain plants, certain birds."

I sometimes wonder if Holmes was already under the spell of the woman we were going to meet. As Mason undoubtedly was. Even though I am an admirer of the fair sex, I think I was the one who remained almost untouched. As if she were an actress playing on a stage. Something very personal, but only for a while.

The cottage was quite isolated but looked cozy. Just as in some streets of London we have the impression of being in the country and almost expect to hear the sound of the church bells around the corner, this cottage gave the impression of being in a village street, with neighbours across the hedge, children playing, and laundry drying in the air. The red tiles, the pink walls, almost covered with red leaves, the garden, where some plants were blooming even now.

"Violet said she was in love with the garden."

"Which Violet?" asked Holmes.

Our young friend shuddered.

"The woman who is pretending to be my wife. I have to call her something." He was clearly defensive.

A middle-aged man appeared behind a fence. He was tall and well-built and limped a little; he saluted us with a quick movement of the head. A woman with grey hair and vestiges of beauty appeared at a window and gave us a tense smile. It was as if we were reviving Mason's arrival on the day his life had changed. For a moment, I wondered if the girl who was coming downstairs to meet us could be the small brunette he had married months before. And what we were going to do if that happened. Take Mason to a psychiatrist in London and consider the case solved?

But the girl who came downstairs was not a small brunette "not prettier than the others." She was tall and slender, her copper hair cut short in front and almost touching her waist in the back. She wore a simple blue dress that played with the violet of her eyes. Her mouth was small, and her slightly irregular teeth gave her smile an endless charm.

I looked at Holmes and for a moment I saw his face as it was years before, when I first met him. Good-looking and young, still open to new things, new changes, that never came. I wondered what he would be like if he had met this girl then. The only time I had seen Holmes taken by a woman was in the case of Irene Adler, and even then I suspected it was really her photograph that seduced him. The photograph he still kept in a drawer of his desk. Perhaps to remember that he once had felt something.

The dog that followed the girl was a spaniel, little more than a puppy, and responded to his owner's caresses with a wave of tail.

"It's nice to meet you Mr. Holmes," said the girl. "I've read some of the reports Dr. Watson wrote of your cases."

"I have a feeling they didn't impress you."

"Oh, not as much as the adventures of Prince Florizel of Bohemia."

"I thought young ladies just read Jane Austen."

"That was years ago. I'm more interested in Mr. Bram Stoker."

Holmes told me, when we were taking our overcoats off, "That girl is laughing at us."

"I'd say at you, Holmes."

"Perhaps. She is not stupid, so she must be extremely clever."

We had a drink in the drawing room. I noticed how cozy it was, with curtains and pillows that could have been brand-new, some nice paintings, vases of red autumn roses.

"You have a lovely home, Mr. Mason," I observed.

"Violet has bought some paintings. And she has green fingers, just like Danvers. It's as if the garden was transformed these last few weeks."

Dinner was good, the wine well chosen. Holmes was staring at our hostess in a way that bordered on indiscretion, but she was clearly a woman used to being looked at by men.

They talked about London theatres and plays. The girl seemed to have seen most of them and even to be acquainted with the actors and the original books when they happened to be adaptations. No common typist. Remembering a girl who had been our client some time ago and the way Holmes had deduced her profession because of the spatulate finger-ends, I examined Violet's hands. This girl was neither a typist nor a music teacher. An actress? Could she be acting even now? A member of the Diogenes Club, who happened to be a well-known actor, had told me once the secret was not acting at all but becoming the character. Had she become Violet? But she made no attempt to be like the young quiet woman she had replaced.

She put a red shawl on her shoulders when she came to say goodbye to us.

"So, we expect you tomorrow for lunch, Mr. Holmes. And you too, of course, Dr. Watson."

"It's an offer difficult to resist. Your cook makes wonders," I said.

"I give her a hand, Dr. Watson."

"That's easy to believe."

"I think you can do anything, Mrs. Mason," remarked my friend. "That's amazing in such a young woman."

"That's not how we measure a life, Mr. Holmes. In years."

For a moment, I thought he would ask how we do measure a life. But he didn't.

Lawrence came with us part of the way to the village. He and Holmes looked grim and immersed in their thoughts.

"Well, Holmes, what did you think of the second Mrs. Mason?" I finally asked.

"Does she sing often?"

Mason didn't look surprised.

"Yes, all the time, around the house and the garden. Sometimes she is just humming, but other times she does sing. She has a beautiful voice."

"As if it had been trained?"

"I suppose so. I...I remember her singing when she was putting up the curtains."

Holmes gave him one of his half-smiles.

"The curtains are new?"

"Yes. She bought the cloth and made them with the help of Mrs. Danvers."

"Was there anything wrong with the other ones?"

"I don't think so. They weren't even old."

"That perfume she wears...is it the same your wife used?"

"No. My wife used a faint lavender cologne."

"This one is a mixture of orange and some flower. Very pleasant, but not discreet."

"I suppose so. I like it."

"Just one more question. Do you think she is happy?"

"Sometimes she seems tense, almost scared. But yes, she is definitely happy."

He said goodbye at the bridge. We stood there for a minute, watching him go at his fast pace. Then we made the rest of the way. When we entered the inn, Holmes said, "Watson, before you go to sleep, I want you to send a cable to Inspector Lestrade."

"Do we really need to get the police involved?"

"You know we do, Watson. There's been foul play."

"Yes. But I won't sleep well tonight."

"I'm afraid I won't sleep at all. It's the first time I have been hired to break a spell. And I don't like it."

The next morning a light but persistent rain was falling. Holmes didn't come for breakfast, and I thought he was still in his room. But when I was having a last cup of coffee, I saw him arriving, his overcoat slightly wet, his dark blue scarf carelessly loose on his shoulder. He sat and asked for a coffee and grumbled, "Why do people who don't have murder in their nature decide to attempt it?"

I closed the newspaper.

"Because they have a chance to get away with it?"

"They won't, if it's not in their nature."

"I thought you believed anyone could be a murderer."

"Nonsense, Watson. I never said that."

He drank his coffee and stood up.

"Hurry up, Watson. I have a cab waiting for us."

The cab couldn't go by our shortcut, so it took us about half an hour to arrive. Mason and the girl came to the door. I couldn't help thinking they made a beautiful couple, more or less the same age, more or less the same height. The girl was wearing a simple red dress that brought up the colour of her hair, loose as ever.

"We weren't expecting you so soon," said Mason. "Lunch won't be ready before one."

"It doesn't matter. Could you tell the Danvers to join us in the drawing room?"

"Yes, of course. But Mrs. Danvers is busy with lunch."

"I don't know if any of us will be in the mood for lunch, my dear friend. At least not lunch as a celebration, as I think yours are."

Mason looked at the girl and his eyes softened.

"Yes. A celebration."

A few minutes later, we were all in the drawing room. There were fresh roses on the table. Heavy, scented. The scent of the girl was there too. I thought sadly that it would be there long after she was gone.

"There are so many scents in this house," said Holmes, as if he could read my thoughts.

"I'm afraid I have common tastes," said the girl. "I like dense perfumes, strings of fake pearls…"

"And red dresses." said Holmes.

She stared at him.

"Yes, Mr. Holmes. I like lovely dresses. Blue and red are my favourite colours."

"Maybe your life would be different if you hadn't worn a red evening dress a week ago."

"Oh, so that was my mistake!"

"As strange as it may seem…yes."

She looked at Mason.

"You don't like me in red?"

"I do."

Holmes interfered. He had to.

"This morning, Inspector Lestrade from Scotland Yard and the local police found your wife, my friend. Your first…your real wife."

Mason's lips tightened.

"Where?"

"In the cottage that belongs to Mrs. Danvers and her sister. Don't worry. She was frightened, but otherwise quite well. And Jasper is there, too."

Mason looked at the dog sleeping on his feet.

"This is not Jasper. I suspected that from the first day. Jasper was crazy when I got home. This one was just friendly."

"They are probably from the same litter. And very much alike. But Jasper would miss his owner and look for her."

"I see."

"Haven't you noticed the resemblance between Violet and Mrs. Danvers?"

"Yes... I think so."

I looked at the two women and suddenly it became quite obvious. The same bone structure, the same tall figure. The girl's eyes were of a rarer colour and the mouth plumper, as if an artist had perfected his picture.

"She is your daughter, isn't she, Mrs. Danvers? Mr. Danvers."

Nobody answered.

"And I suppose she has been living in London these last few years. Working in the theatre, perhaps some musicals? What happened? She was unemployed? She lost the sympathy of a generous lover?"

The girl's face didn't move.

"Both."

"So, you planned everything. To get rid of the young bride and take her place."

"But that makes no sense, Holmes," I said. "They don't look at all like each other."

"That was the touch of genius, Watson. If this young lady was plump and had brown hair, there was no possibility of success. Mason would just go to the police. But like this..."

"Like this..." repeated the girl. She stood up and went to the window. The rain had stopped and the garden was full of autumn light. There was a small tree outside covered with peach blossoms. I noticed the new curtains, of a darker peach colour, were a perfect frame.

"Like this," Holmes went on, "Mason was faced with the inexplicable. He started to doubt his own mind. Don't forget, Watson, that Mrs. Danvers had known him since he was a child. She knew how dreamy he was. If unreality was a disease... He would suspect foul play, of course. But he would hesitate. And that hesitation would give them time."

"To get rid of his wife."

"And of him, I suspect. His wife would inherit everything he had. And his real wife had no connections. A few forged documents would be enough."

The girl at the window caressed the curtains, almost unconsciously.

"I wouldn't let anyone hurt him."

"No?"

"I just wanted to live here with him."

Holmes asked her, slowly, "Did you know him as a child?"

"Yes. But he was kept away from the village children. We spoke twice…but he didn't really see me."

"So… You cared for him."

The girl grasped the curtains.

"Mr. Holmes, I made these curtains. I bought seeds in the village. Next spring, even before spring, there will be crocus and daffodils under these windows. White and yellow flowers."

"You just wanted to live here with him," repeated Holmes.

"As long as I can remember, I never wanted anything else."

I looked at Mason. And what I saw in his eyes was more terrible than anything that had happened or could happen afterwards.

Danvers was following the scene, as if he were just an observer. Mrs. Danvers was the one who spoke, and her voice was firm.

"My daughter didn't do anything but give a false name. We were the ones who kidnapped Mrs. Mason."

"Is that relief I detect in your voice, Mrs. Danvers?"

She shrugged.

"Relief…tiredness."

"I know. The weak point of your plan was not its implausibility. It was the fact that you didn't have it in you. You are not murderers."

The bell rang. Mrs. Danvers got up instinctively but sat down again.

"You can go open the door, Mrs. Danvers. It's Inspector Lestrade and the police from the village. You will go with them."

"Yes."

"May I change, Mr. Holmes?" asked the girl. "This dress seems somehow inappropriate."

She came back a few minutes later, wearing a grey dress and with her hair caught in the back. She barely looked at us. She smiled at her mother, as if to comfort her. A real lady, I thought. Why didn't that idiot notice her when she was a very young girl in the village?

The police and the Danvers left the house without any drama. And suddenly we found ourselves in a dark place. Yes, it was a matter of lighting.

"Your wife is at the village inn, Mason," remarked Holmes. "She needed a good rest, but she is all right."

Since there was no answer, he went on.

"She will want to see you."

Mason nodded.

"Mr. Holmes," he said. "What do you think will happen?"

"You will have two or three children. You will publish two or three books of poetry that no one will read and will bring you neither fame nor money. You will live."

"Mr. Holmes...I don't even know her name."

John took the sheet of paper from the writing machine. He hesitated for a moment and, with a pencil, wrote "Alice" and underlined it. Then he put the sheet on top of the others.

The bottle of whisky was almost empty. There were signs that the night was over: a faint, very faint light, voices from the street.

He took another glass of whisky. It would be nice to have something to eat, but one can't have everything.

He stood up and washed his face in the bathroom. The water was freezing. He looked at his face in the tarnished mirror and smiled ironically.

"I wonder if they will ever publish this."

He put on his overcoat, his dark blue scarf. He went out and, for the first time, heard footsteps upstairs.

It felt good to see people in the street. It felt good to see that rising light behind the buildings. It felt good to touch a tree and emerge in a well-lit street. He made a sign to a cab that was just passing.

Twenty minutes later he was in front of a tall modern building. As usual, he didn't wait for the elevator and ran upstairs. As usual, he didn't use his key and rang the bell. A moment later she was opening the door in her peach negligée, her long hair cut short in front, a copper mess. Her blue eyes were sleepy, but she put her arms around his neck and whispered something. She didn't smell like the rain. She smelt like oranges and wildflowers, and that was even better.

The Wargrave Resurrection

By Matthew Booth

Over the years of my acquaintance with Sherlock Holmes, I have seen a great number of illustrious clients in those Baker Street rooms which we shared, although it is also true that I have seen many members of the lower classes consult the eminent criminologist with whom I was associated. I think that I have remarked elsewhere that it was the peculiarity of the case upon which Holmes concentrated, to the extent that he would refuse to help those of the most exalted positions where the problem failed to engage his interest, whilst applying the most intense applications of his remarkable powers to the affairs of a humble parlourmaid, whose case appealed to his unique and capricious nature. It was one such client who called upon us early one brisk spring morning in the year 1888.

Recent months had been somewhat sterile with us, and I had begun to grow concerned at Holmes's lack of activity. I knew well to what dark alternatives he could turn when his mind was not engaged and he merely sneered at those crimes which had been reported in the newspapers.

"What is the use of seeking a master's views and opinions on the mere sketches of a schoolboy, Watson?" he would say.

"The last few months have not been entirely devoid of interest. We had the Keswick haunting and the madness of old Cranston."

"One cannot live on one's past glories alone."

This was the Holmes with whom I was sharing rooms at the time. It was, then, with some relief that I ushered Mr. Henry Collins into our chamber, for I hoped that whatever storm had blown him to our door would blow away the dust of tedium which was settling on my friend. Collins was a small, ruddy-faced man, whose complexion was intensified by the stark whiteness of his hair and whiskers. He stared from one to the other of us with wild grey eyes, and it was evident to me that he was in the grip of some sort of great fear.

"There is no cause to be hesitant, sir," said Holmes. "Perhaps my colleague here can get you some refreshment, for I observe that you are somewhat distressed."

"If I am not too much of a trouble for it, sir," said Collins. "A small whisky, if I may, for my nerves have had a terrible shock."

I obliged the little man and handed him a measure, which he accepted gratefully as he sat back on the cushions with a small sigh of gratitude.

"I trust that you are now feeling a little more composed," said Holmes. "Perhaps you would be able now to say clearly and concisely what has brought you here."

"Henry Collins is what they call me, Mr. Holmes, and I have made my living in many trades over the years. With no formal education, I've had to take money where I could find it and in whatever way I could. But it is not a matter of my own personal circumstances which force me to trouble you, beyond the fact that one of my jobs a few years back was doing some building work at a publishing house in the city.

"You may have heard of the Wargrave Publishing Company, gentlemen. It was one of the biggest names in its field, well-respected by academic folk and well-liked by those who read for pleasure. It was run by Theodore Wargrave, a man who built the company up from scratch. He made it into one of the foremost producers of books and journals which this country has ever seen.

"Mr. Wargrave was married to a beautiful woman called Sophia, but there were no children. He was a very tidy man, always dressed in immaculate clothes, and from the one time I saw Mrs. Wargrave, it seemed to me that she shared her husband's preference for beautiful and expensive things. I suppose when you have made your own money, you don't feel ashamed to show off the fact, but it's not the way I look at life. As long as my belly is full and my mouth watered, I reckon I'm as lucky as I need to be.

"I left Wargrave Publishing as soon as the building job was done, for another opportunity had come my way by that time. That was four years hence, and I've only heard the name Wargrave on two occasions since. The first was when he sold his company for a huge sum of money. The second is more pertinent to my experience this morning.

"I am currently working down at the Victoria docks. To get there, I cut down the old Merchant Road in Whitechapel, saving a good ten minutes' walk to the docks. If you know the area, you will know that there are several lodging houses down that particular road which offer modest rooms at what they might consider to be a reasonable price. This morning, I saw something outside one of those lodging houses which gave me such a start, I doubted my own senses.

"Walking toward me was a man who was in something of a hurry. He was muffled against the wind, but when he stopped outside one of the lodging houses and opened his coat to get his key, I saw something of his face. The man I saw walking into that grim tenement in Whitechapel was none other than Theodore Wargrave himself. You will better understand my confusion at seeing him,

Mr. Holmes, when I tell you that three years ago Wargrave took a revolver and shot himself in the head."

A heavy silence fell, and the three of us were like a painting of the scene, motionless and caught in time by the thrill of the matter. I was amazed and enthralled by the turn of events, but Holmes, who seemed immune to such amazement by years of overstimulation, retained the controlled and composed attitude of a specialist who sees a particularly sensitive and complicated experiment come to fruition.

"You are sure it was him?" he asked, keenly.

"Four years since I saw him last, but I am as sure as I can be."

"How frequently did you see him during your tenure at his company?"

"Every other day, perhaps."

"Is that sufficient for you to be certain of his face?"

Henry Collins looked at Sherlock Holmes with the defiant air of a man who is sure of his own mind. "I have seen a dead man walking the streets of London, Mr. Holmes, and I shan't have my word doubted on it."

Sherlock Holmes contemplated the older man for some long minutes before he spoke once more. "Quite so. It is a remarkable starting point for an enquiry in any event. What number lodging house was it?"

"Number 38."

"Did you make any enquiry there?"

"I was too shaken to knock on that door."

"What became of Mrs. Wargrave?"

"No clue, Mr. Holmes."

"It is of no matter. I have at least seven means of tracing her without undue exertion. Well, this is a fascinating problem, Mr. Collins, and I shall be happy to look into it for you. I shall advise you of any progress which we make in a day or so."

When our elderly client had gone, Holmes sat curled in his armchair, the smoke from his pipe creating a dense cloud of acrid fumes around his form. At last, he leaned forward, and his grey eyes fixed themselves on me.

"A pretty little problem, is it not, Watson? What do you make of it?"

"Your first priority must be the house on Merchant Road, to see this man of whom we have heard."

"My dear fellow, the man could walk into these very rooms in the next few seconds and we would be no better placed to know if he is Wargrave or not, having never met the fellow. Merchant Road will yield nothing to us at present. There is only one course of action open to us, and that is to examine the facts of the man's suicide. I shall consult the back files of the *Times* and see what I can ascertain from the reports at the time. You may stay here, Watson. It is in the moment of action, not research, that I call for your support and courage."

It was a little after twelve when Holmes returned. He was eager, bright, and in an excellent mood, far different from that black depression which had begun to descend upon him over the past few days.

"Sophia, Mrs. Wargrave, is now Lady Sophia Galsworthy," said he. "She married a man by the name of Sir Benjamin Galsworthy last year, and they reside now in Kensington. Galsworthy is a successful financier, so the lady would appear to have kept true to form in her choice of spouse."

"Did you learn anything about the Wargrave business other than tracing the wife?"

Holmes shrugged. "Nothing of substance. Having identified the body, Mrs. Wargrave, now Lady Sophia, could provide no explanation for her husband taking his own life."

"Were the features of the body disfigured by the gunshot wound?"

Sherlock Holmes chuckled at the suggestion. "I see where your mind is taking you, my dear Watson, but it was a single shot to the temple and the features were not mutilated. You must look elsewhere for a solution. We can do no better than to call on Lady Sophia and learn what we may from the lady in question."

We had a pleasant drive through London on that afternoon, alighting at Kensington Park Gate as the bells of St. Mary Abbot's chimed the half-hour. We arrived at an attractive town house set back from the main road, with steps leading up to the front door, framed by two austere pillars. As soon as we had turned the corner to approach the house, I felt Holmes's fingers close around my forearm. He pointed to the familiar blue figure of a London constable.

"There has been some devilry here, Watson," said Holmes.

My friend's name was sufficient to assure entry, and we were soon in consultation with our old friend, Lestrade, who was clearly surprised to see us.

"The crime was only committed in the early hours of the morning, Mr. Holmes," said he; "how did you hear of it so soon?"

"You are under a misapprehension, Lestrade," said my companion. "We are here on a private errand in the course of a small enquiry. I have reason to speak to the lady of the house."

Lestrade shook his head in bewilderment. "Do you mean to say that you are not here in connection with the events of last night?"

Holmes's eyes narrowed. "I know nothing of them."

Lestrade's eyes flicked from one to the other of us. "Sir Benjamin Galsworthy has been stabbed to death."

A flush of colour burst onto the ascetic cheeks of Sherlock Holmes and his brows creased over his intense eyes. "Fascinating. Would you have any objection to some interference in the case on my part, Lestrade?"

"Not at all, Mr. Holmes, although it is early days. I have made only scant progress. Come this way."

The room into which we were shown was large and expensively furnished. There were two glass-fronted cases, each containing leather-bound volumes on such diverse topics as the fall of the Roman Empire, the history of taxidermy, and the memoirs of the surgeon of a whaling ship. There were three small windows which looked out onto the street outside, although there was a hole in one of them and splinters of glass were scattered around the floor. A modest fireplace was set into the wall, and in front of it was a bearskin hearthrug. The purity of the white fur was tinged with that sickening scarlet intrusion which we knew too well.

The body on the rug was that of a well-made man of about fifty years of age. He lay on his stomach, his face turned toward us. One eye glared in painful defiance, as though our presence was an unwelcome one. A knife protruded from between his broad shoulders. There was an almost understated elegance about the piercing of the skin and tissue which made the violence of the attack seem even more terrible.

"A burglary gone wrong," observed Lestrade. "You see those shards of glass from the window behind the desk?"

"I observed them as I entered the room," said Holmes. "You think the murderer came in that way?"

"I think it is probable."

"Who discovered the body?"

"The lady of the house. She raised the alarm at once."

Holmes walked to the broken window. "Rather a public place for an illegal entry. Why did the burglar not try to gain access to the house from the back, where there is less chance of him being observed?"

"The street may well have been empty," countered Lestrade. "The doctors say that the murder occurred in the early hours of this morning, so there would not have been very many people about."

"It still seems to me to be an unnecessary risk."

Any further debate on the subject was prohibited by the entrance of one of the most remarkable women I had ever seen. She was tall, stately, with a proud expression upon her noble features. Her cheeks were sallow, so that her dark eyes seemed almost black. She was undeniably attractive, but there was a cruelty about her features, a subtle slyness which it was impossible to ignore.

"What is the meaning of this, Inspector?" she said. "Who are these gentlemen?"

My friend stepped forward. "My name is Sherlock Holmes, Madam. I am here to assist in any way I can."

"I have heard of you, Mr. Holmes, and I know something of your reputation."

"Do I have the pleasure of addressing Lady Sophia Galsworthy?"

The lady bowed her head in response. "As I have told the inspector, Mr. Holmes, nothing has been stolen, although this was clearly an attempt to rob us which my husband foiled. He lost his life in his attempt to protect us. I suppose the chances of catching whoever did it are slim."

Holmes smiled. "You must have more faith in our skills, Lady Sophia. The matter may not be as bleak as you suggest."

"I am glad to have your opinion, sir."

"I wonder if I might ask you one or two questions."

"The inspector can enlighten you, since I have told him all I know."

Sherlock Holmes gave a curt smile. "My presence here is connected to another matter with which you might be able to assist me."

Lady Sophia bowed her head. "Very well, but I should prefer to be interrogated away from this room."

We followed her through the hallway and into the drawing room. The lady showed us to two comfortable armchairs in which we sat. Holmes remained motionless, composing his thoughts, and I waited in anxious silence for one or the other of them to speak.

"I imagine the events of this morning have been difficult for you, Lady Sophia," said Holmes at last.

"Finding one's husband murdered is hardly likely to have been anything else."

"It must have been twice the tragedy for you. A question of the past repeating itself."

For a moment, the lady's dark eyes flickered, as though she were startled by the extent of my friend's knowledge of her life. "I have had the misfortune to lose both my husbands, if that is what you mean."

"You also discovered the body of your first husband?"

"Yes, although that tragic part of my life has no bearing on my present grief. Why do you recall it to my memory in this crude fashion?"

Holmes placed his hand on his heart. "You must forgive me, Madam, but a strange circumstance has brought me to your door."

"That being?"

Holmes deflected the question. "There is no doubt, I suppose, that Mr. Wargrave took his own life."

"None whatsoever."

"What would you say, Madam, if I told you that a man swears that he saw Mr. Wargrave alive and well, only this morning?"

"I would say that he is mistaken. Which man?"

"His name is Henry Collins."

"It means nothing to me."

"He once worked for your husband."

"Then he did not know Theodore personally. This man Collins is in error, Mr. Holmes. I can assure you that my first husband is dead."

Sherlock Holmes rose from his chair and paced to the window. He spent a few moments staring out into the street, and I knew from his demeanour that he was turning over in his head each fact of the matter which he had learned.

"One last question, if I may," said he. "What reason would your husband have for taking his own life?"

Lady Sophia shook her head. "I can think of none."

"He had no financial troubles?"

"No. He had sold his publishing company for a sizeable fortune."

"Which you inherited on his death?"

Her eyes became fierce and her lips parted in an angry snarl as she turned back to my friend. "Do you wish to make some accusation, Mr. Holmes?"

"There is no indictment, Madam. I merely seek the truth."

"By answering your question, I shall excuse your impertinence. In return, I must ask you to leave my house."

Holmes's eyes were no less aggressive. "I shall honour that agreement."

Lady Sophia rose from her seat and glided across the room with a purposeful step. At the fireplace, she turned back to face us with an expression of controlled defiance. "I inherited my first husband's fortune. Now, with the present tragedy which has befallen me, the Galsworthy fortune will also pass into my hands."

Sherlock Holmes contemplated the woman, his eyes darkened by distrust and suspicion. I expected him to make some parting remark which would betray his emotions, but he said nothing. Instead, he gave a brusque bow of farewell and ushered me from the room. A few final words were said to Lestrade, and we left the house. Once we were some distance away, Holmes's austere composure dissolved into an expression of savage outrage.

"I have had to deal with many murderers in my time, Watson, but none of them have repelled me quite as much as that woman. In her assured demeanour, I see only the wickedness of the Devil himself."

"She is stoic, no doubt, but she has suffered a great shock."

"Watson, is it possible that you are so naïve? Do you not see a curious coincidence at play? We have heard of the deaths of two wealthy men. In each case, the wife is the same woman and she stands to inherit a significant sum of money by each death. Mark my words, Doctor. I have no doubt that old Collins was mistaken and that Wargrave is dead. Nor have I any doubt that his wife was responsible."

"But Galsworthy was a heavily-set man, Holmes. That woman could not have overpowered him."

Holmes dismissed my objection with a wave of his hand. "A woman can easily stab a man in the back, Watson, and a man is less likely to be afraid of turning his back in the company of his own wife than he is in the presence of an enemy."

"But you said yourself that Wargrave's death was suicide," I insisted.

"So the facts appeared to suggest, but facts are capable of manipulation. Come, Watson, we must set ourselves very seriously to investigating the death of Theodore Wargrave."

We spent a busy afternoon making various enquiries. Holmes was seized by that keen energy which I have observed before, but it seemed intensified by his personal determination to prove Lady Sophia a murderess. Our initial investigations took us to the dark, dank corridors of the Scotland Yard archives, where Holmes was a familiar presence. The attendant constable had no difficulty in obtaining the Wargrave file, and he handed it to my companion with a keen eagerness. Holmes found a small table in the corner of the room and opened the file on his knees. I leaned over him in the dim light afforded by a single lamp on the desk beside us. After a few moments of flicking through the pages, Holmes handed me the medical examiner's report.

"Does anything strike you as important in there, Watson?"

I scanned the contents. "Wargrave was not in the best of health. He was below average weight at the time of his death, and his teeth showed some signs of deterioration. He was a heavy drinker, too, judging by the state of his liver. Otherwise, the report confirms the facts as we know them. Death was the result of a single bullet wound to the right temple, powder blackening on the skin around the wound indicating a close-range shot."

Holmes snorted in disappointment. "I had hoped to find some clue, Watson, some piece of previously overlooked evidence which would indicate the guilt of Wargrave's wife."

Frustrated, he assumed that abstracted expression which I have come to associate with the supreme manifestation of his extraordinary gifts. So intense was his expression that I dared not speak. At last, with a sudden release of suppressed energy, he sprang from his chair with an exclamation of triumph.

"Come, Watson, come! The game is afoot! We must hurry if we are not to allow a devious murderer to evade justice."

We stopped at a telegraph office where Holmes dispatched a hastily worded telegram, whose details I could not see but whose importance was evident. We hailed a cab and Holmes gave Merchant Road as our destination. Daylight was failing as we approached the heart of Whitechapel. The maze of streets were narrow alleys of sin and decay, the air hanging heavy with the stench of poverty and deprivation. Decaying husks of human beings, in various stages of drunkenness, tottered around the filthy cobbles, and the closeness of the surrounding tenements gave the impression of the whole area closing in and swallowing us. Shadowy figures of children hung out from the open doors of the lodging houses, their hands outstretched in fraught pleas for food or shillings. It was hard to believe, amid that mire of insufficiency and desperation, that the thriving heart of opulent and wealthy London beat strongly a few scant miles behind us.

We knocked on the door of number 38, and our summons was answered by a rough-looking character with a scar down the right-hand side of his crimson face. The promise of a sovereign was enough to ensure his cooperation, and he confided that he had had no new tenants since the arrival of a certain Mr. Chappell. A second sovereign ensured our entrance and the landlord's consent to wait for Mr. Chappell in his room. We made our way up the narrow wooden staircase, which threatened to give way beneath our feet at any moment. Suspicious eyes glared at us from cracks in the various doorways as we passed. At last we reached the door of Mr. Chappell's room, and Holmes gave a brief knock.

The room was deserted and reeked of damp. It was a meagre space, furnished in the most rudimentary fashion, with a small table in one corner and an old wooden chair beside it. The bed was little more than an old mattress and a soiled, discoloured sheet. The curtains were sheets of old lace, torn in some places and moth-eaten in others.

"We must possess our souls in patience, Watson," said Holmes.

"What is the meaning of all this?"

"Greed, Watson. Undeniable, unpalatable, and unrelenting avarice, resulting in the death of two entirely innocent men."

Before he could elucidate further, the door was flung open in a gesture of rage. Into the room there stepped a tall and strongly built man with closely cropped hair and the dark eyes of a scheming villain. His teeth snarled at us from behind his cruel, thin lips, and his voice came out in a harsh, guttural whisper.

"What the devil is going on here?"

"Mr. Chappell, I believe," said Holmes.

"That wastrel landlord downstairs said I had men intruding into my privacy. Who are you? What business do you have here?"

Sherlock Holmes remained at the window, where he had positioned himself. He looked out through those miserable lace curtains into the street below. "Perhaps we had better wait for the person whom I have summoned here."

"Who are you?" repeated the demon in the doorway.

Holmes offered no reply. In the silence which fell between us, we heard the hurried footsteps on those old stairs. Within seconds, standing behind the apparition who had burst in on us, there stood Lady Sophia Galsworthy. Never before have I seen a woman's expression change from anxious panic to abject hatred as quickly as her face did that evening. Upon seeing Sherlock Holmes, her eyes turned to fire, and her mouth let out a shrill shriek of betrayal.

Holmes walked to the centre of the room. "Close that door, Madam. We shall have the privacy which Mr. Chappell so desires."

She obeyed my friend's authoritative tone. When she turned back to face Holmes, she threw a piece of paper at his feet. "You sent that telegram, luring me here to trap me."

Holmes picked up the slip of paper and handed it to me. The message was clear and concise: *THE CHARADE IS EXPOSED. COME TO MERCHANT ROAD AT ONCE.*

"It was no trap, Madam. If you were innocent, it would have meant nothing to you. Only this man's accomplice could possibly have construed any message of importance from those words."

Chappell stepped forward so that his face was only inches from my companion's. In response, I moved from my position and was beside Holmes in an instant. Chappell's eyes were on me, but I held his gaze, tightening the grip on my cane.

"There is much to explain," said Sherlock Holmes. "It might be as well for me to give my version of the extraordinary events which have brought us together in this room, and you can elaborate or correct me as you see fit.

"From the moment I learned that Sir Benjamin Galsworthy had been murdered, I suspected that Lady Sophia was somehow involved. It is the naïve detective who does not admit the possibility of coincidence, but the detective who fails to recognise a pattern in a series of events is a fool. I could not ignore the obvious connection between the death of Theodore Wargrave and the murder of Sir Benjamin. That connection, the common denominator, was Lady Sophia, who was married to both men and inherited a fortune in the event of each of their deaths. For that reason, I had concluded before I left the Galsworthy residence that you, Lady Sophia, had murdered both your husbands.

"But Theodore Wargrave had committed suicide. It was inconceivable that the wound to the head could have been forcibly administered without a struggle taking place, and yet there had been no evidence of such a struggle. It is not easy to put a gun to a man's head and shoot unless that man is unprepared or somehow restrained, but there was no evidence of any restraint, and there was no evidence of any attempt by Wargrave to defend himself. The suicide verdict had been accepted as the truth and the matter had been closed. My task, as I saw it, was to determine how Lady Sophia

had managed to commit murder and make it appear so convincingly
as suicide.

"A sensible place to start was the original police report into the
investigation. I confess that I was disheartened when I found no
clue, but my friend, Watson, summarized the medical examiner's
report, and I saw the first glimmer of light. Watson, do you recall the
contents of that summary of yours?"

"Liver damage from alcohol excess, signs of tooth decay, below
average weight, if I recall correctly."

Holmes went to the window and drew aside one of the curtains.
"The London streets below us teem with people suffering from a lack
of food, a dependence on drink, and similar horrors. But Theodore
Wargrave was a wealthy man, the owner of a successful business
which he had sold for a small fortune. Why should a man of the
higher class of society suffer from the ailments of a man from the very
lowest rung of that same ladder?"

Lady Sophia had regained her composure. "Must we listen to this
discourse on medical reports and society's troubles?"

Holmes's eyes blazed. "You must, Madam! It goes to the
very heart of the matter. There was no reason why such a man as
Wargrave would have displayed those medical conditions more in
tune with a life of poverty and deprivation. Therefore, the body
which was found with a bullet hole in its temple was not Wargrave,
but a man whose name we shall never know, who had fallen into the
depths of misery and despair."

"I identified the body as that of my husband," said the lady.

"That could only mean that you were involved in the
crime," I said.

Holmes nodded. "Precisely, Watson. It was not your husband
whose body you identified, Madam; instead, it was the body of a
vagrant whom you had enticed into your grasp, with the promise
of food, warmth, and the presentation of a suit of clothes of your
husband's which served as proof of your benevolent intentions.
Whilst he was admiring himself in his new attire, the real Theodore

Wargrave came up from behind and shot him in the temple, before he could either react or acknowledge what was taking place.

"All that was required was for Wargrave to vanish and for his wife to discharge a suitable period of mourning, inherit the money, and move on with her life. The fear had always been that one fortune would be insufficient to slake your thirst for wealth, and so it proved. It occurred to you both that, if Mrs. Wargrave here could again marry a man of equal or better wealth than Wargrave, then that man could return from the dead and murder the new husband without any fear of suspicion being aroused. Death is the greatest of all alibis. Lady Sophia would inherit the second estate and move abroad to distance herself from her grief."

I was beginning to see some light. "The 'dead' Mr. Wargrave would then join her under an assumed name, and they would marry once more."

Holmes nodded gravely. "An ingenious plan. Unfortunately, a man whom neither of you had ever noticed in the past saw Wargrave only this very morning, no doubt returning from the murder of Sir Benjamin Galsworthy. I had concluded that Harry Collins had been misguided, and I became convinced of it when I began to suspect Lady Sophia of the murders of her husbands. Collins had not known your first husband well and he was elderly, so it was entirely possible that he had been mistaken. And yet, he had believed it absolutely. Only when I read the post-mortem report on Wargrave did I begin to suspect the truth."

Chappell stepped to one side, distancing himself from the woman who stood by his side. "You talk of people I have never heard of, of murder, and things I know nothing about. I took these rooms because they are all I can afford. Be gone and leave me in peace."

Lady Sophia glared at Chappell with the eyes of a woman who sees the wolf discard the fleece of its disguise. "You devil! Do you not see that the telegram condemns us both?"

Sherlock Holmes spoke with the calm, controlled manner which showed that he was master of the situation. "She is quite right, sir.

There must be a connection between you, or else the telegram would not have brought her here. Not just to this house, mark you, but to this very room."

"And you know the connection, of course," said Lady Sophia.

"I think it is clear to us all, my lady. This man is Theodore Wargrave. Collins was not mistaken. He had seen Wargrave, but it was not a case of a miraculous return from the dead, for Theodore Wargrave had not died. In his place, a common man whose life was thought by both of you to be expendable had been sacrificed so that you could murder a richer but no less innocent man for his money."

Theodore Wargrave, since no longer could he be called Chappell, walked to the small wooden chair in the corner of the room and sat down.

"I doubted we could pull it off a second time," said he, his head in his hands. "But the allure of money has always been strong for both of us. When you come from nothing, Mr. Holmes, the desire to have everything swells within you. I had built up that business honestly, and I had made something of it. I knew I could never again go through the sacrifices and the toil required to build a new company, not at the age I had reached. But, still, I had this passionate lust for money. We both had."

The lady took his huge hand in hers and kissed it. "We knew that it would have to be the last time. We were fearful of the very coincidence which you had identified, Mr. Holmes, but we felt that the death of Theodore would be sufficient protection."

"It might have been, Lady Sophia," said Holmes. "Women have lost both husbands before, even to violence. In the case of Wargrave, it was necessary for you to find the body because you had to identify it but, with the Galsworthy murder, anybody in the house could have discovered the crime and my suspicions would not have been aroused. Indeed, it would have been better for you had someone else discovered the body, but like many criminals before you, you overplayed your part. The coincidence of a wife finding the bodies of both her husbands was too much to be credited."

"And the supposed burglary?" I said.

"It was my idea," said Wargrave. "I hoped to suggest that the killer came from the outside, so that the police would search amongst the masses rather than within the closed household."

Holmes nodded. "And so they would, if it had not been for the bad luck of Collins seeing you."

"Even if I had looked him in the eye, I would never have known him."

"No, your nature shows that much is evident, sir," said Holmes. "Of the murderers I have confronted in my career, you pair are amongst the worst. Your indiscriminate disregard for human life in all its variety disgusts me beyond your greed. You may have appeared to cheat death once before, Wargrave, but I promise you that you shall not do so once that rope is around your neck."

He moved back to the window and opened it. Within seconds, the shrill cry of his police whistle declared that there would be no more words spoken on the matter and that the wheels of justice must begin to turn.

Late that night, we sat together on either side of the fireplace in our Baker Street rooms. The air was heavy with tobacco smoke, and we sipped our brandy with the comfortable silence of a close comradeship. At last, as we were knocking out the ashes of our pipes, Holmes turned to me.

"It seems to me, Watson, that the motives and desires of mankind are very possibly insoluble mysteries, although these little problems which come to our door offer an opportunity to attempt to understand those larger questions whose answers will only be known when our time of grace has come."

The Case of
the Waterguard

By Jan Edwards

There had been little chance to approach Mr. Holmes in the hurly-burly of packing. For a man who claimed not to care about the past, he was mightily attached to all of the knick-knacks and gee-gaws picked up in his years as a consulting detective; and as he kept reminding us, his intention of writing on the science and logic of crime would require reference material. Finally, however, as evening came around, some sort of quiet returned to Baker Street.

I waited until Mrs. Hudson had served supper and the maid was clearing away before I approached Mr. Holmes for his advice.

He puffed at his pipe and regarded me carefully. "So, young Billy, what is this burden you are carrying?"

"Me, sir?"

"Yes, you. You have been distracted all afternoon. I assume it has something to do with the letter in your pocket?"

My hand strayed to the envelope without thinking. "How did—"

"I can detect the outline quite clearly. You've developed brawn, as a young man should, but your button-boy livery was sewn for a stripling." He beckoned with his fingers. "Hand it over."

I did so, hardly daring to breathe, and pondered on the fact that I would be the last in a long line of people who had sat or stood in this very room waiting for the judgement of Mr. Sherlock Holmes, as he read.

Dear Billy.

I've no easy way to say this so I'll be quick. Your old dad's banged up in Lewes Gaol. Murdered a waterguard from the Customs Service, so they say, though he swears he never done it. We knows you don't owe Caleb nothing. The Lord knows he's not been any kind of father, but I heard your Mr. Holmes is going down that way soon, and if he can't help then your pa'll be dancing on a rope come the new year.

I haven't told your grandma as I think it'll finish her off. If you can you find it in your heart to ask Mr. Holmes, at the very least the Good Lord will bless you for all your days.

In hope.

Your loving aunt,

Violet Thomkins

"You've never met your father?" Mr. Holmes said at last.

"He went to sea when I was in the cradle."

"Yet your family are convinced of his innocence?"

I shrugged. "Aunt Vi thinks so."

"Then perhaps we should go and see for ourselves." He smiled at my surprise. "I suspect Mrs. Hudson will oversee the carriers moving our belongings far more efficiently without our help. We can catch the six-fifteen to Eastbourne, alight at Lewes, where we shall ascertain the basic facts, reboard the noon train, and still be at the farmhouse before Mrs. Hudson and our furniture arrive."

"Thank you, Mr. Holmes. I can't tell you how much—"

"A parting gift for all of your years of service, my boy. I promise nothing at this juncture, but we can at least speak with your wayward father."

When we stepped through the doors of Lewes Gaol, it was the stench that struck me first. A pall of old mutton and cabbage that almost, but not quite, covered the stench of humanity at its worst. As we moved further in, it was the noise that assaulted my senses—the clanging of doors and the clattering of buckets and cries of fear and pain laced with a large helping of anger.

The governor declined to see us himself, but Mr. Holmes and I were guided to a small room close to his office, a mean and grubby space without any windows. At its centre was a table at which sat a small, wiry man. His ankles and wrists were shackled; his rough-spun prison garb was torn and spattered with blood—old brown patches mixed with fresh bright reds. His head was bowed so that I could see scabs and bruises on his shaven scalp. It was obvious that he had been ill-used, and I glared at the two guards standing over him, their billy clubs drawn.

"That will do," said Mr. Holmes and, as he waved the uniformed thugs away, I was not entirely sure he had meant me to stay. He took the only other seat, opposite the prisoner, placing his elbows on the table, his fingers steepled together against his chin. "Mr. Caleb Thomkins," he said, "I am Mr. Sherlock Holmes."

My father grunted, still staring fixedly at his shackled wrists.

"I have been asked to look into your case on behalf of your family. I am told that you are charged with the killing of a customs service waterguard. Your sister insists you are not guilty, and I suspect your son here would like to hear that from your own lips."

Mr. Holmes sat back as my father slowly raised his head to look at us both. Caleb's skin was leathery, burned by years of salt and sun. His features were lean and pinched and would have been thinner still had his face not been swollen from a half-dozen livid bruises. "William?" he whispered.

I could only nod. The man was a stranger to me, yet I could not help but see the family resemblance, despite the injuries, most especially in those silver-grey eyes so like Aunt Vi's.

He seemed to recognise my feelings, and the momentary hope that had lit his eyes fell away as he switched his attention back to Mr. Holmes. "I've a few mates back in the old streets. They said as the lad works fer you."

"Almost ten years now. A bright boy. He'll go far."

"I'm glad of that." The shackles clattered on scarred wood as he reached as if to touch Mr. Holmes's hand.

"Say no more on that. Tell me about this murder."

"I never snuffed that waterguard, sir. I swear. I'm no angel, but I ain't no killer."

"Do you know who did?"

"I do not, Mr. Holmes. God's honest truth."

"Yet you were found standing over his body."

"I'll not deny that." He sighed. "A smuggler I am and I'll expect time for that, but I've never killed that man."

"Why Cuckmere Haven? It might be isolated, but there is a coastguard station right there in the shore, is there not? What was your cargo that it was worth such a risk?"

"Dunno. The captain just told us he'd had special orders."

"And the customs office had a squad of waterguards waiting for you that night."

"They allus seems to know."

Mr. Holmes fixed Caleb with an acid stare. "Tell me what happened. Miss nothing out." He sat perfectly still, eyes closed now.

My father glanced at me, and I nodded.

"Well, sir. The beach was quieter 'n a cat's paw. Not a soul on the beach, nor along the river. We only had two trunks. Big an' fancy. Leather-bound, like a toff would have. No idea what was in 'em as warranted the trip." He shook his shaven head. "It were the dark of the moon, and thick cloud with it, and we could barely see hand to hand, so we come ashore a bit downstream from where we should've. Dorrin were at the tiller. He'd said he knew the river, but the lads were cussing him for havin' to haul those big trunks up the bank and across the marsh a ways."

Mr. Holmes didn't move, nor open his eyes. "And you?" he murmured.

"I was standing lookout. When I heard whistles and shouting, I knew the lads were in trouble. I started to run. And I tell you this—" he raised his shackled hands to point at Mr. Holmes, his chains rattling like a ghoul's "—that poor cove was stone cold afore I ever tripped over him."

"You could not, perhaps, have shot him in error?" Mr. Holmes's eyes snapped open. "It was dark after all."

Caleb returned the detective's glower. "I never fired my weapon, Mr. Holmes. Not once." He jerked his head toward the door. "Rozzers never gave that any thought. They had me there with a pistol in my hand and one of their own layin' dead. They never looked no further."

"You saw nobody other than your compatriots?"

"There were only me and Dorrin on the bank."

"The rest of the crew had made good an escape?"

My father slumped forward for a long moment. "Took off like rabbits. I place no blame. I'd've done the same in their place." It was Mr. Holmes to whom he spoke, but my eyes that he stared into, as he added, "I'm not a good man, but I'm no cutthroat."

I saw full well this man expected some reply. My understanding, perhaps, or even forgiveness, and I felt a hot anger slicing through me. Under the shrewd gaze of Mr. Sherlock Holmes, however, it seemed wise to keep silent.

My father seemed to know that, and he sat back, rubbing filthy hands across his face, clattering his chains as if he were a phantom already. "I'm a dead man, I know," he groaned at last, "but I got to meet my son afore I left the world, an' that's worth it, mebbe."

Mr. Holmes rose abruptly, his chair scraping across the stone flags. "I believe you are an innocent man," he said, "of murder at least, and I intend to see that justice is served."

"Thank you, sir." Caleb looked to me. "And thank you, lad. Thank you for bringin' Mr. Holmes, though thou don't owe me nothing."

My mouth opened, but yet again, I was unable to speak. There was a great deal that I could have said. I could agree that he was right, that I owed him nothing but I owed his mother and sister a great deal; that I came because it was wrong to allow any man to go to the gallows for a crime he did not commit; that the fact the accused was the man my mother had married was nothing to me; that looking at this pitiful wreck was frightening because he was me. The same eyes and nose and way of jutting his chin. Without Mrs. Hudson lifting me off the street, this could so easily have been me twenty years hence. I nodded without uttering a word and hurried after the sounds of Mr. Holmes's brisk footsteps vanishing down the corridor.

We caught the midday train to Eastbourne, as Mr. Holmes had planned, and arrived at the new house a full hour before the carriers. Looking around the place was an odd experience. The house been empty for some time and our breath hung as cold mist as we entered the hallway, so I busied myself lighting fires in the kitchen and drawing room, and in all that time neither or us said more than four words together. I recognised Mr. Holmes in full thought and knew better than to disrupt his ruminations. Besides which, I had no idea what I could possibly say.

When Mrs. Hudson arrived with the carriers, Mr. Holmes was prowling from room to room, trailing pungent clouds as he smoked pipe and cigarettes in turn, barely aware of the chaos around him. I recognised the signs. Had all his possessions been unpacked, I have no doubt he would've been scraping away on that violin of his, and, as he was still pacing at past eleven that night as the rest of us staggered off to our beds, I suspect Mrs. Hudson had secreted the instrument somewhere safe for that very reason.

Knowing when he bought the farmhouse that there would be no hansom cabs at his disposal, Mr. Holmes had purchased a trap and sturdy pony and hired a local lad as groom and assistant gardener. So on the next day, we were able to set off under our own steam for Cuckmere Haven. It was no more than a couple of miles as the crow, or perhaps I should say the gull, flies, and some seven by road. Seven miles with a freezing wind whipping in from the sea was quite far enough, however, and I was glad of the good coat Dr. Watson had bought for me, but I still had my collar turned up and muffler wrapped tightly around my face.

The Cuckmere coastguard, one Dick Waite, and his son Robert, led us to the spot where the body had been found, just a short way up the tiny Cuckmere river. I stood between them watching as Mr. Holmes flitted across the scene in fits and starts.

Customs and police officers alike had trampled the grass flat, and a full week had passed since the murder; I could not help wondering what Mr. Holmes might gain from being here. But he searched—and we waited. My feet were frozen, and I could not even stamp them when we stood ankle-deep in seeping mud. All I could do was slap my arms around myself against a biting sea wind that the

Waites seemed not to notice beyond sinking their chins deeper into knitted mufflers.

Mr. Holmes was oblivious to our discomfort as he quartered the ground like a bloodhound, bent low to the saturated landscape, all but crawling in places, his face so close to the frosted sedges that they rimed the peak of his deerstalker in spangles of glistening white. At one spot he paused to pick at something in the mud. Waite stood a little straighter, his jaws clamping impatiently on the pipe clamped between his teeth.

"Looks like your master's found somethin'," he said.

"P'rhaps," I replied. "P'rhaps not. You never can tell with Mr. Holmes. He's a dark one."

"Ah, so I heard." Waite nodded. "I hope as he's found what he wants. I'm fair shrammed, standin' about here."

I didn't have time to agree because Mr. Holmes finally appeared satisfied with his search and came loping across the boggy ground like a greying wolfhound. "Tell me, Waite." He took out his own pipe and lit it, as seemingly oblivious to the cold as the coastguard. "Is it normal to have contraband ferried so far upstream?"

Waite shook his head. "Mostly they sticks to the beach, but it was a rough sea on a high tide, so they came right up the river."

"And their contacts knew that would happen?"

"They must've, sir."

"So these villains moved their rendezvous according to the weather?"

"Most like," Waite replied. "The crew o' them boats don't generally put themselves in any more danger 'n they can help."

"Indeed." Mr. Holmes glanced at me, his nostrils flaring a warning to stay silent. "And the vessel that came upstream: did the customs take that as well?"

"No sir. It'd already slipped its moorings when the waterguards came down to rummage."

"And you?"

Waite waved his pipe at the cottages down near the shore. "I lives
here. Not much gets past as I don't see. Owling's not the trade it
were, but we're allus prepared fer it."

"The waterguards arrested just two men that night?"

"Ahh, that's right. First sign o' trouble 'n the rest of the gang
vanished faster than a sea mist in May."

"Did you know of the man who shot the officer?"

"No sir. I knows his kind an' they'd take a life without
a thought."

Mr. Holmes heard my intake of breath and laid a finger on my
arm. "Had you come across either of them before?"

"I know of Sam Dorrin. Not the brightest spark." Waite tapped
his head significantly. "Common gossip 'as he's one o' Colter's men
from way over Chichester."

"Colter the smuggler?"

"Ahh," Waite agreed.

"Did you know the dead man? Hutton?"

"Seen 'im. Newhaven's a small port. You gets to know most of
the faces workin' out of there."

"And you?" Mr. Holmes fixed the younger Waite with
sharp stare.

The lad shrugged. "Bain't my job, be it?"

"No. Indeed. Well, thank you both for your help. I shall not
keep you any longer." Mr. Holmes looked out toward the sea that
was as grey as the sky so that it was hard to see where one met the
other. "One last thing," he said. "Is it usual for Colter's gang to use
this river?"

"These days they mostly ply out of Chichester and west to
Dorset." He frowned and shook his head. "It were a wild night.
Mebbe they just wanted to offload at the nearest place they come to."

"Is that why you were abroad? Because of the wildness of the
weather," said Mr. Holmes.

Waite laughed and shook his head. "No need. I heard 'em
passing up the river so I was duty-bound to look."

"Just so," Mr. Holmes said as he pulled on his gloves. "Thank you again, Mr. Waite. Good day."

Mr. Holmes took the reins from me as we headed home. He urged the horse into a brisk walk with a slap of the reins and we said nothing until we reached the main road home.

"What was it you found in the mud?" I asked him at last.

"The remnants of a clay pipe," he replied. "Somebody had waited there some time. Alone, I suspect. I called the customs office before we left London, and they swear they had not set men waiting to claim excise on that occasion. Just as Waite's claim that he came out because he heard the boat passing into the river has a ring of truth, yet Caleb maintained the man was cold as mutton when he stumbled across him. The police surgeon's report bears that out." He grunted at my surprise. "The telephone is a remarkably useful apparatus, Billy. I had the surgeon read it to me."

"So why don't the magistrates act on that report?"

"Because they have a man charged and, until we can prove that the facts are not as first stated, they will proceed with the case they already have."

"I can't see how we can prove my father innocent when they ignore the surgeon."

"Your father was out on that river for nefarious reasons, by his own admission, which makes him a guilty man. Just not guilty of murder. It is the teasing of one crime from another that is the task at hand. Those local magistrates will not act otherwise until somebody comes forward to disprove their theories."

"My father's shipmates would let him dance from a noose?"

"Colter's band of rogues are no different from any gang in Limehouse. Has your father named a single man other than the one caught with him? Of course not. There is a code, and each man knows he is alone should he make the mistake of being caught."

"Meanwhile he hangs for a crime he did not commit."

"We may yet gain him a reprieve. Firstly, we must have a few words with the Senior Customs Officer."

We drove back to the farmhouse with flecks of sleet biting at our faces. Mrs. Hudson told me off good and proper for keeping Mr. Holmes out in all weathers, but she knows as well as any of us, maybe the most of us, that you can't stop Mr. Holmes when the chase is on him.

"There's a good fire in the drawing room." She took his hat and muffler and Inverness coat and bustled him toward along the short passageway. "Supper will be ready directly."

She opened the drawing room door with a flourish, to display a scene that made even Mr. Holmes halt on the threshold to gaze around him. I don't know how she and Elsie, the new maid, had managed it all in the few short hours we had been gone, but the room was as close to being the old room in Baker Street as the place itself allowed: leather armchairs flanked the roaring fire, and various tables and cabinets were ranged around the walls. Mrs. Hudson steered Mr. Holmes across the carpet and sat him down in his favourite chair. "Come along, Billy, jump to it. Pour Mr. Holmes a glass of port and stoke that fire."

"Yes, Mrs. Hudson." She had bustled away by the time I had said even that much, and I noted that Mr. Holmes was amused at the byplay.

"I do believe I shall miss your sparring with Mrs. Hudson," he said, "but you'll do well as Watson's protégé. He's a good man."

"Yes, sir, he is that," I agreed. "I shall try to do him justice."

"I have no doubt you shall." He cut my words short with a wave of his slender hand and fell to filling his briar from the familiar Persian slipper, hanging in its new customary place on the fire surround. I have no doubt that Mr. Holmes noticed Mrs. Hudson's attention to such details, but he would never make any sign of it.

I poured the port as directed, but carefully, because it had not yet settled from the move, and set to coaxing life into a fire.

Mr. Holmes frowned at my clatter. "Leave that now," he said. "I have a puzzle that needs unravelling. Good night, Billy." I withdrew, leaving the great detective wreathed in smoke from his briar pipe, those sharp features outlined against the firelight as he stared at the empty chair across the fireside from him. As I settled down to sleep, the plaintive tones of his violin wafted on the night.

I should have gone back to London the next morning, but somehow it felt as if I would be deserting my post to leave Sussex there and then. I had rung Dr. Watson's surgery the previous evening to inform him that I would be a few days more.

"Just to help Mr. Holmes settle in. I shall be back by Christmas Eve."

"Is everything all right?" Dr. Watson asked.

"Well…" I drew breath. I felt awkward telling him the full reason for my delay.

"Say no more." He chuckled. "Holmes is very good at inveigling people into joining him in the chase. Take care of yourself. And take care of Holmes. We shall expect you in a few days."

Guilty, though I had not lied as such, I replaced the receiver.

We set out early for the customs office in Newhaven, where Senior Officer Abercrombie took it upon himself to speak with Mr. Holmes.

"I am astonished that you're investing your time in this matter, Mr. Holmes." Abercrombie carefully preened his waxed moustaches into place across the centre of each red-veined cheek and leaned back in his chair, lacing his sausage fingers across his ample girth. Looking at that pot belly, and the mottled, bulbous nose beneath which

those moustaches began, I could not help wondering how much
contraband passed under his desk.

Mr. Holmes smiled and settled his gloves carefully on his crossed
knee. "I am always interested in cases where the facts are at odds, Mr.
Abercrombie."

"At odds, sir?" The moustaches quivered as he worked his upper
lip. "No odds to be at, I'd say. Chap was found standing over the
body, pistol in hand. Waterguard said he chased Thomkins halfway
across the marsh."

"Did he, indeed." Mr. Holmes glanced at me, sensing my anger.
He shook his head minutely. "I am told Thomkins's gun was fully
loaded when he was arrested."

"Was it?" Abercrombie scowled at us both. "I was not
aware of that."

"Mr. Waite didn't seem to know it either, so you are in good
company," Mr. Holmes replied. "You had waterguards standing
watch, I understand?"

"By pure chance there was a small patrol of customs officers in
the locality," Abercrombie mumbled, his emphasis on the rank of his
officers, a part of the newly emerging customs service, expected soon
to reach beyond the old Admiralty waterguards. "They were going
about their usual business."

"So they happened across the event?"

"Exactly so."

"Was the victim part of that patrol?"

Abercrombie hesitated. "Hutton? He works...worked at this
port," he said at last. "But he was not on duty that night."

"And you can't explain what he was doing down there?"

Abercrombie shook his head. "I've wondered that myself.
Hutton was known to fish, but..." He spread his hands.

"Not on such a stormy night?"

Abercrombie sighed. "I am told he may have been checking nets
up-river. Not all of them for fish."

"Poaching? So it could have been sheer misfortune that he happened on the villains as he did."

"That would seem to be the case."

"Poor chap," Mr. Holmes agreed. "Fortunate the coastguard was also on hand, or the murderers might have got clean away."

The customs man shifted uneasily. "The Revenue cruiser *Adeleine* was keeping the smuggler's ship in sight, but we did not imagine they would offload anything at Cuckmere."

"Just so. I hear the coastguard was instrumental in arresting the second man." Mr. Holmes looked down to check his gloves, to hide a smile, I am fairly certain.

"He assisted my men."

"And you believe you have the correct suspect under lock and key?"

A steam whistle sounded somewhere out in the docks, and Abercrombie rose abruptly. "We are quite sure. Now, if there is nothing more to add, Newhaven is a busy port and I am a busy man."

"Of course. Come, Billy, we must leave Mr. Abercrombie to his duties."

I was aware that Mr. Holmes was pleased with himself from the melody he hummed as we made our way back to our pony and trap, but far from sure why that would be. "You think you may have solved it?" I asked as we drove away. "You've proof of my father's innocence?"

"There is a final piece to this puzzle still to come. I have Lestrade making enquiries, since it's obvious the local constabulary are not willing to be of any real help." He turned to look at me, grinning like the hunter that he was. "I'm confident we shall have the real culprit in our grasp very soon."

We arrived back home just as dusk was falling. Mr. Holmes made sure that the pony was settled for the night before we went into the house to be met by Mrs. Hudson. She was not in the best humour. "Your friend Inspector Lestrade called on the telephone and

left you a message," she said. "And a rather scruffy sort of creature
came with that." She pointed at a grubby envelope on the hall
stand. "I thought you were retiring," she grumbled. "Leaving all this
malarkey behind us in Baker Street."

"That was my intention, but could we ignore young Billy's *cri de
coeur?* I am very sorry."

"Of course not."

"You are an excellent woman, Mrs. Hudson." He smiled after
her as she left the room muttering under her breath. He handed me
his coat and hat before scanning Lestrade's message and slitting the
envelope open to read its contents. "It would seem our victim was
not all he appeared to be, my boy, and we have our quarry at bay."

"Yes, sir." I knew better than to expect him to explain further.
Perhaps he still needed to sort the facts for himself. Or, as Dr.
Watson often complained, Mr. Holmes gained as much pleasure in
revealing a denouement fully formed as he did in arriving there. I left
him to peruse the note and letter and went in search of my supper.

Frost had hardened the muddy roads, and the pony and trap was able
to cover the miles in good time, reaching the Cuckmere coastguard
cottages a little after eleven, just as the tide was on the ebb. The cove
itself was calm, but dark clouds were gathering over the sea as we
took the narrow lane toward the cove.

Waite was down on the shore, sorting the ropes of a small
sailing boat half-beached at the edge of the waves. He paused as we
approached, as though playing a child's game of statues. His profile
was clear as the smoke exhaled from his clay pipe whipped past his
ear, vanishing in a blink. He did not turn toward us, only looking
out at the murky grey-brown waves.

Mr. Holmes halted ten yards from him, and for a half-minute I imagine we made a perfect diorama, should anything but the gulls have been watching us. "Mr. Waite." Mr. Holmes had to raise his voice against the surf, and I wondered he did not move closer. For a moment I wondered if Waite had heard when he did not reply; he continued to gaze out to the entrance of the bay. Both his arms were draped on the gunwale of his little boat.

Mr. Holmes took out his own pipe and packed it casually, taking his time to tamp the bowl before shielding it from the wind as he applied flame. "I had an interesting note sent me last evening." Mr. Holmes took the envelope from his pocket and waved it briefly. "You were quite correct when you told me that young Dorrin was a part of Colter's crew. I am also informed that your son was at school with Dorrin."

"Ah," Waite agreed, nodding slowly.

"And," Mr. Holmes went on, "that Hutton was also on Colter's payroll."

Waite knocked his pipe with his left hand against the edge of the boat and let the charred tobacco residue fall into the water.

"You knew he was working for Colter," Mr. Holmes continued. "You knew that a valuable consignment was coming in from Amsterdam aboard the *Garamond*. Sent as luggage for a passenger who, apparently, never went aboard. The unclaimed bags were then to be left on the dockside, and one of Colter's men would collect them after a suitable time had lapsed." Mr. Holmes tilted his head and smiled when no reply came. "Smuggling any quantity of diamonds through a port is always a risk. When Mr. Colter had word that His Majesty's Customs were aware of his plans, he sent word to the captain before the *Garamond* left port to launch a small skiff close to Cuckmere. Am I correct so far?"

"These smugglers try all sorts," said Waite. "Like a barrel of monkeys."

"Indeed. You heard that such was afoot and lay in wait." Mr. Holmes held up the broken remains of a clay pipe. "A bowl or two helped pass the time, but the wind changed and your smoke reached the nostrils of some other cove skulking in the dark."

Waite stared at the pipe, his ruddy complexion paling. "There's many a man smokes a pipe," he croaked.

"Not many hereabouts would have a pipe stamped *H&C, York*. I had word from Inspector Lestrade that your wife and son visited the North just a month ago, when her poor mother passed away. He also found out that Hutton had booked passage to America—for two people."

"I…" Waite dropped his head forward.

"But Hutton was not in league with you, was he, my friend? Nor was it you who dropped that broken pipe." Mr. Holmes took a step closer, and another. "Hutton was to collect the trunks from the river, ferry them to Eastbourne, and place them on the next train to Chichester. But he was not alone…was he?"

Waite bowed his head.

"Hutton was to see the goods onto the train as planned. But not before he had lifted the diamonds that were at the heart of the matter. He needed a partner in his crime, however, and that man was your son."

"Them Huttons were always a bad lot," Waite snarled. "I never guessed till Robert said he'd go an' check the river for me. 'Twas never like him to volunteer."

"So you followed him? And what then? You murdered Hutton? Hid on the marsh and shot him in cold blood?"

Waite hesitated. "Hutton fired the first shot."

Mr. Holmes tilted his head to gaze at Waite. "No. You are not our killer. Though you are ready enough to point the finger at another man and let him hang for your son's crime."

"You knew all that from a broken pipe?"

We all turned to look at Robert Waite. He had used the swathe of kelp and detritus, left above the usual tideline by a recent storm, to muffle his approach, and stood now just twenty paces from us. In his right hand was a revolver.

"I did, Robert," said Mr. Holmes. "What puzzles me is why you killed Hutton."

"Because he thought I was too stupid to see he were never goin' to share. He wanted the lot fer hisself." The younger Waite was shouting, his face contorted in rage. "But he were the one as died."

"And you shall pay the price for that. The police will be here very soon to arrest you."

Waite looked toward the lane, shaking his head, close to panic. "You should leave, lad!" he shouted.

Robert Waite looked past him to the cottage. "I ain't got—"

"Never mind them. Go. While you can."

He stumbled down to the boat and leaned in to take a second gun from inside, which he handed his father. "Dad, I could still—"

"No time, boy."

The younger man looked from his father to Mr. Holmes, indecision plain in his face.

"They've sent for the police," Waite said as he shoved his son against the stern of the boat. "You've no choice, Bob."

Robert Waite's face crumpled as the realisation of his plight hit him, and he threw himself at the little craft, pushing it off into deeper water.

"You." The older Waite waved the gun at me. "Help him."

I looked to Mr. Holmes, wondering if he were carrying his own Webley pistol.

"Do as he says, Billy," the detective murmured. "Can you swim?"

"Yes, sir."

"Then be ready at my signal."

"No time for chatter," Waite bellowed.

I went forward and braced myself against the boat's stern. Being already half afloat, it quickly rose free of the rocky beach, and Robert Waite and I were soon waist-deep in the icy Channel waters.

"Get aboard, Bob!" Waite yelled.

I looked back at Mr. Holmes once more. He stood ramrod-straight on the edge of the water, tense as a pointer dog, quivering with intent. Then came the crack of gunfire from the older Waite, and that that had the detective on the move, his Webley revolver in his fist now and returning the old man's shot.

The younger Waite used the distraction to haul himself over the craft's gunwale and begin pulling at the sail's rigging.

"Leave that, y'dummock!" screamed Waite. "Row!" His son looked at the dinghy's sail now flapping against the mast. "No time. Row!"

Realising the slack sail would be of no use this close to shore, Robert Waite rammed the oars into the rowlocks and began pulling away. Shots were fired on the shore, and he let go of one oar to scrabble for the gun tucked beside him.

I heard a shout, "*Now*, Billy," and looked toward the shore— at Mr. Holmes dashing along the edge of the water. I needed no second asking. Pushing hard at the boat to unseat Robert, I hurled myself backward. Icy seawater closed over my head, and the sudden immersion hit as hard as any cudgel. I couldn't hear Waite fire his gun, nor Mr. Holmes's returning shots. I was too busy thrashing my limbs to pull myself free of the brine that flooded my nose and mouth. The tidal wash sucked at my limbs, pulling my feet from under me, dragging me down into oily brown waters. I flailed about in blind panic, pulling myself toward the shore, driven by the power of my own terror. I was almost sick with relief when my feet grazed the beach's shallow shelf, which stretched some twenty yards out to sea. With a final gargantuan effort, I leaned into the tide and staggered up the beach.

A hand grabbed at my shoulder, hauling me forward, and once water no longer held me upright, I collapsed onto the shingle. That same strong hand was soon yanking me to my feet. My teeth were chattering from shock and numbing cold. Mr. Holmes's left hand was still gripping my jacket, the Webley revolver in his right.

Old Waite was laid out like a bedraggled starfish on the shingle, staring at the sky, his mouth open and slack-jawed. There was a hole in his forehead and another in his chest, each of them awash with his own blood.

Mr. Holmes paid the corpse no attention, and I followed his line of sight toward the tiny dinghy rising and falling on waves that grew ever larger as the boat began to leave the shelter of the cove.

"He's getting away," I said. "We should—"

"He won't get far," Mr. Holmes replied. "A fit man would be hard pressed to row in those seas. A man with a bullet in his shoulder stands little chance at all. And even if he did, the *Adeleine* is poised to pick him up."

"You knew Waite would try to escape? That he had a weapon?"

"It was always a possibility, and a risk we had to take."

"We?" I said. "We?"

Mr. Holmes chuckled and turned me to face the cottage. "Yes, we. And now *we* shall search the cottage for those diamonds while we wait for the constabulary. With luck, you shall be back in London in time to help Watson buy a fat goose for Christmas, and he can write up your case with me."

"And yours, sir. Now you are retired."

"Perhaps," he said, and clapped me on the shoulder. "Perhaps."

The Adventure of the Bloomsbury Pickpocket

By David N. Smith

I loaded my old service revolver, then snapped it shut and stood ready beside Sherlock Holmes.

"You told me that Mason Lassiter was a dangerous man, so why did you not bring a weapon of your own?" I asked.

"I did," my friend replied, a thin smile slipping across his hawkish features. "One that is more powerful than any handgun and sharper than any knife."

"Your power of deductive reasoning, I suppose?"

"You deduce correctly." Holmes gave a small chuckle. "Our quarry will not resort to violence tonight."

"I am glad you are certain of that fact," I replied, "but for me, feeling the weight of my trusty revolver in my grip makes me feel far more confident that I can control the outcome of tonight's proceedings."

Holmes cocked a critical eyebrow.

"Yet nothing could be further from the truth, Watson."

Using my free hand, I pulled out my pocket watch and flipped open the lid, having to angle it to catch the light of the new electric streetlamps that lined the Embankment, so that I could read its face.

"It's almost midnight," I muttered, "and there's still no sign of this villain."

Holmes gave an almost imperceptible nod, his eyes remaining locked on the dark waterfront before us, focused on a length of pavement that ran alongside the unlit bulk of a three-mast merchant ship which was tethered to the wharf.

"If he waits for the chimes of Big Ben," Holmes mused, "that will tell us everything we need to know about his character."

Holmes had a distinct habit of leaving such assertions unexplained, knowing full well that I could never resist enquiring further. I, like a fish, always took the bait and found myself hooked. He, like a fisherman, delighted in reeling me in. Once done, he would cast me back into the depths of my ignorance, so that he could be assured his sport would continue.

"And, pray tell, what great deductions could you make from such behaviour?" I asked dutifully, making no attempt to conceal how much it delighted me whenever he expounded his incredible insights from seemingly irrelevant details.

"It tells us that Mason Lassiter relishes playing the villain. Most criminals are driven by desperation and necessity, often working with urgency, but not him. He holds his clandestine meetings at the very stroke of midnight, like a piece of choreographed theatre, obeying an etiquette of how he believes things should be done. For this man, crime is a leisure activity; doubtless he enjoys the thrill of the game as much as I do." Holmes paused, as the chimes of Big Ben rang out across the silent city. "There he is now. Right on cue."

A man had appeared on the wharf, walking briskly through the pools of light made by the streetlamps, headed directly toward the gangway of the ship. He was a tall figure in a long blue topcoat with its collar turned up, which shielded his face from view.

Holmes, fearlessly, stepped out in front of the man and blocked his path.

"I thought I should introduce myself, Mister Lassiter," he announced jovially, like a businessman making the acquaintance of a rival. "I am Sherlock Holmes, a consulting detective, frequently called upon by Scotland Yard."

"I know who you are, Mister Holmes," Lassiter responded, speaking with a thick American accent. "I've read about your capers in the *Strand*, which I at first mistook to be nothin' but tawdry fiction for entertainin' the masses, but now realise are nothin' more than an exercise in self-aggrandisement."

I felt riled by the flurry of insults, but Holmes showed no sign of affront.

"I should have expected you would know of me," he replied. "A criminal of your standing, would of course be well-read and well-informed."

Lassiter paused, unaccustomed to being both accused and complimented in the same sentence.

"You know me?"

"Naturally, I have heard of you." Holmes gave a small shrug. "I keep a catalogue, chronicling the most interesting crimes, both in this country and abroad. I have come to believe you are the mastermind behind the Charlestown bank robbery, the Kentucky gold heist, and a series of thefts from the National Gallery of Art in Washington."

Lassiter chuckled.

"If it were true, I'd be a fool to confess it to Sherlock Holmes himself!"

"You are no fool, sir. Quite the opposite. You are an intelligent, audacious man, capable of anything. Which is why, when I discovered you were in London, seeking to charter a merchant vessel, I thought it prudent to intercede. I deemed it best to warn you that, here in London, you are outmatched, that I have eyes on both you and every vessel you would seek to hire."

Lassiter took a step backward, rattled by Holmes's words. His gloved hand instinctively reached inside his coat, which bulged with the distinctive shape of a revolver, but he hesitated and did not draw.

"Why'd you warn me?" Lassiter enquired.

"I do hate to see a sharp mind go to waste. I know how addictive crime can be. It is a vice like any other; it can become a habit, which only grows worse, if left unchecked. I therefore felt compelled to intervene, to give you one final chance to turn your intellect to more noble endeavours, to encourage you to add to the edifice of humanity's achievements, rather than remain a stain upon them. As, if you continue, I shall become the architect of your undoing, and I would rather see you redeemed than be responsible for your downfall. With my warning issued, I will bid you goodnight."

Holmes abruptly turned on his heel, striding back down the pavement toward me, his walking cane striking the ground with each step.

Lassiter watched him go, then glanced at the ship, before turning and stepping silently back into the darkness from which he had emerged.

"Extraordinary!" I remarked, as Holmes arrived back at my side. "Why would you show this villain such a kindness!?"

"Empathy, my dear Watson," Holmes replied. "There, but for the grace of God, go I. If a passion for solving crimes had not seized my mind, I often wonder to what I would have turned my hand. Acting, perhaps. Science, possibly. However, both lack the allure and thrill of crime. Had I not chosen one side, perhaps I would have chosen the other. I am also a firm believer that all men, no matter how far they have strayed, deserve a chance to change tack and make amends for their past."

I gave a small snort of derision in response.

My right hand still bore the heavy weight of my revolver. Despite my friend's confidence, I felt sure that we had been but a villain's whim from exchanging gunfire, ending the night with at least one corpse left lying beside the Thames.

"Do you think he will heed your warning?"

"No," Holmes sighed.

"Why not?"

"His shoes were freshly polished."

I grinned.

"And what can you possibly infer from that?"

"He cares deeply about how he is perceived. However, nobody he met tonight, in this darkness, would be likely to notice his shoes; meaning it was done purely for the satisfaction of his own ego. The thrill of crossing swords with me will therefore be more of a temptation than a deterrent, particularly if there is a chance that your pen will immortalise his deeds, enthralling the public in the process. He has obviously enjoyed repeated installments, despite his protestations to the contrary. He is arrogant enough to think he can score a victory over me, but even a defeat at my hands would suffice, giving him the recognition and validation he craves. He would become renowned as a criminal mastermind, whose plans could only be foiled by a legendary London detective."

"Then he has little to lose."

Holmes nodded.

"He will surely press on with his plans. I expect that we shall have a busy morning ahead of us."

I awoke in my old room at 221B Baker Street.

I was fortunate to have a very understanding wife. Mary knew that when Holmes and I worked together, I could not be expected to keep regular hours. Still, I felt a pang of guilt at waking up in my old bed. Given the late end to our business, and with Holmes's clear intention to have an early start, it had simply seemed more prudent to return to Baker Street than to return home.

An old dressing gown, so threadbare I had not bothered to take it with me when I moved out, still hung on the back of the door. I pulled on the comfortable old robe, and ventured down to the sitting room, in search of breakfast.

Much to my surprise, Holmes was already risen and dressed. Traditionally he would rise late, so for a moment I wondered if this was a new habit, or simply a spasm of activity triggered by the thrill of the previous night's confrontation.

Holmes shot me a surprised look, as he tucked into a spread of eggs, rashers, toast, and tea, which had been laid out for two.

"Why are you not dressed?" he enquired. "Our next client will arrive at any moment."

"There is no appointment scheduled," I retorted, joining him at the table.

Holmes laughed.

"No. They did not have the foresight to book, but nonetheless I expect them. Their desperation will have built throughout the night, and as soon as they feel the hour is appropriate, I am sure they will come calling."

Before I could respond, I heard the front doorbell jangle.

"I really should get dressed."

"There is no time. I cannot have my biographer miss such an important meeting! Given the client's distress, and the early hour of their call, they will understand and disregard your appearance. If last night taught you anything, it should be that such things are rarely as important to the observer as they are to the person being observed."

Before I could protest further, I heard the front door open and close, and the tread of footsteps hurrying up the steps to our flat. A hand, light and hesitant, knocked on the door.

"Enter!" cried Holmes, dabbing crumbs of toast from his lips.

The door creaked open, revealing a stocky middle-aged woman, in a faded dress and a woollen shawl.

"I do beg your pardon, sir," she said, hesitating on the threshold of the door. "I would not normally call on anyone so early."

Holmes waved away her words.

"Think nothing of it. The matter is pressing, is it not?"

"Yes, sir!"

"Then sit," he said, gesturing toward a wicker chair, as he relocated himself to his favourite armchair. "Let us begin, as is proper, with introductions. I am Sherlock Holmes."

"I am Lillian Green," the woman replied, as she entered the room, glancing at me with a frown. "A widow from Notting Hill."

"That is Doctor Watson, an intimate friend, who frequently assists and chronicles my most remarkable cases."

"I am aware of who he is, sir," the woman responded, taking the seat to which she had been directed. "I just presumed, now that he was married, he would live elsewhere."

I gave the woman a rueful smile.

"My wife and I were under the same misapprehension."

"You are mistaken, Madam." Holmes interjected. "He is a guest here, not a lodger. You have seen the evidence and drawn the wrong conclusion; it is a very common mistake, which serves to illustrate exactly what I do. I see the truth where others do not. Now, tell us, what has brought you to my door?"

"It is my daughter, sir. Sally Isobel Green. She is an unmarried woman, of two and twenty. She did not come home last night."

"You fear something terrible has happened?"

"I do, sir."

"Then why do you not call on the police?"

Lillian hesitated, then looked away, unable to maintain eye contact.

"Sally has fallen in with a bad crowd. Since the death of my husband, we have been short of money, and she has pursued an unorthodox remedy to our situation." There were tears in Lillian's eyes, as her shoulders crumpled under the weight of her shame. "She has been conspiring with thieves and robbers."

Holmes smiled.

"You want her to be found, but wish to avoid any unnecessary legal complications?"

Lillian nodded.

I gave a small cough, interrupting their discourse.

"Do we really have time for another case, Holmes?" I enquired, as I could see a gleam of interest already alight in my friend's eyes. "Are we not busy enough with our pursuit of Mister Lassiter?"

Holmes dismissed my concerns with a wave of his hand.

"Tell me everything you can about these criminals," he said, steepling his fingers and closing his eyes, so he could focus on every word she spoke. "Leave out no detail, no matter how irrelevant you deem it."

"Sally told me they were uneducated men, over a dozen in number, who hail from the workhouses in the East End. They are primarily pickpockets, who target women in the Bloomsbury area, as many of the ladies that frequent the area are often wearing or carrying expensive jewelry. Sally has been helping them dispose of their ill-gotten gains in pawn shops across London; I presume she makes for a more convincing seller of such wares, than some burly, uneducated brute. Such behaviour is not part of her true nature, but I fear she has fallen for the roguish charm of the gang's despicable leader, a man named Silas Ramstone."

Holmes's eyes snapped open.

His hand instinctively reached for a wooden filing box, which always resided beside his armchair, so that he could flip hurriedly through the papers inside, which he used to catalogue both crimes and criminals.

"This is not a name I know," he said, grabbing a pencil, as he set about creating a new page for his archive. "What more can you tell me of Silas Ramstone?"

"Nothing. She mentioned him only once."

"She admires him? Emulates him?"

"Yes, sir."

"And what more can you tell me of your daughter?" Holmes asked, placing the paper to one side, and once again steepling his fingers.

"Up until she went astray, I believed we had brought her up well. My husband paid his weekly penny so that she could have an education, right up to the age of ten. Remember, this is before such schooling became mandatory. She can read and write. She is very gifted with numbers. She held a respectable position as a parlourmaid, until three months ago, but was sadly let go due to a misunderstanding over some missing silverware. Now, I wonder if she was quite as innocent as I had at first presumed. She certainly became inordinately upset, when I questioned her about it. She cried for hours."

Holmes nodded.

"You need not feel ashamed, Ms. Green. You have raised an ambitious and resourceful young woman, whose moral compass is quite intact, despite your inability to see it. You should be proud of her."

"But the things she has done!"

"In this story, it is the tears that count. They testify to her distress at her predicament. She did not embark on her path to crime willingly, but as an act of desperation."

"Will you take my case then, sir?"

"Indeed I will, Madam. I shall not only find your daughter; I will also endeavour to save her from the misguided path she has chosen. I cannot think of a more deserving case."

I coughed again.

"Perhaps that business with Mister Lassiter?" I reminded him.

"This business must take priority," Holmes replied, reaching for his clay pipe. "Although I am rather surprised we have not yet had our second caller. He should have arrived several minutes ago."

"Second caller?" I queried.

The moment I asked the question, I once again heard the jangle of the doorbell.

"Ah, there he is now," Holmes smiled.

"How could you know someone was to arrive?" I asked, feeling as amazed as ever by my friend's seeming omniscience. "And with such precision in timing?"

"Elementary maths, Watson. You take the standard start time of a shift, allow a little time for communication, then add the time it takes for a hansom cab to travel from Whitehall to Baker Street, allowing for the early-morning traffic on Regent Street. I should have added a few minutes, given the individual concerned, as he is never the quickest to ask for aid."

"You know exactly who it is, then?" I asked, as I listened to the tread of heavy footsteps climbing the stairs, and the rat-a-tat strike of a confident fist on the wooden door.

"Enter, Inspector Lestrade!"

The door immediately opened, revealing the self-same police detective, wearing a pea jacket and derby hat. He bore an uncharacteristically harried expression.

"Holmes, I have come to fetch you."

"As you will note, I have a client," Holmes replied, gesturing at Lillian, who remained sat in the basket chair, dumbfounded by this latest turn of events. "I am currently employed on a case for her and can accept no other."

Lestrade gave him a sour look.

"Holmes, you know I would not have beat a path to your door so early, unless it were something vitally important. This woman can wait. I am here about a national crisis. A robbery of unprecedented proportions."

"What has happened, man?" I asked, rising to my feet, alarmed by his tone.

Holmes sighed.

"I rather suspect he is referring to a robbery from the British Museum," he declared, as he filled and lit his pipe.

Lestrade's eyes bulged with surprise.

"How the blazes do you know that?" he cried, then waved away his own question, uninterested in the answer. "Yes, numerous invaluable items have been taken. Priceless and irreplaceable relics of antiquity, apparently. There is uproar. You must come at once!"

Holmes puffed on his pipe, building the flame within.

He did not move from his armchair.

"Holmes!" I cried. "This really does sound important. We should make haste! We do not have time for you to just sit there smoking your pipe!"

"Indeed," Holmes replied, blowing smoke. "Yet, contemplation seems like the best use of my time, given that we need to wait for you to get dressed."

I frowned.

I had completely forgotten I was still wearing a dressing gown, and there I was, stood before a detective from Scotland Yard!

"I will be but a moment!" I cried, feeling hot embarrassment aglow in my cheeks. "I shall dress as quickly as I can!"

Holmes nodded.

"It is curious, is it not, how quickly one may become accustomed to a situation," he mused, suckling at his pipe. "How what we once deemed impossible circumstances, which we would never enter willingly, can so swiftly and easily consume us."

We took a four-wheeler to Bloomsbury Street, with Lestrade repeatedly urging the driver to whip the horses, despite the road being filled with early-morning wagons transporting goods to market, which kept the poor beasts at nothing more than a two-beat trot. Ms. Green had headed home, reassured by a promise from Holmes that he was attending to her case, despite the severity of this more pressing matter.

We disembarked directly outside the British Museum, made our way up the steps, passing a squad of police officers, and strode between the vast Ionic pillars that comprise the façade of the British Museum.

Inside, we found a small huddle of men, all looking distinctly distressed.

One, noting our approach, broke away to greet us. He was an exceptionally thin man, in a cream-coloured suit, with a scraggily grey beard.

"Is this him?!" cried the man. "Is this finally someone with some intelligence?"

Holmes glanced at him.

"I should think there was no shortage of intelligence here. If I am not mistaken, I see numerous highly qualified professors before me, all directing their vast intellects to solving the crime that has been committed here."

"And yet they have not had a single useful thought between them!" The bearded man sneered. "Do you believe you can do better? Can you help us recover these priceless artefacts?"

"I can," Holmes nodded. "I am an expert, sir, in the field of crime, just as you are in the antiquities of ancient Greece."

I coughed.

"How could you possibly know this man is an expert in the antiquities of ancient Greece?" I asked, knowing the part I should play, as well as any theatre actor. He needed a moment to impress them, to gain their confidence, so he could set about his work without further interruption and debate.

"It is obvious. I noted the cream suit, commonly worn in hotter climates, but still worn now out of unbroken habit, implying he spent considerable time in Southern Europe or North Africa. His mannerisms, though, acquired from mixing with the local population, are purely Greek. Furthermore, when this gentleman spoke of priceless artefacts, he gestured toward a specific, empty, plinth. According to the information plaque, it once held a bust of the Goddess Athena, discovered by a Professor Ernest G. Blackwell. Which, based on his possessive gesturing, I presume is the very gentleman to whom I have been speaking."

"Goodness me," muttered Professor Blackwell.

Holmes clapped his hands together.

"I must have a list, gentlemen, of everything that was taken."

"The bust of Athena, obviously!" declared Blackwell.

"A Japanese katana blade, from before the early-Edo period," cried another.

"A mummified cat!" yelled a third.

Holmes clapped his hands again.

"I said a list, gentlemen!" He glanced around the group of agitated professors. "Surely you have at least thought to compile a catalogue of your missing objects?"

There was an embarrassed silence.

"I shall set my assistant upon the task at once!" cried Blackwell. "Miss Reilly!"

A young woman, wearing a grey dress, obediently scuttled to his side. The two immediately fell into an animated discourse, with him detailing exactly what was needed, which she dutifully noted down.

"Well, hop to it, gentlemen," Holmes declared, as he glanced around at the remaining professors. "Each of you is responsible for a department; check what is missing, and bring the information to Agnes. You cannot expect her to do all the work!"

The professors, having been given their orders, dashed away.

Lestrade watched them depart.

"Well, that will keep them busy, while we get on with the proper detective work. Well done, Holmes." Lestrade nodded with reluctant admiration. "But, of course, I am sure you will have already deduced something vital from it all, which I have foolishly missed. Come, have at it! What vital clue have you noticed?"

"Only the obvious," Holmes laughed. "That all the objects mentioned were small enough to be carried by one person alone. They have not taken the Rosetta Stone or the Elgin Marbles, which have significantly more value, but which would require more than one set of hands to move. The list, once complete, should support this supposition."

Lestrade's eyes widened.

"Are you saying that everything was stolen by one man?"

"No, Lestrade, I said nothing of the sort. You should listen more carefully; observation is done as much by ear as by eye. However, you may rest assured, I shall have my investigation resolved by this time tomorrow."

By the time we returned to Baker Street, the sun had slipped beneath the horizon. Our hansom cab rattled to a halt, with Holmes leaping down to the pavement before the carriage had come to a stop.

I moved to follow him, but he stopped and turned, blocking my path.

"What the blazes do you think you are doing?" he asked.

"We are on a case of national importance," I responded. "I cannot go home now. Whatever deductions you make tonight will be of the greatest interest to my readers."

"You have a wife and home to attend to, Watson. Your duty is there." He declared, pushing me back into my seat.

"But the case, Holmes! It is important!"

"But it is not more important than your marriage, is it?" Holmes asked, his eyes narrowing. "Besides, the case is solved."

I frowned.

"But we have so many cases!"

Holmes shook his head.

"I have pledged myself to only one case."

"I count three separate cases!"

"Three?" Sherlock laughed, a mocking twinkle in his eyes. "Your maths is askew."

"I count the business with Mister Lassiter, the disappearance of Sally Green, and the thefts from the British Museum. There, that is three cases."

"You are mistaken, Watson. They are all just pieces of one puzzle, which I assure you will be resolved in the morning, when I shall reveal the full picture to you."

I stared at my friend.

"I cannot go now, Holmes!" I protested. "If there are answers, I must have them!"

Holmes shook his head.

"*Demain matin*, Watson. You will have your answers then. If this whole business should teach you anything, it is that we must strive to break our compulsions. Habits are easily acquired, but infernally difficult to break, so we must be wary which ones we allow to thrive. If I allowed you to stay here a second night, you would think nothing of staying a single night in future, and your marriage would suffer. I therefore pledge you will not sleep under my roof again, not while your wife is so close, no matter how fascinating the case. If I allowed it, I would be no friend at all, and you are very dear to me, John. I must therefore send you away. I must send you home."

I returned to the British Museum the following morning to find numerous police officers still guarding the front entrance.

Holmes was stood just inside, looking decidedly pleased. On the plinth beside him, restored to its rightful place, was a bust of the Goddess Athena. Elsewhere, I could see other ancient objects which had not been present the previous day.

Professor Blackwell and Miss Reilly, trailed by a gaggle of professors, were dashing excitedly from exhibit to exhibit, their faces lit with joy.

Lestrade was stood by the main doors, his arms folded, managing to look both begrudgingly impressed and annoyed.

"Everything has been returned?" I asked, astonished. "How is that possible?"

Lestrade gave a little grunt.

"Inside job and a guilty conscience, would be my guess." He eyed the roving professors suspiciously. "However, Mister Holmes seems reluctant to furnish us with an explanation."

"No crime has been committed. What is there to account for?" Holmes responded.

"Blast it, Holmes! I need to explain all this to my superior officers. Is there nobody I can arrest?"

"Outside, Lestrade, you will find an agitated man in a blue topcoat. I would be most grateful if you would arrest him. Be aware, he will be armed."

Lestrade blinked, shocked by the sudden revelation. To his credit, he did not waste time with questions, but turned and dashed out through the main door. I moved to follow, but Holmes blocked my path with the handle of his cane.

"Let Lestrade do his job."

"Then let me do mine," I retorted. "Tell me what is going on. How can I chronicle these events, if I have no clue what is happening?!"

Holmes nodded, lowering his voice to a whisper.

"I regret not bringing you into my confidence sooner, but I had to be sure of a satisfactory resolution before I risked revelation. The man outside is Mason Lassiter. It was he who masterminded the Bloomsbury pickpocket gang, for the purposes of scoping out the area around the British Museum, so that he could plan a much more audacious raid. The target was obvious, as soon as Ms. Green told us the area the gang were working."

I shook my head.

"We have it on good authority that those scoundrels are run by Silas Ramstone."

Holmes laughed.

"Watson, criminals rarely use their real names! They are one and the same man."

"How can you be sure?"

"At our first meeting, we established that Mister Lassiter would do things purely for the benefit of his own ego. So, when choosing his alias, he could not resist the urge to mock his opponents, purely for his own amusement; and he made it an anagram of his own true name."

Holmes reached into his breast pocket and produced the piece of paper from his meeting with Lillian Green, upon which he had written two names, one atop the other.

Silas Ramstone.

Mason Lassiter.

"Written down, side by side, it is easy to see that the two names contain exactly the same letters."

I hurriedly checked the names and confirmed their symmetry.

"This made it exceedingly easy to find Sally Green. Knowing from her mother's testimony that she admired and emulated this rogue, I knew she would seek to copy this frivolous charade. So, when searching for Sally Green, and encountering a woman of an appropriate age working within the museum named Miss Reilly, I quickly extrapolated that if they were the same person, her new forename must be Agnes. The additional *i* is accounted for by her middle initial; you will remember that her mother gave her full name as Sally Isobel Green. Having made my deduction, I was able to innocuously verify it, by using the name in conversation when talking to the professors."

"So simple, Holmes!" I cried, as delighted as ever by my friend's deductive reasoning. "So simple! Lestrade will be delighted to have another culprit in his clutches."

Holmes looked taken aback.

"I will not have that! I accepted the task to find the girl and retrieve her from the temptations of a criminal life."

"Nonetheless, she has committed serious crimes, Holmes."

"She was penniless. She sought only a means to survive. She has a shrewd and able mind, and naturally seized upon the only opportunity open to her. Lassiter, impressed with her talents, deployed her here, getting her a job within the museum. It is a job she takes pride in, whereas her criminal activity left her ashamed. Lassiter was so antagonised by my confronting him at the docks that, after the robbery, he kept every member of his gang close, fearing one of them would speak out. An action which sent Ms. Green to our door. It was of course my intention, by applying such pressure, to force something loose. I did not know who would come to our door that morning, but it was probable that someone would, as every member of the gang would know someone concerned by their absence, who would seek some other recourse other than the police."

The implication of his words was obvious.

"You have spoken with Sally. You convinced her to return everything she stole."

Holmes nodded.

"When we interrupted Lassiter's attempt to acquire a ship, we foiled their attempt to remove the goods from the country, so they were still stored in a neighbouring property. It was as simple for her to return them as it was to remove them."

"You are very generous to give this girl such a second chance."

"Not at all. It would be wasteful not to provide one. As I have said, she has a sharp mind, which is now being put to better use. She of course succumbed to crime when offered no alternative, but now she has the taste for a new habit, in the form of a regular and well-paid job, which stimulates her intelligence rather than degrades it. She has become accustomed to working here and wishes to continue; she seeks to leave her criminal habits behind."

I nodded thoughtfully.

"I see only one flaw in this scheme."

"I see no flaw."

"Do you think Lassiter will let the girl go free from her old life so simply? Once caught, do you not think he may name her as a co-conspirator?"

Holmes shook his head.

"This I have anticipated. It is with this that we shall let Mister Lassiter determine his own fate, through the very nature of his character. Having found the treasures returned and his plan foiled, his bruised ego will have compelled him to come here and confront me, but he will instead find Lestrade and his officers waiting for him. If Mister Lassiter has but a tiny fragment of decency, honour, or humility in his soul, he will easily survive the encounter. If he does not, his damaged ego will be unable to contain his temper, and he will doubtless lash out against them."

There was a sadness in Holmes's voice as he spoke, and, as he prided himself on being an expert in the criminal character, he undoubtedly knew what would happen next.

The gunshot rang out, as loud as a church bell, the distinctive sound driving everything else into silence. I leapt forward, hurrying toward the noise, my hand reaching for my own revolver. I crashed through the doors, stepping out into the dazzling daylight.

I was too late.

A man in a blue topcoat lay dead in the street, a revolver still clasped tightly in his right hand, his eyes staring blankly upward. Lestrade was stood over him, his own revolver still smoking from the shot.

"He would not surrender, even though he was surrounded by officers," he muttered. "Instead, he pulled a revolver. He left me no choice."

"He chose his own fate, long ago," Holmes told him, as he looked down on the body. "From the day he committed his first petty crime, his fate was set, because he would let nothing dissuade him from his path."

Lestrade reached down and drew the man's eyelids closed.

"He said he wanted the world to know, it was Sherlock Holmes who defeated him."

"No. This time, the credit remains yours."

"Who was he?" Lestrade asked.

"Silas Ramstone. An unremarkable pickpocket." Holmes lifted his eyes, to stare at the empty street. The public had fled when the shot was fired, but from the shadows of doorways and side streets, a handful of pale faces were still staring at the scene with wide-eyed horror. "Those still close by will testify to that identity, as they were his comrades in crime."

Lestrade turned to look.

"Well, I guess I had better go and have a word with them then."

He stepped away, with two uniformed officers falling into step beside him as they approached the cowering witnesses.

I turned to face Holmes.

"Why did you give Lestrade his fake identity?" I asked. "Why not let him know this man was Mason Lassiter?"

"The story may be told in two ways: either a criminal mastermind planned an audacious robbery of international significance, only to be undone by the renowned consulting detective Sherlock Holmes, or a common pickpocket died in the street."

"I very much intend to chronicle the first, not the second!"

"That would undoubtedly be the more popular tale. It would make crime seem glamourous and exciting. The villain himself would have taken pride in it. Others would be lured to take their first bite of the apple; and as we have seen, one bite is never enough. Let us not encourage people to take their first step upon such a dark road."

"Then I may not document these events for the *Strand*?"

"Write them up if you must. Then lock it away, until all his kith and kin have passed from this world. Let him not be celebrated as a paragon. Let the passage of time expunge any glory that might have been afforded to him by the press or public; let his history be dictated by your pen alone, when no other voice remains. Then let him be remembered only as a criminal, who died an undignified, dishonourable, and pointless death; for in truth, that is all he ever was."

I nodded, respecting my friend's wishes.

"Then all is well. The world has one less villain preying upon it. The museum has her treasures. Sally Green has a new life, filled with opportunity, and is free to return home unashamed. You may congratulate yourself on a job well done."

"And what should I do now?" Holmes asked, finally meeting my gaze.

I hesitated. Anyone else would have filled the rest of their day with friends or a lover, but not Holmes. He had only his violin, his pipe, and a large supply of alkaloids.

"I am sure another case will be along soon," I said.

"I do hope so," Holmes replied, as he strode away. "I should hate to become bored."

The Dulwich Solicitor

By Martin Daley

One

Of all the cases I presented to *The Strand* magazine that involved the singular talents of my friend Mr. Sherlock Holmes, its editor chose to publish what might be described as the more lengthy, complex adventures. I should stress that this is not a criticism of his judgement, nor of that wonderful publication. After all, I have personally been involved in, or have had knowledge of, over a hundred cases during my acquaintance with him, and Holmes once stated that he had been involved in five hundred investigations of capital importance before we even met. Decisions had to be made therefore as to which adventures were deserving of publication, and I believe Mr. Greenhough-Smith's judgements were as good as any.

I was reminded of this recently when I had cause to visit my bank, Cox and Co. at Charing Cross. I had misplaced a keepsake given to me by my beloved Mary not long after we first met, when I suddenly remembered I had placed it with other valuables in the vault of the bank. While I was there, I could not fail to be tempted by the contents of my old, battered dispatch-box, containing the notes of my adventures with the great consulting detective. I sat for over two hours glancing through the piles of papers and recalling every possible emotion experienced as a result of my association with Sherlock Holmes.

As I did so it struck me that, as well as the adventures that the public are familiar with due to the aforementioned judgements of our editor, there were many others that probably were not considered, due simply to my friend's brilliance in resolving the matter in double-quick time. The keepsake I referred to earlier reminded me of one example, and I found myself sifting through my old papers until I rediscovered the record of the investigation concerning Mr. Silas Wagstaff.

It was late September 1888 and Holmes had, two weeks earlier, completed the strange case of Mr. Jonathan Small and the great Agra treasure. During the course of his investigation, I met the sweet and sensitive Miss Morston for the first time, and once the matter had been concluded, I was delighted when Mary accepted me as her husband in prospective. A few days later, I received a letter from her, inviting me to be a guest of hers and of her employer Mrs. Forrester's family at their home in Lower Camberwell. I am not ashamed to admit that my heart skipped with joy upon receiving the letter, and I had no hesitation in accepting.

As a matter of courtesy, I asked Holmes if he could do without my assistance for a few days. He had been lukewarm at the news of my engagement and further demonstrated a lack of feeling as he barely looked up from his newspaper and sent me off with a dismissive wave, announcing, "I have all the company I need in the form of the cocaine-bottle."

Ignoring the reference to this foul habit, I left and enjoyed enormously a wonderful week in the company of Mary; I was even more delighted to find that she enjoyed my company just as much as I did hers. On the final day of my holiday, she gave me a signet ring belonging to her father, which was apparently a gift to him from her mother on the day of their wedding. I was touched that she would even consider parting with such a memento and was honoured to accept it.

I returned to Baker Street's brooding autumnal skies the following morning, but even they could not dull my feelings—as far as I was concerned, it could have been the first week of May. That was to change, however, upon entering our old rooms at 221B. Such was my demeanour that I virtually bounded up the stairs, eager to see my friend and share the news of my holiday. Not for the first time, however, I was to be disappointed.

"Morning, Holmes!" I shouted from the landing as I hung up my hat and coat on the stand. There was no reply.

I entered our sitting room, only to be engulfed in a cloud of thick pipe smoke. Coughing, I made my way over to the window and raised the sash. After regaining some composure, I looked across the room to see my friend with his eyes closed, sitting in the wicker chair by the fire with what seemed like several days' worth of newspapers strewn all around him. He was in his grey house coat and sat with his knees up under his chin. Protruding from his mouth was the small oily clay pipe he would invariably turn to when he was in pensive mood.

"Good *morning*, Holmes," I repeated.

Raised eyebrows and a creased forehead were all that I received by way of a response. Already feeling my jovial mood dissipate, I sat down opposite, snapping open one of the newspapers as loudly as I could in order to elicit some form of acknowledgement. Again, I was to be disappointed.

My eyes inevitably travelled toward the Persian slipper that hung to one side of the fire, and then to the morocco case I knew contained a hypodermic syringe, sitting on the mantelpiece above it. I was appalled at the thought of Holmes stagnating like this over the past week.

The newspaper was folded open at the obituaries page. It was one of the few pages that was not dominated by the two stories that had horrified the nation over the previous few weeks: the

theft of the favourite for the Wessex Cup and the tragic murder
of its trainer was now rivalled by the recent dreadful murders in
Whitechapel. I wondered if either of these matters were the cause
of my friend's noncommunicative mood. Without remembering
the detail, I did recall him making some comment about the first of
the Whitechapel murders some weeks earlier but, when he was not
consulted by Scotland Yard on the matter, and then when the case
that was brought to our door by Miss Morston took the following
three weeks to complete, his attention and mine were naturally
focused elsewhere.

No sooner had Holmes embarked on the case, which I
subsequently titled *The Sign of the Four*, than another brutal murder
took place in Spitalfields. Little did we know that the following week
would see a further two horrific attacks. Again I wondered if Holmes
was reproaching himself for not getting involved in the matter.

Just then, the doorbell rang, and my friend instantaneously leapt
from his chair, as if propelled by a giant spring hidden under the
wicker seat.

"*Ha!*" he cried, "*Mrs. Hudson! MRS. HUDSON!*"

I heard the footsteps of our long-suffering housekeeper on the
stairs as Holmes made it to the door.

"Yes, yes, Mr. Holmes," said Mrs. Hudson's voice as she turned
and hurried across the landing. Handing a telegram to Holmes at the
threshold of the room, she saw me and attempted to add, "Oh, hello
Doctor, I didn't hear you come—"

But the poor woman was gone, the door of the sitting room
having been closed in her face by surely the most infuriating lodger
in London. Completely oblivious to his rudeness, Holmes was
ripping open the telegram.

"Excellent!" he cried, "Watson, back into your coat, we have
work to do!" He headed toward his own room to collect his outdoor
wear but stopped in the doorway and turned, "Oh and by the way,
no, I wasn't contemplating the actions of the Whitechapel maniac

when you entered—nor indeed the interesting developments at King's Pyland."

I stood there for the umpteenth time, open-mouthed. "How on earth…" I began, and then realised there was no point in trying to extricate myself from the mischievous trap I had fallen into yet again. Holmes turned again toward his room with that familiar twinkle in his eye.

Among the thousands of words I have written over the years to describe my friend, the one I mentioned earlier deserves a prominent place—infuriating.

Two

"Where are we going?" I asked as our hansom picked its way through the busy traffic of Baker Street.

"First we must call at the Post Office on Marylebone Road," replied Holmes, "and then it is on to Dulwich, Watson; we are going to Dulwich to trap a villain who is more cunning than Roylott and more cold-hearted than Rucastle."

"Good heavens!" I was shocked by the reputation afforded to this man by Holmes. After gaining some composure, I couldn't resist adding icily, "I'm pleased you haven't spent the whole time locked away with your cocaine and tobacco."

A brief smile plucked at the corners of my friend's mouth as he prepared to tell me about the matter.

"You will remember when I employed the Irregulars to find the steamboat *Aurora* two weeks ago, during the Jonathan Small case?"

"Of course," I replied. "I've never seen such a group of sad, grubby-looking characters. What their lives have been like to date, I cannot begin to imagine."

"And that brings us to the point at hand, Watson," said Holmes, leaning forward to elaborate on his narrative. "When the boys entered our sitting room, did you notice any*one* or anyth*ing* in particular?"

"Not particularly," I said, "they all descended like a plague of locusts! I remember poor Mrs. Hudson was none too pleased at the intrusion."

Holmes smiled at his recollection of the event. "Yes, but among the excitement there was one boy who stood out from the rest."

"You mean Wiggins? He seemed to be doing all the talking."

"No, no. Like the rest of his companions, Wiggins had bare feet, rags for clothes, and an eager sparkle in his eye, attracted as he was by the prospect of earning himself a guinea. But there was one boy who was distinct from the rest. He was the last to enter; he stood slightly apart from the others, as if he didn't really know them. Most distinctive of all was his appearance: he wore shoes, his clothes were not as worn as his friends', and his skin and hair were not as pitted with the grime and filth of London as the other poor wretches."

"I can't say I particularly noticed," I said, not for the first time in my long association with my friend.

Holmes widened his nostrils and exhaled loudly in disappointment at my failure. "No," he drew out the word before continuing. "The sight of the boy troubled me, and I later called Wiggins back to ask about him. It transpired that he had only been with Wiggins and his associates for little more than a week prior to us receiving them in Baker Street.

He's called Simon," said Wiggins, "Simon Rutherford. I found him begging down Rotherhithe way, where I had a bit of business."

"A bit of business indeed!" Holmes threw his head back and roared with laughter as he recalled the conversation. "The little tyke!"

"Simon Rutherford?" I queried. "Hardly the moniker of your average street urchin."

"Exactly, Watson. His name, his appearance, everything was incongruous with the situation he found himself in. It transpired that the boy was recently orphaned. Wiggins told me he thought he was from a quite well-to-do family, but his parents died, leaving him destitute."

"Surely a decent middle-class family would have provided for their offspring with a will?"

"And this is what intrigued me still further. In the absence of my trusted biographer, I resolved to carry out some further research into the matter and discovered that the boy's father had died suddenly within six months of his mother, and he did indeed leave a will."

Holmes reached into his inside pocket and brought out a piece of newspaper torn from the *Times*. It was part of the obituaries page and recorded the:

Sudden passing of Mr. Gerald Rutherford of 13 Tewkesbury Avenue, Dulwich. Husband of the late Sarah Rutherford and father of Simon James Rutherford. The reading of the will is due to take place at the offices of solicitor Mr. Silas Wagstaff on August 15, 1888.

"So presumably this took place and, as a result, the poor child received nothing and was kicked out onto the street?" I asked with some alarm.

"I am certain of it," replied Holmes through gritted teeth. "There is something quite despicable about crimes against the most vulnerable of our society, Watson, and they are invariably perpetrated by the wealthy and privileged."

"And you obviously suspect this Wagstaff is guilty of wrongdoing against the boy Rutherford?"

Holmes looked squarely at me. "I know it Watson," he said, "I know it."

At that moment, our hansom drew to a halt outside the post office, and Holmes leapt from the vehicle onto the pavement and into the building in a single movement. I saw him through the window speaking with the postmaster behind the counter, and he took an envelope from him, in exchange for some form of payment.

Within seconds, he was back in the hansom and with a rap on the inside of the roof with his cane, we lurched back up to speed.

"I know it, my dear Watson, because of this," he announced, showing me the envelope he had just collected. "It is the final piece in the puzzle of evidence against this wretched creature."

The envelope was addressed to a Mr. John Radford, c/o Marylebone Road Post Office, NW1. "I don't understand," I said. "Who is Mr. John Radford, and how have you come to receive his mail?"

Holmes once again flashed me that mischievous glance of his before announcing, "*I* am Mr. Radford. I have already visited Wagstaff during your absence, Watson, and this letter is the result."

Naturally, I was at a complete loss as to what Holmes was up to and asked my friend to elaborate.

"Every fibre in my body told me that there was something sinister concerning the passing of Gerald Rutherford, so from the newspaper room at the British Library I went straight to the Registrar's Office in Dulwich to view the recorded deaths. In Rutherford's case, the cause of death was listed as a heart attack and organ failure."

"What age was he?" I asked.

"Forty-six," replied Holmes, "an unusually young age for one's organs to completely shut down, wouldn't you say, Doctor?"

"I agree."

"And less than ten entries before that of Gerald Rutherford was the recording of his wife's passing. The cause of her death was typhoid fever.

"I leafed back through the ledger still further and found no less than six entries during the previous three years where causes of death were listed as either a heart attack, organ failure, or both. Six weeks prior to each death, it would appear that the respective spouses of the deceased had also passed away. I made a list of the names concerned and then visited neighbouring registry offices. I found a similar pattern of spousal deaths in Norwood, Kensington, and Norbury:

one passing away first and the surviving spouse outliving them by no more than two or three months. All enough to form a pattern but not enough to particularly arouse any suspicion of wrongdoing.

"From there I returned to the library to discover that, in each case, there were children orphaned by their parents' passing, and of those cases that were heard at a coroner's inquest, it was judged that the deaths were as indicated on the respective death certificates."

"You naturally do not believe this?"

"I do not," Holmes said gravely, as our cab rattled over Waterloo Bridge, "and in each case, the solicitor involved in dealing with the deceased's estate was the same."

"Silas Wagstaff."

"Precisely."

"But surely it should be a matter for the police, Holmes," I suggested. "After all, no one has actually commissioned your services in the matter."

"I am not interested in money when it comes to such matters, Watson. There are some cases worth pursuing simply because it is the correct thing to do. If this ends up with this odious specimen at the end of a rope, then that will be my reward.

"But you are correct about the police; the telegram I received earlier was from Inspector Stanley Hopkins, who has obtained a magistrate's warrant and will meet us at Wagstaff's offices this morning."

Three

For the remainder of the journey, Holmes completed the gaps in his narrative concerning his meeting with Silas Wagstaff.

"I first contacted him claiming to be a Mr. Radford, who had recently lost his wife. As it was too painful for my young daughter and myself to remain in the family home in Dulwich, we had moved out and were temporarily staying with friends north of the river. I explained that I had not made a will, and my dear wife's sudden passing had prompted me to give the matter some serious thought.

Not surprisingly, he was all too willing to help. I visited him first last Monday in the guise of the grieving widower."

Having witnessed—and been taken in by—many of Holmes's disguises over the years, I could picture him playing the part to perfection. I have thought on many an occasion that the stage lost one of the finest actors when Holmes turned his attentions to the art of detection.

"Like most villains of his kind," resumed my friend, "Wagstaff is certainly a plausible character. You have often complimented me on my thespian abilities in the past, Watson, I must grudgingly pay tribute to his.

" 'Come in, my dear Mr. Radford,' he said when we first met, 'and let me express my heartfelt condolences to you and your daughter for your devastating loss.'

" 'Thank you, Mr. Wagstaff, it has been an extremely difficult time for us both.'

" 'Let me get us some refreshment. *Mr. Kent!*'

"The solicitor's clerk answered his employer's call.

" 'Ah, Kent, would you be so kind as to bring us some refreshment please? There's a good chap.'

" 'Very good, sir,' replied the clerk with a nod.

"He returned some moments later with a tray, upon which was a pot of tea and two cups, and a plate of what looked like a most appetizing fruit loaf, cut into slices.

" 'Oh, how lovely, Kent, thank you,' said Wagstaff when he saw the tray, 'and we've got some of my dear wife's beautiful recipe; we are in for a real treat, Mr. Radford.'

"Kent placed the tray carefully on the corner of Wagstaff's desk. 'Would you like me to pour it, sir?' he asked.

" 'No, I'll deal with it Kent, thank you,' said his employer. 'Now, Mr. Radford,' he said turning back to me, 'you would like to make a will. May I ask how much your estate is worth?'

" 'Well, I'm not really sure—a reasonable amount, I suppose, as I do own my own house on Hartington Place, and I have some savings.

"I saw Wagstaff's eyes gleam behind the lenses of his spectacles. 'And presumably you want to secure your daughter's future in case something unthinkable happens to yourself?' he asked.

" 'That's right, but I don't know what I can do, that's why I contacted you. I remember a neighbour said how kind you were after her husband passed away. Your assistance appeared timely as, sadly, she herself died shortly afterwards. Thank goodness she managed to put things in place to protect her young son.'

" 'Well, I can't talk about individual clients, you understand,' said Wagstaff, bowing and shaking his head, 'but it is true that I have experienced such tragic affairs.'

" 'What would you recommend in my case?' I asked.

" 'I think the sensible thing to ensure that little…erm?'

" 'Katy.'

" 'Of course, Katy, how delightful. To ensure that little Katy's inheritance is secured.'

" 'That sounds perfect,' I said.

" 'What I suggest therefore is that we make your will, which will list Katy as the sole beneficiary. In the unlikely event of your passing, your estate will be held by a trust called the Dulwich Children's Fund until Katy reaches an appropriate age when she can access her inheritance. In the meantime, the trust would identify a family home in the area where Katy would be raised commensurate with the high standards demonstrated by yourself and your dear late wife.'

" 'I see,' I said, rubbing my chin in thought. 'In the unthinkable event of myself *and* Katy passing away, what would happen to my estate?'

" 'I have known clients in the past requesting that their estate be given to the fund to continue their excellent work in supporting orphaned children.'

" 'I suppose that would be as good a solution as any, although I'm sure that doesn't happen very often.'

" 'Oh no, no, no, hardly ever,' replied Wagstaff, 'The tragic events involving your neighbour comprise the only occasion I can ever remember. Oh, perhaps I shouldn't have said that,' he added in mock horror."

Holmes broke off momentarily from his narrative. "I must say, Watson, he is amongst the most wicked of creatures."

He resumed.

" 'There is one thing I would like to alter,' I said, in the role of Radford.

"Wagstaff looked slightly chagrined at this revelation. 'Alter?' he repeated.

" 'Yes. I was speaking with the friend Katy and I are currently staying with, and he suggested that he could act as Katy's guardian in the unlikely event of me passing away before my daughter comes of age. I wonder if we could include that in the will?'

"Wagstaff sat down and was silent for a while. 'Yes, I don't see why not,' he said at last.

" 'Oh, thank you, Mr. Wagstaff, that would be most kind and a great relief to me. I would therefore like you to make the necessary arrangements to that effect.'

" 'Excellent, excellent,' cried the solicitor, 'now let's have some tea.'

"He poured the tea and delicately put two slices of loaf onto separate plates.

" 'I have a model will here, Mr. Radford,' said Wagstaff, bringing a document out of his desk drawer. He offered it to me and then reached across to the tray. He put a cup of tea and a slice of loaf in front of me and attempted to do the same for himself. As he did so, however, the saucer of his cup collided with the teapot, causing him to spill the contents over his own piece of loaf and part of the blotting pad that covered half of his desk.

" 'Oh dear!' he cried, 'I am so clumsy. Do forgive me, Mr. Radford, I will go and get a cloth to clean this mess up. In the meantime, please carry on reading the document and don't stand on ceremony when it comes to your refreshment. I will return shortly.'

"During Wagstaff's absence, I folded the piece of loaf on my plate, and another from the cut slices, into a handkerchief. I also took a small sample of tea from my cup in a vial I was carrying and poured the remainder back into the pot. It was ten minutes before the solicitor returned.

" 'Sorry about that, Mr. Radford, I was looking for the maid. How are we getting on?' he asked as he started dabbing away at the excess liquid.

" 'Yes, I'm sure that will do fine,' I replied referring to the sample will.

" 'Good, good. And I see you have enjoyed your refreshment in my absence?'

" 'Yes, it was delicious, please compliment your wife on her wonderful baking. I hope you don't mind, but I helped myself to a second piece.' I indicated the plate that was still on the tray, containing the remainder of the sliced loaf.

" 'Oh, no, not at all, sir.' Wagstaff seemed positively excited. Then, observing my empty cup, he asked, 'Can I get you some more tea?'

" 'No, thank you, it was most refreshing.'

" 'Splendid, splendid,' said Wagstaff, rubbing his hands lightly.

" 'Could I make a suggestion?' asked the solicitor. 'If you give me the details of your friend, I will write out the will and invite you back to have it signed up. I can ask my clerk and maid to act as witnesses. You could even bring your friend along.'

" 'That would be fine, thank you.' I gave Wagstaff details of my fictitious friend Robert Wilson, and he told me that he would hope to have the document completed for the end of the week.

" 'Excellent, excellent. One thing I should add, in the interest of fairness and disclosure. I myself am one of the trustees of the Children's Fund, along with three other solicitors.'

"Wagstaff gave me a piece of paper with three names listed and then added, 'We could be listed as your executors if that would be convenient. I appreciate that I myself appear slightly older than yourself, but two of my colleagues are considerably younger and therefore the chances of everyone pre-deceasing you are extremely remote.'

"I assumed Wagstaff was amusing himself inwardly at this last comment, as he would make sure that he would not pre-decease me, but I played along at face value. 'Yes, that sounds like a good idea also.'

" 'Wonderful. In that case, I will draw the documents together. Would it be convenient to call again toward the end of the week?'

" 'Yes, I suppose that would be fine.'

"I gave Wagstaff all of my details as John Radford and—given my supposed temporary living arrangements—asked him to correspond with me via the Post Office on Marylebone Road.

" 'I will indeed, my dear sir; I will confirm it by letter, but let us provisionally say Friday morning at ten o'clock?'

" 'That would be ideal Mr. Wagstaff,' I said shaking his hand heartily. 'I will look forward to hopefully seeing you then.'

"Prior to returning to Baker Street, I set about doing some research into the so-called Dulwich Children's Fund. It transpires that it is listed in the index of London charities, but that is where any legitimacy begins and ends. The three names of fellow-trustees given to me by Wagstaff turn out to be a deceased gas-lighter, a retired tailor who knew nothing about the matter, and a plumber's mate from Bermondsey. *Ha!* The effrontery of the man!"

"I'm sure all of his other victims were too grief-stricken to think so lucidly," I said, almost to myself.

"Indeed," said my friend as our cab slowed to its destination. "Now let us see how he reacts to someone who can."

Four

The office of Silas Wagstaff was on Wyndham Avenue, a stylish
Regency thoroughfare with a long sweeping crescent and trees either
side of the road. It was this elegant tranquillity that afforded the
solicitor a perfect cover which allowed him to carry out his heinous
activities unmolested and unsuspected.

We climbed the few steps to the front door and Holmes rang
the bell. Moments later, a tall thin man with a ramrod-straight back
opened the door. Upon seeing my friend, his self-assured demeanour
appeared to alter slightly. I assumed from this that he recognised
my companion from his previous visit but—knowing my friend as I
do—no doubt Holmes had altered his own attire and demeanour in
order to confuse and distract his opponent.

"Good morning, Mr. Kent." Holmes ignored the clerk's
uncertainty and strode past him with characteristic confidence across
the hallway. "I assume Mr. Wagstaff is in his office?"

I followed Holmes across the reception area toward the door
at its furthest point. Kent came scampering behind us and, as
Holmes entered, the clerk bundled past us to announce, with some
uncertainty, the arrival of his employer's client.

Silas Wagstaff was a short, rotund man of around sixty, with
a high forehead and a wide nose on which was perched a pair of
tortoiseshell spectacles. As he looked up from his desk, his expression
mirrored that of his clerk some moments earlier.

"Mr…Radford," he said hesitantly, "and this must be your
friend, Mr. Wilson." He rose from his desk and appeared to regain
some composure. "Gentlemen, please, sit down. Kent, please bring
us some refreshment."

The clerk left and we remained standing. Again, Wagstaff
attempted to break the uncomfortable silence. "Please, gentlemen, sit
down. I have drafted your will, Mr. Radford, and I think you'll find
everything is in order, including Mr. Wilson here acting as Katy's
guardian in the unlikely event of your passing." He had a strange
manner of speaking which was both obsequious and patronising;

all the while I sensed that he was inwardly amusing himself by deliberately misleading his vulnerable clients.

"Unlikely?" queried Holmes. "Come, come, Mr. Wagstaff, I think my passing would be extremely likely if I continued to allow you to act for me."

"I'm sorry, I don't understand," said the solicitor, whose disposition appeared to be changing from one of uncertainty to one of concern.

At that point Kent entered with a tray on which there was a steaming pot with three cups and a plate containing what appeared to be slices of fruit loaf.

"Ah, please come in, Kent," said Holmes. "I see you have some of that distinctive loaf I so enjoyed earlier this week."

Kent put the tray on Wagstaff's desk and, with a dismissive nod from his master, left the room.

"Shall I pour the tea, Mr. Wagstaff?" asked my friend. "I wouldn't want you to accidentally spill it again."

The solicitor sat in silence, unsure of how to respond, as Holmes poured one cup of tea and placed it in front of him. He then lifted one slice of the loaf onto a plate with the serving tongs and put it beside the tea.

"I don't think I am particularly hungry, actually," spluttered Wagstaff.

He reached down to the bottom drawer of his desk, as if to retrieve some papers that were pertinent to the matter, but Holmes was alive to his intentions—he slammed down his cane on Wagstaff's wrist, trapping it in the open drawer. Under the solicitor's splayed fingers I saw a revolver.

Holmes eyes darted from the weapon to its owner. "A pretty affair this is turning out to be, Mr. Wagstaff."

"Who are you? What is this all about?" Wagstaff attempted to keep up the façade of confidence and authority, but it was draining away by the minute.

Holmes moved his cane from the solicitor's wrist to under his chin and pushed him back in his seat, closing the drawer with his foot as he did so. "My name is Sherlock Holmes, and this is my friend and colleague, Dr. Watson."

Wagstaff's eyes went wide behind his thick lenses.

"I see my name is familiar to you," added Holmes.

"You have deceived me." Wagstaff tried his best to sound like the wronged party.

"I salute your effrontery, but it simply won't do. *You* are the deceiver, the thief, and the murderer."

Rarely have I seen Holmes so angry, as he jabbed his cane under Wagstaff's chin to emphasise each accusation.

"I…I don't know what you are talking about," Wagstaff said, desperate now.

Holmes released the cane and took a calming breath. "I notice you haven't eaten your cake," he said. "Of course, neither of us should be surprised by that; when I visited the other day, I took some away with me, along with the tea you served. It was not made by your wife as you claimed; amongst other things, I discovered that you are unmarried. I tested the…*refreshment* and confirmed my suspicion that it was poisoned—both tea and cake laced with aconitine.

"What a nice person you are, Wagstaff; you pray on the bereaved by poisoning them and stealing their estates, while leaving their children starving and destitute."

"That is a serious charge," blustered the solicitor.

"One that you can discuss at length with Inspector Hopkins, who has a warrant for your arrest," replied Holmes.

As if on cue, I heard a four-wheeler pull up outside, and a kerfuffle in the hallway resulted in Stanley Hopkins barging into the office with three uniformed men.

"Good morning Mr. Holmes, Doctor," said the inspector, and then, turning his attention to the seated Wagstaff, "So this is the man you informed us about, Mr. Holmes."

"It is indeed, Hopkins," replied my friend. Holmes proceeded to repeat his findings to the inspector and informed him of the solicitor's *modus operandi*, including handing over the letter he had picked up from the post office that morning.

"Thank you, Mr. Holmes, another triumph. We'll take it from here."

His men marched the criminal out in handcuffs, and we returned to Baker Street.

In the weeks that followed, the body of the unfortunate Gerald Rutherford was exhumed, along with three other suspected victims. As Holmes had predicted, traces of aconitine were found in each body, and it was enough to convict Wagstaff, who went to the gallows as Holmes had hoped.

His clerk was found guilty as an accessory and sentenced to hard labour, after it was established that, after Wagstaff had murdered the surviving parent in each case, Kent had taken the orphaned children and discarded them in some far corner of London to fend for themselves.

In the days following the conclusion of the case, I read in the *Pall Mall Gazette* of the latest atrocity in the East End, and it struck me for the first time that two such killers were operating in different parts of London simultaneously. The methods of Wagstaff and the affluent setting of South London may have been very different from the horror and violence perpetrated by the so-called Ripper in the slums of Whitechapel, but the net result was the same: multiple deaths of innocent people. Unfortunately the latter murderer has yet to be apprehended, but at least the good people of South London have had *their* threat removed.

As for Holmes, I recall him commenting of his exhaustion following the Jonathan Small case and that of the Dulwich Solicitor, and how he would welcome an escape from London for a while. We would be in luck, as the following weeks would be taken up by not one, but two cases in the fresh air and spectacular setting of Dartmoor.

The Adventure of the Missing Master

By Phillip Vine

Islington, London, September 2021

The knocking seemed familiar, but I could not put a name to the rat-a-tat-tat tune that was played by a cane walking stick upon the oak veneer of the front door of our Islington flat.

"Aren't you going to get that, John?"

My wife's urgent voice threaded its way from the bathroom, through the living room, and into my study.

"Alright, Mary, alright."

I heard the impatience, the unkindness in my words.

I had hoped, with the assistance of my wife's planned expeditions to the coffee shops of Upper Street and to the Estorick Collection of Modern Italian Art in Canonbury Square, to enjoy undisturbed time to complete my monograph on the polyphonic motets of Orlande de Lassus, the subject closest to my heart since the completion of my doctorate in Renaissance Musicology at Brunel University.

I shuffled through the apartment, pausing to admire the Modigliani sketches recently purchased by my wife and hung in the hallway, hoping all the while that the knocking on our door would cease.

"Hurry up, darling, or we will miss our visitor."

I glanced behind me to see Mary, her body enveloped in a brilliant white bath robe, her hair wrapped in a turban of towel. I waved unfriendly arms at my wife, signalling that her state of undress was inappropriate with a stranger at our door.

The knocking, meanwhile, had become a constant hammering.

The man—and the postulant had to be male, I was sure of it, with the unabated violence of his demands for entry—was persistent, aggressive, and rude. I determined to send him away with a flea in his ear, or worse, if necessary.

"I'm coming," I shouted.

"You don't recognise me, Watson?"

Before me stood a tall figure, upright and straight as a flagpole, gaunt, emaciated, his countenance as white as chalk, as cragged as a rock face.

"Surely you must remember me."

The visitor's voice was thin as wind, yet bold enough to command the silencing of a storm.

"I don't know, I, er..." It was unusual for me to stumble over my words. After all, I now lectured for a living, sharing my wisdom relating to all things historical-musical and musical-historical.

"Come now, Watson, aren't you going to invite me in?"

The stranger was already removing his old-fashioned bowler hat and offering me his walking cane and his tweed overcoat.

There *was* something familiar about the man.

"Mary," I called, anxiety and puzzlement in my voice.

I hoped my wife was now dressed and that she would unravel the stranger's mystery.

"I'm glad you made an honest woman of her at last, Watson."

The visitor's face lit and lifted at the emergence of the beautiful woman from the shadows at the far end of the hallway.

"Mary Morstan," said the stranger.

"Holmes," said Watson's wife, "how delightful to see you again."

The newcomer bowed his head in acknowledgement.

"You must remember Sherlock Holmes, John, surely you must."

"You don't mean to tell me you don't believe in reincarnation, Watson?"

"All that Eastern guff, it's all poppycock, stuff and nonsense, whoever you say you are." My voice was a bluster of wind.

"If not through the enjoyment of previous lives, how else, Watson, would you explain the subject of your study, de Lassus, his genius, his ability to become *maestro di cappella* at the Basilica of Saint John Lateran in Rome at the astonishing age of twenty-one?

"How else explain my own particular, peculiar genius?"

The man my wife had called Sherlock Holmes paused, as if to admire the strength, the compulsion of his own arguments.

My eyes turned toward my wife, took in the lush extravagance of her blonde hair, her powdered face, her striking blue eyes, and signalled to her for assistance.

Instead, Mary Watson—nee Morstan—turned to the newcomer.

"In all our time together, Holmes, John and I have never discussed our spiritual beliefs."

"Most, interesting, Mary, a most curious lack, too, if I may say so."

"Yet, for myself, Holmes, I never doubted either the art or the science of reincarnation. It is the sole philosophy, to my mind, that makes sense of *everything*."

I heard the passion in my wife's words and saw the intensity in her eyes and my old enemy, my jealousy, flared in my breast.

"I say, Holmes," I said, and I knew I was trapped in whatever web my visitor was weaving, in whatever story the newcomer was about to tell.

"Well, I'll leave you boys to catch up on old times."

Mary's voice was now light as air, as happy and relaxed as a child's, and I understood she had once—in a former lifetime perhaps—been in love with Holmes.

"Enjoy your visit to Estorick's, Mary," our visitor said.

"How did you know, Holmes?"

"Elementary, Mrs. Watson, a merely superficial example of the deductive process."

I watched as my wife's smile widened and my own memories—from another lifetime indeed—began to coalesce.

"Well, Mary, I have seen the way you have been casting longing glances at the Modiglianis on your wall, and I know Estorick's contains more fine examples of the modern master's work."

I, meanwhile, was attempting to tame the twin beasts of my anger and my jealousy at the way my wife had been captivated and manipulated by this stranger who I now understood was not a stranger after all.

"In addition, Mary, there is a complimentary ticket for a private viewing at the aforementioned gallery waiting for you to pick up from your hall table as you leave."

Both my wife and my friend from a former lifetime shared in the rush of their laughter.

"I see, too, Mary, from the manner of your dress and your lipsticked mouth that you are meeting an old flame at Estorick's."

"What?" My voice was unbrooked anger now. "This really is too much, Holmes."

"I am joking, Watson, merely showing you how ridiculous that untamed possessiveness of yours can still be, even now, even after all your lifetimes of learning.

"Your lovely, loyal wife, who adores you more than you deserve, is meeting a colleague from work, Jennifer Cross, MA, and an expert in Etruscan terracotta sculpture, for coffee and then for shared artistic appreciation at Estorick's."

"Holmes, I am sorry, but you astound me." There was unbridled relief as well as admiration in my words.

"Simplicity itself, Watson."

"How so, Holmes?"

"In your travels up and down this hallway, Watson, you have failed to notice Ms. Cross's business card lying next to the invitation from the gallery."

My face fell, collapsed into mortification.

"I see your observational skills, Watson, appear to have lapsed totally since our previous adventures together."

"But what about the coffee, Holmes?" Mary's voice was triumphant. "How do you know Jennifer and I are meeting for coffee?"

"Ah, Mary, you have me there, but how could anyone live in the vicinity of Upper Street and be unfamiliar with the delights of the Euphorium Bakery, the Gallipoli Bistro, or those of the Ginger & Lime?"

After admiring my wife's cheery wave of departure, I settled to a study of the man who called himself Holmes.

Naturally enough, I was aware of the fictional character created by Arthur Conan Doyle in the late nineteenth century, recalled even a film I had watched at the Aubin Cinema in Shoreditch with Mary when she was merely my fiancée. It had been in black and white, and there had been a murderous hound somewhere in the story. I recalled that I had fallen asleep and awoken to find myself abandoned and alone in the back row of the picture house.

It occurred to me now for the first time—slow-witted as I undoubtedly am—that my name was the same as the great detective's accomplice.

I raised myself from both my reverie and my armchair.

Holmes was perusing my bookshelves on the far side of the room.

"I say, Watson, these old volumes here are most interesting."

The tall stranger was blowing dust from a leather-bound book.

"Oh, those, I've never read them," I said.

"But you should, Watson, you really should."

"Well, they were my grandfather's volumes—he wrote them actually—he left them to me in his will."

"This one, for instance, Watson, it's called *A Study in Scarlet, being a reprint from the reminiscences of John H Watson, MD, late of the army medical department*."

"Gosh, that's right, that's him, my grandfather. He was a doctor-doctor, unlike me, who isn't really a doctor at all, except in an academic sort of way."

"You underestimate yourself, Watson," said the man calling himself Holmes. "You enjoy the possession of some enviable talents."

"I do?"

"You do, Watson, you do indeed, and I require your assistance in a peculiar case I have been invited by my brother to solve."

"It was just yesterday morning when Mycroft came to see me."
Holmes's voice was a siren song, and I knew I would be unable to
resist any demand made of me by the newcomer.

"My brother is a powerful man, Watson."

"Did you say *Mycroft*, Holmes?"

Something was stirring in my mind, something shifting from the
back to the front of my brain.

"I remember," I said. "Your brother, Holmes, you said he *is* the
British government, a man who moves and shakes behind the public
utterances and public actions of the administration."

I watched as a stealthy smile formed on my visitor's bony face.

"We worked together, Holmes, on a case involving the theft of
plans for a submarine that would revolutionise naval warfare."

"You are correct, Watson; the recovery of the Bruce-
Partington plans proved crucial in the defence of the Empire in the
previous century."

"The last century, Holmes? But how is that?"

"Reincarnation, Watson, that is how, and your memory of at
least one of our adventures together proves my point precisely."

"I still don't understand, Holmes."

I heard the uncertainty, the frisson of fear in my voice.

"My dear friend, on occasions you are as dim as ever you were
back in your previous lifetime." There was impatience in the visitor's
countenance and his suspicion of a smile was a ghost from former
times together. "Watson, wake up, please."

Holmes's face was a tangle of irascibility and frustration.

"How could you recall names and events from the past if you had
not also lived in those times?"

"I suppose you must be right, Holmes."

My words staggered from my mouth.

"I am *always* right, Watson, and you should know that by now."

Memories were stirred and shaken inside my head.

"But we are wasting our time, Watson, and there is work to do."

Holmes's ridiculous bowler hat was already on his head, his cane in his hand, and his gloved hand upon the door of our flat.

"Wait for me, Holmes."

My friend moved fast, leaping from stone step to stone step down the staircase, almost overtaking time as he ran into the street beyond.

I recollected now other occasions when I had followed Holmes, breathless, red-faced, muscles straining in pursuit of my friend. *The Adventure of the Solitary Cyclist, The Disappearance of Lady Frances Carfax, The Adventure of the Sussex Vampire.*

When time permitted, I would have to read the volumes bequeathed to me by my grandfather.

"Wait, Holmes," I called in despair, "you haven't told me yet what Mycroft wanted when he came to see you yesterday."

Holmes was seated, his back to the wall, in a dimly lit corner of a public house adjacent to the underground railway station of Highbury and Islington.

He was drumming his long fingers against the table, impatient, while I chewed upon a ham and mustard sandwich.

"You should eat, Holmes."

"I have no time for triviality, Watson, for inconsequentiality."

"You cannot live on fresh air, Holmes."

"I can assure you that the air in this part of London is no cleaner than it was one hundred and more years ago when we last moved in these quarters. The pollution is merely of a different singularity."

I saw no benefit in arguing with my friend and filled my mouth with the last crusts of my sandwich.

"Holmes," I asked, "now, what was it Mycroft wanted?"

"It concerns reincarnation, Watson, the rebirth of a figure crucial for the future of the world."

I sat bolt upright in my chair, the last crumbs from my meal tumbling to the floor as I straightened my back and tightened my stomach muscles.

"I see you are ready for action, Watson, and action you shall see indeed."

I smiled a weak smile, fear finding one small unfilled part of my bulging stomach.

"Have you a gun about your person, Watson?"

"Holmes, whatever I was in my previous lifetime, I am that man no longer."

"A pity, Watson, you were a companion of matchless bravery when I last called you to my side."

"I am a lecturer, Holmes, in medieval music, and find no need for weapons."

"I recollect one thrilling adventure, Watson, involving the apprehension of several German spies and, if I recall it aright, you omitted from your account of our capture of Von Bork more than one incidence of your own valour and self-sacrifice."

"I cannot call it to mind, Holmes, reincarnation or no reincarnation."

I found myself the subject of intense scrutiny.

"No, Watson, but you'll do for me now, you'll have to do."

I thought we were an odd couple, one who seemed as if he ate no
fat and the other as if he ate no lean, and we hurried from the bar,
hastened onto the street where crowds poured like wine from a
bottle, from the opening of the tube station, where street vendors
called out their wares.

Holmes took an *Evening Standard* that was thrust in his
direction, paused to glance at the headline, shoved the newspaper
under my nose.

"There's our problem, Watson, damn it."

The headline was stark, as dark and full of menace as
Holmes's face.

MISSING MASTER MAY MEAN WAR

"I don't understand, Holmes, you still haven't explained…"

"How can you be so dumb, Watson?"

"But you never told me…"

"Curses, Watson, but my brother was depending on me to solve
this problem *before* it became fodder for the press."

Inside one of the dark recesses of the Stranger's Room at the
Diogenes Club, I glimpsed, through a thick fug of tobacco smoke,
the recumbent figure of Mycroft Holmes.

"You remember Dr. Watson?"

"But of course, Holmes."

"And our adventures together?"

The seated man made no effort to rise from his armchair and
his cushions. His face was enveloped in a grey-blue smog, making it
difficult for me to picture him clearly.

"Indeed, Holmes, there was an affair, I seem to recall, of a Greek interpreter."

"You are correct, Mycroft, a most singular problem that Watson helped me to solve."

The hurried journey from Islington to the Diogenes, situated in the secret heart of Whitehall, had left me too tired to protest at any praise from my friend. By now, too, with the clouded vision of Mycroft Holmes before me, I had no further doubts on the matter of reincarnation.

"I am sorry, Mycroft," I heard Holmes whisper, "but someone on your side has leaked this information to the press."

I watched as Holmes placed his copy of the *Evening Standard* face-up on the table between us.

Mycroft picked up the paper, glanced at the headline, returned it to Holmes in what I regarded as a most insouciant manner.

"It is a sad indictment, indeed, Holmes, of our modern, degraded age."

"There is no more I can do, then, Mycroft?" Holmes's voice was edged with sadness, wistfulness at the apparent loss of an adventure.

"On the contrary, my dear brother, the spy within our department is the man we need to apprehend, the traitor whose tracks you need to follow, Holmes."

Mycroft rose unsteadily to his feet, his rotund physique lending him the momentary appearance of a great ape awakening from deep sleep.

"Come with me."

I followed the two brothers into an unlit corner of the Stranger's Room and heard a key turn in a lock. "In here, Holmes, in here, Dr. Watson." Mycroft's voice was barely audible. "No one can follow us here."

A dim electric light bulb, hanging, naked, from the centre of a whitewashed ceiling provided sufficient illumination for the task of talk, for an explanation of the current problems bedevilling the

British government, and all that related to the *Standard's* headline concerning a missing master.

"For the last dozen years or so, Dr. Watson, we have been sheltering a Tibetan *tulku*, a reincarnation of the warrior emperor, Songtsen Gampo, a man so ruthless he had his argumentative younger brother, Tsansong, burned to death."

I noted the passage of a serpentine smile and a knowing look between Mycroft and Sherlock Holmes.

"This man," Holmes interjected, "believes it is his destiny to free Tibet from the clutches of the Chinese communists."

"And he has support from within the highest echelons of the British ruling classes," Mycroft added, "and possibly that of the PM himself."

I felt myself blushing in the small, locked room with the dim light and the lack of furniture. I could not but be flattered by my inclusion within the orbit of these startling revelations.

"The problem is, as the world and his wife now know, Watson, that our *tulku* has disappeared from his safe house."

"There is, of course, no real danger of war," Holmes's brother added. "That is mere paper talk, but, as I understand it, if the Chinese have taken our Tibetan friend, it may lead to all our clandestine efforts on behalf of subjugated peoples inside the Chinese Empire coming to nothing and, if our man talks when questioned, it could mean the arrest and torture and even deaths of hundreds of our agents working in the East."

"But what can we *do*, Mycroft?"

I was taken aback by the sound of my own voice—concerned, strident, ready for action, anything at all that was required to preserve the interests of my country. It was as if, I thought, I had returned to inhabit my previous life as a military man who had served the Empire in India and Afghanistan.

"What you can do, Dr. Watson, with the able assistance of my younger brother, is find the traitor within our midst."

"I must phone Mary," I said, "let her know I shall be away for a few days."

The reunited pair of private detective and willing assistant found themselves at London Bridge, awaiting the departure of the next train to the Sussex countryside.

"Please don't use that mobile device, Watson."

"But, Holmes…"

"The Chinese will be on our tail, Watson, and they will be waiting and listening for any further information regarding our movements and our whereabouts."

"But, Mary…"

"If Mary Morstan is the woman I know she is, Watson, and she remembers her previous incarnation, she will already know we are about our nation's business."

I followed Holmes from the first-class carriage, stepped down onto the platform at Three Bridges, watched as Holmes appeared to conjure a taxi as if from thin air.

"Forge Wood," Holmes said. His voice was both soft and imperious.

"Will that be the Big House, guv'nor?"

"It will, and there will be a generous tip if you make it there within five minutes, and further remuneration if you can tell me who else has made this journey earlier today."

There was an initial, and surprising, silence from the driver.

"You see, it's like this it is, guv'nor, one gent gave me an extraordinarily generous reward on the understanding I would say nothing about his direction of travel."

"I will double it," said Holmes, his words fired quickly as bullets from an army revolver.

"Well," said the taxi man, slyly, "he was a toff—bowler hat like yours, guv'nor, that's what he was."

"And…"

"He had a broken nose, he did, like an eagle's beak, a bald eagle he was too, beneath his hat, which he raised from his head when he bid me goodbye."

"That's our man, Watson," Holmes whispered in Watson's ear.

The Big House turned out to be a conference centre in deciduous woodland reserved exclusively for the Ministry of Defence.

Inside—and awaiting course leaders and guest speakers—was a gaggle of civil servants, including four men and two women suspected by Mycroft Holmes of betraying state secrets, including the whereabouts of the Tibetan master.

"Time was, Watson," said Holmes, "when women knew their place."

In my role as the detective's assistant, I did not know whether to answer in my modern man married to a working woman incarnation or from the depths of my darker, unreconstructed, Victorian self.

I said nothing.

A ripple of applause greeted us as we entered the building.

"Good God, Holmes, they think we have come to lecture them."

"Well, that's your preserve these days, Watson, and you can tell them all about de Lassus and his Franco-Flemish school of polyphony."

Half an hour later, after Holmes had given a meticulous account of the importance of mastery of both disguise and of foreign languages in the role of a spy, when the conference attendees, including Mycroft's six suspects, were gathered in the refectory, my friend murmured in my ear in extremely muted tones, "I've been such a dunderhead, Watson."

"What do you mean, Holmes?"

"I've been played for a fool." The detective's voice was full of regret, empty, all of a sudden, of ego.

"But, Holmes, he's here, the bald man with the boxer's nose, and he looks a suspicious cove, if ever I've seen one."

"It's true, Watson, he may well be a double agent, but that is of no concern to us now."

Holmes rose to his full height, thanked the gathered men and women from the ministry, apologised for his impending and unavoidable absence, and rushed from the eating hall. I followed behind as if tied and towed by some invisible rope.

"Back to London, Watson, as fast as we can."

"But Holmes..."

"It was something he said, Watson, something he said..."

On the return journey, Holmes was so distracted he sat down in a second-class carriage of the train.

He refused to say anything about the case in hand other than a handful of words to the effect that a switch was about to be effected and that there was so little time to prevent it.

He smoked a pipe of Balkan Sobranie tobacco until a guard appeared and threatened him with the transport police unless he extinguished his disgusting bonfire.

I stayed silent for the duration of the journey, lest my words should either offend my friend or disturb the depths of his thoughts.

"You can use that infernal telephone of yours now, Watson," Holmes said at last as the train approached London Bridge. "Phone Inspector Lestrade at New Scotland Yard and tell him to meet us at the Diogenes."

Outside the exclusive London club, I studied the police inspector closely, struggling to come to terms with my fragmentary memory of a previous lifetime over one hundred years ago.

Lestrade was short to Holmes's tall, but both men were lean as racing whippets, both men's eyes and brains restless, the policeman's eyes shifty to the private detective's deep and still pools of concentration.

I thought I recalled a case in which Lestrade turned up at a lodgings house in Baker Street with an apparently insuperable problem involving broken busts of the Emperor Napoleon. One sentence of the policeman's ran around and around inside my head.

"Now, Mr. Holmes, you have got the facts."

A century and more later, Lestrade was again providing Holmes with crucial information. I strained my ears but could not make sense from the stray words I heard.

Soon, Holmes was hammering on the front door of the Diogenes, arguing with the doorman attempting to prevent the entry of Lestrade, who was not a member of the club.

A flash of the police inspector's credentials proved more effective than Holmes's reasoning.

I followed the two men upstairs and into the heart of the Diogenes.

"To the Stranger's Room, Watson, as fast as you can."

Holmes's voice provided encouragement to my tired limbs and overworked lungs.

"In there, Lestrade, quickly."

Holmes was pointing at the door on the far side of the room.

The police inspector's shoulder, however, proved inadequate to the task of breaking down the door. "Watson," Holmes cried, "your extra weight should prove sufficient to the task."

I doubted my strength but, nevertheless, ran full tilt at the locked door. The wood splintered and I fell to the bare floor of the room where once, in what seemed at least a lifetime ago, I had listened to Mycroft Holmes explaining the problem of the missing master.

The same pallid electric light leaked from a dirty bulb hanging from the ceiling but, seated in the centre of a circle of faint luminescence, was the bound and gagged figure of Mycroft Holmes.

"It's Moriarty," Holmes hissed.

"It *was* Moriarty," his elder brother insisted, once the gag of rags had been removed from his mouth. "His disguise was impeccable."

"It was something he said…"

"Even I thought he was me," Mycroft exclaimed.

"He called me *Holmes*," the great detective said, "and you never do that, Mycroft, you always call me Sherlock."

I watched, still uncomprehending, as Holmes beat his breast.

"Oh, I have been the king of fools, Mycroft."

I saw a sly smile spread across the wizened face of Lestrade, watched as the smile was folded away by the policeman, as Holmes turned to him for help.

"We must close all the ports, all the airfields, Lestrade, we must not let them get away."

"Indeed, Mr. Holmes, indeed."

Now it was my turn to smile as I understood the proper relationship between Holmes and Lestrade, of master to apprentice, had been restored.

"Yes, hurry, do, Lestrade," said the real Mycroft Holmes. "Moriarty and Songtsen Gampo intend to rule and ruin the world, and I believe that, with the professor's evil genius and the *tulku's* Tibetan magic, that is a real possibility."

"Watson," said Holmes, "we must return to Sussex, where I
suspect a man with a bald head and a broken nose may lead us to
our prize."

In a Rolls-Royce borrowed from Mycroft Holmes, and with a
chauffeur seconded from the Metropolitan Police, Holmes and I
sped south through Surrey and Sussex toward the conference centre
near Three Bridges.

"You recall Professor Moriarty, of course, Watson?"

It was as much a challenge to me as a question, a throwing down
of a gauntlet, a test and a trial of my credence of reincarnation.

I felt my head nodding in assurance.

"You're lying, Watson."

"Sorry, Holmes, it's all been such a whirl of events, it's been
difficult to deal with the philosophy at the same time."

"It's memory, Watson, that's all it is." Then the dark clouds
of Holmes's face cleared and were replaced by the sunshine of a
rare smile.

"I'm sorry," the detective said, "I've been expecting too much of
you too soon, my friend,"

"Who was he, then, Holmes, this Moriarty?"

"Who *is* he, Watson?" Holmes permitted his eyes to savour the
contours and the living colours of the passing countryside. "Moriarty
is the only man with talents worthy of my own, Watson. He killed
me once, and I killed him, yet here we are both alive once more."

"I do recall now..."

"He must be stopped, Watson. At all costs, he must be stopped."

The car slewed to a halt in the conference centre's car park.

"Come, Watson, come."

There was no other vehicle parked on the tarmac.

We raced toward the building, flew through an open door that flapped in the breeze, and Holmes called out, "Police, ho!"

The response was a silence so deep it might have swallowed the world.

"There's no one here, Holmes."

"He's here," Holmes whispered, "the man with the broken nose."

"What is he?"

"He's the link, Watson, the link between civilisation and chaos, and he has betrayed the former in favour of the latter, and we can only trust he will see the error of his ways before it is too late."

"How do you know all that, Holmes?"

"Keep quiet, Watson, and listen."

Still, though, the only sound was silence.

"If he's not here, Watson, he will be at the airport."

Returned to the Rolls-Royce, Holmes issued directions.

"How can you come to these conclusions, Holmes?"

My voice was reverential.

"I noticed a private airfield behind the woods as we approached the conference centre."

"I didn't see…"

"No, Watson, you were asleep."

"I was not, Holmes."

"All people, Watson, who are not awake, are asleep," he said. "Over there, driver, that's right."

I was hurt by my friend's jibe but still understood this was not a time to cling to resentments.

On the field ahead of us was a Cessna jet, crouched and ready to fly.

"The old Watson," Holmes said, as we began to run across the field, "would have had his service pistol loaded and ready to fire."

I heard a manic laugh escape from my friend's throat, and understood it as the thrill of the chase.

"At least, I'm here, and I'm ready to help," I said, gasping for breath as I tried to keep pace with Holmes.

"And I'm glad of it, Watson, so very glad indeed."

Shots rang out from the direction of the Cessna, bullets flew past our heads, and a low, red sun hung in the Sussex sky.

To me, it did, indeed, feel as if the future of the world hung in the balance.

"Take cover, Holmes."

"No time, Watson."

We were at the foot of the steps leading into the belly of the plane.

The Cessna's engines roared like a wounded animal.

I found my right hand in Holmes's as the detective hauled me deep inside the pit of the beast.

"And so we meet once more, Mr. Holmes." Moriarty's voice was sly as sin and his Glock .22 pistol was pointing at the great detective's head. "It is so good to see you again."

"You too, Professor," Holmes said with understated irony.

"You may take us up and away now," Moriarty instructed the pilot, his eyes never leaving Holmes for a second. "Mr. Holmes and his friend, Dr. Watson, will be leaving us once we reach twenty thousand feet."

Shamefully, I tumbled to the floor of the jet as the Cessna began to accelerate down the runway. I was distraught at my fall. I had hoped somehow to throw myself in front of Holmes and take the impact of any bullet meant for my friend's heart or head. Now I was on all fours like a dog. When I tried to raise myself, Moriarty commanded me to stay where I was and not to move on pain of death.

Holmes was as silent as the grave.

The Cessna was in full flight, its destination unknown to me, unknown too, in all likelihood, even to Holmes.

"Where is Songtsen Gampo?"

At last, the private detective's question broke the silence the way a stone splits the surface of a lake.

"He is safe, Mr. Holmes."

"And where is the man with the boxer's nose?"

"Safe too." Moriarty's voice was hypnotic, soothing yet sinister.

"I think not," said Holmes, and his voice was cold as time.

Behind Moriarty, I could see the man with the flattened, crooked nose, his arm raised, baseball bat in hand, held hard above the evil professor's head.

Too late, the master criminal turned.

What happened next I struggled to recall when I returned home to our flat in Islington.

Mary was all questions and I was all forgetfulness.

It was as if my determination to come to terms with the ramifications of reincarnation had obliterated all else from my mind.

"Holmes will be here shortly, Mary."

I wiped the sweat from my brow.

"He will explain everything,"

In fact, within the hour, a party had gathered in our compact living room.

Holmes led the way, followed by his brother, Mycroft, and by Lestrade and his Tibetan companion, Songtsen Gampo.

One moment later, another knock upon the front door, brought the arrival of a man with a bald head and a beaten-up face and broken nose.

"Well, well," I said, "if only Moriarty were here, we would be complete."

No one laughed, no one even smiled at my feeble attempt at humour. It was ever thus, I thought, and resigned myself to wordlessness as my part in the proceedings. I guessed it would be the great detective who broke the silence, and I was not disappointed.

"Thank you, Mary Morstan," Holmes said, and his eyes sparkled as he spoke. "Thank you for permitting the loan of your husband in this enterprise, in this adventure to cap all adventures."

I had rarely seen my friend so flirtatious, and my stomach tightened in preparation for battle against my old enemy.

"As it turned out, Watson was an invaluable ally, in spite of losing consciousness at the climax of the affair in midair above the coast of Normandy."

I looked shame-faced and my wife squealed with delight and amusement at this information.

"For your benefit, then, Watson, what happened after our brave and noble boxer here bashed Moriarty over the back of the head, was a sequence of events, one tumbling over another, the sum of which was a narrow avoidance of descent into the North Sea, the arrest of a revived Moriarty by Lestrade, and the delivery of our Tibetan friend to a hospital where his stomach has been pumped clean of the noxious drugs administered to him by the Professor of Evil.

"And here we are, Watson, enjoying the coffee and company provided by your delightful spouse."

"But, Holmes…"

"I know, Watson, like your predecessor, the medical doctor, you will wish to write up these events, to secure their publication, and their pride of placement alongside the volumes bequeathed to you by your grandfather."

"And, in order to do so, I shall require some further elucidation of some points concerning this adventure…"

"Of course, Watson, your questions will be most welcome once we have all recovered from this ordeal."

I looked across the room for support and encouragement from my wife.

"Go on, John," said Mary, "you know you've always longed to write something a little less dry as dust than your studies of de Lassus," and Watson's beautiful wife blew a kiss across the room at her beloved husband, who could not fail at that moment to smile a smile that would have charmed the gods from their heavens.

"Holmes," he said, "I shall begin immediately, and you must come and see me again to review my progress, to correct any errors in the narrative, to fill in any gaps in my knowledge due to my inadvertent and unfortunate failure of my duty to pay full attention to events."

"Remember, though, Watson," Holmes said, "to be kind to all the characters in your story.

"My brother here deserves great praise for his work in saving both our nation and our world, and Lestrade here is surely the finest detective in all of modern London, and the saintly *tulku*, Songtsen Gampo, who will return now to his homeland and work for peace with China, and, not forgetting our heroic friend, who wishes fervently to remain anonymous, the man with the boxer's nose who saved us all from the loss of our current lifetimes."

"You are always welcome here, Holmes," said Mary Watson.

"Thank you, my dear," said Holmes, "and, when I return, there may even be further adventures, further crimes to solve, and these I would wish most ardently to share, with your permission, with my brave friend, Watson, who may yet prove to be as good a writer, and as good as a detective's apprentice, as I'm sure he is a husband."

The Pale Reflection

By L. C. Tyler

"This is a monstrous imposition!" I exclaimed. "Do you see what I was handed in the street, just now, right by your front door? Look at it! Does everyone who comes to visit you receive one of these?"

Holmes glanced up from a half-completed monograph on the secular music of Lassus, which he had been working on for some days. "Monstrous? It is scarcely more than a slight inconvenience," he said. "Do you think that I need to explain to my readers the difference between a sonnet and a sestina?"

"Almost certainly," I said. "Are you intending to do nothing about these people who hang around your door?"

"They are harmless," said Holmes, finally putting down his pen and turning toward me. "Whose advertisement is that?"

"Herbert Merrivale. Detective work of all sorts undertaken. Reasonable rates. Complete discretion. The most scientific and up-to-date methods of investigation guaranteed. Master of subterfuge and disguise."

"Ah, I have not come across him before."

"Well, there are at least three urchins with wads of paper like this by your front door even as I speak. Each represents a different imitator of yours. They trade, Holmes, on your good name and reputation. They seek to steal your own clients with promises of lower prices and I know not what else."

"Well, you may depend on it that none has as fine a chronicler as I have. Do you think I need explain to the readers of my monograph who Petrach was?"

"I fear that you will," I said. "This is your own fault, Holmes. Once you had achieved success in the field of detection, there were bound to be others who copied you. But when you disappeared for three years following your struggle with Moriarty at the Reichenbach Falls, they really grew in numbers. They hoped to take your place. They sought to mimic not only your methods, but even your dress and mannerisms. Though you are, at last, happily back with us, they have not retired from the scene, but actually have the impudence to distribute their grubby handbills on Baker Street."

"There is crime enough in London for us all," said Holmes. "Do you think anyone will notice if I make no reference to Lassus's Dutch songs?"

"Nobody at all," I said. "And you plan to do nothing about these inferior versions of yourself and their (doubtless) equally inferior assistants and narrators? Because if you won't, then I shall."

"Not for the moment," he said. "Neither of us has the necessary time. There is somebody coming up the stairs that I want you to meet."

"Who?" I asked.

"A gentleman who visited me earlier and rather melodramatically told me that we had perhaps only days to save the British Empire from a terrible fate."

"What did he mean by that?"

"I have no idea. I was in the middle of writing about Lassus's motets. I told him to go away and take several circuits of Regent's Park to calm down, then come back at the hour I was expecting your arrival. Any considerations of sixteenth-century choral music apart, I wanted you to hear what he has to say and to let me have your opinion of him."

"You mean you think he may be mad?"

"He did not strike me so."

"Then what help can I give you? I have defended the Empire in my own small way in the hills of Afghanistan. But of broader threats I happily know nothing. If it really is a matter that concerns the safety of this country, then surely your brother Mycroft, at the very centre of the government, would be a better judge of whether the man is speaking sense?"

A knock sounded at the door.

"Too late, I think, to send for my brother, who never ventures north of Oxford Street in any case. That urgent tapping will be Mr. Cromwell. Please be so good as to let him in, Watson. I shall tidy away my notes on Lassus. I don't think they will interest him much, do you?"

"Not in the slightest," I said.

Cromwell proved to be a man of middling height and well-dressed, though, I noted, with a small darn in the right knee of his trousers. I was pleased I'd seen it, because Holmes would expect me to notice such details.

My friend ushered our visitor into a chair by the fire. Though it was late spring, the afternoon was chilly and overcast and a brisk breeze was blowing down Baker Street.

"This," said Holmes, "is my trusted friend, Dr. Watson. You may say anything in front of him that you would say to me alone."

Cromwell nodded. "May I smoke?" he asked.

"Of course," said Holmes.

Cromwell produced a large, curved pipe, already filled, and lit it, expending three or four matches in the process. He sucked at it tentatively, coughed, inspected the glowing tobacco and coughed again.

"Where do you wish me to begin?" he asked when he regained his voice.

"Tell us about yourself," said Holmes.

"There's not much to relate," he said. "My name is Richard Cromwell. I am a bachelor and live in Clapham, near the common. I have a small private income—enough that I can please myself what I do. I therefore spend most of my days at the British Museum—I have a fancy to study Etruscan art."

"Commendably obscure," said Holmes with a nod. "So, how did you come across this intelligence that the Empire is in danger? From where we are sitting now, everything appears to be in order."

"Do not mock me, Mr. Holmes," said Cromwell. "I have chosen to come here, but I could as easily go elsewhere." He took a crumpled piece of paper from his pocket. "Merrivale sounds as every bit as good as you. Cheaper and employing the most modern methods. I've heard he's pretty clever. A master of disguise."

"Then go to Merrivale by all means," said Holmes suavely. "Since I have no idea who he is, I cannot say whether any of his claims are justified. As for the price, if the matter really concerns the safety of the Empire, I would scarcely charge you or anyone else."

"You've really never heard of him?"

"Not until I saw a similar piece of paper in Dr. Watson's hand earlier."

Cromwell scowled. "Very well. In any case, the matter is urgent, and I suspect Merrivale is a busy man. You are aware that the Queen is ill?"

"A slight cold, so I'd heard."

"At her age that could be enough to carry her off. She could be stiff as a board by tomorrow morning."

"There was a time when saying that could have had you hanged for treason. But in this decadent era, your remark is merely in poor taste. The nation would grieve if Her Majesty were to pass away, but the Prince of Wales has been waiting all his life to succeed her. The Empire would be in good hands."

"In the hands of a murderer?"

"You claim the Prince of Wales is a murderer?" said Holmes. He raised an eyebrow.

"It is certain. I will swear to it."

"Ah, then you seem determined to commit treason even by today's debased standards, or slander at the very least. Do you have proof of what you say?"

"No, but my cousin does. You must interview him."

"And he lives in Clapham too?"

"In Cambridge. He is a pharmacist there."

"And when do you claim this murder occurred?"

"More than thirty years ago."

"Your cousin witnessed it?"

"No, but he was an unwitting accomplice."

"And who was the victim?"

"Prince Albert, the Prince Consort."

"But Prince Albert died of typhoid," I said. "Sir William Jenner, whom I have the honour to know, was with him when he died. Jenner is our greatest expert on typhoid. He could not have been deceived."

"Not deceived, merely silenced," said Cromwell with a sneer. "The Queen knew well enough. She forbade an autopsy for fear that the truth should come out."

"Even so, what possible motive could there have been?"

"The Prince of Wales was then an undergraduate at Cambridge. He had attended military training in Ireland the summer before and formed a liaison with one Nelly Clifden. His father found out, a little too late, and travelled to Cambridge to reprimand him. They argued bitterly. Very heated words were exchanged. Prince Albert returned to Windsor, where he died shortly afterwards."

"More than two weeks afterwards," I said.

"It was a slow-acting poison."

"That sounds unlikely."

"I see that you doubt me, Dr. Watson, but what I say is true, nonetheless. You, Mr. Holmes, must go at once to Cambridge and speak to my cousin. After all these years, the matter weighs heavily on him. He wishes to confess. It was he who sold the Prince of Wales the poison."

"Then why does he not go to the authorities himself?"

"Because he does not wish to hang as an accessory, Mr. Holmes. But if he can persuade you that what he says is true and give you the name of a further witness, then you can take whatever action you see fit. Your word would be respected. The prime minister would act."

"And remove the Prince of Wales from the succession? I am not sure even Lord Rosebery can do that."

"The prince would need to stand down or be exposed. Perhaps even hanged."

"Or you could go to Merrivale," said Holmes with a smile.

"He too is respected," said Cromwell. "You may claim not to have heard of him, but one day his name will be as well-known as your own. And see here on this handbill: 'complete discretion.' That's what I need. That's what my cousin needs. Can you promise as much?"

"If what you say is true, then, other than to inform the authorities, not a word will pass my lips or the pen of Watson here."

"I don't need that," said Cromwell. "You may write it up as you choose. I merely want my name and that of my cousin changed when you do."

"Very well, Mr. Cromwell," said Holmes. "Please write down your cousin's name and where we are to find him. We shall travel to Cambridge by one of the mid-morning trains tomorrow. Then, on my return, I shall visit my brother, who is at the very centre of the web that makes up our Empire, and take his advice."

"No!" exclaimed Cromwell. "On no account must Mycroft Holmes be involved! He is part of the conspiracy that has long concealed the Prince of Wales's crime. You must go straight to

Lord Rosebery, or the Home Secretary at the very least, and inform him yourself."

Holmes nodded. "Very well, I shall do that, if your cousin confirms your story. Now, since our business is concluded, can I persuade you to join us for a simple bachelors' supper?"

Cromwell took out a silver pocket watch but scarcely glanced at it before announcing that he had another appointment. He seemed anxious to be on his way.

"That is a great pity," said Holmes. "A very great pity. We have veal pie. No? Are you sure? Very well, I would suggest that we meet again here at noon, in exactly one week's time. I shall let you know what I have discovered."

"So," said Holmes, when Cromwell had departed. "What do you make of that?"

"I do not think he is mad," I said. "He seems quite rational in everything except his faith in Merrivale as a detective. But surely his story is nonsense?"

"The outline is true enough. It is well-known—at least in the circles in which Mycroft moves—that the prince was enamoured of an actress of the name of Clifden at the time he was at Cambridge. And I fear, though it is not widely reported in our own newspapers, there have been many other ladies since then. The Prince Consort did indeed travel to Cambridge on the twenty-fifth of November, a few days before he died, to reprimand young Albert Edward. And though typhoid was given out as the cause of death, no autopsy was ever performed, at the Queen's personal request. But let us consider the man himself—Mr. Cromwell, I mean. I think he has told us a number of lies. He is not, for example, a bachelor."

"How do you know? Do you mean the neatness of the darning in his trousers?"

I was pleased that I had observed this, but Holmes shook his head.

"Well spotted, but not just that. There was also the question of the pipe. Like me, he is what you describe as a self-poisoner with tobacco. But a single man amongst other single men will take it for granted that he may light up. His request for permission suggests that he normally lives in more civilised circles. And his feeble attempts to get the pipe going show he is not allowed to smoke very often. Then there was his response to my invitation to sup with us. A bachelor breakfasts without knowing where he will dine. Any invitation is welcome to him. But a married man knows he is expected home for a meal in the evening and woe betide him if he is late—unless he already has his wife's permission to be out."

"Indeed," I said. "So you knew he would not accept your offer?"

"I very much hoped he would not, because he seems a rather tedious individual. There would of course have been veal pie to spare if he had—I am not completely heartless."

"So that is one lie."

"I think so. He has also looked more into my personal life than he admitted. He knew for example that my brother was called Mycroft—few do unless they are very well acquainted with me. I was not an arbitrary choice for this task."

"So his threat to go to Merrivale…"

"Was a mere bluff? Yes, it was not simply professional pride that convinces me that is correct. Merrivale would not have served his purpose. Let us call Mrs. Hudson and tell her that we shall eat early. Writing about Lassus always gives me an appetite."

I received two telegrams at my practice the following morning, both reply-paid. The first was from Holmes, instructing me to be on the ten fifty-five train to Cambridge. I sent a message back to say I should be there. The second telegram I read, smiled at, and stuffed into my jacket pocket. Then I hailed a cab and asked to be taken to Liverpool Street.

Holmes was already lolling on his first-class seat, his long legs stretched out before him, with his pipe lit and issuing almost as much smoke as the engine.

"This is a very late train for us to be catching," I said. "We could have almost completed our work by now and be setting off back to London."

"Perhaps," said Holmes. "But I have had a profitable morning at the British Museum."

"You wished to ascertain whether Mr. Cromwell was really studying Etruscan vases?"

"I had not thought of that, though I suspect you are right that I would not have found him there. No, it was the library that I needed to visit, and for a rather more prosaic volume than Mr. Cromwell might have selected for his own reading."

Holmes drew on his pipe. He would doubtless tell me in due course which book he had needed to consult.

"I too have had a potentially profitable morning," I said.

"Potentially?"

"Much seems to depend on today's expedition. As you know, I write up our investigations, and they are sometimes published in *The Strand* magazine. I received this telegram at nine o'clock. Like your own message, the reply was pre-paid."

Holmes took the slip of paper. "A thousand pounds!" he exclaimed.

"Indeed. The editor is offering me that sum for my next report. He needs it by the end of the week. He offers to send a messenger round to collect it from my consulting rooms the moment it is finished. Payment on publication a few days later."

"And he casually suggests writing up whichever case we are currently working on?"

"Just so."

Holmes drew on his pipe and chuckled. "Do you think by any chance that he has been tipped off as to the nature of our present investigation?"

"I don't see how he could have been," I said.

"A thousand pounds is a lot of money."

"I never said otherwise."

"And what did you reply?"

"As yet, nothing. I obviously wished to consult you. The matter seemed too delicate to be the subject of any account—even if, as Mr. Cromwell wished, I changed the names of the parties."

"On the contrary. Take the reply slip to the post office in Cambridge and tell him that he may send his boy at the end of the week—Friday morning at ten. I think we shall be ready for him by then."

It was almost one o'clock when our train finally pulled into Cambridge station, but Holmes insisted on a leisurely stroll into the centre of town and then an equally leisurely luncheon at a public house close to Trinity College. Two o'clock had already struck when we paid our bill and set out to locate the pharmacist's shop in a back street in the northern part of the city, though even then we stopped off at the post office to deal with the reply-paid telegram. Holmes must have consulted a street plan of Cambridge at the British Museum, because, once we had left the busy town centre, he did not pause or hesitate as we worked our way between the rows of low and dirty terraced houses. Eventually we came to a shop, on its own in a small cul-de-sac. The paintwork was blistered and the glass was covered in grime, but the sign above the large window was freshly painted. "Cromwell's Pharmacy," it read, then underneath in much smaller letters: "Late Fairfax."

"We have found our man," said Holmes.

The sign on the door still said CLOSED, but I tried the handle and it swung open. The inside was as dingy as the exterior and as deserted as the street, but the large jars on the shelves and the pill bottles on the counter all appeared to have been cleaned and dusted recently. The owner clearly cared more about his profession than he did about appearances.

The man behind the counter looked up eagerly as we came in—I wondered if we were in fact his first visitors that day. He was of middling height, grey-haired, and with large grey mutton-chop whiskers and a very black moustache. He wore horn-rimmed spectacles.

"Can I help you, my good sirs?" he said.

"I believe you can," said Holmes. "You are Mr. Cromwell?"

"I am, sir."

"And you have a cousin living in Clapham of the same name?"

"He is Richard, I am Henry, but yes, the same surname, to be sure."

"My name is Sherlock Holmes," said my friend.

"Ah, then he could not get Merrivale?" asked the pharmacist. "That is a pity."

"I do not know Merrivale, so I cannot say how much of a pity it is. But since I am here, and since you seem to know why I am here, perhaps you would be good enough to tell us what happened to you on the twenty-fifth of November 1861?"

"I shall indeed, because the matter lies heavily on me. I was not the murderer myself, but merely the unwitting accomplice. I was then working for Mr. Fairfax, who owned this shop in better times— you see how little trade we do now. Late one afternoon, he took me to one side and said: 'Now then, young Cromwell, I have something I want you to do and you must follow my instructions to the letter, do you understand?' 'Yes, Mr. Fairfax,' I said. 'Very well,' Fairfax continued. 'Tonight, after the shop has closed, a fine gentleman will call. He will ask you for something and, whatever that thing is, you must give it to him—no questions asked. And there is no need to enter what you give him in the sales ledger. He has already paid

me very well. Then, when he has gone, you will forget that you ever
saw him.' "

"Did that not arouse your suspicions in any way?"

"It now seems to me a strange way to do business, but I was then
only an apprentice and did not question my master's judgement."

"Go on," said Holmes.

"At six o'clock there was a knock at the door. A very well-dressed
and quite portly young gentleman entered the shop. His hair was
fair and curled and he wore a nobleman's gown—in those days,
noblemen wore silk gowns that were very different from the normal
student's gown. I asked him what I could do for him, and he said
that he needed some cyanide to kill rats that were troubling him in
his rooms. I measured out a little of the powder, but he demanded
that I double the amount, since the rat he wished to kill was a large
old one. It had come over on a ship from Germany some years
before, he said, and it was high time somebody dealt with it. I did
as he asked and would have done so even if Mr. Fairfax had not
ordered me, because the gentleman had an air about him of one who
was not used to having his instructions questioned. He took the
cyanide powder in a small phial. I bowed to him. Then he handed
me a guinea. 'It's all paid for, sir,' I said. 'That's to make sure you say
nothing,' he snarled. 'And if you do, you'll regret it all your days.' "

"And you never saw him again?" I suggested.

"Not exactly," said the pharmacist.

"What do you mean?" asked Holmes.

"I mean that I was very troubled," said the pharmacist. "By the
guinea as much as anything. I recognised the gown as being a Trinity
College one and so, the following day, after my duties here were
done, I set out for Trinity to see if I could spot him again and find
out who he was."

"And did you see him?"

"No, sir, I did not. But I met with a bedmaker from Trinity,
who lived close to the shop and whom I knew well. I described my
customer and his request to her and she let out a gasp. 'But that

can only be the Prince of Wales,' she cried. 'You know him well?' I asked. 'Indeed. By a remarkable coincidence, I am his bedmaker,' she replied. 'This is terrible.' 'Terrible that he wishes to kill rats?' I enquired. 'No, Mr. Cromwell,' she muttered. 'I now see what he plans to do. Oh, Lord have mercy on us both.' And with that, she fled."

"Did she clarify what she meant?"

"No, though later I worked out what must have happened. But it is better that she explain it to you herself."

"How will we find her?" I asked.

"She is still a bedmaker at Trinity College," said the pharmacist. He looked at his watch. "Her name is Mary Fleetwood. She finishes her work at three o'clock. If you walk back slowly to Trinity, you should catch her as she leaves. She has grey hair and wears a red dress and a black shawl."

"Thank you," said Holmes. "We shall do that. By the way, your sign says CLOSED. You will not get many customers that way."

"Ah," said the pharmacist.

But he made no move to change it.

"A strange shop," I said to Holmes, as we proceeded southwards again.

"But very much as I expected," he said. "Even down to the closed sign on the door."

"And have you already formed an opinion of the lady we are going to meet?"

"I am not sure. She will be one of two things. Let us see which of those things she is."

"And will that help us solve this puzzle?"

"No, it is purely incidental. But it will tell us something about the methods of our adversaries."

"Adversaries?"

"Oh yes. As we try to work upwards toward the light, there are those who are trying to pull us down to our destruction. But fear not. I think we are ahead of them, Watson, and I plan to stay ahead."

We were outside the gates of Trinity at three precisely and, at one minute past three, a small grey-haired lady in a red dress emerged.

"Is that what you expected?" I asked.

"It is the less likely of the two possibilities, but I now understand something that Mr. Cromwell—Mr. Richard Cromwell—told us." He turned in the woman's direction and called, "Mrs. Fleetwood! A word with you, I pray!"

She stopped abruptly. "And who might you be?" she demanded.

"I am Sherlock Holmes. I am a consulting detective. I think you may be able to tell me about a murder that occurred a little over thirty years ago."

"Lord have mercy on our souls!" she exclaimed. "I always feared this would happen."

"You have nothing to be frightened of for the moment," said Holmes. "Perhaps if we stepped into that public house, we might be able to find a quiet table at which we can talk."

"I'll have a gin," she said. "A large one."

At that time in the afternoon, the barroom was almost empty, and drinks were quickly ordered and a quiet table secured.

"You say you've already spoken to Mr. Henry Cromwell," she said. "So you know the worst of it. Early that afternoon, Prince Albert had shown up at the college unexpected and in a fine temper. He and young Albert Edward, as I always called him, had had a row and Prince Albert had gone for a walk by the river to cool down. The moment he had gone, the young prince summoned me. "I have need of some very special medicine," he said. "Do you know a pharmacist who can be trusted, somebody you know personally?" I nodded. Lots of my young gentleman got a dose of the French pox from time to time, so I was used to requests of this sort. "Take this money," he said, "and this note explaining what I want. Say I'll call by early this evening and collect the special powder. When you're done at the chemist, I want you to go to the confectioners over by St. John's and buy a dozen marrons glacés. My father loves them, and I need some sort of gift to pacify him. He usually eats one a day, so a dozen will last him the better part of a fortnight. Then bring them back here." I thought little of it at the time. I wasn't sure a dozen would be enough, but otherwise everything seemed in order. Then the following day I met Mr. Cromwell—Mr. Henry Cromwell, I mean—and he told me about the cyanide. But Prince Albert had already left for Windsor with the poisoned sweetmeats in his greatcoat pocket. Of course, I read the newspapers with trepidation. Within days there was news of his indisposition, then that he had taken to his bed with sweats and stomach pains. Finally came news of his death. His face and hands were black, sir—cyanosis. I could not doubt that he had been slowly poisoned with the cyanide that Mr. Cromwell had sold Albert Edward."

"But..." I said.

Holmes held up his hand to silence me. "Thank you, my good woman," he said. "Here is half a crown to buy enough gin to drown your sorrows very thoroughly."

"I shall do so," she said. "But you do believe me, don't you, sir?"

"Why should I doubt you?" he said.

"Well," said Holmes, when we were again seated in a first-class compartment and his pipe was poisoning the air, "I think that we have had a very satisfactory day."

"But that woman…" I said.

"She is not an expert on poisons," said Holmes.

"Even so…"

"I have brought my notes on Lassus," said Holmes. "I shall occupy the journey to London rereading them. I would not want anything to delay the delivery of my monograph to the printer."

"And the case we have been investigating?"

"It is solved. There is nothing more to be done. On Friday at ten I shall be at your consulting rooms to await the arrival of the man sent by *The Strand* magazine to collect your latest case report."

"But I still do not know the ending."

"It will take you only a moment or two to add the necessary paragraphs, once the man has arrived. I shall dictate them to you, if you wish."

"And what will be in those paragraphs?"

"I cannot yet say."

"But surely all is clear. Some foreign power, anxious to discredit the heir to the throne, has sent us on a wild goose chase to Cambridge where we were to unearth what are, frankly, some very spurious facts from some very doubtful witnesses. We were expected to make them public, without informing Mycroft, who would most certainly have been able to tell us the truth and stop us. The editor of *The Strand* magazine has been tipped off and has most disloyally decided to profit from it by being the first to publish the rumours. Royal scandal always sells well. I shall not send him any further cases and shall tell him in no uncertain terms, when his messenger arrives, that he may not have this one."

"Oh no, I think you can let him have it. Though the fee may sadly be less than you expect. You have spotted some of the clues, Watson, but you have clearly missed others. All will be revealed on Friday."

For the next hour, my friend silently read and occasionally hummed some rather archaic tune. Later he relit his pipe and for a long time stared out of the window with apparent satisfaction at the flat East Anglian countryside. Slowly pipe smoke filled the compartment. It was a relief when we arrived at Liverpool Street and I could open the carriage door and get out into the relatively fresh and pure air of London.

"I wonder what sort of dinner Mrs. Hudson has prepared for us this evening," he said, as we joined the queue for a cab.

"I think she said it would be some sort of pudding," I said.

"Let us hope she has not over-egged it in the way that our adversaries have," said Holmes.

On the Friday after our visit to Cambridge, Holmes arrived at my consulting rooms at ten o'clock.

"I am not too late?" he enquired. "The messenger has not been and gone?"

"No," I said. "Are you going to explain to me now what the end of the story is?"

"Once the messenger is here, I can begin. Ah, the doorbell is ringing—hopefully we can now conclude this."

A man of middling height with a dark, bushy beard and enormous eyebrows was ushered in. His hat was pulled down low over his face.

"You are from the the *Strand* magazine?" asked Holmes.

"That's right, guv. Give us the story and I'll be on my way."

"You shall indeed have the whole tale," said Holmes, "but in exchange I'm having your beard."

Before the man could even protest, Holmes had grabbed one side of the beard and tugged it, with a ripping sound, from his cheek. The man made to pull away, but that only aided Holmes in removing the false hair entirely.

"Mr. Cromwell!" I exclaimed. "I mean, Mr. Richard Cromwell…"

"And Mr. Henry Cromwell," said Holmes. "For a while I thought that he might prove to be Mary Fleetwood too, but that was somebody else. Your wife, I assume, Mr. Cromwell? I could not at first understand why you, as a married man, insisted you were a bachelor. Then of course it occurred to me: your wife had a part to play in the plot that you were weaving and you did not wish us even to suspect her existence."

"How did you know who I was?" he said.

"How did I know that Henry and Richard were the same person? First, I took the natural precaution of checking that Cromwell's Pharmacy really existed. To that end, I visited the British Museum and consulted various trade directories. There was not and never had been a pharmacy of that name in Cambridge. It was clear therefore when we visited you that you had taken a derelict shop for a few days and smartened it up as much as you could and added a few jars and other suitable props. Of course you wanted no real customers, so the closed sign remained firmly in place. It amused me to let you stew for most of the day behind your fake shopfront, while you added unnecessary embellishments to what you planned to tell me. That it really was you behind that rather pathetic disguise was confirmed by some of the things you said—for example you, as Henry, repeated word for word some of Richard's remarks about the matter lying heavily on you and being an unwitting accomplice. Your wife was good in her supporting role as the ancient bedmaker. But she slipped up by clarifying at one point that she meant *Henry* Cromwell, when she had no reason to know that Richard Cromwell even existed—

much less that I might have ever met him. She also made a mistake that Watson immediately spotted concerning cyanosis. You'd think, from the word itself, that it would be a feature of cyanide poisoning—and they do both derive from the Greek for 'blue'—but cyanosis has nothing at all to do with the poison. It was a tempting little detail thrown in at the last minute, but completely wrong. Over-egging the pudding. The thousand pounds for the story was also a little too much—none of Watson's tales are worth half that. The reply-paid telegram was a good idea though—Watson's reply went to you as the sender, not to the real *Strand* magazine, which remains innocent of the whole thing."

"So," I said, "Cromwell here—Richard or Henry as you choose—would have obtained a full account of the Prince of Wales's guilt, from an impeccable source, and then sold it to a foreign power to bring down our next king? I can see why that source had to be you and not Merrivale. His word would have counted for nothing."

"I beg to differ," said Cromwell, indignantly.

"I'm sure you do," said Holmes, "because Richard Cromwell is not your real name either, is it? Shall I pull off those eyebrows before I name you?"

"I'd rather you didn't," he said. "They are stuck on very firmly."

"Very well, false eyebrows and all, this is that master of disguise and employer of modern techniques, Mr. Herbert Merrivale."

"But…" I said.

"Like so many of my cheap imitators, Merrivale was aware that he could not compete with the real thing. He needed to discredit me. So, he hatched a plot to make me denounce the Prince of Wales, publicly, as a murderer. The denunciation would take the form not only of an ultimately embarrassing meeting with the prime minister, but also of the write-up of the investigation by you, Watson—an utterly improbable tale of slow cyanide poisoning with impossible symptoms and a dying prince continuing to stuff himself with marrons glacés—a tale that I would apparently have been taken in by. And it would not have appeared in *The Strand*, but in some inferior magazine or newspaper that Merrivale would actually send the manuscript to. And in case you hesitated, he was prepared to offer, though almost certainly not actually pay, a thousand pounds for your cooperation."

"How did you see through me?" asked Merrivale (as I must now at last call him).

Holmes laughed. "Who, other than Merrivale himself, would have spoken as highly of him as you repeatedly did? Who, other than a man who was trying to imitate me, would have sat there pathetically trying to light and relight such an enormous pipe? Who…"

Merrivale held up a hand. "There's no need to rub it in," he said.

"Just clear off and take your eyebrows with you," said Holmes.

"So," I said. "I do now have the end of the story. Thank you, Holmes. I shall write it up for *The Strand*."

"You just need a title for your account," said Holmes. "What about *A Scandal in Cambridge*? Or what about *The Slandered Prince*?"

"No," I said. "I've thought of a better title than that—one that applies to all imitators of your work…and indeed of my own."

Sherlock Holmes and the Butterfly Effect

By Cristina Macía with Ian Watson

Few people are aware that certain actions which Sherlock Holmes undertook on behalf of the British Admiralty in China's Shandong province during the First World War unintentionally led to the founding of the Chinese Communist Party in 1923.

Thus the reigning Chinese Politbureau of the mid-twenty-second century regard Holmes with a certain respect, as for an ancestor—at the same time as they abhor all the help which Holmes constantly gave to the ruling houses of Europe, resulting in the creation of the United Kingdom of Europe, capital in Brussels, adversely affecting China's growth.

To ensure the continuity of the Chinese Communist Party while preventing a pan-European Kingdom will require fine-tuning of events every bit as skillfully as for a Stradivarius, preferably with the cooperation of the virtuoso though vain detective…

The two time-travellers, David Mason and Rajit Sharma, lie semi-hallucinating on adjacent tolerably clean and comfortable mattresses upon bed frames of carved Burma teak in an opium house in London's Limehouse district, near the docks. Comfortable damask cushions cradle the users' heads. A maid passes softly by, seeing that the clients' long pipes remain upon the oil lamps, all flames turned low. Brown smoke hazes the air. Reality trembles like a child prostitute meeting their first client.

Opium expands time and space. Mason trails a hand through the air, copies of itself staying visible to his gaze in a disconcerting way. It is and it isn't there, many times over. At least Holmes supposes that is what is going through the Oxonian's mind. Such assuredly is the burly man's clipped, but nevertheless plummy, accent. An accent shared, be it noted, with self-proclaimed Doctor of Philosophy Sharma—although a nasal whine of Birmingham Brummie faintly underlies the Hindu's impeccable English, which is odd.

"Where?" murmurs Mason. "And when? It's…fasc-in-at-ing."

"Fascinating indeed," agrees Holmes, who sits contemplating in a rattan chair nearby. He's wearing his belted half-cape coat and deerstalker because, with childish glee, the darker visitor "from the future" specially requested this costume, even though no moor nor vile landscape is nearby unless one counts the foul mud along the Thames at low tide.

Nor does Holmes indulge himself in opium. Truth be told, not ever. When he needs cerebral stimulus, he'll use cocaine, morphine, or shag tobacco. Right now, Holmes requires no such stimulus, since his visitors provide this fully.

The relaxing effect of opium might—or might not—loosen the tongue of even the best-trained spy. Which is why Holmes acceded to the enthusiasms of the taller, dusky young man. Downstairs at Holmes's digs earlier on, bizarrely this "gentleman" shed a short frock coat—now resumed—as though that were some overcoat. Beneath, a double-breasted waistcoat was unaccountably loosened and flapping, as if there were a heatwave this present October. The other fellow—for so Mason claimed to be *academically*—wears a lounging jacket woven of Harris tweed with incongruous plus-fours below. Neither man has been near a tailor, yet they are kitted out as if to impress.

Holmes leans toward Mason. "Tell me again where you come from. And from *when?*"

In the Oxford of 2050 a week ago, or 170 years ahead depending upon how one looks at it, an elegant woman from Guoanbu, the Chinese State Security Ministry, instructs Mason and Sharma. She's tall and slim in her smartly tailored future-blu uniform, two gold stars on the epaulettes. Raven hair, chestnut highlights, divide on the left to expose a wide brow. Jet-pupil almond eyes transfix from behind full horn-rimmed glasses, which may be Armani, from the Dukedom of Italy. Perfectly drawn red lips. She's a bit like a lovely mantis.

That woman's name is Maggie Mo. Chinese officials often have "English" first names for use with Westerners. This adds a level of mystery and masquerade.

Incidentally, when not used as a surname, Mo 莫 means *Don't.* Maggie is General Don't. And also General Do. Supposing that stars denote a general.

Right now, Maggie Mo would gladly surrender a star from her shoulder to be the person receiving instructions rather than giving them. She might even sacrifice two stars.

For her personal passion happens to be the late Victorian period of what would become the Great British Battenberg Barony—or

GB-BB—within the UK of Europe. The period when Herbert George Wells envisioned invisibility, for instance—oh, to be a security officer unseen, yet with public fame as a Shanghai film star. The period of artist extraordinary Aubrey Beardsley and of forbidden absinthe.

Guoanbu's Seventeenth Bureau—its Enterprises Division— oversees Beijing's Time Institute that built the "pod" which can carry people into the past. Tampering with time is a sensitive political matter. This is restricted Chinese knowledge, but they use the best tools to accomplish each mission, in the sense of recruiting the best agents. In this case, as previously, Mason and Sharma fit the bill.

Although soon to be displaced by more than a century, Mason and Sharma are part of the same milieu which Holmes and Watson navigate confidently, pistols in their pockets, fists ready to box. Mason and Sharma both are Oxford men, the former a historian of ideas, the latter a specialist in the literature of the Victorian era which culminates in Arthur Conan Doyle. Lanky and dusky, Rajit Sharma could be the son of a Raja of the Indian Empire, Mason a portly stockbroker.

There's only one person better prepared than them for the mission, not merely as regards cultural knowledge of the late Victorian period, but also of the intricate web of events which even a minor time-change might affect. Yet two-star Maggie Mo is an official too high in rank and too valuable to risk losing in the past without any rescue technology available. For you cannot dip a toe twice into exactly the same eddy of the timestream without you originating there first of all, though the time-pod can travel autonomously.

Amply compensated, Mason and Sharma will be well advised to keep absolutely mum about what Maggie Mo confides. Likewise, other worthies of useful Oxford University. The time-pod is presently stationed in the university's vaulted medieval Divinity School, a spacious, closed-off location attended by élite Han technicians. The pod is a giant egg of shimmery pearl with three fat wheels in case it needs pushing by hand, a single porthole to see out of. On an easel rests a blackboard which Mo quickly cleans of some scribblings, chalking up instead, almost derisively, three letters followed by a couple of characters, like a primary teacher on the first day of class:

UKE

中国

"The United Kingdom of Europe," she declares. "Down below, there's the Middle Kingdom; in other words, Zhōngguó, namely China. Due to its unshakeable unity, the UKE impedes China somewhat. To a significant degree, whose fault is that? Our own scholars and myself alike believe that a crucial figure is the detective Sherlock Holmes, who constantly bolstered European monarchs and noble houses by solving crimes and muting scandals which otherwise would have resulted in hostilities and revolutions which would have torn apart the network of royal relationships."

Does her voice tremble at mention of those times out of reach? That's unacceptable. Private yearnings cannot interfere with the mission. But how Maggie yearns to visit Victorian London in person. Indeed her expertise is why she is here, so frustratingly in charge of this particular mission.

"I promise we will bring a certain vital person from that past to meet you," Sharma says consolingly. He understands.

"Thank you! I shall merely miss experiencing the actual streets, the weather, the buildings, the sounds, the smells, the Savoy operettas—" Would the lorgnettes of ladies in other red boxes swivel at sight of her oriental face? "The Criterion restaurant, Simpson's in the Strand," she concludes, as much bitterly as sarcastically.

And if Sherlock Holmes refuses to accompany Mason and Sharma for a quick trip to futurity? Surely everybody wants to step ahead a century and more! Especially when the future is pleasant enough. A no-brainer.

As Mason and Sharma proceed along Baker Street, reading the numbers on doorways, suddenly the next door swings open and from the shadows within looms a sizeable moon-faced female in fulsome black drapery, a bustle jutting out behind like a cushion stitched to her backside. Upon her head, a lace cap. Endow her waist with a bunch of keys and for sure, she's a landlady. She beams. "It's here," she informs the startled duo.

They look behind, they look across the way. People pass by, but no, she is addressing themselves, and she doesn't seem to think that any more explanation is necessary. She draws aside so that they can enter.

The hallway is small. There's nowhere for Sharma to hang his frock coat except for the arms of Mrs. Hudson, which she proceeds to offer after her dusky visitor begins to divest himself, seemingly to her mild amusement. On top of the frock coat go both men's matching grey Homburg hats, of stiff felt, with dented crowns. Mrs. Hudson, she must be Mrs. Hudson, has to be. Sharma can scarcely stop staring at her. She's unlike her many imaginary portraits, having a touch of the washerwoman about her.

"He's upstairs." Burdened by the coat and hats, she gestures with her chin at the steep stairs. "He'll be expecting you."

"But how did you *know*?" begins Mason.

How many times has someone asked that very same question in this hallway? Enough times for Mrs. Hudson to recite automatically:

"You came along Baker Street, checking the house numbers with mounting urgency the closer you got to here."

"Amazing!" Mason exclaims with true admiration. Mrs. Hudson sketches a smug smile. "And how is it you've been on the lookout so much?"

"Lately there's been little enough—" The landlady's smile fades. She clams up; she *shan't* go down in history as a gossip. The stairs await.

Holmes does not rise from his armchair by the fireplace, since visitors first need to galvanise his curiosity; otherwise, they'll be dismissed. The coarse shag he's smoking in a meerschaum pipe smells strong; you can suck meerschaum pipes more vigorously than briar pipes, reaching higher temperatures. There's a dizzying fug in the air.

"Mr. Holmes, sir, the honour is ours!" Mason presents their visiting cards printed in 2050, both cards in unison, which is wise since Sharma almost capers like a giant gangly puppy. In this big sitting room of high windows, here's the sideboard with the Persian slipper that keeps Holmes's shag tobacco from getting dry and leftovers of a woodcock to snack on. Here's the stick rack and the bearskin hearthrug and the cocaine cooker kit.

Also, the framed portrait of "Chinese" Gordon who put an end to the bloodiest war of the nineteenth century, the Taiping Rebellion, God-crazy proto-communists versus an established dynasty; Maggie Mo might have mixed feelings as to sides.

Over there is the chemistry corner, with side table stained by acids and a microscope of modest power. On the mantelpiece of the black marble fireplace correspondence of no value is impaled, ready to set fire to kindling.

And in the wall nearby are the famous initials V R, topped by a crown, made by bullets during precision target practice. To achieve such accuracy, Holmes must have used a long-barrel service revolver and intense concentration on several occasions.

And there's the problem: *Victoria Regina*. Holmes's extreme royalism extending protectively to any minor European princelet.

"Mr. Holmes," says Mason. "I shall be frank. We come from the future."

"Certainly you do not appear to be from the present," replies Holmes, setting his pipe aside. "At least as regards discarding a frock coat downstairs instead of wearing it while visiting, as I presume has happened. Do you suffer from a nervous disease, Mr. Sharma? Something exotic brought back from the Indian Empire?"

"Not at all! I'm just thrilled to meet you at last, sir. As my colleague says, we are from the future."

"Perhaps you are influenced by a piece of fanciful fiction?"

"Fiction? What fiction? Not in the slightest!"

No no no. They're completely safe. Wells's *Time Machine* hasn't been published yet!

Holmes's languid gesture indicates his chemistry corner. "I happened to notice a squib in the Royal College of Science's journal for science students. I too am a student of science. Now what was the title of the piece? *Chronic* something…" Holmes raises his pipe and puffs. "*Argonauts?*"

In a hissed aside, "Damn it, Mason, I forgot, but that's Bertie's *first* use of a time machine."

"So the idea of travel through time is not unknown to me. The problem is whether *you yourselves* accomplished this or are feigning, and why so."

Sharma responds brightly, "Once you eliminate the impossible, whatever remains, no matter how improbable, must be the truth."

Holmes snorts. "What poppycock! Whoever came up with such stupidity? To eliminate the impossible would take centuries. Raise your game, gentlemen. If you come to me with this bizarre story, I don't doubt you foresaw that you'd need to show some proof. So what will you show me from 'the future'?"

This is going faster than expected. From his jacket pocket Mason produces his Huawei 340 Pro, as planned. There's no signal, of course, but the phone packs plenty inside of itself, such as molecular

MiniSinoSiri. Sharma and Mason exchange nods. Mason switches on. The screen with its apps brightens.

Sharma instructs clearly, "SinoSiri, recite *The Charge of the Light Brigade* by Alfred, Lord Tennyson."

The sweet familiar voice commences:

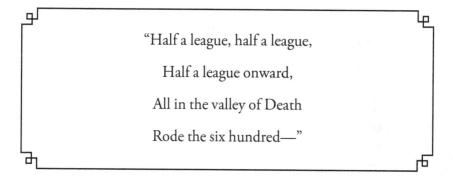

"Half a league, half a league,

Half a league onward,

All in the valley of Death

Rode the six hundred—"

Now Holmes arises, placing a hand over his heart. "Since our beloved laureate is quite recently interred in Westminster Abbey, he shall *not* be used as emotional bait."

"Didn't you know Tennyson died recently?" Mason hisses at Sharma.

"SinoSiri, stop!"

"But do let me hold that device."

"Yes, of course."

Holmes's fingers dance nimbly at random, then pause as bright red British uniforms, white helmets, and rifles appear; before leaving 2050, Mason was watching *Zulu*, the original movie.

"Surely," Holmes says wonderingly, "this is the Battle of Rorke's Drift, for which eleven Victoria Crosses were awarded! Surely no kinetoscope exists which can possibly…the colour, the clarity, the continuity…unless invisible chronic argonaut carriages *do* exist… which must also be miniature… If this be a conjuring trick…"

"No," Mason assures, "it's a motion picture from seventy years in the future from now. No invisible time machines are involved. No blood is shed, nobody dies."

"But the Zulu savages—"

"—Those Black actors live in a rainbow nation. *Lived*, I mean—by now, they must all be dead of old age. Sorry if I confuse."

Holmes's fingers fly again and a menu of names and numbers appears.

"As well as much else, this may *primarily* be some kind of *telephone*, although without any line to connect it."

"Mr. Holmes, how can you possibly deduce that!?"

"Personally, I need no telephone. Telegrams serve me better. Telegrams are concise and permit time for analysis. Yet certain numerical principles regarding webs and networks must apply to telephony…"

Holmes's astonishment level is still low.

"Let me show you another 'trick' this device performs." Mason recovers the Huawei and snaps a photo of Holmes. He turns the screen to the detective.

"Hmm! I see myself and my background a couple of seconds ago. This is faster than any tintype photography of which I know hitherto—"

Damn it, that photo per se is not astonishing.

Yet, oh, the value of a genuine photo of the great detective in this historic room! In case of accidental deletion, Mason slips back to the previous photo in memory, which happens to be of two-star Maggie Mo beside the blackboard in Oxford's medieval vaulted Divinity School.

"An *oriental woman* military officer!" exclaims Holmes. "And not lacking in charms. You have indeed now piqued my interest. Congratulations, gentlemen. Let us work on the hypothesis that I believe you. My diary is clear for the rest of the day. In what may this modest consulting detective, first and only of his profession, help you?" Few times can the word "modest" have been pronounced with such disingenuousness.

Sharma shuffles. "We want to help to make a better future world… Dear me, do I sound as if I'm taking part in a beauty pageant?"

"I think," replies Holmes enigmatically, "you can safely leave such activities to the Belgians." A discreet cough. "I intend no disrespect to the royal house of Leopold, despite what is noised about the Congo."

Worse than Poland under the Nazis. "To be sure," agrees Mason hurriedly.

They cannot reasonably request Holmes to accompany them to the pod hidden by bushes in Regent's Park. Even if Holmes agrees to go for a stroll, an egg on wheels with three seats and a few buttons and levers might strike the most brilliant brain of the age as of dubious proof compared with contraptions from the Grande Fête of the Future in Paris, as shown in the *Illustrated London News*.

"If only," muses Mason, "you might go with us on a quick *hop* into the future. That Chinese lady explains things so vividly, compared with ourselves."

"You sound like a pimp," says Sharma, which briefly shuts Mason up.

Holmes takes up his pipe and puffs shag. "Tempting. Your Chinese lady sounds intriguing. But there are cogent reasons for not straying from town…reasons beyond your ken."

"Beyond our Kensington, ha ha." Sharma becomes excited. "This town! I have spent half my career studying your era. Would it be too much to ask…"

"To look around town? I don't see why not. In due course, you may confess your true motives. It's cloudy today, but there'll be no rain."

"The Criterion, Simpson's, Bart's Hospital, Piccadilly…" Sharma might be writing a letter to Santa Claus. "To meet the Irregulars, to call at your tobacconist, to ride in a carriage—"

"To visit an opium den?" Holmes suggests.

To uphold the decorum of the street, no regular cab stand is nearby, but a vacant "growler" carriage happens to have halted by the curb thirty yards away. Its top-hatted driver is consulting a newspaper while his horse occupies itself feeding from a nosebag now flat on the roadway.

"As seeming admirers of myself," Holmes remarks, "you may know that I favour a two-seater hansom for speed. However, for comfort, three persons require a carriage. And conveniently…" Holmes raises his cane to catch the cabman's attention.

Out from behind the still stationary four-wheeler suddenly comes a nimble hansom. A flat-cap cabbie lays on to his horse with his long lash, cutting around the front of the heavier growler cab.

"What the deuce?" Holmes glances at Mason, at Sharma, at the four-wheeler, at the hansom—analysing the situation with the speed of a supercomputer which doesn't yet exist.

"Looks like he's desperate for a fare," says Mason.

"A fare for three fellows crammed in his two-person cab?" Holmes tsks. "Plainly kidnap by hansom isn't any plan of *yours*, Futurians. Yet is kidnap itself the plan? The plan of someone expecting one man, not three. Willing to risk finding out? At a push, three chaps *can* share a hansom. The destination must be very near to here; otherwise, alone, I would soon jump out irrespective of twisting an ankle—curiosity would keep me in the cab for two minutes at most—so the plan may be a serious bashing with broken bones to keep me at home for months."

The hansom stops perfectly beside the trio. The cabman's nose is squashed as if well acquainted with fisticuffs, and under the brim of his cloth cap a short forehead soon meets bushy brows.

"I'm game," declares Mason. "I'm a former Oxford Martial Arts Blue."

"So! The game is afoot… Hmm, words worth remembering."

They board, Mason squashing against skinny Sharma, which pretty much immobilises both men. Holmes throws open the trap door up behind his head and calls, "Limehouse, Cabby."

"Guv," growls the driver and takes off at a fair lick. Scarcely has the cab sped a hundred yards than abruptly it quits the main thoroughfare.

"Well, that was fast," says Holmes, in a voice that says, "as I told you it would be."

Perilously the hansom corners, narrowly missing a post and going up momentarily on one wheel before slumping back. Surely at least one horseshoe skidded. Poor horse could easily have gone down, breaking a leg. In that case, curtains for the hoss. Thus the "cabbie" doesn't care a hoot. Now they're in a cobbled mews, rattling them horridly. No one is in sight ahead, although the door to one stable is open.

"Hey up there, cabman!" calls Mason in protest.

Overhead, the reins pull back tight, wrenching the horse's head. "Whoa!" bellows Beetlebrow. Though not in response to the Oxford man.

Before the vehicle can fully stop, Holmes has kicked aside the low rain-door and is outside, slashing upward with his cane as the cabman comes to a halt, now parallel with himself. The cabman's cursing cry of surprise and pain accompanies him dropping a freshly seized bludgeon.

"Join me, gentlemen! With all due dispatch!" Holmes's nostrils flare. "I smell stout. Let us wallop the opposition."

Out of that dim stable stagger two evident ruffians, both of them clutching strong sticks. One still also holds a bottle from Fuller's brewery. They've been drinking to pass the time, maybe for hours, till their presumed solitary victim arrives. Mason and Sharma disentangle themselves and provide reinforcement, Sharma less boldly, since the stick he confronts is knobby and knotty. Mason rushes at the assailant who clutches the bottle of stout—and manages to execute a full hip throw, oh gosh! This leaves Mason panting, his hands upon his knees, but the cobbles have bashed the assailant's cranium.

Holmes pushes in front of Sharma. The detective's walking cane counters the knobby shillelagh as the weapon whacks at Holmes. It's easy for a master of singlestick to hit his drunken foe across the side of the neck, causing collapse due to half the brain fainting. Holmes swings smartly around, but the ex-cabman is already legging it away, favouring his sore limb.

"Did you *see* me there, Rajit?" Mason gasps as Holmes grips the shillelagh villain by the scruff, since the other miscreant appears to be concussed.

"Tell me the name that hired you!" demands Holmes.

The ruffian hides his face with his arm and blubbers. Exasperated, Holmes addresses his companions, for want of other audience: "Of course this creature will not know any useful name. But I swear to you, if London be a giant web and if myself be a spider sensitive to the twitches, that there lurks another spider, cunning and malevolent." Sharma certainly takes this in, though Mason may still be preening.

"Well," Holmes continues more calmly, "it's said that opium brings peace to the troubled, although many of the Chinese nation may not agree. So let us continue our journey."

"But the driver has skedaddled," Mason observes.

Whereupon Holmes makes strange clicking noises at the horse, then confidently mounts the rear of the hansom and gathers up the reins.

"Gentlemen, your carriage awaits. We can leave the horse and hansom at a cabman's shelter nearer to Limehouse and continue on foot."

Before stepping up inside, Sharma winks at Mason. "*Sherlock Holmes*, no less, is about to chauffeur us by cab through Victorian London. Best that Maggie Mo never knows—she'd never forgive us."

"Perhaps another pipe of paradise?" Mason implores Holmes. "I don't feel stupefied at all."

"I did ask Li Yi—the maid—to prepare mild doses for newcomers. But anyway, you have not eaten since arriving at Baker Street. Maybe you've worked up an appetite by now?"

Needless to say, neither has Holmes snatched a bite even of the cold woodcock on the sideboard since the pair first knocked on his study door. Nor is opium normally any booster of appetite. But for Mason, deduces Holmes, a variety of pleasures should ideally succeed one another.

"I do feel a bit peckish myself," mentions Holmes suggestively.

Sharma speaks up. "Mr. Holmes, I don't wish to seem brash, but I have some sovereigns to burn—in a manner of speaking. Let yourself be our guest this evening, if you would do us the honour."

"Well spoken, sir. Where else should one go but to Simpson's in the Strand?" One of Holmes's favourite restaurants.

So here they are. The great dining room is bright with illumination from wall sconces and pendant lamps and white table linen covering the dining tables. By the doorway a grand piano plays unobtrusively, its music mostly drowned by laughter and chatter amid the clink of cutlery upon porcelain. Some theatrical-looking ladies dressed to the nines sip champagne, for it is evening now. A gentleman repairs to the smoking divan upstairs, unlit cigar in hand. The trio have a table halfway down the room, over to the right.

"Oh, there's one of the famous carving trollies," enthuses Sharma. Big domed solid silver dishes cover succulent roast beef of Old England, guided around the tables by a master carver.

"Indeed. Sirloin of beef, or saddle of mutton? I believe roast beef is appropriate. To accompany which, I would recommend the Quinta do Noval Petit Verdot, a very respectable Portuguese vintage. Do we agree?"

Thus is the sommelier instructed presently.

The wine arrives cradled in a towel. Holmes approves first the label and then the bouquet. The sommelier pours what one might call a study in ruby red.

The meat presently carved from the joint is also a study in red rarity—thick succulent slices, soon joined by the finest horseradish sauce in London, potatoes roasted in goose fat, bright orange carrots, crispy Yorkshire pudding, and a port-wine gravy.

This done, Holmes leans forward. "I am not unacquainted with pharmacology. So I am well aware that opium *by itself* does not loosen tongues when smoked. And when dissolved in alcohol as laudanum, any 'indiscretion' effect is largely due to the alcohol. At what one might call the 'molten caramel' stage of the opium, Li Yi obligingly added a few grains of a substance I provided, the name of which I shall withhold."

Sharma gapes at Holmes.

"Do eat. As shall I."

"I never imagined you capable of drugging a pair of strangers," says Mason.

"Doubtless because you little know me." Holmes slices beef, loads his fork, commences.

Nonplussed, Sharma does as Holmes did, but then covers his mouth with his napkin to speak.

"In the accounts of your exploits which have come down to us, nothing indicates this as your style." Sharma's tone may be bitter; it's hard to tell, given a juicy mouthful of food competing.

"Many aspects of my exploits are withheld simply due to lack of a constant chronicler."

"But Watson?" asks Mason. "Whom we have not yet met. Does he not write up your deeds?"

"My dear fellow, Watson is a fiction—a doctor companion invented by Doyle. That is Arthur Conan Doyle, the Scots author who has begun to publish accounts of my cases for ridiculous amounts of money, when he would very much rather be penning," and he snorts, "historical fictions. Scribbling about my own humble doings to satisfy public demand robs him of time."

Mason raises an eyebrow to hear the word "humble" coming from Holmes, but he also raises a lavishly loaded fork. To be served such a bounty of beef is far from normal in 2050, even at a college feast or gaudy when maybe a single slice of rare Angus might be plated along with nicely boiled Jersey potatoes.

Mason gestures. "So there *is* no Watson?"

"If only I did have a devoted Watson, how useful he would be. Someone who can listen to me think aloud and prompt me with suitable questions. To remind me of the obvious which sometimes escapes me while I'm deep in a knotty problem. Not indispensable, of course, but…useful."

Holmes lays down his fork. "What I did deduce in the opium establishment, from stray words of yourself and Mr. Mason, is that your mission here is intended to assist an unexpected great power of the future by altering aspects of the present day, although I know not how, nor why, nor where, nor when. Too many questions, not enough answers. Consequently, I am sorry, gentlemen. In order to avoid that future which you will not tell me about in any detail, you will need another plan. For I am not leaving London. There is an enemy at large, scheming evilly. I neither wish nor dare to leave London except for a quick dash to, say, Dartmoor or Norfolk."

Just as salient, perhaps, is that, in the London of the Victorians, Holmes is godlike. He knows all the ashes of tobaccos, the droppings of horses, the printers' fonts for setting headlines. What would he be in 2050? An object of study. Admiring study, but study nonetheless.

"Do you have somewhere to spend the night, gentlemen, where a cab may pass by on our departure? Or will you merely disappear into fog?"

Mason tells Holmes, "In truth, we left our vehicle hidden amidst bushes in Regent's Park. You are very welcome to visit our 'egg.' To come aboard for a while, purely to satisfy curiosity."

Holmes smiles. "As you have witnessed, I am well able to evade abduction. I suggest that for now we should devote ourselves to this excellent nutrition." He raises his glass of Petit Verdot from Portugal, England's oldest ally.

"So what do you call this if not a bungle, a botch, and a balls-up!" Maggie Mo is steaming. Maybe not literarily, but scorching vapour is all that's missing from her fury of frustration. Her eyes blaze at Sharma and Mason like a cinematic dragon's. Maybe those aren't actual flames that are roasting Sharma and Mason, it just feels so.

"It wasn't a simple mission." Thus Mason tries to excuse them. "Sherlock Holmes isn't silly."

"Oh, really? That's the conclusion you arrived at? Using the most advanced ultra-secret technology to send a pair of experts a century and a half into the past to bring back the news that Sherlock Holmes, the most astute, clever, and perceptive of men…'isn't silly'! Wow, that's money well spent."

The two Oxonians are seated in a soundproofed private chamber at one end of the long gloomy vestibule which gives access midway to the Divinity School. Their wooden chairs are unpadded. No table protects them from Maggie Mo righteously upright before them. She is an indignant schoolma'am, a pissed-off boss, a colleague cheated— and a caged tigress certain that *she* would have succeeded if not for sodding bureaucracy.

Placatingly, Sharma says, "Here's the problem. We couldn't tell Holmes anything. If we lied, he'd have known right away. If we told the truth, given his regard for any old royals, why should his interests align with ours? A UK of Europe might have seemed like a champion idea to him."

"What's more," adds Mason, "our arrival coincided with the first signs of Moriarty. And lo, the bloodhound sniffed the wind." Mason can be the king of metaphors when he cares. "No human power could drag Holmes aside."

"Of course Holmes caught a scent!" bawls Maggie Mo. "He just didn't express this in his usual forthright and unsubtle manner."

Mason can tell that Maggie was about to say "like Westerners do," but nobody gets to the rank of Comrade Mo without being aware that politically correct diplomacy must clamp down occasionally.

The pair should have kept close to Holmes. Theirs should have been a long, subtle, meticulous job. Morons! They had enough authentic period banknotes rolled up tightly. Men! Running back to Mummy! Scared by a bit of street violence too, no doubt.

Finally, she growls in a low voice, "Too much to ask you to spend more time with Holmes, eh? Coming back after one damn day!"

"Well, we couldn't really keep the time-egg safely parked in the park for too long... Could we? Risk of discovery. Dog runs into the bushes; child runs after the dog..."

They don't need to be great detectives to deduce how much she herself would have given had she been tasked as they had been.

Mason and Sharma exchange glances, nerving one another. Mason nods approval, so Sharma leans forward in his chair in an almost Sherlockian fashion.

"The mission isn't a failure yet. We have an idea. As you say, it'll take time and a lot of fancy spadework to divert Holmes from his course. He's a glacier. We don't want to disappear him, just to divert him gently. That's a job for someone who's at his side day after day. Someone who knows him and understands him, someone who knows where to push gently or let fall an opportune remark. Sherlock Holmes needs a Watson."

"But Watson never existed! That's the pen-name of Conan Doyle."

"That can change. We just need to come up with the perfect person and plant her at Holmes's side."

"Did you say *her*?"

"Well, I wouldn't wish to sound sexist… We need a person who can entice him with a more challenging and seductive case, if he's about to rush instead to the aid of some European princess who's being blackmailed or some heir to a minor throne's mistress. A person willing to devote years to being Holmes's shadow."

Maggie Mo gazes at Sharma now, her eyes no longer blazing but with a different bright gleam in them.

"Continue," she says. Does her voice tremble a tad?

"Did we mention the candid interest that Holmes showed when he saw your photo?"

In London it's getting dark, though fog already took possession of the city a while ago. Streetlamps are lit. Those don't yet compete with the gloaming, but in less than an hour they'll be like fireflies or holy haloes. Sherlock Holmes puts his key in the lock. Mrs. Hudson has already withdrawn to her own rooms, and he doesn't care to disturb her. Whatever that idiot eye-doctor Doyle says, Holmes isn't inconsiderate.

"Good night, Mister Holmes."

Holmes freezes. It is not the first time somebody utters that same sentence at his back. How didn't he hear this unknown someone approaching? What a poor show. Unless the someone is really subtle. He turns and regards the newcomer.

Maggie Mo, dressed as a gent in striped trousers and a short frock coat suspiciously reminiscent of Sharma's, her black mane in a bun tight under her topper, feels in her pocket for two stars, her lucky charms.

Holmes beams. "Good night to you too. I was expecting you. Your room is ready."

And he opens the door to admit Maggie Mo. With a nod, she enters this Baker Street house as if to the manor born and ascends the stairs.

Sharma and Mason regard the plates before them without enthusiasm. After pints in the Dowager Duchess of Deutschland pub in Queen Street, they're in one of the cafés inside Oxford's Covered Market, the name of which can stay mum. They'd ordered its traditional beef and two veg with boiled spuds and a micro-Yorkshire pudding accompanied by gravy from granules.

A ghost of what they took in Simpson's in 1894. The two humble slivers of beef are grey. The Yorkshire pud is part burned, part soggy. Sharma sniffs, cuts, forks, chews, swallows without relish.

"They might be eating there right now." Mason has read his thought. "I wonder when the consequences will reach us. Supposing that we realise. With Holmes diverted from his previous course, I do hope there aren't any stupid conflicts in a patchwork Europe. Oh, why the devil did we come here to eat?"

"Them. Lunching. At Simpson's." Sharma sighs and sets down his fork. "There's no worse nostalgia. *A La Recherche de Palate Perdu.*"

"I do wonder what Holmes would think of the USA falling apart and the non-stupid states all unifying with Canada."

Sharma raises a cup of tea, for this café lacks an alcohol license.

"Yes, indeed. Here's to Her Majesty Meghan Markle, long may she reign over them."

The Case of the Secret Assassin

By David Stuart Davies

Starring Basil Rathbone as Sherlock Holmes & Nigel Bruce as Doctor Watson

On rising one morning in the early spring of 1942, Doctor John H. Watson was somewhat surprised to discover that his friend and associate, Sherlock Holmes, had already gone out. His long overcoat and tweed fedora were missing from the coat rack by the door.

"What's all that about?" he mumbled to himself. "Didn't say a bally thing to me last night about scooting out at the crack of dawn."

He rang for Mrs. Hudson to arrange for his breakfast. "Did you see Mr. Holmes this morning?" he asked, as she handed over a bowl of porridge and he shook his napkin before tucking it into his collar.

"I did, Doctor," she replied. "A message came for him around six o'clock. I think it was from Mr. Holmes's brother. He was out of the house in quick sticks."

"Mycroft, eh? Something important, then. Can't think why he didn't tell me."

Mrs. Hudson raised an eyebrow and gave him a fleeting smile before departing.

After Watson had finished his breakfast and perused the morning paper, he was about to tamp down a post-prandial pipe when he heard light, quick footsteps moving up the stairs. He easily recognised that tread. Moments later, Sherlock Holmes entered, his eyes sparkling and his finely chiselled features alive with energy.

"Ah, the wanderer returns," observed Watson pithily.

"Indeed, he does," said Holmes, slipping off his hat and coat. "Is there any tea left in the pot? I could do with a strong brew."

Watson poured him a cup.

"Where have you been? And why wasn't I allowed to go with you?"

"Oh, don't pull such a petulant face, old fellow. All will become clear in due course."

"Will it?"

"If you must know, I've been with Mycroft at Number Ten."

"Number Ten? …Downing Street?"

Holmes nodded.

"You mean to say you've been with…"

"The prime minister—yes."

"Great Scott, what's that all about?"

"It's a case, Watson, a very top secret case. If I tell you, you must swear not to reveal any of the details to a living soul."

"You know me, Holmes, the model of discretion."

Holmes peered over the rim of his tea cup. "Yes," he said without much conviction.

"So, go on, what did Mr. Churchill want with you?"

"News has reached British intelligence that Alex Brunner has been smuggled into the country and is in London at the moment."

"Alex Brunner? Never heard of him."

"He is the Nazis' ace assassin—responsible for the death of the resistance leader Colonel DuPont in Paris earlier this year.

Brunner is here on a special mission that could possibly turn the tide in the war."

"And what's that?"

"To assassinate our prime minister."

"Great heavens, Holmes, that's terrible."

"Certainly a successful outcome of Brunner's mission would be."

"He must be stopped."

"Always quick off the mark, eh, old fellow?"

"Just saying…" huffed Watson.

"Perspicacious, as ever," said Holmes, kindly. "Indeed, he must be stopped, and that is my job: to track him down and hand him over to the authorities. That will not be an easy task. Brunner is the master of disguise—a virtual chameleon."

"If anyone can do it, it is you, Holmes."

Holmes gave a bleak smile. "Thank you for your vote of confidence, Watson. Mr. Churchill shares your belief, but I fear we commence this journey looking for that proverbial needle in a very dense haystack."

"Where on earth do you start? It seems an impossible task."

"Nil desperandum, old boy. Someone must be harbouring Herr Brunner. If I can locate him…"

"But how?"

"Mycroft has given me the name and address of Hugo Oberstein, the key German agent currently residing in London. That is my starting point."

"Oberstein? You mean the musician, the violin player."

Holmes nodded. "Yes, that is his brilliant cover. He fiddles by day and carries out acts of espionage by night."

"You obviously haven't seen the newspapers. The fellow is dead."

"What!"

"He was dragged out of the river in the early hours of this morning. He had been beaten up rather badly about the face and was identified by his papers. Here it is in the *Stop Press*."

Holmes ran his eyes over the print and then, jumping to his feet, he snatched up his coat and hat.

"You going out again? Thought you wanted that cup of tea."

"The tea can wait. There isn't a moment to lose. I have to get to Scotland Yard posthaste."

"Well, wait for me old boy. I'm coming, too."

In less than an hour, Holmes and Watson were entering the police morgue in the bowels of Scotland Yard. They were accompanied by Inspector Lestrade.

"This is the one," said the inspector, indicating one of the stone slabs which housed a body covered by a white sheet.

"How did he die, Lestrade? Was it drowning?" asked Holmes.

"More brutal than that. He was shot in the back."

"What a cowardly act," observed Watson.

"Indeed, old fellow, but we're not dealing with gentlemen, you know. Nazis don't play the game by the Queensberry rules." So saying, Holmes pulled back the cloth to reveal the naked corpse beneath. Withdrawing a magnifying glass from the inner pocket of his overcoat, he carried out an examination of the body. After five minutes' close scrutiny, he turned to his companions with a dark smile on his lips.

"What d'you make of it, Mr. Holmes?" asked Lestrade.

"Very little, apart from the fact that this man is not Hugo Oberstein."

"Blimey! How can you be sure?"

"Look at his hands, those stubby fingers with thick ingrained dirt. They have never held a violin, let alone played one. Oberstein had a reputation as bon viveur, yet this man is obviously malnourished and his teeth are rotten. He is obviously some unfortunate down-and-out who has been dressed in Oberstein's clothes to create the impression that he has been assassinated. That is why his face has been rendered unrecognisable. As he was shot in the back, such violence was unnecessary unless it was to mask the man's identity."

Lestrade leant over the body and examined one of the hands. "I see you what you mean, Mr. Holmes. What's it all about?"

Watson was about to make a remark, but Holmes silenced him with a glacial stare.

"It is too early in the game for theories. What I would like to see are the belongings and clothes that this poor creature was wearing when he was fished out of the Thames."

Holmes examined the tweed suit, the cigarette case bearing the initials H. O., the wallet, and a silver card case containing a set of visiting cards which announced the owner as Hugo Oberstein. He pointed with some distaste at the man's boots. "Another *faux pas* committed by the killers. No doubt the clothes belonged to Oberstein, the maker's label would indicate as much, but I am sure our fiddle-playing friend wouldn't be seen dead in these crude boots. And of course, he wasn't. This is further confirmation of my deduction that the body in the morgue is not that of Hugo Oberstein."

"Then who is it?" asked Lestrade, scratching the back of his head.

"Sadly, that is not important for us now. We must leave you to follow that trail in your own inimitable way. The key question for us is why have they tried to create the impression that Oberstein is dead."

"Who are *they*?"

"When we know that, the mystery will be solved," Holmes replied tartly as he headed for the door. "Come, Watson, we have work to do."

It was approaching noon when Holmes and Watson stood before the front door of 13 Caulfield Gardens, Kensington.

"I wish you'd tell me why we're here," said Watson, with an edge of petulance in his voice. "You haven't said a word to me since we left Scotland Yard."

"Sorry, old fellow. I was thinking. You know how I am when I sink into one of my brown studies. This is Oberstein's last known address—the obvious starting point of our investigations," he said as he rang the doorbell. They heard the clanging noise echo through the interior of the house and waited for a response, but none came. Exchanging glances, Holmes rang the bell again and hammered on the door with his fist.

Then they heard a feeble cry from inside: "I am coming. I am coming. Please be patient."

At length the door was opened by a tall woman wearing a maid's outfit. She had tightly permed hair and a long doleful face. Her large eyes peered out through a pair of thick-lensed spectacles.

"Good afternoon, gentlemen," she said in a tremulous voice that seemed older than her years.

"I'd like to see Mr. Oberstein," said Holmes passing his card to the maid. "It is a matter of great importance."

The maid examined the card and then shook her head. "I am sorry, but Mr. Oberstein is not at home. He went out late yesterday afternoon and has not returned. To tell you the truth, I am somewhat worried about him. It is not like the master to stay out overnight without informing me."

"I see," Holmes said. "Then perhaps I could have a word with his guest."

With a bewildered glance, the maid shook her head again. "There is no guest."

"Oh, come now. Why bother with the charade if there was no guest, a certain Alex Brunner?"

"Charade? I don't understand."

"Oh, yes you do, my good sir!"

The maid's right hand moved swiftly toward the pocket in her pinafore, extracting a small pistol, but Holmes was too quick for her and landed a sharp uppercut to the chin. The blow sent the creature flying backward, crashing onto the tiled floor of the hall. In an instant, Holmes swooped down and snatched the revolver from the maid's grasp.

"What a devil of a woman," gasped Watson, shocked by the sudden dramatic turn of events.

"A devil certainly, but not a woman, I assure you." With a deft tug of his hand, he relieved the maid of her wig. "Let me introduce you to Hugo Oberstein."

"Great heavens!"

"Now, sir," said Holmes, addressing Oberstein, who had pulled himself up into a sitting position, "I will be obliged if you would inform me where I can locate your guest."

"Go to hell!"

"That particular journey is out of my hands. I am aware that you are in league with Alex Brunner."

"I do not know what you are talking about…"

Holmes pursed his lips. He had dealt with Nazi agents before and knew of their iron reserve. They would rather die than betray the Fuhrer. With a sigh, he handed the pistol to Watson. "Keep this fellow covered while I search the house. Don't hesitate to shoot the scoundrel if he tries anything funny."

Watson waggled the gun in the direction of Oberstein. "You can rely on me, Holmes."

The detective began his search of the premises. It was a very well-appointed town house with smart and expensive furnishings. The downstairs quarters revealed nothing of any significance. After an exhaustive search of the bedrooms upstairs, Holmes was growing frustrated. He had examined drawers and bookshelves and other locations where plans or secret documents could be concealed. Also, there was no sign that anyone other than Oberstein was in residence. "I feel like the dog barking up the wrong tree," Holmes muttered, on the verge of resigning himself to failure, and then he spied a dirty mark on the pale wallpaper in the smallest bedroom by the side of a large chest of drawers. On closer inspection, he determined that the mark was a dusty fingerprint. On instinct, he pulled the chest away from the wall to reveal a small door just over three feet in height. It was obviously an entrance to the loft area. Pulling the door ajar, he squeezed through and entered a large space illuminated by daylight falling through the skylight. It was open, allowing a cool breeze to filter into the chamber. There was a chair placed beneath the skylight. Holmes stood on it and stared through the open window at the panorama of rooftops beyond. It was clear to him that Brunner had made his escape this way, no doubt after overhearing the altercation downstairs.

Stepping down from the chair, he focused his attention on the room. It contained a bed and a small trestle table and certain items of men's clothing. There was no doubt in Holmes's mind that this had been Brunner's bolthole. With practised thoroughness, Holmes searched for clues, anything that would give him some indication of Brunner's plans for the assassination attempt and his current whereabouts.

What immediately caught his eye was the ashtray on the table at the side of the bed. There were two cigarette stubs lying in a thin layer of grey ash. He lifted one of the stubs and examined it, his eyes widening in surprise as he did so. He slipped it into his pocket and continued his search.

On the trestle table he found a notepad. The top page was blank, but he observed that there were faint indentations that had been pressed through from the previous sheet before it had been removed. Bringing the ashtray over, he gently smeared some of the ash over the notepad, which allowed the indentations to appear in relief. In this way he was able to make out some of the letters: "Ambass...tel...ar."

Just then he heard a series of loud cries from the ground floor, followed by a gunshot. In an instant Holmes was racing down the stairs into the hallway, where he found Watson and Oberstein lying on the floor, their bodies entwined. Neither was moving.

"Watson," Holmes cried, "for God's sake, say you're not hurt!"

Watson raised his head slowly. "Just a bit winded, that's all. This fellow tried to make a dash for it, grabbing my gun, which went off in the struggle. I'm afraid he's had it, Holmes. I'm so sorry."

"As long as you are all right, that is what really matters. Here, let me help you to your feet."

"He tried to wrestle the gun from me, but I held on tight. As we struggled... I'm sorry."

"Don't blame yourself," said Holmes with some warmth. "What happened, happened. At least you are unharmed. It's a pity that we've lost a key link in this mystery, but you did the right thing in trying to prevent his escape. There's a telephone in the sitting room; I'd better ring Lestrade and tell him to scoop up the body—the real Hugo Oberstein this time."

As they were leaving, a tall grey-haired, bearded fellow was making his way up the path. He was dressed in a smock which was spattered with paint. "Is everything all right?" he said. "I thought I heard a disturbance and something that sounded like a shot. I reside next door, you see."

Holmes smiled ingenuously. "Everything is fine. My careless friend here knocked a small table down the stairs—but all is shipshape now. No cause for alarm."

"What a relief. So pleased. Well then, I'd better get back to things." With a gentle wave, he retraced his steps and entered his own property.

"My careless friend," chided Watson indignantly.

Holmes smiled and gave him a gentle pat on the back.

Later, as they travelled back to Baker Street in a taxi, Watson sought some explanations from his friend. "What puzzles me, Holmes, is why they carried out the fake murder of Oberstein."

"No doubt it was to put the police off the scent. If Oberstein was presumed dead, he could not be involved in the planned assassination, and therefore the Scotland Yarders would focus their attention elsewhere, leaving his guest Brunner to get on with his assignment unhindered."

"With Oberstein remaining incognito as his own maid!"

Holmes gave a grim smile. "So it would seem. He was there to repel inquisitive boarders."

"Amazing. And it all could have been successful if you had not deduced that the body fished from the river was an imposter."

"Well, certainly that led us down the right path, but it is one that remains convoluted and enigmatic. Brunner is still at large, and I fear we are running out of time."

On returning to Baker Street, Holmes sat smoking in his chair by the fire while staring at the sheet of notepaper containing the letters "Ambass…tel…ar." At length he passed it to Watson.

"What d'you think of that? I'm having some difficulty making sense of it."

Watson stared at it for some moments. "Well, I think it possibly refers to some ambassador, some dignitary or other, and possibly the 'tel' was part of his telephone number."

"Yes, that was one of my early thoughts, but I'm not convinced. What about 'ar'? "

"Not a clue, old boy. Sorry."

"This is a certainly a three-pipe problem requiring my strongest shag."

Watson groaned. "Gracious. It's like a pea-souper in here as it is. If it gets any thicker, I'll have to feel my way out of the room. If you're going to persist in polluting the atmosphere further, I may have to book myself into a hotel for the night."

At these words Holmes froze, his eyes sparking with excitement. "By George, I think you've got it."

"Have I? Er, what have I got?"

"Hotel! Of course! The 'tel' is not a reference to a telephone number, but to the word 'hotel.' And when you have the letters 'Ambass' before it, it seems logical to me that we have the Ambassador Hotel which, as my memory serves me, is located at Marble Arch, which also covers the letters 'a' and 'r.' "

Watson scratched his head. "Well, I can see that your theory fits, but it is rather a stretch of the imagination."

"If we did not stretch our imagination, we would never find the solution to any puzzle."

"If you say so."

"Make a long arm, Watson, and pass me my London gazetteer. I want to look up the Ambassador Hotel."

Holmes skimmed the pages and read the entry he was seeking.

"What does it tell you?"

"Very little of consequence. A luxurious hotel built in the eighteenth century. Fully modernised in 1875. Favoured by the aristocracy and royalty. Used occasionally for state banquets." Holmes gave a sharp cry of excitement and then, snapping the gazetteer shut, he rose quickly from his chair. "What time is it, Watson?"

The doctor consulted his watch. "Four thirty."

"Excellent. By the time we get to the Diogenes Club, brother Mycroft will be ensconced in his favourite chair, nursing a brandy and soda. I have a few questions to put to him."

So it was that, just as Holmes and Watson entered the Members' Room at five minutes past five, they discovered the corpulent Mycroft Holmes, as predicted, sitting near the window with a glass in his chubby hand. "You can set your clock by Mycroft's movements. Five o'clock on the dot he will enter this room and very shortly a drink will be served to him," whispered Holmes, ignoring the frowns of a few members for breaking the absolute rule of no talking.

On observing Holmes, Mycroft indicated with a wave of his hand that they would have to move to the Stranger's Room, where conversation was permitted. It was a large, airy chamber, overlooking Pall Mall.

"You have made progress, Sherlock?" enquired Mycroft, once they were seated in their new quarters.

"Possibly." Quickly he recounted our adventures of the day.

"So near and yet so far, brother mine. Despite everything you have uncovered, Herr Brunner is still at large."

"Actually, I believe that Herr Alex Brunner could also be Fraulein Brunner."

Mycroft almost dropped his glass. "What on earth leads you to this conclusion?"

"A few indications I noted in the room our German friend occupied. There was an aura of feminine perfume lingering in the air and, more particularly, in the ashtray there were cigarette stubs smeared by lipstick."

"But, Holmes, you told me there were some men's clothes about as well," chimed in Watson.

"Indeed. I believe that Brunner is a chameleon and is able to assume a male persona when the situation requires it. Remember our late lamented friend, Irene Adler, and her skill at dressing in male attire."

"Ah, yes 'the Woman.' "

"This is hardly good news to me, Sherlock," said Mycroft crossly. "You are now telling me that we are searching for someone who can appear as either a man or woman, and this individual is loose in London with the aim of killing our prime minister."

"Your analysis is simple but correct. However, I think we may be able to narrow things down a little. Tell me about the function at the Ambassador Hotel."

Mycroft stared at his brother in surprise. "How on earth do you know about that?"

"I am a detective; it is my business to know things. Tell me what is going to happen at this prestigious hotel and how Mr. Churchill is involved."

Mycroft studied his glass of brandy and soda for some moments before responding to Holmes's request.

"What I am about to tell you is not in the public domain and must be kept from that arena. Is that understood, Sherlock, Doctor Watson?"

The two men nodded their acquiescence.

"Tomorrow night there is a private dinner to honour the Soviet Foreign Affairs minister, Vyacheslav Molotov. He has been visiting London secretly to discuss the territorial concessions regarding Poland and the Baltic States before flying to Washington to see Roosevelt. He has given Churchill a tough old time in the negotiations, but it seems a satisfactory compromise is on the horizon. This farewell dinner is aimed at keeping him sweet."

"How many guests will be attending this dinner?"

"About fifty. Members of the cabinet and Molotov's entourage, along with some civil dignitaries."

"Then this, I deduce, is where the assassination attempt will be made."

"What makes you reach this conclusion?"

"That matters little now. Take me at my word, Mycroft."

"Very well. I trust you. You are seldom wrong."

Holmes gave a dry smile. "Seldom is correct. You recognise that I am not infallible."

"That's true," mumbled Watson *sotto voce*.

"So, Sherlock, how is this attempt on the prime minister's life going to be carried out? Brunner has used many different methods in the past. He or she could be acting as a sniper or planting a bomb or…by some other means."

"Because of the location, Brunner will need to be absolutely certain his victim has no chance of survival, so I believe bombs or other explosive devices are out of the question. These cause destruction, of course, but cannot be guaranteed to eliminate one intended victim. Similarly, acting as a sniper, Brunner cannot be assured of securing an ideal concealed position to carry out such an operation and to be certain of fleeing the scene without being apprehended. Mr. Churchill will be targeted in a more subtle way."

"Poison," said Watson.

"Bravo, my friend. I believe you have it. There will be drinks and toasts galore, no doubt, at this function."

"So, all one needs to do is ask Mr. Churchill not to touch a drop," said Watson.

Mycroft shook his head. "Trying to stop Winston taking a drink is like Canute attempting to hold back the waves. Besides, if it is poison, it could be in the food or the coffee."

"Good point, Mycroft. It seems to me that the only way Brunner can be sure of success is to deliver the poison to Churchill personally. And who could do that?"

"A waiter."

"Or…a waitress. She ensures the poison has been administered to her victim and then slips away unnoticed before the effects of the deadly draught become evident."

"The serving staff is vetted scrupulously before these events, but I will ensure that the procedure is extra-vigorous this time."

"Nevertheless, we are dealing with one of the cleverest agents in Europe, who has the talent to squeeze his way through the smallest loophole."

"What are you suggesting?"

"That Watson and I will attend this function, so that we can be extra eyes at the feast."

"The problem is that you don't know who you are looking for. Brunner could turn up as a man or a woman, and in either case, you don't know what the devil looks like."

"That is a problem, I agree, but it is one that I must overcome," said Holmes with grim determination.

On leaving the Diogenes Club, Holmes suggested Watson return to Baker Street. "I have a little mission of my own, which I hope will bear fruit," he said.

"Huh, leaving me out of things again."

"Only briefly. I'll make certain you'll be in at the kill, as it were."

"Unfortunate words under the circumstances," mumbled Watson, wandering away in search of a cab.

Later that evening, Holmes returned to Baker Street, a broad grin on his face.

"What's amused you, Holmes?" asked Watson.

"It is always satisfying when an inspired hunch plays off."

"And what hunch was that?"

"You remember Oberstein's neighbour this morning, who was so concerned about the noise next door?"

Watson nodded.

"You will also remember his paint-spattered smock."

Another nod.

"Well, it struck me that the fellow must be a painter, an artist. And I was right. I've just paid a visit to him, Hubert Grace by name, and he was kind enough to show me some of his works. They are competent studies, but not of the finest quality. He is no Constable or Rembrandt. However, he does have the facility for capturing a likeness."

"What has all this to do with the case?"

"I enquired whether he had seen Oberstein's visitor in the last few days—and indeed he had. As you may have gathered, Mr. Grace is somewhat of a nosey neighbour, and so he had a very good gander at the person in question. So I asked him to draw an accurate sketch of the visitor—it was a man, by the way. I said I would pay for his work, so he was happy to oblige. Starving artist and all that. In fact, he obliged brilliantly, and then as an added favour, I asked him if he would provide an extra drawing for me of the same face as though it were a woman with long hair and the usual female accoutrements of lipstick and eyeshadow. Again, friend Grace came up trumps." So saying, Holmes drew two sheets of paper from his coat.

"Feast your eyes on these, old fellow. These are fairly accurate likenesses of Mr. or Miss Brunner. The only distinctive feature is that broad fleshy nose."

"Not very feminine. Don't know how he gets away playing female with that hooter."

"My friend Grace was also able to tell me that the fellow was small of stature, about five foot, and somewhat on the plump side. Certainly information, along with these drawings, which will help us in seeking out Brunner at the banquet."

The following evening, Holmes and Watson arrived at the Ambassador Hotel an hour before the guests and were met by Mycroft, who led them immediately to the banqueting suite. There was a small top table reserved for the prime minister, the foreign secretary, Molotov, and his personal aide.

"That must be the focus of attention when the dinner is served," observed Mycroft, "but there will be mingling with drinks and canapes beforehand, which is a problem. Churchill has been warned to abstain from both food and alcohol at this stage, but I'm afraid he cannot be trusted to abide by this. He really believes he is invincible."

Holmes nodded, but said nothing.

"Now, gentlemen, I must leave you. As I am responsible for making sure this affair goes smoothly, I have other tasks to perform elsewhere. I will have to leave the safety of our premier up to you."

"That's a daunting prospect, eh, Holmes?" said Watson.

"Yes," Holmes replied darkly.

It wasn't long before the serving staff began appearing, all smartly attired and silent; they were followed shortly by the guests. Holmes and Watson separated and stationed themselves at either end of the room, surveying the proceedings with keen eyes. At seven thirty the doors of the suite were opened by two flunkeys, and the familiar figure of Winston Churchill appeared. All eyes in the room turned in his direction. There was a round of applause, and he responded with his trademark V sign. He made his way down the few steps into the main area, followed by the Foreign Secretary, Anthony Eden. A waiter stepped forward with a tray of drinks. Churchill's hand hovered over one of the glasses and then he withdrew it, with a shake of the head. Then, slipping his hand into the side pocket of his dinner suit, he produced a silver whisky flask and took a quick drink from that. He flashed a smile at Eden, who seemed to share the joke.

The maître d' approached Churchill and whispered some instructions in his ear. The prime minister listened attentively and nodded. Once the Russian delegation had arrived and had been greeted by Churchill and other members of the cabinet, the maître d' consulted with Churchill once more, before banging a gong and requesting that the diners take their seats. As the guests made their way to their allotted seats, with Churchill shepherding Molotov toward the top table, Holmes approached the maître d' to ask him the location of table seven. The fellow, a short, lean individual with large blue eyes, seemed somewhat flustered at this request. He waved an arm vaguely as an indication. "Over there, sir," he said. "You will excuse me; I have my duties in the kitchen." With these words, he rushed away. Holmes waited until he had disappeared through the swing doors that led to the kitchen before following in haste. The maître d' had not got far before Holmes caught up with him.

"Oh, Alex," he cried.

On hearing the name, the maître d' froze, his back stiffening, before slowly turning around to face Holmes.

"Don't move, Brunner, or I will be forced to shoot you," said Holmes, producing a pistol.

The man's features twisted with anger, the mouth uttering a Germanic oath. His hand moved toward his jacket pocket.

"I wouldn't if I were you," snapped Holmes, firing his pistol so that the bullet landed inches from Brunner's feet. "Next time, my aim will be more accurate. Just make sure there isn't a next time. I'm afraid for you, my dear sir, the game is up."

"So you think," snarled Brunner, but Holmes could tell that this was an empty threat.

At this moment he was joined by Watson. "What's going on?" he asked.

"We've hooked our fish, old fellow," he said, stepping forward and relieving Brunner of the pistol lodged in his jacket pocket. "Just keep him covered for me, Watson, while I have a quick word with Mr. Churchill."

Holmes emerged from the kitchen and headed for the top table. He was just in time to see Churchill retrieve his hip flask and prepare to take a drink from it.

Holmes lunged forward and knocked it from his hand.

"What the devil!" cried Churchill.

"It's poisoned," cried Holmes.

Churchill gazed up in surprise at the intruder. "Why, Mr. Holmes, it's you. What is all this nonsense about? It can't be poisoned. This flask was filled with my own single malt before I left Number Ten tonight."

"It has been tampered with. The maître d' is our spy. He took the flask from you, picked your pocket, and then returned it after adding the poison."

"He took it without me knowing."

"It is a pickpocket's skill."

Churchill stared with some incredulity at the silver flask which lay on the table, and then his features creased into a broad smile. "Bravo, Holmes. A very neat piece of work."

"Thank you, sir."

Later that evening, Holmes, Watson, and Mycroft were seated around a blazing fire in Baker Street, enjoying a nightcap.

"Now all the fuss is over and Brunner is safely stored away, I would be most obliged if you would explain how you knew the maître d' was our man," said Mycroft.

"It was a collection of small details. When I saw the maître d' being so familiar with Churchill, standing so close to him, my suspicions were aroused, and when I got to the fellow and spoke to him, there were other indications that he was not who he seemed to be."

"What indications?" said Watson.

"Well, you remember those sketches, and that rather interesting nose, which was effectively captured by Oberstein's neighbour. This fellow had such a nose. He also had pierced ears—ideal for wearing earrings when disguised as a woman. I noted specks of red on his fingernails which I suspected were the remnants of nail polish, again used when Brunner was in female mode."

"But Oberstein's neighbour said that the fellow was stout. The waiter chap was slim."

"Padding used as a kind of camouflage, no doubt. The more Brunner could change his appearance, the less chance he could be identified."

"Amazing."

"Elementary, my dear Watson."

Mycroft chuckled with delight. "Well, it seems I may have to alter my view of you, Sherlock. You are infallible."

"Well, we have conquered this time, but I fear there will be many more instances when the enemy will threaten our democracy and freedom. But as a nation, as individuals, I am sure we will persevere and survive. The dark hours may be long, but one day we will emerge into the bright sunshine of peace once more."

Two days later, a parcel was delivered to Baker Street by special courier. It contained a solid silver hip flask bearing the inscription: "To SH from WC with gratitude."

Cast:
Sherlock Holmes: Basil Rathbone
Dr. Watson: Nigel Bruce
Mycroft Holmes: Sydney Greenstreet
Inspector Lestrade: Dennis Hoey
Mrs. Hudson: Mary Gordon
Hugo Oberstein: Henry Daniell
Mr. Grace: Miles Mander
Brunner: Gerald Hamer
Winston Churchill: ?

About the Editor

MAXIM JAKUBOWSKI is a London-based former publisher, editor, writer, and translator. He has compiled over one hundred anthologies in a variety of genres, many of which have garnered awards. He is a past winner of the Karel and Anthony awards, and in 2019 was given the prestigious Red Herrings award by the Crime Writers' Association for his contribution to the genre. He broadcasts regularly on radio and TV, reviews for diverse newspapers and magazines, and has been a judge for several literary awards. He is the author of twenty novels, the latest being *The Piper's Dance*, and a series of *Sunday Times* bestselling novels under a pseudonym. He has also published five collections of his own short stories. He is currently Chair of the Crime Writers' Association.

www.maximjakubowski.co.uk

About the Authors

MATTHEW BOOTH is the author of *Sherlock Holmes and the Giant's Hand* and one of the authors contributing to *The Further Exploits of Sherlock Holmes*. Matthew was a scriptwriter for the American radio network, *Imagination Theatre*, syndicated by Jim French Productions. He was a regular contributor to their series *The Further Adventures of Sherlock Holmes*. Matthew is the creator of former criminal barrister and amateur detective, Anthony Rathe, who appeared in a radio series produced by Jim French Productions. Rathe now appears in *When Anthony Rathe Investigates*, published by Sparkling Books.

Born in Haworth, West Yorkshire, ERIC BROWN has lived in Australia, India, and Greece. He has won the British Science Fiction Award twice for his short stories, and his novel *Helix Wars* was shortlisted for the 2012 Philip K. Dick Award. He's published over seventy books, and his latest include the seventh and eighth crime novels in the Langham and Dupré series, set in the 1950s, *Murder by Numbers* and *Murder at Standing Stone Manor*. He lives near Dunbar in Scotland, and his website is ericbrown.co.uk.

MARTIN DALEY was born in Carlisle, Cumbria, in 1964. He cites Doyle's Holmes and Watson as his favourite literary characters, who continue to inspire his own detective writing. His fiction and nonfiction books include a Holmes pastiche set predominantly in his home city in 1903. In the adventure, he introduced his own detective, Inspector Cornelius Armstrong, who has subsequently had some of his own cases published. For more information, visit www.martindaley.co.uk.

DAVID STUART DAVIES is the author of eight Sherlock Holmes novels and *Starring Sherlock Holmes,* which details the detective's film career. David's three successful one-man plays, *Sherlock Holmes: The Last Act* and *Sherlock Holmes: The Life & Death* have been recorded on audio CD by The Big Finish. *Sherlock Holmes: The Final Reckoning,* premiered in Edinburgh in February 2019. David is the author of other works of crime fiction, including seven Johnny Hawke novels—the latest being *Spiral of Lies.* Other recent titles include *Sherlock Holmes: The Instrument of Death* and *Oliver Twist & the Mystery of Throate Manor.* David is a Baker Street Irregular and a member of The Detection Club and edited *Red Herrings,* the monthly magazine of the Crime Writers' Association, for twenty years.

O'NEIL DE NOUX is a New Orleans writer with forty-one books published and over four hundred short story sales in multiple genres. His fiction has received several awards, including the Shamus Award for *Best Private Eye Short Story,* the Derringer Award for *Best Novelette,* and the 2011 Police Book of the Year. Two of his stories have appeared in the *Best American Mystery Stories* anthology (2013 and 2007). His latest book is *12 Bullets,* a police thriller. He is a past Vice-President of the Private Eye Writers of America. His website is www.oneildenoux.com.

JAN EDWARDS is a UK author with several novels and many short stories in horror, fantasy, mainstream and crime fiction, including *Mammoth Book of Folk Horror* as well as various volumes of the MX *Books of New Sherlock Holmes Stories.* Jan is an editor with the award-winning Alchemy Press (includes the Alchemy Press Books of Horror series). Jan was awarded the Arnold Bennett Book Prize for *Winter Downs,* the first in her WWII crime series *The Bunch Courtney Investigations.* To read more about Jan, go to janedwardsblog. wordpress.com.

PAUL A. FREEMAN is the author of *Rumours of Ophir*, a crime novel which was taught at 'O' level in Zimbabwean high schools and has been translated into German. In addition to having two crime novels, a children's book, and an 18,000-word narrative poem commercially published, Paul is the author of hundreds of published short stories (of various genres), articles and poems. He currently lives and works in Abu Dhabi.

JOHN GRANT is the author of over eighty books, including *A Comprehensive Encyclopedia of Film Noir* (2013), the largest of its kind in the English language. His stories have been collected as (so far) *Take No Prisoners* (2004) and *Tell No Lies* (2014). He's the author of a loose series of books on science issues, including *Discarded Science* (2006), *Corrupted Science* (2007; revised 2018), and *Denying Science* (2011). For his work editing the Paper Tiger imprint of fantasy/sf art books, he received a Chesley Award. For his own nonfiction, he has received two Hugos, a World Fantasy Award, and others. He died in February 2020.

BONNIE MACBIRD (BSI, ASH) has written three critically acclaimed Sherlock Holmes novels for HarperCollins: *Art in the Blood, Unquiet Spirits*, and *The Devil's Due*, to be followed soon by *The Three Locks*. A passionate fan of Holmes since the age of ten, she writes in traditional style and voice, though in novel form. Thirty years in the film business as a studio exec, screenwriter, playwright, and Emmy-winning producer inform her character-driven storytelling style. Bonnie lives in LA and London, just off Baker Street, with her husband, computer scientist Alan Kay.

After cutting her teeth translating comics, CRISTINA MACÍA is now Mother of Dragons due to her hugely popular Spanish translations of the *Game of Thrones* books (as well as of many Terry Pratchetts and other genre authors). Her bestselling YA novel *Una casa con Encanto* (*A Haunted House*) is now in its nineteenth edition, and she writes cookbooks too. A leading Spanish Sherlockian, CM is codirector of Spain's principal SF, Fantasy, and Horror fan convention, Celsius 232, now in its tenth year. Her partner, SF novelist IAN WATSON (www.ianwatson.info), spent a year eyeball-to-eyeball with Stanley Kubrick, resulting in the Screen Story of the movie *A.I. Artificial Intelligence*, directed by Spielberg. IW and CM live in rainy Asturias Province, rich in cheeses and crabs.

ANA TERESA PEREIRA is a Portuguese writer and translator. She is the author of more than twenty novels, novellas, and collections of short stories. A reader of Henry James, John Dickson Carr, and Cornell Woolrich, she likes to think of her stories as "abstract crime fiction." Her last novel, *Karen*, has won the Brazilian Oceanos Award—for the best book in the Portuguese language published in 2016. Her novella "O Atelier de Noite" was published in January 2020. She lives in Funchal, Madeira.

DAVID N. SMITH is a UK-based writer, who has had over a dozen short stories published in various anthologies. He's recently been writing and coproducing a multi-cast audio drama series, based on the classic *Fighting Fantasy* gamebook range, which is currently available through Audible and iTunes. He's also written a number of corporate training videos, but people tend to be a lot less interested in these, as they involve considerably fewer dragons. He's also recently completed work on his first novel, which will hopefully be published in 2022. You can find more information about his writing at www.davenevsmith.co.uk.

This is the second piece of short fiction NICK SWEET has had published in an anthology edited by Maxim Jakubowski, a previous story of his having appeared in *The Mammoth Book of Jack the Ripper Stories*. Other stories have appeared in the crime-fiction anthology *Sunshine Noir*, the *Evergreen Review*, and *Descant*. His crime novel *The Long Siesta* received a positive from critic Barry Forshaw in his book *Brit Noir*. Details on Nick's other books can be found by clicking on the link to his website, here: www.nicksweetbooks.com.

L. C. (Len) TYLER is a former cultural attaché and chief executive of a medical royal college. He writes two crime series: the Herring Mysteries and a historical series featuring seventeenth-century lawyer and spy, John Grey. He has had short stories published in a number of magazines and anthologies. He has won the Goldsboro Last Laugh Award (twice), the Ian St. James Awards, and the 2017 CWA Short Story Dagger. Len has also been twice nominated for an Edgar Allan Poe award in the US. He has lived and worked all over the world but has more recently been based in London and West Sussex.

PHILLIP VINE's short stories have been published by Solaris and appeared in numerous anthologies of prize-winning tales. He is a former ghostwriter and editor of the literary magazine, *Words International*. His most recent publication is *Visionary: Manchester United, Michael Knighton, and the Football Revolution* (Pitch Publishing, 2019). He is currently working on a novel, *The Last Song of Elvis Presley*. Phillip lives in Norfolk, England, with his wife Liz, and has been a lifelong fan of Sherlock Holmes.

Mango Publishing, established in 2014, publishes an eclectic list of books by diverse authors—both new and established voices—on topics ranging from business, personal growth, women's empowerment, LGBTQ studies, health, and spirituality to history, popular culture, time management, decluttering, lifestyle, mental wellness, aging, and sustainable living. We were recently named 2019 *and* 2020's #1 fastest growing independent publisher by *Publishers Weekly*. Our success is driven by our main goal, which is to publish high quality books that will entertain readers as well as make a positive difference in their lives.

Our readers are our most important resource; we value your input, suggestions, and ideas. We'd love to hear from you—after all, we are publishing books for you!

Please stay in touch with us and follow us at:

Facebook: Mango Publishing
Twitter: @MangoPublishing
Instagram: @MangoPublishing
LinkedIn: Mango Publishing
Pinterest: Mango Publishing
Newsletter: mangopublishinggroup.com/newsletter

Join us on Mango's journey to reinvent publishing, one book at a time.

CPSIA information can be obtained
at www.ICGtesting.com
Printed in the USA
JSHW020239030921
18400JS00003B/3